A PLACE OF

A PLACE OF SPRINGS

Hannah Colby

Blessed are those whose strength is in you,
whose hearts are set on pilgrimage.
As they pass through the Valley of Sorrow,
they make it a place of springs;

Psalm 84

MARTINEAU

MARTINEAU

First published in Great Britain in 2018
by Martineau
an imprint of Unicorn Press
60 Bracondale
Norwich
NR1 2BE

www.aplaceofspringsthebook.co.uk

Designed and typeset by Nick Newton Design
Printed in the UK by TJ International Ltd, Padstow, Cornwall

A CIP record of this book can be obtained from the
British Library

ISBN 978 1 911604 53 2

The symbol ❀ = piano pedal up
Frontispiece: *Girl with viola*. Charcoal drawing by Hannah Colby
Cover photograph: 'Crestfallen' copyright © James Kerwin

*To Gill whose friendship and reliable
orthography have been there all the time*

ACKNOWLEDGEMENTS

There are so many people I want to thank for their help, support and expertise during the five years it's taken me to complete this book: Patricia Mullin for inspiring me to start writing; Carol Smith for her experience as a published author; Gillian Graham Dobson for her kindly eye and uncanny ability to find typos, spelling mistakes and worse; Mary Gibson for her sympathetic professional editing; Nick and George Newton for their help and expertise with design and typesetting; David Owen Norris and David Neil Jones for their invaluable advice on piano technique and repertoire; Frances Wilson for editing the musical content; Paula Best for showing me around backstage at the Wigmore Hall and Josepa Štadlera for receiving me at the Sarajevo Academy of Music; Professor Antonio Damasio for allowing me to quote from his writings on Schubert; Martin Bell for letting me take liberties with his name and Roger Cohen for allowing me to quote from his 1984 *New York Times* article *War Comes to Sarajevo*; Harmin Sijerćic for helping me with Serbo-Croat and Bosnian names, words and phrases; Janey Bevington and Jullien Gaer for medical facts; Richard and Margaret Seebohm and Lisa Watts who read the MS in its last phase and spurred me on with their enthusiasm and frank observations; the beautiful Roisin Callaghan who, with her fiddle, was the model for my drawing of Irena.

My loving thanks go to my family, who have never lost faith that I would eventually finish the book and that they would live to see it in print: to Nicola and David Moore, Charlie and Elisabetta Robinson, Polly and Jullien Gaer, Barnaby and Heidi Robinson and my sister Ann Buxton.

Hugh, my publisher husband, spends his life amongst books, but the ones he usually nurses into life are not works of fiction; his help and advice were therefore all the more touching.

If, in spite of this support and guidance, I have strayed from absolute accuracy in my story-telling, it is entirely my fault.

CONTENTS

PART ONE

1.	THE MAESTRO	3
2.	IN A BLUE STUDIO	13
3.	GATHERING CLOUDS	20
4.	BESIEGED	30
5.	DANIEL'S QUEST	34
6.	A DANGEROUS PLACE TO BE	48
7.	INTO THE LION'S DEN	59
8.	LOOKING FOR A PIANO	67
9.	NEW WORLD, NEW LIFE	77
10.	A LETTER FROM AMERICA	80
11.	A PARTY ENTERTAINER	90
12.	A HELPFUL NEIGHBOUR	94
13.	HEDI COMES TO CALL	105
14.	MEZZO PIANO	112
15.	A SERPENT'S TONGUE	119
16.	EXPECTATIONS	133
17.	ANOTHER POINT OF VIEW	140
18.	REPAIRING THE DAMAGE	161
19.	UNRAVELLED	175
20.	INTERLUDE	178

PART TWO

21.	REVELATIONS	187
22.	MAROONED	196
23.	JOURNEY'S END	204
24.	PASSION AND PAVLOVA	212
25.	VARIATIONS	216
26.	PETER HAS NEWS	224
27.	TYING NEW KNOTS	229

28.	RETURN TO SARAJEVO	233
29.	IRENA'S QUEST	240
30.	SECRET SORROW	250
31.	ARRIVALS	264
32.	PLAY IT AGAIN DAN	278
33.	CRESCENDO	288
34.	UNRAVELLING	298
35.	PERFECT PITCH	307
36.	PORTRAIT	310
37.	TO HAVE AND TO HOLD	321
38.	THE MUSICIAN'S DAUGHTER	330
39.	AUTUMN FLIGHT	335

PART THREE

40.	ASHES AND ICES	341
41.	SCISSORS	348
42.	AN OUTING	360
43.	UNCERTAIN JOY	372
44.	A FITTING MEMORIAL	378
45.	SAM'S FUTURE	388
46.	RETURN TO ST BEDE'S	396
47.	REFUSAL	404
48.	INVITATION TO THE DANCE	417
49.	PICKERS' PARTY	425
50.	MOVING ON	435
51.	BRAVE NEW LOVE	444
52.	SAYING YES	449
53.	DISCOVERIES	453
54.	A SORROW SHARED	470
55.	WRITING IT DOWN	476
56.	ASHES TO ASHES	483

| Further Reading | 488 |

PART ONE

1.　THE MAESTRO

I met a lady in the meads,
Full beautiful, a faery's child;
Her hair was long, her foot was light,
And her eyes were wild.

John Keats (1795–1821). From 'La Belle Dame Sans Merci'

SARAJEVO 1991

T HE PIANO ARRIVED the day after my fifteenth birthday. My mother and I watched its precarious progress through the orchard to the studio, its black varnish reflecting ripening plums and apples under the bright September sky.

'Oh dear, that's going to be very loud … We'll hear it over in the house.' Mamija said anxiously. 'When Tata said he was going to hire a piano for Dr Danuczek, I didn't know he was thinking of a full-size grand.'

We watched four sweating men heave the piano through the French windows and lay it on its side. The foreman screwed on three sturdy legs, his team lifted the huge instrument onto its feet and they all stood back, mopping their brows.

I was helping my mother to get the studio ready for the arrival of our latest house-guest. As our lodgers always did, the newly appointed Director of Keyboard Studies at the Conservatory would be sleeping on the gallery, reached by steep wooden steps.

'Let's just hope Dr Danuczek can manage the stairs better than poor old Professor Bronowski,' Mama went on. 'There isn't any room now downstairs for a bed.'

'And what if Dr What's-his-Name is fat? He'll have to squeeze round that gi-normous piano to get in and out. Oh Mum, I can't bear those seedy old musicians – they're so boring and ugly. Why can't we have someone fun for a change – someone young – you know, students would think the studio was a really funky place to stay.'

Mama laughed, put her arm around my waist and kissed me. 'Professors tend to be oldish, darling, but they're more likely to pay the rent than students. And Maestro Danuczek is a wonderful pianist – he's famous all over the world. Your Tata is thrilled and the Conservatory is buzzing with excitement.'

She told the removal men to go over to the kitchen for their beer, flicked a duster quickly over the piano, positioned the stool under the keyboard and shut the studio door. 'We'll soon see if he's fat or thin. His flight from London will get him here in time for lunch tomorrow.'

I stumped gloomily upstairs to my room, knowing the stultifying boredom of those endless lunches with the aged academics. I shuddered as I remembered Frau Doktor Tunkel, female of the species, a clarinet teacher with frizzy hennaed hair, who practised endlessly by the open French windows and emptied the spit out of her instrument onto the flowerbeds. Disgusting. And, oh, her embarrassing attempts to talk to me – always asking about my school work and what music I was studying. Always saying how important it was to practise and read the classics, so I would grow up to be a cultured person. On and on until I could have screamed.

The house where I was born, the Vila Dolena, had been designed and built in the 1930s by my grandfather. The exterior was austere and unwelcoming, for the stucco walls had long since lost their pristine whiteness and were streaked with grey

and ochre, but their severity had been softened by a Virginia
creeper which my mother had planted the year I was born.
All summer its leaves were bright green hands which autumn
would turn to scarlet, cheerfully framing the eccentrically
placed windows and scrambling up into the slates of the roof,
under which house martins nested every summer above my
bedroom window. It was this roof that everyone remembered
of the house, for it was unlike any other to be seen in Sarajevo: a squat, four-sectioned dome clothed in diamonds of
hand-cut slate with a tall square chimney standing guard at
each corner. In my childish imagination it was the helmet of
a benign giant, sheltering and protecting the people I loved
as it glowed and changed colour against the restless sky of
Yugoslavia.

Inside, the house was full of surprises, from the wide,
cantilevered staircase, which curved up three floors like the
inside of a snail's shell, to the spiral layout of the rooms,
each in itself quirky and eccentric. Floor-to-ceiling bookcases crowded each landing, cheek by jowl with rustic painted
cupboards and a jumbled accretion of family memorabilia,
and the walls closely hung with pictures. In the music room,
which formed half of the ground floor, my grandfather, a
fashionable portrait painter, had veered from the contempor-
ary theme of the architecture and painted the ceiling in an
exuberant baroque style.

Our tree-lined drive gave onto Nevinosti Street which ran
through a quiet suburb above Sarajevo. Beyond the stone gate-
posts was a wooded slope through which the river Miljacka
glinted in the distance. Behind the house was my mother's
garden, planted with bright flowers and crowded fruit trees
and, beyond them, the tall pavilion that had been my grandfather's studio. I loved this building, with its high windows
and paint-stained floor which reminded me of the tempera-
mental but loving old man, who was Dedo to me. He had

visited Monet in his studio at Giverny and had copied the blue
paintwork which gave the whole structure a luminous quality,
its big windows glittering at the far end of the orchard.

My mood did not improve when the piano tuner arrived
early the next morning and I was subjected to his monoto-
nous strumming and charmless arpeggios as I tried to finish
my homework. I heard a taxi draw up and my parents greeting their new lodger and calling for the gardener to help with
the luggage, of which there seemed to be a great deal. My
bedroom window overlooked the garden between the house
and the studio, but I didn't look out as they trooped back and
forth. Half an hour later, Mama called up to me, 'Irena, hurry
up. Lunch is nearly ready – and our guest is here.'

I dawdled down to the salon. Several of my parents' close
friends had been invited to meet the new incumbent of the
conservatory. My mother's family lived in Ireland, but my
father's, who were mostly Muslim and nearly all academics
or musicians, were bursting to see our illustrious new house-
guest. With them came my well-behaved cousins, with whom
I seemed to have little in common. Lati, whose mother was
my favourite aunt, Hedi, was the only one who could share
a joke. I was relieved to see her getting out of the car and
hitching up her skirt to a more fashionable length behind her
mother's back.

When I entered the salon, my parents were by the unlit fire
and a tall man stood between them with his back to the door.
Mama held out her hand to me. 'Darling, come and meet Dr
Danuczek. Maestro, this is our daughter, Irena.'

The man turned towards me and held out his hand, smiling
and saying: 'Hello – how lovely to meet you … ,' but I was
overcome with shyness and could not find my voice to reply.

We sat down to lunch, our guest on my mother's right on
one side of the long table, my father, Tata, opposite her and
the rest of the grown-ups flanking them. My cousins and I

took up our places at one end and looked at each other con-spiratorially. Although we all knew how excruciatingly long and dull these lunches were, that day there was a new electric-ity in the air.

'Are you sure he's really a professor? He doesn't look like one,' Lati whispered, gazing unashamedly down the table. I, who was considered to be an expert on this matter, was also confused.

'He must be – his stuff's in the studio and he's spread music all over the piano.'

'He's really tall ... makes your mum look like a little girl.'

'And his hair's really long – like Liszt's ... '

'He hasn't got any warts, though ... and Liszt didn't wear glasses.'

We stifled our giggles as we continued to stare as much as we could without attracting the attention of the learned Doctor.

'Maestro Danuczek, we drink to your time with us in Sarajevo', said my father, raising his wine glass, and all the grown-ups followed suit. Our guest bowed his head in acknowledgement protesting:

'Oh, thank you so much ... but please call me Daniel.'

'If you wish, of course.' But Tata was uneasy with this informality; "Maestro" was a title denoting reverence and proper respect.

We were speaking English, my mother's native tongue. I am bi-lingual, having spoken both Serbo-Croat and English all my life, but some of our guests struggled with the language and would lapse from time to time into German or Russian, or even Turkish. Dr Danuczek had a smattering of European languages and my critical adolescent ear had already picked up his slight foreign intonation. Although he lived in London and had been educated there, it seemed that he was not English, but Czech. He laughed a lot at the frequent misunderstandings that crept into the conversation, throwing back his head and showing his white teeth.

'Maestro Daniel, will you play for us after lunch?'

My mother, who seemed more interested in our new house-guest than she had ever been in his predecessors, had unconsciously christened him with the name by which we would know him in the months to come. Maestro Daniel was what I, too, called him during the time he stayed with us, and he teasingly followed our formality by calling me by turns 'Contessa', 'Bellissima Infanta', 'Grëflin' or 'Sultana'.

'I'm sure you'll very soon have had quite enough of my playing …'

This was a change; most of the aged musicians couldn't wait to perform for my father.

'How old were you when you first played in public?' asked Uncle Bahro.

'Six, I think, but my parents didn't want me to become known as a child prodigy. So I didn't give any real concerts until I was quite a lot older.'

'But you were performing internationally by the time you were a teenager?'

'Well, yes … I really enjoyed playing in public – particularly when I was finally allowed to make my own programmes …' He paused and then laughed. 'I was a terrible show-off!'

Lati and I nudged each other, hanging on his every word. He carried on, more seriously:

'It was a very rich experience and essential for learning the repertoire, as I played all sorts of things including many of the moderns.' He was beginning to look around as he spoke and, seeing me, he smiled and asked:

'Tell me about your life. I'm sure it's much more interesting than mine. What do you like doing here in Sarajevo?'

Surprised and embarrassed, I stammered, 'Oh, there's lots to do. I like going to the cinema, oh, and skating and swimming and riding my bike in the woods.'

Encouraged by the Maestro's obvious interest in my reply to his question, I went on, 'They're full of wolves, you know – though I've never seen one but I'm not allowed to go alone in case I get eaten.'

'It'd be a shame to be eaten by a wolf, of course. Maybe I could get a bike and you'd show me the best places to go? If your parents would trust me to fight off the wolves effectively I mean.' He paused and then asked: 'And what about music – are you learning an instrument?'

My heart sank. Here it came, the interrogation, the advice about practising. I answered as politely as I could.

'I'm learning the viola. Tata plays it, too, in his quartet. It's my favourite instrument.'

'Ah! Do you know, I love it too. We must play together some time. If you think I'm good enough to accompany you.'

Everyone laughed and I hung my head, embarrassed. But he was not making fun of me, of that I was sure – his smile was gentle and encouraging.

Later that afternoon, the Maestro was persuaded to play the piano for us. He sat down at the keyboard and took off his big horn-rimmed glasses, tucking them into his breast pocket.

'Wow!' whispered Lati, looking at him admiringly. My mother had asked him to play Schumann's *Kinderstücke*. She held the sheet music in her hand and had pulled a chair up close to his stool, intending, I think, to turn the pages for him, but he shook his head, said something I couldn't hear and turned to his audience.

'This is a piece Maestro Andá loved and it's become a great favourite of mine – Ernst von Dohnanyi's arrangement of the *Valse Lente* from Delibes's ballet *Coppelia*.'

I have heard that enchanting piece many times since, but that afternoon it was new to me and the music was like flowing water. The Maestro's hands seemed to gather up the notes, spilling them delicately, precisely and sweetly before his audience. I could not then have put into words what it was that made his playing such a revelation. All too soon, he reached the final delicate, harp-like phrases and, dropping his head, sat for a moment with his hands on his knees.

A hush descended on the gathering as they took in the reality of the legend that had come amongst them before they started to clap and shout 'Bravo!'

He bowed from side to side before turning to Lati and asking her: 'And what music do you like?'

Blushing with embarrassment, she blurted out: 'Oh I like Mariah Carey best.'

What a liar that girl is: Lati was into Heavy Metal and Grunge, but she didn't think the Maestro was likely to know about them – if indeed, he'd heard of the chart-topping singer either. He looked down at the keyboard for a moment, disapprovingly we feared. Then he launched into a vigorous medley of songs from Carey's newest album, *Emotions*, which he embellished with elaborate ornaments, so that the result was classical enough for the uncles and aunts to be confused as to what they were hearing. When he had finished, with several alarming and un-Baroque *glissandi*, and affecting a very serious expression, he put his glasses on again and stood up. He bowed from the waist to the group of young people around me on the window seat, his right hand on his heart.

That evening I found our new lodger standing in front of one of my grandfather's portraits in the hall on his way to joining us for dinner. I suspected he might have preferred, after the long lunch and incessant questioning, to have been given a tray to take over to the studio, but Mama had urged him to join us and to dress informally, so he had exchanged his suit for a bright blue, open-necked shirt and chinos – a great improvement in my eyes on the cardigans and baggy flannels favoured by his predecessors.

'Do you like pictures?' I asked, standing beside him before the portrait: a woman in a low-cut evening dress, her hair waved in the pre-war style and her scarlet lips parted in a half smile.

'I'm pretty ignorant about art, but these are fascinating. They are so different from the pictures I have of my family.'

'Oh, why?' I asked.

'Well, – we've only got a few photographs left now – our family portraits disappeared in the war. Most of my forebears had long beards and black hats and the women were shrouded in shawls – they were all Jews, you see, from Central Europe and Russia. They don't look a barrel of laughs ... Not like these charming people. Where do your grey eyes come from?'

'My Irish Granny, I suppose. She was an actress – that's her.' I pointed at another portrait, whose sitter had a mischievous, coquettish gaze, her large grey eyes seeming to be full of fascinating secrets. 'Dedo – my grandfather – painted this just before I was born – in Paris. My Irish relations refused ever to come to Yugoslavia – they were cross that my Mum had married a foreigner. Anyway, Dedo designed this house, you know, and you're sleeping in his studio.'

Maestro Daniel was looking down at me as I spoke, his head tilted to one side. My parents thought I talked far too much and often didn't even let me finish a sentence, but our new lodger seemed interested in what I was saying.

'The studio's great – I never imagined I'd be put up in such a wonderful place. And that amazing piano – I usually get an upright. I just hope I won't drive you all mad with my practising. I'll have to start early to get a couple of hours in before I go down to the Conservatory ...'

'Oh, nothing wakes me and my parents sleep at the front.

Anyway, I have to practise my viola before school – in the music room, so Tata can hear if I'm working properly.'

'Where I played this afternoon? It's got the most amazing ceiling …'

'Yes, Dedo painted that, too. There are rude bits in it, you know.'

'Really? Lucky I didn't spot them while I was playing, or I might have played wrong notes – or stopped altogether!'

'Well, you'd taken your glasses off, so you mightn't have been able to see them?'

As I spoke, I wondered if I had gone too far, but the Maestro laughed, 'That was so I couldn't see you lot giggling at me'.

'I wasn't giggling – not when you played. It was really wonderful'.

'It was an honour,' he replied, and was executing an elaborate bow when the door opened and my father appeared.

'Ah, we should have warned you about our resident Belle Dame Sans Merci, Maestro Daniel. Has she already got you in her thrall?' he asked as he ushered his guest into the dining room. The Maestro looked confused. I wondered if he had read any Keats. Maybe it was just Tata's difficulty pronouncing the word 'thrall'.

2.   IN A BLUE STUDIO

WEARING A DJELLABA and Turkish slippers, our resident musician would stride across the orchard every morning, a towel over his shoulder, to take his shower in the primitive washroom behind the kitchen. We no longer had the staff for whom the downstairs plumbing had originally been installed, just Amela, who had always worked for my father's family. Now she was old and blind in one eye, with pendulous breasts and a waddling gait; my mother overlooked her poor dusting and sweeping, for we intended to give her a home for the rest of her days. She was still a wonderful cook and I would go with her to the market and bear home the baskets of vegetables and fruit she no longer had the strength to carry.

Mama's birthday was soon after our new lodger's arrival and we had a family party in the music room under the painted baroque ceiling. Tata and I had asked Maestro Daniel to play for her. Immaculate in his best suit, his hair brushed back sleekly, he sat down at the piano, stretched out his hands and played the Schubert *Impromptu* he must have heard her struggling with when she thought she was alone in this house. He smiled across to her as he finished the piece and Mama clasped her hands to her breast, tears in her eyes. Then, as everyone was still applauding, he stood up, put his glasses into his top pocket, pulled a lock of curly hair down onto his forehead and, standing crouched over the keyboard, began to play again. His right foot banged out the beat and his hands alternately pounded the keys and ran up and down in repeated glissandi until he stood up, turned his back on the piano and played the final notes of 'Great Balls of Fire' by sitting on the keyboard.

'Jerry Lee Lewis was a great hero of mine – a natural pianist – completely self-taught.' And Maestro Daniel was laughing as he pushed back his hair, acknowledged our applause and began to take requests from his audience.

'I hope he shows as much enthusiasm when he lectures on Bach …' muttered Tata dryly when the guests had left. 'The boy's a clown – I can't think why the Board gave him that job.'

'He's not a boy', I said. 'He's thirty – I've seen his passport – passports – he's got two, you know.'

My mother laughed. 'One of these days you'll think thirty's quite young.'

Happily, our lodger was able to reclaim his gravitas in my father's eyes a few weeks later when he gave his first concert at the Conservatory. He was to play a Mozart Piano Concerto with the city orchestra – most of whose members were old at that time and several were my relatives; he would direct it himself from the keyboard. I was used to seeing him at the piano as I looked across at the studio, but in the days leading up to his concert I watched fascinated as he practised conducting too, the score in front of him as he sang the orchestral part to himself and his hands brought in the imaginary players. He stopped from time to time, making pencil notes on the page before leaving to rehearse with the orchestra. I missed him at mealtimes and wished the concert over and normal life resumed.

Tata, remembering the embarrassment of my mother's birthday party, had scarcely spoken to our lodger for several days afterwards. But, a musician himself, he could not restrain himself from asking Maestro Daniel as he drank his breakfast coffee a few days before the performance, about the cadenza he would be playing. 'I believe Mozart's own for this concerto was lost?'

'Or he just didn't write it down – he often improvised when he performed his own work. There is a Beethoven cadenza which is frequently played, but I find it somehow intrusive – the voice of another great composer, yes, but one whose style and weight are so different from Mozart's. This is one I've been working on for some time. It's an awe-inspiring challenge to attempt to add anything to this glorious concerto.'

'And you prefer not to have a conductor?

'The great Mozartian, Geza Andá, thought it the best way to keep piano and orchestra singing with one voice.'

'Did you study under Andá?'

'No, I was too young … and he lived in Vienna or Budapest … but he stayed with us once. I heard him direct and play several Mozart concerti in London … and I've never forgotten those performances. He was great fun and women adored him. He died far too young – of cancer – even when he was teaching he always had a cigarette hanging out of his mouth. I really worshipped him – and he wore specs too, so I didn't mind when I got mine!'

On the evening of the concert, I looked out of my window and saw Maestro Daniel leave the studio, his tail suit on a hanger in one hand and a fat music case in the other. This time he didn't go by bicycle; a large black car swept him away.

With its huge chandeliers and sagging blue velvet chairs, the Conservatory concert hall had a still elegant, but slightly shabby, grandeur. That evening the ornate Bösendorfer piano had been put centre stage so that the pianist could be seen by all the players. I was filled with breathless anticipation, hardly able to contain myself until the performance began.

The orchestra filed in and began to tune up. Then Maestro

Daniel appeared, immaculate in white tie and tails, shook hands with the leader and bowed solemnly to the audience. It was the first time I had seen him perform in public and my heart swelled with pride. His large, graceful hands performed their subtle ballet, tiny indications and inflections of his arms and fingers bringing in the different sections of the orchestra. And when he played the lilting, tripping airs, the delicate, immaculate runs and ornaments of the solo piano part, his fellow musicians were coaxed, by the play of his mobile face, into bringing the familiar music to life with all the freshness and intensity of pilgrims.

The standing ovation that followed left no doubt that the Maestro's reputation in Sarajevo was assured, even to those who, like my father, had doubted that the new Director of Keyboard Studies was a serious and exceptional musician. Although his working days were long and busy, Maestro Daniel was always approachable and patient when he was questioned about music, so Tata started to invite him into his study for a nightcap. I could smell the smoke of Turkish cigarettes wafting up the stairs and heard their animated voices long after I had gone to bed. I wondered what they talked about when my mother and I were not around.

The following day I was told that Maestro Daniel would be resting in the studio. Seeing Amela start out unsteadily across the garden with a tray of food, Mama told me to take it myself and save her the journey. I found the Maestro at the piano, writing rapidly on manuscript paper, playing the odd phrase or bar as he wrote and singing quietly to himself. I hesitated by the open French window, but he looked up and saw me.

'Czarina Irena, what's this? Are you now to be my own personal slave?'

'Mama thought you'd like your lunch in here so you can rest.'

'That's very kind, but I could have fetched the tray myself. This looks delicious – and far too much – come and share it with me.' Amela's helpings were always on the large side and she had fallen hard for our house-guest. Thinking he was too thin, she was constantly giving him little treats, until he said; 'Madame Amela, you're going to make me fat and I haven't got time to go shopping for new clothes.' The old woman didn't understand what he was saying, but when he pecked her on the cheek her pasty, wrinkled face assumed a glow not seen in many years.

I sat down on the doorstep next to the Maestro who gave me his fork while he used a piece of bread to scoop up the fish stew which Amela had flavoured lavishly with garlic and pimento. We waved our hands in front of our mouths as the hot spices hit our tongues. Then he peeled a peach very seriously and meticulously, cut it in two and gave me the rosier half.

'Your concert was wonderful' I ventured.

'Ah. I'm glad you enjoyed it. The orchestra were perfect, don't you think?'

'Yes. But it must be very hard to play the piano and conduct as well.'

'Hard, but well worth it. You see, that way we're all on the same wavelength. Pianists and conductors don't always want the same things from a piece of music.'

The steam from the hot food had clouded his glasses and he took them off and put them down beside his plate. How surprisingly blue his eyes were, for his skin was olive, his hair almost black.

'Your eyes are an amazing colour,' I said before I could stop myself.

'Thank you, but they're amazingly short-sighted, too I'm afraid.' He polished his spectacles, held them up to the light and put them on again, smiling at me as he did so. So I went on: 'Do you like talking about music? My family do.'

'Well, that's part of my job, you know. I have to give lectures about it. For instance, this week my theme is the use of the pedals – so very important playing the piano and something people don't always work at enough – Chopin said the sustaining pedal was the "soul of the piano" you know.'

'Do you like teaching? I mean don't you want to be travelling around and giving concerts everywhere?'

'The travelling's not really that much fun – I don't often get to see more than hotel rooms and concert halls. Anyway, I really love teaching and trying to tell the students things that will help them in their interpretations. But it's impossible to describe in words what sound means to a composer or performer – or just a lover of music – and we don't really understand how the brain processes music into such great emotions. Your parents love music, so you mustn't blame them, Irenita, if they also love to talk about it. Just you learn your instrument as well as you can – then it will say for you what you have in your heart and you can leave the talking to other people.'

I was brought back to earth by my mother calling me for lunch. 'You must have a very good memory – for all those notes, I mean.'

Maestro Daniel piled up the dishes and put the tray into my hands.

'Ah, but you see I can't remember a lot of other things. For instance, your name. Petrushka, isn't it?'

I giggled and he went on: 'I need some fresh air – Amela will want bread later – come down to the baker with me when you've had your second lunch?'

'Oh yes. And we can get cakes.' I knew he had a sweet a tooth, as I did.

I hurriedly returned the Maestro's tray to the kitchen. Amela was gratified to see the cleanly wiped plates, but anxious when she saw me picking at my food. She would dose me later with a disgusting herbal potion that her peasant grandmother had given her as a child.

Our lodger always seemed to be in a hurry. I would watch as he cycled off every morning to the Conservatory, and laugh when frequently he returned a few minutes later for something he had forgotten. His students and the Conservatory staff were of all nationalities and lessons were mainly conducted in English, so he had no need to learn Serbo-Croat, but he thought it couldn't be too hard as it had many similarities to his native Czech. I volunteered to help him if we could go on the promised bicycle rides when he was free at weekends. I was not allowed to go to the vast dark forests alone, and this arrangement pleased the Maestro who liked the change from sitting at the piano.

We would set off, Maestro Daniel on my father's bicycle, for which his legs were rather long. First, we would go to the market, where we bought sausages and tomatoes and fruit and little dishes of local specialities, which we chose with care. There, I would laugh unkindly at his valiant efforts to speak to the stall holders and tell him wrong words for the things he was trying to buy.

Then we would take the main road and enter the forest which extended, dark and mysterious, over acres and acres of the mountains around Sarajevo. I loved the dappled light on the tracks we followed between the huge dark trees, singing as we rode, down to the swift, tumbling stream below, where we would sit on the bank and eat our picnic, skimming flat river stones across the water to see how many times they would bounce.

3. GATHERING CLOUDS

MAESTRO DANIEL had a good grasp of the complicated politics of the region and would join in the discussions that came to dominate our dining table that year, most of it fraught with an unspoken fearfulness for the future of Yugoslavia after its federal units had become independent states. Since then, the various factions had been enlarging and reinforcing their home guards into increasingly threatening armed forces. My parents did their best to protect me from their anxiety for as long as they could, but the papers were full of reports of increasingly frequent attacks on the Yugoslav People's Army, some not many miles from where we lived. I knew that all was not well when my father became uneasy about our Serbian neighbours in the northern suburbs of the city, where we had many family friends. Brought up as I had been under Tito's government, I was used to the constraints and difficulties of living under Communism, but my life was still thrilling and varied and I could not at that time imagine that anything would change it.

The winter snows melted and spring began late – and reluctantly it seemed – that year of 1992. Maestro Daniel and I, in thick coats, fur hats and boots, had been determined to brave the cold and go for the first cycle ride of the year.

As we set off for home we rounded a corner and saw that a road block had been set up across our way, manned by armed men in combat uniforms. They made us dismount and the Maestro handed over our papers, shielding me behind his bicycle and himself. Earlier he had surprised me by insisting

I bring my identity card with me and I had seen him put a passport into his coat pocket. The soldiers took a long time examining the documents, making crude comments as they looked at my photograph. Then they took all the money my companion was carrying and let us pass.

We were not held up for long, but I could see that Maestro Daniel was more upset than I was by the experience. From what I'd heard from visiting members of the family, these road-blocks were becoming a regular feature of travelling in and around Sarajevo. We would soon cease to venture far from the house. So began the closing in of our lives, as we became prisoners in what had once been a peaceful suburb above the city.

That evening at dinner, Tata wiped his mouth, put down his napkin and planted his hands on either side of his plate. We all looked at him expectantly, knowing that he must be about to say something of importance to which he expected every-one to listen.

'It's time we tried to understand what's happening around us. Irena and Maestro Daniel, you were stopped today and this is happening all over Sarajevo now. I suspect that the Serbian militia are going to become more and more aggressive – they are determined to reclaim – as they would put it – our city and its surroundings – and create a Serbian-ruled state. That in itself is serious, but their hatred of Muslims is something we need to fear, as a community and as a family.'

I interrupted him: 'But Mum's not a Muslim – she's an Irish Protestant, a Christian … '

'Don't interrupt, Irena, this is serious. No-one knows what the Serbian army has planned for us, but they've begun to position snipers and build up an arsenal of weapons in the hills above us.'

I stared at him in disbelief.

'That's where Dsopan and Marina live ...' And, as I said these names, I thought of the many other Serb pupils at my school.

Mama said, gently 'Yes, darling, but they are Serbs and so are many of our friends. They will find themselves very torn in their loyalty now.'

Maestro Daniel, who wore a more serious expression than I had ever seen before on his usually cheerful face, spoke slowly. 'I have heard that Muslim families are preparing to leave the city and stay somewhere safer until they know which way things are going. Would you consider leaving the city for a while, Adam?'

My father shook his head. 'I can't think that we need to take such action yet – if at all. I think we'd all prefer to remain here and see how the wind blows. But what about you, Maestro? You have no need to stay, have you?'

Mama looked up, her face suffused with some strong emotion that I could not read; she looked across at Maestro Daniel, seeming to be willing him to look in her direction. But he was answering my father, his voice slow and measured.

'I would prefer to stay – if you'll have me. I haven't finished the work I came here to do. And now, if you'll excuse me, I have something to prepare for tomorrow.' He rose, bowed slightly to my father and said goodnight to my mother and me. I saw Mama's eyes follow him out of the room and, after a few minutes she hurriedly piled up our fruit plates and carried them into the kitchen. I heard her speaking then, her voice high-pitched and pleading, and Maestro Daniel's voice replying. He seemed to be calming her down. Then the garden door opened and closed and Mama reappeared, her face flushed and streaked with tears, as she summoned me to help her clear the table. Tata watched us for a moment and then rose and, refilling his wine glass as he passed the sideboard, went across the hall to his study.

As I was going up to bed, Tata called out to me and I leant over the banisters and looked down at him.

'You're not afraid, are you, my little Wren? I didn't frighten you with what I said?'

I looked down at his broad, dark-eyed face with its bushy black moustache under a surprisingly delicate nose – fine-drawn and narrow. I had never seen him afraid before, but I knew that he felt helpless and unable, for the first time, to protect his family from whatever was to come. Why, I wonder, as I look back now, did I not run down to him and try to reassure him or at least go into his arms and let him feel my love for him? Instead, I began to turn back up the stairs.

'I'm not scared, Tata. But please let's stay here with our friends. Don't take us away, will you?'

I was thinking only of myself and of another person I had become accustomed to seeing every day.

My mother was in her mid-thirties then, a pretty woman and a foreigner. I knew she always felt she would never really belong away from her native Ireland. I had begun to notice, that spring, that she often sought the company of Maestro Daniel, but I suppose I was so enraptured with him myself that I paid little attention. I probably thought, anyway, that she must be far too old to be attractive to him. He had discovered that she had a lovely, high soprano voice and took to accompanying her in the Schumann *Lieder* that my father had taught her in Dublin. She found that she remembered the words of *Im wunderschönen Monat Mai* and her eyes were fixed on those of Maestro Daniel as her sweet voice, winged and ecstatic, floated above the water-like rippling of the piano part.

She, in turn, taught him the Viennese waltz. I watched them whirl round and round the music room, his head bent to hers. He was a good dancer and learnt quickly but would forget to execute a reverse turn from time to time, so that they would stagger, clutching each other, dizzy and doubled up with laughter when the music stopped. Mama would leave the room hurriedly when she heard Tata return from work and then Maestro Daniel would change the record and dance with me, leaping around the room as he taught me to jive and jitterbug. He introduced me to the frenetic moves of the Lindy Hop, too, and I loved it, but I secretly wished he'd ask me to waltz and hold me in his arms as he held Mama.

Maestro Daniel was a busy man and I suppose we cannot have spent very much time together. I was busy too. I had my school work, at which I was expected to do well, and my own music. I rose early every day to do an hour's practice on my viola before breakfast and there had to be at least another two hours found somehow during the rest of the day before I had satisfied my father that I'd done enough work on my instrument.

One morning, struggling with a piece that I found particularly demanding, I saw Maestro Daniel's reflection in the looking glass over the fireplace. He came over and stood beside me as I continued to play. I could smell his delicate English shaving soap as I played and there were flecks of it still on his chin, which I had to ignore so as not to laugh. When I reached the end of the piece, he said, 'This Walton really throws everything at you, doesn't it?' Then, taking the viola from me, he asked, 'May I?'

I nodded, wondering if he knew how to play a stringed instrument.

'Oh, good old C clef, of course, let me see ...'

He raised the music stand to his height, tightened the bow a little, put the instrument under his chin and started to play.

It was as if a sigh were going around the room, a rhythmic purring sigh which then flowed into an air of great sweetness. When he reached the passage of double stopping, he bent sideways over the instrument, pounding the strings with the bow. Then he plucked them as delicately as a bird pecking at grain as the pizzicato passage led to the return of the theme and the final legato bars which flowed towards the low, questioning conclusion.

My father had been listening to my practising as he got dressed. Hearing the change in what he took to be my playing, he came running into the music room just as the Maestro completed the piece.

'I didn't know you played the viola,' we both said at once.

'Well, as a conductor I need to have some knowledge of all sections of the orchestra, but I've always particularly loved the viola and studied it for a while.' He paused and added, smiling at me, 'I'm not very good at instruments you have to blow through …'

'You mustn't let Irena take up too much of your time, Maestro Daniel. You have far too many calls on it already,' said my father.

'It's a pleasure to hear a musician in the making,' was his reply.

He never told me how I ought to play or gave me outright instruction, but his gentle suggestions left me with an inspiration that was to last all my life. He taught me subtleties of sound that were new to me, using words and expressions which were not like those of my tutor, who listened to my progress with surprised delight.

One evening after dinner, Tata brought a battered black case into the music room and held it out to me. I could see that he was excited; his eyes glowed and his thick moustache quivered as he told me to open it. Mama and Maestro Daniel stepped forward to watch as I lifted out a small viola, its varnish softly bright and the figured walnut of its back like some beautiful animal's pelt.

'It's like a tabby cat!' I exclaimed.

'Maestro Daniel thinks you need a better viola, Irena, and my old friend Dr Lubowić, who is an expert on stringed instruments, found this for you, my darling girl. It's a rare three-quarter-size viola from the Guarneri workshop – possibly made by a pupil of the great Andrea. It's been in my friend's collection for ages, as it's too small for most adult viola players. It's perfect for you.'

'But won't she grow out of it?' asked my mother.

The Maestro said: 'Oh, I think she'll always be petite, like you, Nolly.'

Nolly? This was the pet name that only close friends and family called Mama and it had come out as if he was accustomed to using it. I saw my mother's eyes widen and Daniel reddened. They both looked towards Tata, but he was at the piano, tuning the viola and singing the notes as he did so; he appeared not to have heard. The Maestro excused himself soon after and left the room, just pausing to say to me, without meeting my eyes: 'That's a lovely instrument you have now. You're a very lucky girl.'

Perhaps I would have overlooked or forgotten that incident. Life seemed to go on as usual and Maestro Daniel appeared at meals and made jokes as usual, but the dynamics of mealtimes had changed; there seemed to be a stillness between Mama and him and a new, strained formality in their conversation.

Spring was coming and, one day, as I was approaching the studio to see if Maestro Daniel was there, I saw the door open and my mother coming out. There would have been nothing strange in that alone, but she was walking hurriedly, and I saw that her pale red hair was down, a drift of soft apricot tumbling onto her shoulders, and, as she walked back to the house, she was catching the locks and pinning them up again into the accustomed chignon. She had not seen me and disappeared from my view into the kitchen, tears streaming down her lovely face.

I hesitated outside the studio, confused. Maestro Daniel was standing by the piano, his back to the door, but he heard my step and turned round, his face lighting up: 'You've come back, Nolly!' but then he saw me and stood stock still for a moment, his expression changing from joy to one of confusion. 'Oh Irena. You'd better come in …' He rarely called me by my real name and I suddenly felt apprehensive. He looked very serious, but not with the seriousness that came when he talked of his beloved music. This was something else, more painful, and seemed to fill the air with foreboding.

'Have your parents told you that I have to go back to England – very soon?'

I couldn't answer and he continued: 'The Foreign Office in London has asked me to take the British students back with me as soon as possible.'

I looked up at him, uncomprehending. Surely he couldn't leave us, not yet.

'When will you come back?'

'When I can. I promise. But I need to get back to work in London – I was never going to stay more than a year at the Conservatory.'

I was too immature to know I ought to say I understood, so that breaking this news to me would be easier for him. All I could feel was my own pain and the shock of what I had just witnessed. Yet I could have forgiven him anything if he would stay, if life could go back to the way it had been and he could be in the studio, tease me, go for bicycle rides and make music live for me in my studies.

'Please don't go away.'

'Oh, Irena ... I wish I could stay. It's been wonderful being with your family, but I've got to go back to London. I have no choice.'

'When are you going?' I asked.

'The day after tomorrow.' He turned his head away, took a handkerchief out of his pocket and removed his glasses. I had never seen a man cry.

'Irena, it's time for your lesson,' called my mother from the house and I wondered if she could see us through the studio window.

Maestro Daniel turned back to me, tears now running down his face.

'You'd better go in, sweet one,' he said. He had never called me that before.

The following day I did not see Maestro Daniel at all. He was at the music school winding up his work, but his light was on late into that night. I could see him moving around as he piled sheet music and scores onto the piano and put them into boxes. The next morning, I saw these being carried out to the front of the house and suitcases and bags followed. Then I heard the studio door shut for the last time on our lodger. Although it was spring and warm for the season, I lay down on my bed and pulled the bedclothes over me.

My father called up the stairs: 'Irena, come and say goodbye to Maestro Daniel.'

I ran downstairs and through the house. There was a taxi in the road and my parents were at the gate with Maestro Daniel. My father saw me and beckoned me to where my mother stood, weeping. The Maestro turned and I remembered the first time I'd seen him standing between my parents and holding out his hand to me, smiling. But now the smile he attempted was bleak and sad.

'You won't forget me, will you, Little Wren?' He spoke so softly that I almost didn't catch the words as he took my hand. He lifted it to his lips, as I had seen him do with my mother and other women. Then he climbed into the taxi and was gone.

4. BESIEGED

S ARAJEVO HAD BEEN a lovely place to live, a magical, kalei-doscopic city, steeped in the history of the Holy Roman Empire. My journey to school took me past Orthodox and Catholic churches, synagogues, mosques and temples where the Muslim call to prayer was interspersed with the bells that punctuated the Christian day. In common with many Yugo-slavs at that time, my parents did not practise their religions – except on feast days when they took advantage of all that both faiths could offer for merriment and present-giving. They had taught me passionately about the architecture, the beauty and the history of our city and its buildings, but my education was strictly sectarian, as was common in the liberal, multi-racial Sarajevo of those days. Nor could I possibly have antici-pated the prejudice and hatred that, nominally in the name of these religions, were to turn neighbour against neighbour, friend against friend.

The Siege began a few weeks after Maestro Daniel left. At first, there was sniper fire in the streets. Distant though our house was from the city centre, their guns became a constant background to our lives. Then mortar shells began to burst, leaving behind smoking craters and scarring the city we loved with an arbitrary baptism of shrapnel. More constant even than that – for the shooting ceased at night – fear became a constant companion, entering our minds at daybreak with the fading of our dreams and remaining with us all our waking hours. Electricity and water were turned off for most of the time, so washing and cooking engaged our ingenuity. Food was very scarce and increasingly expensive with meat a rare luxury. A continual hunger – a gut-churning sensation I had never known before – seemed to drive out other thoughts.

The stray dog I had adopted had to be fed on our scraps and then, one day, he disappeared. I searched everywhere for him and was wandering down the road, which I was forbidden to do, as there were snipers on the hill behind the house. Pressing myself against the walls, I made my way towards the little square in front of our nearest church. I could hear laughter and saw, as I approached, a group of men in dirty uniforms, pointing at the main entrance of the church, the fine old doors with iron hinges whose complicated swirls and arabesques had always fascinated me. Then I saw it – I saw her – and the image has never left me, never found any propitiation in my endless reliving of the jumbled memories that brought my childhood to its ugly, sudden end. Hanging on the door from torn, bleeding hands was the body of a young girl, a girl I knew. Looking back, I realise she had been crucified, but I had no recognition or understanding of what I had witnessed as I turned, retching and weeping, stumbling back home over the shell holes and fallen masonry. Behind me were voices and running feet – and more laughter – and an engine starting up. A Jeep overtook me as I half fell against the pile of stones that had once been our front wall to the street. Four soldiers got out and one of them twisted my arm behind my back and dragged me up the drive to the front door.

My parents were both at home, as Tata's office had been bombed and Mama was helping him sort out the papers he had managed to rescue from the ruins. They looked up and tried to reach out to me as the first soldier pushed me through the door, but the other soldiers, laughing again, held them back as they danced me up and down in front of them. It was lunch time and Amela was in the kitchen trying to make a cabbage into an appetizing meal. They found her cowering under the table, and frog-marched us all out into the garden. There, the three adults were lined up against the garden wall, sunbaked on that hot summer's day, so that they screwed up their eyes against the bright gleam of the guns being held in their faces.

I stood helplessly, facing them and held fast by my captor. He now had his hand over my mouth and pushed his fingers between my teeth so I could not scream. They tasted of oil and unwashed flesh. I saw a soldier take hold of my mother, pulling at her clothes and laughing. My father lunged at him and another soldier struck him full in the face with his rifle butt. It went straight into Tata's eye socket and blood gushed out with fragments of bone. I felt I must be having a nightmare; everything seemed to be happening in slow motion and, like a film, in garish colour, for the sky was a pure cobalt blue that day and the garden bright with flowers. Tata was crouching on the ground, cradling his head in his arms and moaning, a stream of blood pooling onto the hot paving stones. Mama screamed and I struggled to go to her, but was held back. I watched the first soldier unbuckle his belt, and, pulling her skirt up with one hand, he pushed her against the garden wall, her arms and legs splayed. He raped her there in front of me, in front of my father, but Tata could no longer see, thank God. I think he was already dead. Then another soldier took Mama too, and the other followed. She just stood there, her face averted as they shot her in the head. She fell across Tata, imitating in death the conjugal embrace they had long ago abandoned in life.

Amela had been thrown up against the wall, too, but the soldiers didn't have any use for her. Shouting with ribald laughter, one of them pulled the wooden cover off the well that stood outside the kitchen door, then covered in pots of geraniums because we no longer used it. He picked the old woman up. She screamed, her toothless mouth a dark chasm in her wrinkled face, her one remaining eye cast up to heaven in supplication. The soldier whirled her round in a macabre imitation of dancing. Then he smiled reassuringly into her face and dropped her down the well, carefully replacing the cover and putting the plants back where they had been.

My captor had passed me to one of the others while he had his way with my mother. I struggled and screamed but my arms were pinned behind my back. Then, as he reclaimed me, he flicked the straps of my sun dress and ran his hand down the front of my body.

'This one's mine,' he said and pushed me into the Jeep.

5. DANIELS'S QUEST

'DARLING, DO STOP looking so serious.'
Felicity ran her fingers through Daniel's dark curls.
'Don't do that,' he said, pushing her hand away. 'I'm trying
to read this.' He had spread the newspaper out on the floor at
his feet and was leafing through the pages.

'You're always reading the papers now – ever since you got
back to London. Always Sarajevo, Sarajevo. Can't you think
about anything else?'

'Flic, you just don't understand. I lived there, with that
wonderful family and they haven't answered any of my letters.
I must get some news of them and I don't know how.'

'I'm sure they're fine – probably escaped and living somewhere safer – lots of people have left the city, you know. There
are pictures of them getting into buses every day on the news
– they get taken to places away from the war. I do understand
that you're worried, but we are getting married, you know.
That's quite important, too. To me, anyway.' She stood up
and smoothed her tight leather trousers over her hips and
turned back towards Daniel. 'You do still want to marry me,
don't you?'

He took her hand and pulled her back onto the sofa next to
him, his eyes on the narrow white fingers he held. Her hands
had always fascinated him; they were so graceful yet so useless.
'Of course I do. But you know I'd rather we just walked down
to the Registry Office – it's really near – in Wright's Lane. I
haven't got any relations apart from my sister and if I had
they wouldn't fancy a church service.'

He held the soft hand against his cheek for a moment.

'Oh Danny – you know Mummy so desperately wants me to have a proper church wedding. It doesn't matter if my side is fuller than yours – anyway you've got all those musician friends, masses of them, haven't you? They'll come, won't they?'

'Saturday's not the best day for them – they're nearly all Jewish. But, you know, darling, I can't really concentrate on this until we get back from Chicago.'

Felicity was silent for a moment, smiling to herself as she savoured the prospect of their first tour together, Daniel being fêted everywhere and staying in the best hotels. She had been a part of his life for a couple of years before he'd taken the job at Sarajevo Conservatory. They'd talked about marriage and he'd often dreamed of her being always at his side, but the dream was always silent, without words or music. Just a vision of her in all her blond beauty floating beside him, lying supine in his bed, her lips parted, her ivory-pale arms held out to him, but when he'd approached her, there would be nothing there. Just the wispy remnants of the dream, like fine white filaments of shredded silken cloth, evading his searching hands.

He detached himself from her embrace, kissed her neck and went back to reading his newspaper. After a few minutes, he tore out a piece from the foreign section, pushed it into his top pocket, got up and went to the window, where he continued to stand for some minutes, staring out at the great opaque expanse of sky that lay between him and Yugoslavia.

Soon after he had left Sarajeveo, Daniel had written to Adam and Finola – a long and affectionate expression of thanks for their kindness and hospitality. He had included in his envelope a note to Irena, telling her to come over to London soon as he needed her to tidy up his scores. Finola's reply was full of anguish and fear; there was nothing from Irena. He wrote back by return of post, begging her to bring her family to London while she could – or at least to send Irena for his sister and him to look after. But there had been no further word. He learnt from the papers that the post was no longer getting through to Sarajevo or its surrounding villages.

There was nothing then to give him any hope that his friends were safe. He thought of Adam, who had welcomed him so generously, almost as a son, for the year he had lived in their garden studio. He thought, too, of the Conservatory, with its pompous *fin de siècle* grandeur, of his earnest students and the hours of teaching and study he'd spent there that year. His fellow professors had all been so kind, so ready to overlook his inexperience. The young musician's professional reputation had preceded him and the fabled Dr Solomon, known for his short temper and gimlet eye would have been prepared to put up with much for the honour of having such a talent under his roof, but even that cantankerous old man had succumbed to Daniel's charm. The old musician had written him a disturbing letter; there was no good news, except that the conservatory struggled on, in spite of considerable damage to its fabric, to provide music and tuition, to keep spirits up in the war-torn city. Maestro Danuczek would always be welcomed with open arms but shocked by what he would find. Many people were leaving the city. Death and destruction were all around them.

Daniel's schedule of teaching and performing had never been so busy. And now this wedding. He hoped that Felicity would understand why he absolutely had to go out to Yugoslavia; she surely would see that he couldn't go on not knowing how the Vidakovićs were and whether he could bring them help. He must find a way to get to Sarajevo. But how? He had tried many times to telephone, but the lines were dead.

Daniel thought of little else, tormented by the alarming articles and hideous pictures that filled the newspapers. He wrote to Martin Bell, whose reports appeared regularly in the British press. The journalist, now a war correspondent in and around Sarajevo, was deeply pessimistic about Daniel's request, but said he would help if he could. He thought that the presence of such a man – who probably had no understanding of what daily life had become in the besieged city – could only be a danger to himself and to others. But a Croatian reporter begged him to find a way of getting Daniel to Sarajevo – music was something that people desperately needed in the city, he said. Bell thought then of a new colleague, Peter Henderson, who was to be going out in the next wave of BBC coverage.

'Dr Danuczek?' The satellite line from Sarajevo kept breaking up and Daniel could scarcely hear the voice on the other end – also there was a lot of background noise that sounded like gunfire. 'Sorry – is that how you pronounce your name? I'm Peter Henderson. I gather you want to get out to Bosnia?'

'Oh, God, yes I do – you're Bell's friend?'

A laugh. 'Not really his friend. Very much an underling, but he's asked me to help you. You want to try to find some missing people, I gather.' And Daniel told him about the Vidaković family and about Professor Solomon's request for music. The words poured out of him and the reporter stopped him, gently.

'Fine. Let's see what we can do. You know, I expect, that you might come back in a box or, if you're lucky, with a leg missing?'

'As long as it's not a hand – I need both of mine!'

Winter had begun when Daniel climbed into Henderson's Land Rover at the airport and was jogged and bumped, frozen to the bone, through the passes that led to Sarajevo, through the burnt and decimated forests where Irena and he had once cycled, laughing and singing between trees that were still tall and green. After endless check points they arrived in the city late in the afternoon and Daniel looked around in disbelief at the hideous changes – at the appalling damage that no building seemed to have escaped. Some had been reduced to mere craters; all were pocked with shrapnel and rocket blast.

Daniel joined Henderson at a hotel made famous by the journalists who met there to file their reports, a square yellow building whose colour and uncompromising shape had shocked the city when it was first unveiled. He spent the evening by candlelight which was the only source of illumination, drinking too much and hearing with a terrible foreboding the stories they told him of everyday life in the city. Arriving at their hotel, Henderson, who was surprisingly young, with an alert, humorous manner, brown eyes and a lean, intelligent face, went with Daniel to his room and warned him to watch where he walked as there was broken glass everywhere. He suggested he sleep on his mattress under the table; Daniel wasn't sure if he was joking. They were to go out into the city early the next day to try to find news of the Vidaković family from the neighbourhood of the Vila Dolena. He had been asked to play at the Conservatory at lunch time, when old friends and colleagues would gather to meet him again. Naïvely, he accepted this invitation, not yet knowing that trying to keep to any timetable was foolishly optimistic in besieged Sarajevo.

As dawn broke, Daniel was woken by a noise he could not at first identify. Then he remembered that Peter had warned him that the snipers rose at daybreak in their hides in the hills above the city, and would begin picking off anyone who dared to walk across the main city roads and the two bridges. Shells burst sporadically, leaving behind a landscape of smoking craters. The dead lay where they fell and the wounded cried out for help. Some were dragged to safety by crouching figures, often falling themselves as they scurried about their tasks. Daniel was terrified – he had never been near real gunfire or anywhere where his life was in danger. He had imagined it would be bad, but this – this was beyond the bounds of any nightmare he had known.

And everywhere an image he was to carry all his life – the endless stream of refugees, anonymous in their ragged clothing and carrying whatever they could, leaving their homes to board buses and lorries which would take them away. Where to? Who could know.

They were accompanied by Sandy, the Glaswegian cameraman, up into the northern suburb where Irena's family had lived. Sandy, shaven-headed and covered in tattoos, looked at Daniel and wondered why the hell he was being asked to endanger his life for this soft, no doubt ignorant passenger – who wore gloves all the time, for God's sake. He had no use for these hangers-on and made this quite plain to Daniel. And Peter Henderson wondered about his passenger, curious to know what it was that drove him to put himself in such danger.

Nevinosti Street scarcely existed any more. Daniel got out of the Land Rover and scrambled over the heaped up rubble to where a single stone gate post still marked where the drive had once curved up to the house. The Vila Dolena had taken several hits. The roof had caved in but the four walls still stood and Daniel put his shoulder to the door until unwillingly it creaked open. Inside the rubble was deep and he saw that the curved stairs and landings had collapsed into the hall, the doors to the bedrooms opening onto a void above him. He clambered over the fallen masonry and found the music room. The ceiling was pitted with bullet holes but still intact and he tried to make out the languorous Baroque figures, now whitened with plaster dust and cracked from corner to corner. He groped through the remains of the kitchen to the back door, past the well and across the garden, where only stumps remained of Finola's precious fruit trees. The studio bore signs of habitation – an old mattress, piles of rags and newspaper and, pushed into a corner, a heap of dusty ivory and ebony keys and tangled brass wire. Plastic sheeting had been nailed to some of the blue window frames but was coming away and hanging like great bats, flapping in the wind. He began to cry, the tears coagulating in the dust on his cheeks. He took off his glasses and wiped his face and eyes; the unfocused view of the beloved surroundings comforting him for a moment. Was he dreaming, he wondered. Was this a nightmare from which he would awaken and find himself again on the mezzanine of the studio and looking down on the grand piano strewn with his sheet music? But the sharp focus as he replaced his spectacles brought the present back before his unwilling eyes and he stumbled back to the Land Rover.

He would have recognized the old neighbours, but everyone had gone – either rounded up and taken away, Henderson said, or killed in their own homes. This was the fate of most people from that area. Daniel asked an old woman who was trying to sell him a few potatoes if she knew where the Vidaković family were. But she didn't understand what he said and, if she recognized the name, she pretended they meant nothing to her, muttering again and again, her dusty, wrinkled face writhing around her toothless mouth: '*Nema nikoga kući, nema nikoga kući.*' (no-one at home, no-one at home).

Daniel gave her some money and stuffed her potatoes into his pockets. The driver took the Land Rover on while Peter and he went on foot along the once familiar streets, past the white mosque and the synagogue, turning down the cobbled lane that led to the market place. Wherever they went there was the stench of death, of blood and the all-pervasive dank smell of decaying buildings and sewage.

The half-covered market place was thronged with people hurrying to get the few available goods before the stalls were sold out. Others, with whatever containers they were able to carry, had formed an orderly line beside the water tanker drawn up in the street.

Daniel and Sandy made their way through the queue. Then the mortar bomb went off. For an instant, Daniel only knew that it was the loudest noise he had ever heard, a sound that seemed to fill his whole head and body and burst out again, tearing at his ear-drums. Then, almost in slow-motion everything was lifted into the air, the water, as it leapt from the disintegrating tanker forming a graceful waving curtain above it, where it billowed around, performing a macabre dance with the canvas coverings of the stalls, with bodies and parts of bodies – chunks of butcher's meat or hunks of human flesh: it was impossible to tell them apart.

Daniel was thrown violently backwards and found himself at the foot of a wall, winded and covered in blood – and something worse than blood, thick and stinking – and his ears were singing. His glasses had gone and it was a moment before he saw that Sandy was lying a few feet away, halfway through an open door next to a heap of something from which Daniel averted his eyes. The photographer was groaning and Daniel crawled painfully to his side.

'Sandy' he croaked, his throat full of dust. 'Sandy, it's OK. I'm here.' He looked around desperately for Peter. He could see little for the still swirling dust and debris. The air was filled with screaming and shouting as the living tried to get help, to find their companions and, if they were still able, to get away from the horror around them.

Daniel wiped the blood and dust from the photographer's face with his handkerchief. Then he saw that Sandy's left arm had been blown off – raggedly at the elbow – and jets of blood spewed rhythmically from the severed arteries.

Daniel felt his stomach heave. His instinct was to get away, anything but look at that pumping blood and jagged stump. He took a deep breath of the thick, rancid air and tried to think. A tourniquet, that was it … He took off his belt and put it around the top of Sandy's arm, pulling it as tightly as he dared. The blood ceased to gush from the wound, just a thin stream now seeping from the torn flesh. He needed a bandage of some sort. Daniel struggled out of his anorak and flak jacket and removed his shirt. He tried to rip it with his teeth, but it was new and he could not tear it, try as he would. He clumsily tied the whole shirt over the end of the limb and wound the sleeves round as tightly as he could. The crisp blue shirting was soon sodden with blood and, leaning away from Sandy, Daniel was sick against the wall.

'Hey. Don't go to sleep. Sandy, Sandy!' Daniel knew he must keep him awake somehow. He wondered what had happened to Henderson and hoped to God he hadn't been blown to pieces. He'd got to get help for the photographer and had no idea how to set about it. And he was pretty sure that, if he released the tourniquet and let Sandy lapse into unconsciousness, the man would die. There were no ambulances. The dead and wounded were being collected on carts and on the back of pick-up trucks, but he was loath to let Sandy join them – his few polite words of Serbo-Croat would hardly have served him now.

It seemed an age before Peter turned up, he too covered in dust and gore, but intact. Coming into the market place a little behind the others, he'd missed the worst of the blast and had been frantically searching for his companions. He found Daniel, naked to the waist and sitting in a pool of blood. He was still holding his belt around the remaining part of the Sandy's arm and, cradling the man's head in his lap, slapping his face and singing: '*I belong tae Glasgae, Dear auld Glasgae toon ...*'

The Land Rover was still where it had been left behind the market. It was covered in debris but it started after a few attempts and Peter drove Sandy and a badly injured woman to the nearest hospital, or what remained of it. Daniel waited outside, watching the stream of cars and vans unload their gory charges. Peter joined him.

'We'll get him flown home tomorrow, if we can. He's luckier than most of these sods. I'm sorry you had to witness that. You did well today.'

'I felt absolutely useless. And I was scared shitless. I hope Sandy makes it. He's got kids, hasn't he?'

Peter nodded. 'You'd better go back to London. I can get you on tomorrow's flight. There's a chopper that'll take you to the airport first thing. 'Meantime, you any good with a camera?'

'A camera? I can't see much, but I'll have a go if you tell me where to point it.'

'Have you got a spare pair of glasses with you?'

Daniel remembered then that Felicity had burst into tears when he was packing to leave London, tipped the suitcase onto the floor and run out of the room. His spectacle case had shot under the bed out of his reach. He'd left it there, hastily re-packed, kissed the tearstained Felicity and run down to his waiting taxi.

Peter repeated his question and Daniel replied lightly.

'It's OK I'll manage. Where's the camera?'

When they returned to their hotel that evening, the hotel manager had shaken his head regretfully. He told Daniel and

Peter that he had been making enquiries about the Vidaković family. He had reliable news that Irena's parents had been killed, although no one knew where they had been buried. He had no news of Irena, but hinted darkly that a young girl could have been taken away. Daniel, who had thought it impossible to feel more pain, heard their abrupt speculations as if he'd entered the very gates of hell. He had seen so much horror over the last few days that he thought he must become inured to it; he'd heard so many stories of unbelievable cruelty and treachery. Now the memory of the girl with grey eyes and dimples in her cheeks had become a question no-one could answer.

Daniel remembered guiltily that he had missed giving the promised lunch-time concert at the Conservatory. His head had begun to ache with the effort of focusing without his glasses and, exhausted and miserable, he packed his bag for the morning and tried to reach Dr Solomon by telephone, finally leaving a somewhat garbled message for him. He and Peter were to meet in the bar for a drink before dinner and he had got as far as the lobby when a note was handed to him. He read it, holding the writing close to his face.

> Please, dear friend, play for us this evening before
> you go back home, I beg of you. We are in such need
> of music and everyone we can find will be there.
> You will know many people and they want to see
> you again and to thank you for coming to us here at
> this terrible time. Thank God you were not hurt this
> morning.
>
> Oskar Solomon

Daniel joined the old musician in the familiar hall, where he was at once surrounded by a group of people he had worked amongst in a life he remembered vividly, but which now seemed to have been quite another existence. For them he played the piano he had once known so well and which still stood in the candle-lit concert hall, a metal leg replacing one that had been blown off. Oblivious of his fatigue, he played for a long time, his eyes closed, finding comfort himself in the music and giving his audience the assurance that beauty, that exultation and wonder still existed in the midst of their suffering and grief. Afterwards he ate with them; people had found food somehow and, hungry though he was, Daniel took as little as he politely could, for he knew that for many in the tarnished grandeur of the hall starvation was not far away.

He slept that night sprawled in one of the dusty blue velvet chairs before setting off the next day in an army helicopter for the airport. They arrived as it was getting dark and Daniel was told to jump onto the runway. It was a fall of several feet and Daniel, who couldn't see where the ground was without his glasses, landed badly.

Two days later he returned to London on crutches, looking somewhat sheepish – his left leg in plaster. He performed that week at the Cadogan Hall, grinning as he hobbled onto the stage.

Martin Bell, curious about Daniel, was in the audience and was moved. This remarkable musician was no soft, spoilt, squeamish man, he'd heard. He had guts.

An article appeared in 1995 in the *New York Times* and was found years later amongst Daniel's papers with a letter from Martin Bell.

Music Helps Stay Sane Sarajevo During War

By ROGER COHEN

Published: October 23, 1994

Among the scarred streets and alleys of Sarajevo there is one comforting crossroads, where the sound of a Beethoven sonata or a Chopin waltz may be heard. The music, sometimes flowing, sometimes betraying a student's faltering hand, cascades from the Sarajevo conservatory. In its lightness and otherworldliness, it offers solace in a city still raw with suffering. People linger in the shelter of the sound of half-forgotten times.

But the music is deceptive in the comfort it offers, for the institution it comes from has been lacerated. Once synonymous with civilization, and the universality of music, the conservatory now shows the barbarous legacy of the Bosnian war.

The solid Austro-Hungarian school contains destruction, physical and spiritual; interethnic suspicions, spoken and unspoken, and tragedy laced with the optimism of youth.

The physical toll on the school of two and a half years of war has been onerous. Seven music students and one teacher have been killed. Last year, two Serbian shells came through the ceiling of the concert room, which with its chandeliers and chairs upholstered in blue velvet contrives nonetheless to retain vestiges of a Viennese plushness.

Dear Daniel,

Thanks for your note. I'm glad to hear the leg is mending well. That was a cruel thing to happen just when you were almost safely home!

Please don't thank me for my part on your search. Henderson's a good man and will have done his best for you, but I'm afraid few of these searches end in anything but terrible disappointment and leaving many questions unanswered.

Sandy sends his best – he's beginning to manage pretty well with one hand and tells me he'll be out in the Land Rover again soon. I'm not sure, but that's up to the powers that be. He owes his life to you and won't forget that in a hurry.

All the best and look after those magic hands of yours. And your head.

Yours Martin

6. A DANGEROUS PLACE TO BE

WHEN HE HAD LAST returned from Sarajevo, Daniel not only had a broken leg, but was haunted day and night by the thought of Irena, and the fate that she must have suffered. Better that she should be dead, than be held captive in God knew what conditions. Then Peter Henderson had phoned him and asked if they could meet when he was next in London. He had news he wanted to tell Daniel, but not over the phone. They met for a hurried drink at the Travellers' Club.

'I don't know if this is good news or not. But I'll tell what I've heard – which isn't a lot. It seems that Irena was captured and was kept by a notorious Serb, Colonel Vukašin Milić for over a year. We haven't any details, but I'm afraid she'll have been through hell.'

'Where is she now?' asked Daniel, the room spinning round him.

'I can't trace her, but it seems she could have got away. There was a girl who did. And there was another who was killed, I'm afraid. I haven't got their names. One of them had relations in the States. She may be there. I'll see what I can find out.'

Daniel didn't know if he wanted any more information. Reports of Bosnian war trials gave vivid descriptions of the hideous crimes perpetrated against women. In a way, he preferred now to believe Irena was dead, that she had died soon after her capture and been spared the horrors he found himself forced to read. He had not made any effort to trace her for a while. Trying to put her out of his mind, he travelled the world, giving concerts, recitals and master classes until exhaustion forced him to take a break; going home, he realized that Irena's fate still occupied his thoughts and dreams.

The following year, Dr Solomon invited Daniel to come out to Sarajevo again – things were a little safer now – to give some recitals and master classes at the Conservatory. Daniel rang Peter and, after a few fruitless attempts, managed to catch him the day before he left for his next assignment. He needed to take another trip to Bosnia and, if Daniel could be there at the same time, they'd meet up again.

The two men enjoyed one another's company, but, for all their light-hearted banter, keeping his charge safe was a responsibility Peter took very seriously.

As they left the airport, Daniel asked if there was any news about Sandy. Peter laughed.

'Making a lot of noise about getting back out here again. They've given him a false arm – with different attachments instead of a hand. He's sure he'll manage just as well as he used to. Oh, sends his regards to you, of course.'

The following morning Peter knocked on Daniel's door holding an extra large flak jacket and an undamaged helmet. 'Better get you kitted out properly,' he said, taking out a marker pen. 'What's your blood group?'

'My blood? It's something peculiar – AB negative, I think. Why?'

'We mark it on your helmet – in case you get shot or blown up. But you'd be lucky to find any of that vintage in these hospitals. So better not get in the way of any bullets.'

Peter threw Daniel the helmet – now inscribed with his blood type next to Peter's addition of a skull and crossbones. 'Ever fired a gun?' he asked as they left the hotel.

'Good God, no.'

'Left handed?'

'Yes. Why?'

'Of course you are!'

'God, Henderson, you really are a bastard!' Daniel said as, both laughing, they headed for the Land Rover.

Daniel told Peter how his wedding to Felicity had been cancelled when the two of them had returned from his latest North American tour. His bride-to-be had travelled out with him filled with excitement about the glamorous time she anticipated but not realising that the life of a concert pianist is not an easy one to share – except, perhaps, with another musician. Felicity had tired of waiting around for someone whose life was filled with rehearsals, hours of practice and foreign cities where all they saw was the inside of yet another anonymous hotel and an indistinguishable concert hall. And the Daniel she had known before had seemed to be quite another man – now constantly exhausted, so that he fell into bed night after night too tired to make love, never wanting to eat at grand restaurants but ordering room service as he worked on his scores or practised on his portable keyboard. Peter wondered why the woman had not anticipated the difficulties this life would present her with, but he had seen the effect that Daniel had on everyone he met. The poor girl had been dazzled at first and, knowing little about music, had seen only the excitement of becoming part of Daniel's fame.

'So you dumped her when you got back?' Peter asked.

'Actually, she dumped me ...' Daniel grinned ruefully as he added, 'Got back from a concert in Usher Hall to find she'd taken her stuff and left a Dear John letter on the hall table. A bit humiliating, but it was rather a relief too. You can't imagine how awful her mother is and you know what they say about cats … Anyway, it didn't take her long to find someone who doesn't spend his waking hours at the piano. She's engaged again, so …'

Later, as they were driving yet again into the suburbs of Sarajevo where Irena had last been seen, Peter said: 'You've told me about Irena, but I'm curious about the rest of her family – her parents. That's an interesting mixture, Yugoslav Muslim and Irish Protestant. What were they like?' and Daniel looked out of the window of the Land Rover and thought for a moment. Not that he needed to dig deep into his memory: these people were always with him while he searched the city, listened to the hideous recitals of murder and brutality, of disappearances and the discovery of people who could no longer be recognized as those who had been lost.

'Her father, Adam, was a very sensitive musician, though you'd have thought he was a labourer to look at him – short and stocky with big square hands and a bushy moustache. He was a strict parent but clearly adored his daughter – and his wife. He was endlessly kind to me. He knew my own father and mother had died when I was a teenager and I think he saw himself and Finola as my proxy parents. I had a responsible job at the Conservatory, but he wasn't above telling me off for being late, or losing things or not dressing in the approved style. London was really swinging in the nineties, but Sarajevo was pretty old-fashioned. Finola took me shopping for an awful brown suit and the sort of tie academics wear on the continent – pleated black silk, for God's sake.'

'Oh and then my hair was long. I think they thought that was acceptable for a musician, but not the horn-rimmed specs I wore. She said they made me look like a rock star and whisked me off to the optician and had me looking like a proper professor of music … at least when I was in class. Finola – that was her name – had a lovely singing voice and was very beautiful – I'd never seen such white skin and her hair was the palest sort of red – fabulous.' Daniel stopped for a moment, his face shadowed with the pain of his memories.

'You sound as if you were rather taken with her. How old was she?'

'Still in her thirties and had a great figure. Yes, I did find her very attractive and I should have behaved better.'

Peter was intrigued. This was not what he had expected to hear. 'But what about your feelings for Irena – what happened there?'

'Nothing, of course. She was only fifteen and I never allowed myself to look at her as anything other than someone it was fun to be with. She had a terrific, mischievous sense of humour – just full of life. And she was also becoming a marvellous musician – I've almost never heard such a sensitive ear. But sex was absolutely off the menu. I did sometimes think that, were we to meet again when she was older … But then, you see, I was already more or less engaged to Felicity, who wanted to get married when I got back to London.'

'Christ, what a complicated life you do lead!' Peter stopped the Land Rover in a deserted farm-yard and took out his map. But he wanted to hear more about Daniel's relationship with Madame Vidaković. 'So did you reach first base with the mother?'

'That's a very vulgar expression! But, since you ask, yes. And it was wonderful at first, but she got very emotionally involved. If I hadn't been sent back to London, I've no idea how things would have gone. She wanted to leave her husband and go off with me. But that would have been impossible on all sorts of fronts. Think what it would have done to Irena.'

'Do you think Irena knew?'

Daniel didn't look directly at Peter. 'She must have suspected – I was indiscreet once – I called Finola by her pet name in front of Irena and her father. I don't think Adam heard, but I'm sure Irena did. There were other occasions too, but that was very near the end of my time with the family. The strange thing is that, after I'd gone back to England, it was Irena I couldn't get out of my mind.'

Peter started the engine and the two men continued their journey without speaking, their silence broken by the distant sound of mortar shells exploding and the rapid, rattling accompaniment of sniper fire. They did not continue their conversation, but Peter suspected Daniel trusted that this information would go no further. And, even when he was amongst other journalists who were intrigued by Daniel's presence and speculated about his life, he never allowed himself to reveal what he knew about the musician. He would say, simply: 'Brave man. And good fun, too …'

It was Daniel's third visit to Sarajevo after the Siege. He had gone out ostensibly to perform in a concert and do some teaching at the conservatory, but, when not involved in music or rehearsals, he took to going to the hospital where Sandy had been treated. There, he would sit, sometimes for hours, talking to the patients, many of them hideously wounded. Peter would pick him up and drive back to the hotel, Daniel frequently overcome with emotion.

'Christ, Peter. Can you imagine? The ones that survive, I mean. To spend the rest of their lives disfigured or crippled. There was a boy there today who was crying his eyes out – he'd just been told he'd never walk again – I don't think I could hack that, you know …'

And all the while, he was still looking for any trace he could find of Irena. After the concert Daniel said goodbye to the orchestra and Professor Solomon. How frail and old he now seemed. The siege of his city and the horrors that had surrounded him over the last years had taken their toll, as indeed they had on all the valiant musicians at the Conservatory. They sat and talked and Daniel felt ashamed of his own comfortable home in London and of the safety and ease of his life there. They had listened so attentively to his playing and to the introduction he'd given first, waiting for each sentence to be translated into several languages before he would continue, sometimes losing his place and doubling over with laughter – the infectious laughter which did them all so much good, the old man reflected. They loved this young man with his strange Czech-Englishness and his constant good humour. They admired the thoughtful, sensitive way he interpreted the old works they would ask for, the piano seeming to sing to them. The new, complicated and difficult works of Eastern Europe seemed to come naturally to him too, weaving the old and the new together. And then they heard something of the sadness of his yearning soul, the sadness behind his big grin and the dance steps he couldn't resist executing as he demonstrated phrasing and style and gave to his lectures a new dimension of understanding.

Peter had made tireless enquiries, still hoping for a clue that would lead them if not to Irena, at least to something that would put Daniel's mind at rest.

'As I told you, Milić was a real brute. Seems he was killed a few months ago, but his family will tell us nothing except that he kept a girl prisoner for a year or so. I think his wife is hiding something, but she clearly trusts no one. Her eyes fill with tears when I mention Irena, but she won't say a thing – just sits there with her little boy in her arms, holding him close to her.'

Peter was afraid that Irena must be dead. He hoped for the girl's sake, and for Daniel's too, that she had died before she'd had to suffer too long at the hands of Milić. Peter would look at him as they went out yet again in the Land Rover, gazing intently out of the smeared windows as if he expected at every turn of the road to see Irena waiting there for him.

He wished that Daniel would give up looking for her, fearing that his obsession could only end in pain.

Leading up to Daniel's last visit there had been a lull in the violence and Sarajevans were daring to believe that peace had come at last. But there were still snipers and Peter was relieved to be safely back that evening amongst his press colleagues within the walls of their hotel.

After a meagre dinner, they went into the bar where a guitarist was playing, incongruously, the overture to *The Magic Flute*. Oppressed by the dreariness of the bar, Daniel stood up and began to act out Mozart's delicious opera. First, Daniel became Papageno, pretending to play the Pan pipes and singing the air in a trilling falsetto. Other guests stopped in their tracks and some of them joined the couple, laughing and applauding, and the guitarist, delighting in this change from the gloomy evenings spent trying to spread a little cheer in the bar, rose to the occasion and accompanied Daniel with renewed enthusiasm.

The anguish of the day temporarily banished, Daniel became lost in the music he knew so well. He caught up a gaunt and anxious-looking woman reporter to partner him, to become Papagena, while a sturdy waitress acted out the Queen of the Night. The surly porter found himself enobled to the High Priest, Sarastro, singing along with Daniel as his répétiteur. Peter watched in admiration, wondering how Daniel could hold all that music and so many words in his head. But he didn't know the opera and was unaware of the fun Daniel was having, for the words were hardly Mozart's or those of the benighted Schikaneder, his lyricist – they were largely of Daniel's own invention.

Peter would hold in his memory this image of Daniel dancing, singing and conducting – the clownish side of him and the accomplished musician woven together in one long-legged young man with dark curls and big glasses, entertaining a group of people for whom cheerfulness was now the rarest of treats.

The evening drew to an end and the journalists and guests made for their rooms. Daniel packed his bag, paid his bill at the reception desk and asked to have his luggage brought down for him. Then he ran upstairs to Peter's room, carrying with him the remains of a bottle of cherry brandy.

This last evening in Sarajevo Daniel wanted to remember Irena's father. Feeling in need of male company, Adam had sometimes summoned Daniel into his study, offering him a Turkish cigarette from a battered brass jar and the two men would sit and smoke, often in silence. Daniel had brought a packet of the oval, black and gold cigarettes with him.

'I didn't know you smoked?' Peter was surprised.

'I don't really. But these remind me so much of good times in Sarajevo. Irena's father smoked them. Won't you keep me company?'

'I'm a Gauloise man myself — when I smoke. I'll stick to the cherry brandy, but you go ahead.'

Daniel lit up and stood inhaling the perfumed smoke, his eyes half closed, before he turned to Peter. 'Thanks for everything,' he said and he threw back the curtains, opened the window and went out onto the balcony to say a final farewell to the city he loved.

'Hey Daniel — for God's sake! There's a blackout.' Peter was shouting at him and Daniel, realising what he had done, turned abruptly. There was a sudden barrage of gunfire and Peter saw the look of open-eyed surprise on Daniel's face as his knees buckled and he sank to the ground, still clutching the curtains which came off their rail and subsided gently on top of him.

Peter knelt down beside Daniel. 'Christ, Daniel. What the hell did you do that for? Are you OK?'

Daniel had heard the burst of fire as the bullets hit him and remembered toppling over, then lying face down. He turned his head and started to cough. Peter knew he shouldn't lift the wounded man, but he needed to get Daniel away from the curtainless window. At first, all Daniel could feel was broken glass scraping his cheek as Peter pulled him across the floor. Then he became aware of pain and, unable to stop himself, began to scream.

Squatting on the helicopter deck next to Daniel, Peter could do little to help the medical orderly but hold the rehydration bag, kneading it from time to time when the fluid seemed to have stopped flowing. The patient had been given morphine and finally ceased to throw his head from side to side. His screaming had given way to an uneven rasping in his throat. At each breath, Peter, who had seen men die too often not to know the signs, wondered if it was to be Daniel's last. They transferred him to an airplane where a doctor took over and examined him as they took off for London.

'Not well, this one. Lost a hell of a lot of blood. I hope they can match his group – I've sent out an alert for some. We don't get much of that – Jewish community mainly. Is he a Jew?'

'Never thought about it, but yes, probably … '

The doctor pulled his stethoscope down round his neck and motioned to an orderly to turn Daniel on his side while he examined the bullet wounds. Blood was still seeping out round the temporary dressings, blood and a greenish yellow fluid. The dressings were removed and Peter found himself wanting to retch. The bullet holes were puffy around the edges and beginning to discolour. The journey seemed endless and Daniel's face was now unrecognizable, yellow and crusted with scratches. His hair was full of dust and blood and Peter started to push it back from his forehead, but Daniel flinched as it caught in the coagulating wounds. He opened his eyes and looked into Peter's.

'What the hell's going on?'

'We're on our way home now. Won't be long.' And Daniel gave a deep sigh and was unconscious again. Peter looked at Daniel's hands and thought of the music that they made day after day at the piano. He covered them carefully with the blanket.

7.   INTO THE LION'S DEN

LEO HASKELL collected a cup of coffee from the machine in the lobby, lit a cigar and settled down to read the papers. His London office was in Soho. HASKELL AND WALDSTEIN, ARTISTS' AGENTS, was engraved on the sign outside an unremarkable building in Golden Square. He didn't usually come in on a Saturday, but today he needed to deal with the intense media interest in one of his clients, a musician who had managed somehow to get himself shot out in Sarajevo. Daniel Danuczek was an old friend as well as one of his most lucrative performers and now his agent was faced with printing a plausible explanation for the pianist's unlikely accident. He had issued a press release and saw that it had already been printed in *The Sunday Times*.

Celebrity Pianist Shot in Error

The internationally renowned concert pianist, Daniel Danuczek, who was out in Sarajevo giving a series of recitals and master classes, was involved in a shooting incident at his hotel on Friday evening. It appears that a sniper mistook him for a visiting BBC correspondent. He was air-lifted back to the UK and is in Intensive Care at St Thomas's Hospital. A bulletin, issued last night, stated that the musician, who is 34, is in a serious but stable condition. He has not yet regained consciousness.

The telephone rang. 'Leo, oh thank God.' It was Daniel's sister, Magda Bloomfield. 'I rang you at home. Gerda told me you'd gone into the office.'

'Yes, I'm dealing with the press at the moment. Are you at the hospital? How's Danny?'

'I'm with him now, but he hasn't woken up.' Her voice broke:

'I knew something dreadful would happen if he kept going out there.'

Daniel was dreaming. In his dream he was chasing Irena down Nevinosti Street, the steep Sarajevo road, that led to the market. They ran past the white mosque and the synagogue and turned sharply down the narrow cobbled lane where her slim legs bore her away from him, her brown hair swirling around her laughing face. He followed her, but, coming into the market place he could not see the girl; crowds of frantic people milled around and there was blood everywhere. Daniel slipped in the gore and fell hard on his back. The pain as he hit the cobbles took his breath away. This was a dream he had again and again.

Days passed and the vague forms that swam in and out of Daniel's vision started to have features. One of them was the face of his sister, and she seemed to be there most of the time. There was comfort in that and he was relieved. His mind began to make links between what he remembered and his present surroundings: clearly he was in hospital and he vaguely remembered Sarajevo and the balcony where some-thing had hit him from behind. But nothing after that. Tubes came out of the back of his hands and from other places that he couldn't see and there seemed to be a heavy weight pressing down on him, which he could not dislodge. The pain came and went, sometimes overwhelming him so that there was nothing else in his consciousness, only pain and a sense of things pulling and twitching low down in his spine. Magda was always beside him and one day, as she reached for his hand, he cried out, suddenly confused and frantic, 'For God's sake get me out of here. It's going to kill me. Please, take me home.' and he burst into tears against his sister's breast. She rocked him in her arms like a babe and spoke gently to him, not knowing what she said or what he needed to hear. Her heart felt fit to break. For Daniel was no longer Daniel. He was a broken thing, so weak and frail that she feared he could not live. His strength, his agility and all the life-force of the brother she loved seemed utterly destroyed and she had no means of comforting him.

Over the days that followed, she sat beside him constantly, grasping at the small changes, the small improvements, that gave her some sort of hope that Daniel might be on the mend. Sometimes it was the removal of a tube or a drain. Sometimes a dressing was replaced with a smaller one. The wounds ceased to seep, so that there were just the puckered, scarlet, slowly-closing bullet holes in her brother's legs and back. He had been operated on soon after his arrival at the hospital, and now there were lines of stitching left after the bullets had been extracted, so that his back came to resemble a black and red snakes and ladders board.

Since the news had broken, Leo had been in almost daily contact with Magda. It had become clear that Daniel wouldn't be performing for a while. Maybe not ever again. Daniel was one of his most valued musicians, whose virtuosity and personal magnetism always pulled in the crowds. He had been at the beginning of a TV series of master classes, which were a good showcase; he was so photogenic and audiences loved his charm, his gentle and humorous way of putting across to the students the essence of the music they were studying.

Above all of this, Leo had known Daniel since he was a boy and he counted him amongst his dearest friends. He needed to see him: he needed to know if all this was lost.

Magda and Leo broke the news of Daniel's condition to all the people who should know and busied themselves with bulletins to those who enquired or sent letters and flowers. They were thankful to have something useful to do while they waited for Daniel to wake up. If indeed he would wake up. To Leo the spectre of his friend spending the rest of his life in bed, attached to tubes and perhaps never to speak again, or laugh – for laughter was the quality friends most remembered of Daniel – was too terrible to contemplate. He constantly saw him in his mind: sitting with his dark head bowed over the keyboard and his hands flying over the keys, spilling out the music that was his life. And then his handsome, laughing face as they shared a bottle of wine in Leo's untidy office, Daniel regaling him with gossip about the music world, and snippets from his own colourful and rather chaotic love life. And the gentleness of Daniel when Leo's son had attempted suicide and he had listened hour after hour as his agent castigated himself for allowing the boy to fall prey to the drugs that had been destroying his young life. Those were the images that came again and again to Leo. What a loss it would be, what a terrible, irreplaceable loss.

Then finally the day came when Magda rang him, her voice changed, almost joyful.

'Leo, he's awake. Yes he really is and he understands what we're saying.'

The next day Leo went to see Daniel, who was lying wedged on his side with pillows. Leo had never known Daniel be ill, even mildly so. The only time he'd seen him out of sorts was when he returned from Sarajevo with his leg in plaster. He'd refused to take any time off and performed in several scheduled concerts, hobbling cheerfully onto the stage on his crutches, but to Leo he appeared emotionally drained. He didn't speak of the time he'd been away but Leo had suspected that Daniel was trying to bury something. Even before he was out of plaster, he threw himself into an unusually busy season of concerts and recording sessions. Daniel's voice was very weak when he focused on Leo and broke into a faint smile. 'What are you doing here? Haven't you taken me off your books yet?'

'I've come to tell you to get a move on – you've got a lot to do this autumn, you know.'

Daniel was glad to have someone speak to him without hushed tones.

'God you're a heartless man! I'm doing my best, but they've trussed me up like a chicken and I can't even sit up. I just want to go home and they won't let me. If I could get out of here and get to a piano again ...'

'Let's get your keyboard in here – you'd better start practising. That'll empty the wards really quickly once you start – I hear they're short of beds.'

Then Daniel laughed and Leo was relieved.

Waking from a restless sleep one afternoon, Daniel became aware of someone sitting near the side of his bed. He felt on the bedside cabinet for his glasses, but his visitor put them into his hand. It was Sam, one of his composition class pupils.

'Thanks – oh, hi Sam– what on earth are you doing here – shouldn't you be at college?'

'No – we've finished for the summer – your sister asked me to stay with you while she did some shopping.'

The young man was clearly ill at ease and didn't make eye-contact with Daniel as he took a box out of the plastic bag he had on his lap. 'I remembered you like smoked salmon and my mother said you'd be glad of a change of food by now ...'

Daniel took the Selfridges box, opened it and, lowering his bearded face, sniffed its contents. 'Fantastic!' he said and, seeing that the young man had got to his feet, 'Do you have to go? Tell me about your music and the others – I suppose someone else is teaching you now?'

He hadn't given his composition class much thought – that normal life in his flat seemed very distant, but the presence of Sam, his most gifted pupil, reminded him of Thursday evenings in his music room which had been followed by pizza deliveries and trips to the pub afterwards with the cheerful group.

Sam sat down again and began to answer Daniel's questions, his surprisingly dark eyes in his fair, narrow face becoming animated with the pleasure of seeing his teacher again and finding him less changed than Magda's gloomy warning had implied. He went away with a list of things that Daniel wanted from his library and messages to give his colleagues when he next saw them. Most of them had gone away on holiday, but the news of Daniel's accident had felled Sam for several days and the thought that he might now see his teacher regularly and help him back to normality spurred him to arrive daily at the patient's bedside, thinking up errands when he had been given none to carry out. Daniel found his presence soothing and was glad to be spared Magda's constant and ill-concealed anxiety when Sam took over some of her tasks, even volunteering to shave off Daniel's beard.

Daniel saw a wheelchair being brought into his room and allowed himself to be lifted into it and watched his feet being arranged on the footrest. He put his hands down onto the big wheels to either side of him. His back hurt hideously as he tried to turn them – his whole body still seemed very sore and weak. He managed to propel the chair across the room and the physiotherapist, Ross, who was young, muscular, and rather in awe of this patient, was delighted.

'Great. Carry on like that and you'll soon get your abs back.'

Daniel pushed himself down the passage between the wards

until he could see the other patients through their doors. He waved weakly at them and tried not to be upset by the contraptions that strung some of them up to the ceiling or held their limbs in various uncomfortable-looking positions. They made him feel queasy and he just said, 'Hi' and pushed himself on until he could go no further, his whole frame shaking. A nurse fielded him in the corridor and pushed him back to his room, his head lolling to one side.

Aware that he had no control over his legs and felt nothing when they were touched, Daniel was confused by the shooting pains that still leapt up and down them, particularly at night. This pain and the thrashing spasms which would follow led him to hope there was sensation returning and that he had only to wait to become his normal self again.

In the meantime, the routine of hospital existence had taken over his life. A fastidious man, he tolerated the indignities of this new existence as best he could, but felt a deep shame as his most intimate bodily functions were discussed in loud voices for all to hear. Frustrated by the cumbersome wheelchair, he wondered how long it would be before sensation would return to his legs so that he could walk again. He spent some of the long, tedious days looking curiously around on his floor of the spinal unit, opening all the doors he could and taking in the workings of the hospital. It both interested and appalled him, but, now that his life and well-being seemed to depend on many of the different departments there, he was keen to see for himself where it all happened.

'You'll be going down to the gym soon,' said Ross, cheerfully.

'Shit,' said Daniel, his eyes wide with horror. 'What the hell do you think I'm going to do there?'

'You'll see. Keep at those exercises I've given you. You'll need to be at your best.'

'My best isn't much good at the moment. I need to get out

of this place. It's driving me mad.'

'All in good time.' Ross replied, hurrying off to his next patient.

'Why won't they tell me when I can go home?' Daniel asked Magda.

'You've hurt yourself really badly, Danny. You've got to get a lot better before you'll be able to manage at home again. I know it's frustrating, but try to be patient.'

Looking sideways at his sister, who would not always meet his eyes these days, he muttered: 'What I need is to get back onto my feet again.'

8.   LOOKING FOR A PIANO

D ANIEL HAD BEEN moved to a new ward and Peter walked down the corridor, not entirely sure he had remembered the number correctly, when a door opened and a nurse came out, smiling and tidying her hair. 'That'll be it,' thought Peter, and he looked through the porthole in the door. Daniel, shaven and dressed, was sitting by the window in a wheelchair, staring out at the stormy sky.

Peter knocked. 'Can I come in? Is it a good moment?' He walked across the room and Daniel looked round at him.

'Peter! My God, am I glad to see you ... but I thought you were abroad – Afghanistan, wasn't it this time?' He reached out his arms and pulled Peter to him in a violent embrace. The brakes were not on and his chair rolled suddenly backwards, so that Peter was thrown off balance and fell to his knees sprawled over Daniel's lap. Daniel started to laugh hysterically and for a few minutes the two men grappled with each other like schoolboys.

Peter tried to get to his feet, but Daniel was still holding him down on his knees. 'You great loon,' he gasped, 'let go. They'll think I'm attacking you.'

The door opened and Magda appeared.

'Danny – for goodness' sake – what are you doing?' she rushed towards the two men. 'Oh Peter – it's you ...'

Peter scrambled to his feet, dusting off his knees and kissed her on each cheek.

'You know each other?' Daniel was surprised.

'Yes. This wonderful man brought you here in a helicopter.

And hung around several days while you were unconscious.'

'Ah, the deathbed scene, the wringing of hands over me – I can imagine it.' said Daniel, making a tragic face, but, seeing Magda's expression, he stopped laughing and pushed himself over to her, took her hand and kissed it, his voice gentle now, 'You're very early, Blossom.'

Peter smiled, thinking that only Daniel would pick such a nickname for this large, bony woman.

'Oh, yes, of course, we're seeing Hussein this morning, aren't we? But Peter's come all this way from God knows where.'

'We're not due for half an hour. I'll go and get a paper. Good to see you Peter. How are things with you?'

'Chasing my tail as usual. Couldn't get here last month … and I'm off again tomorrow.'

Daniel starting laughing again as Magda closed the door.

'Honestly, Peter, attacking a poor helpless cripple – who wears specs, too. You should know better.' Daniel stopped laughing and looked out of the window.

Peter said, his words sounding as if he would have preferred not to say them.

'I got your note. I'm so sorry …'

'It's a bugger, isn't it?'

'Are you sure? It's early days – things might change, heal or whatever.'

'No. Too late, now. My spinal cord's been ruptured and so that's that. I'm paralysed from here down. They tell me I'm lucky it's just my legs … Anyway I've got to accept that I'll be getting around in one of these from now on.' He touched the wheels of his chair. 'I suppose I've known for a while really, but you keep on hoping … but, no. That's it as far as my legs are concerned.'

'God. I'm sorry. I don't know what to say.'

'Don't worry – I don't suppose anyone will be exactly eloquent when I tell them. But I just don't know what to do. I mean, my career is up the spout – people think that you don't need feet if you're a pianist, but actually you do. Except for very early stuff composed before pianos had pedals, there's a lot I'll never be able to play again.'

'I didn't realise that. Oh God …' Peter, appalled, wanted to say something useful, but what was there to say?

Daniel went on, 'And, apart from that, I don't know how to be a disabled person. Things will be completely different. Getting around, driving – oh and girls … Though, mind you, my dick's okay, I've checked that.'

Peter shook his head, smiling in spite of himself. 'Oh well, you've still got your priorities right.' His smile faded as he regarded his friend for a moment and then stood up and went over to him. He put his hand on his shoulder and Daniel's hand came up and covered it.

'Bloody hell – don't make me cry. I do far too much of that. I've got to stop feeling sorry for myself. I'll hate it if people are sorry for me – I know I will. I want to be the same stupid bloke I was before and have people laugh at me …'

But tears were spilling down his cheeks and Peter, hearing Magda come back into the room, tried to shield her brother from her, but she had seen Daniel's distress and met Peter's eyes looking as desperate as she had when Daniel had been between life and death. She lowered her head as she tried to conceal her own emotions.

'Danny – we must go. Peter, I'm so sorry, but we mustn't be late for Hussein – he's come in specially to see us today.'

Daniel looked up at Peter. 'Great to see you – and for God's sake take care. Don't you get smashed up too.' Magda watched the two of them as they said goodbye, Daniel again pretending to punch his friend, who retaliated in kind and the two of them embraced.

'Good luck,' said Peter quietly and Daniel nodded.

At the far end of the department, Daniel's Spinal Consultant, Aziz Hussein, was sitting in his office, apparently ready for a game of golf, wearing a diamond-patterned sweater and checked trousers. He had a lean face and large mournful brown eyes. Magda thought he must dye his hair; it was wonderfully black and glossy for a man who was no longer young. His patient wheeled himself to the other side of the desk and leaned over to shake hands and Magda sat down beside him. The surgeon had woken that morning not looking forward to this consultation. He had grown to like his patient and, being fond of music, knew him as a fine concert pianist.

Daniel looked up at the wall above his desk at the light box with scans and X-ray photographs clipped to it: photographs he now recognised of his own spine, a bullet still lodged against one of the bones.

'So what happens now?' he asked when Hussein had again confirmed his dismal prognosis.

'You'll need to stay here a bit longer – until we are satisfied that your back is stable. Then you should go for a few weeks to Stoke Mandeville Hospital. Have you heard of it?'

'Why do I need another hospital?'

'It's for rehab. They'll teach you how to manage your life and all the aspects of your disability, so you can look after yourself and get about in a wheelchair. And they'll sort out with you the changes you'll need at home so that things are as easy as possible for you. There'll be a lot of very tough physio – so you can make the most of the movement you have left. You have to concentrate now on your upper body and your core muscles to remain as active as you can. It could be worse, you know Daniel, your injury is low down. You still have bowel and bladder control, which is a great bonus. And you should be able to be a father.'

'A father?' Daniel could see no relevance in this.

He was silent for several moments. Then, feeling the

anguish of his companions in the room and not knowing how he could possibly help either them or himself, he put his hands down onto the guide wheels of his chair and asked, 'Do you think there's a piano in this place?'

Hussein looked bemused. This was not the sort of question the surgeon had anticipated. Nor was it a reaction to bad news that he had experienced before. He said, cautiously, 'I think there's one in the main hospital, in the children's ward. Why?

'I need to play. I really need to play. It's been too long.' and Daniel turned his chair. Magda and Hussein watched him as he left the room, turned into the corridor and made his way to the lift.

His head light with the shock of what he'd just heard, Daniel took the lift down to the reception floor, where he consulted the map. Then he wheeled himself through the double doors to the main hospital and took another lift, this time up to Paediatrics. He found himself in a long corridor, brightly painted, and off to one side he saw a light, cheerful room, its walls hung with drawings and mobiles. Against the far wall, was an upright piano. There seemed to be no-one about, although he could hear voices and a child crying.

Daniel wheeled himself across the room, opened the lid of the piano and put his hands on the keyboard. He experienced for the first time since he'd been in hospital a sense of reality, some sort of a link with his normal life before it had been overcome by this nightmare. The piano was out of tune, so, after he'd played a few arpeggios, he removed the front panel and peered at the mechanism inside. Then he became aware of a small person beside him. It was a little girl. Although she was completely bald, he thought it must be a girl as she was wearing a pink dressing gown. Her face had Mongolian or Chinese features.

'Have you broken it?' she asked. Daniel laughed and put the panel back carefully.

'No, I just wanted to see how it works'.

'What's your name?'

'Danny. What's yours?'

'Melanie. Can you play me something?'

'I could try. What would you like?'

The child named a song which had been a recent hit on the charts and started to sing it. Daniel remembered hearing this tune in a café in Gloucester Road. He began to play by ear very softly and then, as Melanie looked delighted, louder and faster, embellishing the tune with runs up and down the keyboard. It didn't matter at that moment that he couldn't use the pedals – he played as he had heard pub pianos played – honkey tonk, he supposed.

The little girl clapped her hands and danced around the room, her pink dressing gown swirling around her, like a diminutive whirling Dervish. Her little flat face was lifted to the harsh lights of the ceiling, a radiant golden disc, glowing with her pleasure in the music. Daniel was enchanted and played on, varying the rhythm as the child changed her steps.

'Who are you? What on earth are you doing here?' An angry voice came from behind him and Daniel turned to see a young woman shouting at him. He thought she might be the child's mother as she was not in uniform. She continued to rail at Daniel as she pulled the little girl to her.

'I'm a patient – from Leinster Ward,' he explained. 'I'm so sorry, but you see I just needed to find a piano to play. It's OK. I'll go back now.'

The woman whispered something to Melanie, who waved at Daniel and trotted out of the day room singing. Then she said, more calmly, 'You're not meant to be able to get in here without a password and a code.'

'I just wanted to play the piano. I'm a musician, you see, and it's been a while since ...' Daniel's hands were still on the keyboard and the desperation in his eyes as he sat there looking up at her from his hospital wheelchair made her anger change to pity.

'I'm sorry ... we have to be so careful these days. I'm the Ward Sister here' she said gently. 'We don't wear uniform on the children's ward,' she added, seeing the surprise on his face. Then she went on, 'Look, play for a bit, since you're here, but not too loud, please.'

She started off towards the nurses' station, but stopped and listened as she heard Daniel begin to play something she recognized from distant piano lessons. Bach, she thought, a piece in the minor key. The beauty and clarity of his playing, the wrenching sadness of the piece, made her want to cry. She turned round, hoping no-one would interrupt the spell that Daniel had woven around her, but she heard footsteps and saw another nurse coming out of a side ward. She hurried back to the day room and put her hand on Daniel's shoulder.

'I'm afraid I can't let you go on playing just now,' she said.

Daniel stopped and looked up at her.

'You've been very kind. I don't want to get you into trouble.'

He carefully closed the lid of the keyboard, feeling, in spite of the horrors of the day that at least he'd be able to play the piano to amuse himself, even if there were other things he couldn't do. He hadn't yet had time to work out what these things were, but Hussein had used the word 'disabled' and it had struck cold.

The young woman held the door of the day room open for him and said, impulsively. 'The children are having a party next week and I was just going to put CDs on. Would you come and play for them? I know you're much too good for that sort of thing, but I might be able to get permission for you to use the piano regularly if you'd play sometimes for the kids.'

Daniel was filled for a moment with panic and then, looking at the young woman, thought that maybe it would be fun. He liked children and was curious to know about Melanie. And anything that would get him out of the ward would be a relief. 'Yes, of course. I'll have a go if you like. When is it?'

'If you wait, I'll get you an invitation and then there won't be a problem getting onto the ward. By the way, my name's Joanna.'

Joanna walked away toward the nurses' station and Daniel found he was noticing what nice legs she had, nice legs and a small waist. Her long hair was pulled back into an elastic band, the sight of which gave him a surprising stab of pain. Oh Irena, he thought, remembering how she, too, had worn her hair in a ponytail when they went out on their bicycles, and would undo the ribbon and shake her hair free when they returned to the Vila Dolena. Once he had picked up a ribbon that she'd dropped in the garden and put it in his pocket, and found it months later when it was all he had left of that magical time.

Joanna returned with a piece of brightly-coloured paper in her hand and gave it to Daniel. 'You're a real pianist, aren't you?' Daniel laughed. 'I was once, I suppose.'

The young woman looked at him questioningly, and he went on hurriedly. 'I'll play anywhere – village halls, schools, old folks' homes – you name it. But I don't know many pop songs ...'

'Don't worry. They'll love anything. It helps to distract the ones who are really ill and the others get so bored – so much waiting around.'

The lift arrived and, pausing before he pushed himself in, Daniel said: 'Would you mind if I send along my piano tuner before the party?' It's hot in here. Pianos hate that.' As the lift doors closed on him, he smiled at her.

Back on Leinster Ward, Daniel realised that it was over an hour since he had left Hussein's office. His arms and back were aching with the effort of pushing himself so far, but he smiled cheerfully at Magda and Sam, who were sitting anxiously in his room. His sister rushed over to him.

'Where've you been? I was so worried about you?'

'I went to find a piano. I told you,' and Daniel reached up to kiss his sister, suddenly remorseful for having left her as he had.

'Did you find one?'

'Yes I did – in the kids' ward. Look, they're having a party next week – and they've asked me to play for them,' and he showed her the invitation.

Magda stared at her brother. An hour ago he'd been given shattering news, changing his whole life and future. But here he was smiling and telling her about a child called Melanie. Sam had dreaded seeing Daniel that day; Magda had told him what Hussein had said and he felt he had no place there after such news had been given to his tutor, but he had brought the CDs Daniel had asked for; he wondered if he should leave them and go home.

'Sam, good to see you. Don't go.' said Daniel, cheerfully, and went on, 'We need champagne. Would you go and find a bottle of fizz at the offy while I get into bed?'

Daniel was propped up in bed when Sam returned and took the bottle from him. Wrestling to open it, he thought angrily how weak he had become. He poured the wine into the hospital beakers and looked up at Sam. 'Have you been told?' he asked.

The young man looked at Magda and back at Daniel. He had no idea what to say to someone who'd just been told that day that he'd never walk again. He stammered. 'Yes. And I'm so sorry …'

'Well, so am I, as you can imagine. But I've got to get through this and I can't face the future if everyone round me looks as though they're getting ready for my funeral. Look, lots of people spend their lives in wheelchairs. You see them everywhere. Even in the Olympics. So we've all got to cheer up and here's a toast: let's drink to not being a footballer.'

'Not being a footballer?' Magda was confused; but Sam began to smile.

'Yes. If I was a footballer I'd have to find another job, wouldn't I? But I'm a pianist and I probably spend a quarter of my life sitting on my backside – so that's something I'm already really good at. Right then, please, no more long faces. I'm going to need a bit of help, but just don't treat me differently. I'm the same person, you know. Or at least I shall be when I can get out of this bloody place. So here's to my new life ...'

'... and all who sail in her,' added Sam, raising his plastic cup.

9.   NEW WORLD, NEW LIFE

1995

NEW YORK from the airplane looked just as Irena thought it would, just like all the pictures she had seen. She could not eat the food they kept bringing and choosing drinks from the trolley was quite beyond her. She was so tired, but when she slept the dreams came back and she awoke several times, shaking and wondering if she'd cried out. Her neighbour, an elderly woman, had looked at her several times, curiously, but Irena didn't care. She just needed to get there now, to arrive and find her aunt and then to go to bed. She kept thinking of the turret room in her aunt and uncle's castle in Moravia, where she often stayed as a child, and the white-curtained four poster bed with its down quilts and pillows. Aunt Hedi might still have that bed and there she would be able to sleep. That was all she could think about now.

Hedija Tanović – Irena's Aunt Hedi – was Adam Vidaković's sister and her daughter, the spirited Lati, had been her best friend. Hedi and Bahro had escaped from Sarajevo and been taken in by friends on Long Island. They knew only a little of the events after the death of Adam and Finola. The British Embassy in Berlin, who had contacted them when Irena had been delivered to them, filled Hedija in a little more. She had been warned that Irena would not be the girl she once had been, but she was not prepared for what she saw when her niece came through from Customs to the Arrivals area.

Although she had only one small bag, Irena had taken a

trolley and walked slowly, leaning heavily on it, like a frail old woman. Hedija's niece had always been slim, but she'd had plump young cheeks, rosy and with two distinct dimples which were much in evidence when she smiled; the child Irena was always smiling. The young woman who walked towards her aunt was emaciated and her once glossy brown hair hung lankly on either side of the cadaverous cheeks where the dimples had become deep creases running down on either side of her mouth.

When Irena caught sight of her aunt she smiled with relief.

'Irena?' Hedija knew this was her niece, but the hand the girl extended was more like a claw and as her aunt took it in hers she burst into tears and pulled Irena to her, feeling the almost fleshless ribs and shoulder blades through Irena's thin coat.

The car journey seemed very long – the Tanovićs lived on Long Island and they skirted the coast for what seemed hours. Sleep – she wanted sleep so badly. And the tears she had held back when her aunt had enclosed her in her arms were now flowing and she couldn't stop them. Hedija, who was driving, gripped the wheel and looked straight ahead at the road, knowing that nothing she said just then would be of any help to the weeping girl.

At last they arrived and Hedija opened the front door of the low, white, clapboarded house, and led her niece to a soft, inviting sofa. Irena knew she was going to be all right now. There would be a room for her and there would be a bed. But first she had to see her uncle. He came bustling in from another room and walked quickly towards his niece, smiling broadly. But the smile froze and gradually faded as he looked down at Irena. She would have stood up, but her legs wouldn't obey her and she merely moved forward in her seat and held out her hand. And Uncle Bahro – whom she had always called Teták – saw the shrunken paw she extended and recoiled from it. Irena saw the look of horror on his broad, benign face and withdrew her hand, pushing it under her, but still forcing herself to look up at this man who had loved her once and cuddled her, perhaps a little too much.

The room she was to occupy had been vacated by her cousin, Mikel, now at college and not expected back for several weeks. The walls were covered with posters, photographs and newspaper cuttings. All about sport, she saw. She sat down on the single bed. Hedija was still explaining things to her – the workings of the shower in the bathroom that adjoined the bedroom, the position of lights and how to pull down the Venetian blinds. Irena listened for a moment and then she lay down, sideways at first with her legs still over the edge of the bed. And then she pulled them up and rolled towards the middle, her head coming to rest on the two soft pillows. She closed her eyes.

Hedija turned around. She shut the shower room door and stood for a moment looking down at Irena and then pulled the duvet over her and bent to kiss her cheek. There was a sour smell coming from the girl – sweat and clothes that needed a wash. She thought of Finola, her lovely sister-in-law, and how she had dressed her little girl so beautifully and how her chestnut hair had shone from being brushed as her own Irish nanny had brushed hers: a hundred brushstrokes every night.

Later, Hedija came again into the room and began to undress Irena, who opened her eyes but did not either resist or help as her aunt pulled one of her own nightdresses over the girl's head, trying not to look too closely at the staring rib-cage and shrunken breasts. She covered her again with the duvet and sat down next to her, holding a cup of hot milk to her lips. Irena was crying again, but making no sound. Hedija's arms around her, she drank a little. Then she fell back on to the pillows again and slept.

10.   A LETTER FROM AMERICA

L EO turned up again at the hospital, but this time he met
Magda in the day room before going in to see Daniel.

'Hang on a minute, I'm trying to work this out.' Daniel
was sitting in bed, playing something on the silent keyboard.
He pulled his headphones down round his neck and extended
his hand to his visitor. Leo, held onto the hand as he began,
'Magda's told me ...'

'That I can't walk any more? It's a cow, isn't it?'

'It's certainly bad news. Are they sure?'

'Cast in stone, I'm afraid. Can't feel anything from here
down. Legs feel as if they belong to someone else.'

Leo pulled a chair up beside the bed. 'Glad to see you're
playing again. How's it going?'

'Well, the hands seem OK – badly out of practice of course
and no pedals ... I'll be playing in pubs now – if I'm lucky.
You won't want me on your books any more.'

Leo leant towards Daniel. 'I'll tell you when you've had it
professionally. Until then you get back on that stage as soon
as they can build you a ramp.'

Daniel shook his head. 'No-one's going to pay good money
to see a cripple pushing himself around.'

'For God's sake Daniel don't let me hear that word again. I
need you back and the sooner the better – we've lost a lot of
work these last few weeks. A lot of money, too. Stop feeling
sorry for yourself and worry about me instead. I don't do this
for fun, you know.'

❋

Daniel was in the hospital gym, struggling along between the parallel bars, his legs encased in full-length braces. They locked and unlocked at hip and knee, so that he could stand upright, and he'd been excited when Ross first got him into them, thinking that now he could start to get around again on his feet. But, as the days passed, these sessions began to be something he dreaded. Every step was a huge effort and the horribly unstable mobility he was able to achieve involved leaning on something he'd always called a Zimmer frame. He felt that he had joined the cohorts of elderly patients who shuffled along the hospital corridors on these things.

He couldn't escape the sight of himself; mirrors lined the gym and reflected him from every side, as Ross had stood in front of him and he put his weight onto the frame and swung one leg forward a few inches at a time. He had been trying to do this for several sessions, but his legs were a dead weight and he never knew quite where they were. The muscles that still functioned were so weak now that they no longer had the strength to do what he asked of them. But Ross smiled encouragingly as he took a few more steps, feeling unbalanced and very afraid he might fall; he'd toppled over once and it had hurt like hell. He knew there was no escape from this torture if he was ever to get anywhere near mobile again, though he wasn't sure he wouldn't prefer just to opt for the wheelchair rather than this clumsy and premature senility.

Today, Ross didn't hand him the frame but a pair of elbow crutches. 'Have you used these before?' he asked.

Daniel nodded. 'I broke my leg and had some then.'

'Well, you'll know what to do. But now you haven't got one good leg to rely on.' Daniel watched Ross demonstrate the technique his patient was to use and, his face suddenly more cheerful, tried to balance himself between the crutches. He felt relieved to be shot of the walking frame – he'd got rather nifty on his crutches with a leg in plaster three years ago. But his confidence was short-lived. This new way of walking was even more clumsy and impossible than with the frame; he felt completely crippled and helpless. Shuffling forward again, he saw Leo standing in the doorway.

'*Do prdele!*' he always swore in Czech when the word was not one to be aired in public.

'For God's sake, Leo – this isn't a fucking freak show!' he shouted, his face flushed with anger and humiliation.

Ross, seeing that his patient had had enough, pushed Daniel's wheelchair up behind him, helped him into it and took the crutches. 'You've done well today. Off you go now. See you tomorrow.'

Daniel was feeling behind his knees to release the bolts that held his legs straight and then he arranged his feet on the footrests. It was the first time Leo had seen him do any of this and he turned away to hide his feelings.

'There's something I want to talk to you about,' he said 'Let's go to the café, shall we? I could do with a cup of tea myself. I know you only drink Belle Epoque, Danny, but the NHS is a bit mean about the bubbly.'

Daniel didn't laugh and propelled himself towards the lift in silence. Once in the café, he pushed himself to a table at the far side and stopped with his back to the room. Leo brought over a teapot and two mugs. He collected some brownies and put them in front of Daniel, who had a very sweet tooth, but they were pushed away angrily.

'Magda says you go to Stoke Mandeville soon – do you know how long for?'

Daniel wasn't feeling like talking, let alone about the feared rehab. 'A couple of months. Sounds like a nightmare.'

'I want to talk about a radio programme I think you should do.' said Leo.

'A radio programme? For God's sake, Leo …'

Seriously Daniel. This is *Desert Island Discs*. We booked

you in a while ago and I think you should do it. People have loved your TV master classes. They know who you are.'

'Who I was, you mean,' said Daniel. 'Oh Christ, Leo … what am I going to do?'

'You'll go to this Stoke place and behave properly while you're there. We taxpayers are footing the bill, you know. Then you'll go home and start your life again, beginning with *Desert Island Discs* to remind the world you're still around.' He put his hand up to stop Daniel from speaking,

'God knows you can do it if anyone can. A lot of your life needn't be that different. You never did play the piano on your feet, did you? Or with them, come to that?'

Leo had hoped to elicit a laugh from his companion, but Daniel rounded on him.

'What about the fucking pedals? You know perfectly well I shan't be able to play most of the stuff I used to.'

Leo had indeed wondered when he'd have to have this conversation and of course Daniel would have been agonizing about this aspect of his playing – he'd have been thinking of little else.

'One thing at a time, Danny.' He said quietly. 'Of course you'll need to look at your repertoire in the light of your … disability.'

The word seemed to stick in Leo's throat but he was a man who called a spade a spade and he swallowed and went on, 'take your time and just keep your head down and tackle things when you need to and not before. Being a musician isn't like running in the Olympics, as you very well know. There is more to your pianism than physical ability. You'll find a way because you won't be able to live without playing the piano. It's part of your inner life. Anyway, your face hasn't changed – don't forget that's your greatest asset – hang the music. It's the CD covers that made me a rich man.'

This time Daniel did laugh and helped himself to a brownie.

Before he left, Leo handed him a fat envelope. 'Fan mail – you'd better read these to cheer yourself up. Seems there are lots of ladies queuing up to look after you. Take your pick. Oh and there's a personal one, I think. From the US. I haven't opened that.'

Daniel sorted the post into piles on his bed. To his surprise there was a lot of fan mail and some kind letters full of encouragement, but also a number of rather disturbing ones about disability and how to cope with it – these he put aside to acknowledge later. He always made a point of dashing off a quick note of thanks no matter what nonsense had been written.

Leo had left Daniel looking more cheerful but inside he was no less afraid. He just couldn't see what his life was to be now that he couldn't get about anymore in a normal way. Even more terrifying was his wrecked career. Yes, there was work he could perform, but people would see him as an object of pity, as a man who was no longer the musician they remembered. He dreaded pity, or dismissal. Either would be alien to him and he wondered at the way he had taken for granted the fame and adulation that had been his for over twenty years. Now everything was hard work and complicated and he seemed to have become horribly clumsy in all he tried to do. He wasn't a vain man, although he knew that his looks were admired, but he'd been able to take his lean, well-made body for granted. His face was thinner and sallow – like something that lived under a stone, he thought – and two long scars, still livid, ran down his left cheek, leaving a hairless track through the stubbly growth of his dark beard. Yes, his looks were going and he badly needed a haircut. There were quite a lot of white hairs now amongst the dark ones. He pulled one out and examined it – it curled back onto his fingers, glistening silver in the evening sun, and he flicked it away. It spiralled down and, following it with his eyes, he was reminded how ridiculously thin his knees and legs had become – he looked like a long-legged bird now – an increasingly muscular torso finishing on these pathetic, fleshless pins. How he hated them.

Returning to his mail, the letter from America aroused his curiosity. There was a name written on the back which rang a bell with him, but he wasn't sure why. He opened the envelope, noticing as he did so that the writing looked continental – although he could not have said exactly what he meant by that.

Dear Maestro Daniel

Please forgive my addressing you this way, but we always called you that when we met at the Vila Dolena all those years ago and in much happier times. Perhaps you will just remember me as Adam's sister, Irena's aunt, as we met only when there were family parties at the Vidaković house during the time you were teaching at the Conservatory.

My family and I were fortunate enough to be able to leave Sarajevo before the Siege took over the city. My brother was not so lucky. I do not know if you heard the terrible end that befell him and Finola – to this day I can't think about them without weeping.

You may also not know that Irena was captured and imprisoned for two years by the Serbs. However, she survived and managed to get to the US, where we were able to take her in and care for her. I shall not dwell on what she went through – I believe she was abused and mistreated in every sort of way – and she is still unable to talk about her sufferings. She arrived here in a terrible state and it has taken all this time for her to be able to face life in a normal

fashion and to be able to move to Manhattan where
she shares an apartment with members of her own
string quartet. You will remember what a good viola
player she was. I think her instrument has saved her
life, as she lives for her music.

Daniel read and re-read the paragraph and then he began
to weep, but it was strange weeping as he smiled at the same
time, smiled and laughed a little, too.

I know you and Irena spent a lot of time together
when you were her family's house guest, and you are
the only person from her past that she will talk about
without becoming very upset, even now. Perhaps you
do not know that she survived? She is a very altered
young woman.

I was very shocked to read of the terrible thing that
happened to you last year in Sarajevo. The papers
have carried quite a few articles about you and the
latest one, in *Music Monthly*, said that you are
recovering from your injuries but will be confined
to a wheelchair. It may have been the wrong thing to
do, but I decided to keep this from Irena, who never
reads the papers. I kept the articles to show her when
I felt she could withstand the shock of reading them.

The reason I am writing now is to tell you that Irena
and her quartet – Vibrati Vivaldi – will be going
to London in May for a concert tour and I have
persuaded Irena to look you up while she is there.
Now that her trip is planned, she has started to ask
me how she can find out where you live and I told
her I would write to you via your agent. She is a very
shy girl these days and also believes that you did
little to keep in touch with her family after you left
the city. So she is torn between wanting to see you
again and other confused feelings about you.

May I leave it to you to get in touch with Irena if
she does not contact you herself? I don't know what
happened after you went back to London, but I
remember you as a very kind man and cannot believe
you put that wonderful family right out of your
mind when the press were so full of the suffering of
what was then Yugoslavia.

I have enclosed a card with the address where Irena
and her friends will be staying north of Kensington
Gardens – and also their schedule in the UK, starting
with a few weeks in London, where they will perform
a series of Haydn concerts. Then they go on to play
in several of your major cities and in Scotland as
well. They plan to be away for about two months and
I shall accompany Irena to London and make sure
she is coping before I go back. The two violinists in
the quartet are sweet girls and I hope will be able to
take over her care when I return to the States.

If you are to meet again, she will need to know what
happened to you. I don't know how she'll take the
news, but it's better she knows in advance.

I do hope you are managing with your new
difficulties – I gather from our musical friends that
you are planning to play the piano in public again.
That is wonderful and I send you all my good wishes
for your life and career.

Yours sincerely,

Hedi Tanović

PS I think you will remember my daughter, Latifa
– we called her Lati. It is a great sadness for us that,
although she survived the war, she fell in love with
a Serbian and now lives amongst the people we
had learned to fear and loathe. I do not know if we
shall ever see her again, as her husband has filled
her head with anti-Bosnian propaganda. They have

twin boys, and I wish so much I could see them, but that terrible war tore apart so many elements of our happy and united country.

When Magda dropped in to see Daniel that evening, she arrived almost simultaneously with Sam, who had brought a bottle of champagne, a bag of CDs and some avocado pears. Daniel greatly disliked hospital food. His sister and the many friends who visited him knew that an offering of something delicious would raise his spirits and set him laughing again, even if only for the duration of their visit. He did his best to appear positive and cheerful, but he felt neither. Magda did not need to be told this and nor, as he spent more time with his tutor, did Sam. They both knew that Daniel was in a very dark place and that there was nothing they could do to help him, other than simply being where he could always find them. Only he would be able to cross the bridges – or to build new ones – to find a way of living that was pleasurable again. Pleasurable and musically productive, for it was his art, they suspected, that would save him in the end.

'Now,' Daniel said, as he poured the champagne. 'There is something wonderful to celebrate.' He paused and looked down at his old Turkish slippers, which didn't stay on his feet very well these days, so he leant down and pulled them on further. The news he was about to share seemed to him so momentous that he didn't know how to begin.

'You know I stayed with the Vidaković family in Sarajevo for nearly a year?' Daniel spoke slowly at first and then he could no longer contain himself, ' I told you that Adam and Finola were killed soon after the beginning of the Siege, but no-one knew what had happened to their daughter, Irena. But look …' and he held out Hedija's letter towards his two companions, his face glowing now. 'She's alive! She's been living in the States and she's coming to London in May.'

'Irena's alive?' Magda could hardly believe what she was hearing.

'Yes. And living with an aunt – one I used to know, actually. She was very ill when she got there but now she's OK. Anyway, she plays in a string quartet – viola, she was always very good. And they're coming over to perform around the UK next summer.'

'So you'll be able to see her?' Magda went over to her brother and put her arms around him and for once he allowed her to hold him for a while so she shouldn't see his tears. And Sam looked out of the window wondering about this Irena who was so important to Daniel.

11. A PARTY ENTERTAINER

THE CHILDREN'S Day Room had been transformed; bunting and balloons were everywhere and the piano, also wreathed with decorations, had been moved into the middle of the room. All around the edge sat the young patients, some able to sit cross-legged on the floor, others in wheelchairs and some had even had their beds brought in from the wards and lay around the room with their drips and dressings. A cheer went up when Daniel pushed himself in, wearing a red cashmere sweater that Magda had given him for Christmas. Joanna came to greet him, relieved that he hadn't let them down and thinking how handsome he looked.

'This is Daniel – he's a really good piano player and he's going to play for us today, so be thinking of your favourite tunes. But first he's going to start with something really fast to get us all going.'

The fastest piece Daniel could think of then was *The Flight of the Bumble Bee*. Although playing without pedals and on a less than perfect piano was something he had dreaded, he looked around at the excited children and forced himself to smile as his hands flew up and down the keyboard. The children had never heard anything like it and the staff listened, astonished. Joanna had told them about the patient who had come to the ward to play the piano when they were wondering how to entertain the children, but this was not what they had expected. They doubted that a programme of classical music was going to give them the fun they had been promised. They need not have worried. Daniel had finished the Rimsky-Korsakov and threw himself into a medley of nursery rhymes and popular songs, beginning to enjoy himself as the children joined in, singing at the top of their voices. He watched them closely, so that everyone was included by his enthusiastic gestures of encouragement. Adding funny words where he didn't know the real ones, he joined in the singing. They loved it. They loved him.

Daniel looked around for Melanie as he played. She didn't seem to be there. Later, a trolley was wheeled in and tea was served and Daniel went over to where Joanna was standing with some of the parents. 'Where's Melanie?' He asked her, accepting a large slice of cake.

'Poor little thing. She's not very well – she had her op yesterday. She was so disappointed not to be able to come to the party. She was longing to see you.'

'Can I go and see her?' asked Daniel, finishing his cake in a few large mouthfuls.

'Of course you can. She'd love it.' One of the younger nurses led Daniel along the passage to Melanie's ward. The little girl's head was swathed in bandages and her eyes were closed.

'Melanie,' Daniel whispered and she opened her eyes; 'Oh Piano Man – I couldn't hear the music,' said the little girl sadly. So Daniel began to sing for her, very softly, the songs he'd played in the Day Room and pretended to be playing the piano, his fingers running up and down her blanket. When he couldn't remember the words he made them up and the little girl began to laugh. Soon she became sleepy, with a happy smile on her face, and Daniel knew he should go back to the party.

'I'm going now. Would you like me to come and see you again?'

'Oh yes, please' Melanie's voice was very faint now and she closed her eyes, still smiling.

Back in the Day Room, Daniel played some more, but the pain in his back, which had been niggling all afternoon, was now making it hard to concentrate. He played one more tune and then explained that it was his bedtime and he'd get into trouble with Charge Nurse if he was late. The children laughed, Joanna made a little speech to thank him and he pushed himself out towards the lift.

The next day Daniel was exhausted, but he remembered Melanie. Abandoning the struggle to dress, he pulled on his djellaba and made his way to the Children's Ward. This time he was recognized and greeted enthusiastically by the staff and spent some time going slowly through the ward talking to the children and making them laugh. Joanna was not on duty and he felt disappointed in a way that surprised him.

Melanie was not fully conscious when he arrived, but she smiled when Daniel sang to her and told her a joke. Her eyes flickered open but they seemed not to focus on him.

'Does she have visitors?' He asked the nurse.

'Oh yes, her parents come every day, but late. They have a restaurant and it's such a struggle for them to get here. But they always come, even when she's asleep they sit and hold her hands. And she seems to know they've been.'

'Is she getting better?'

The cheerful nurse looked at the floor. 'Time will tell. She's a sick little girl.'

The following morning, feeling uneasy about Melanie, he returned to the children's ward. The staff at the nurses' station looked up and came to greet him. Some of the children gathered around him as well, hoping for more music.

'Could I see Melanie? How is she?'

No one spoke and they stood around him looking from one to another. 'I'm afraid' said the little Indian nurse at last,

'Melanie left us yesterday.'

'She's gone home already?' Daniel was surprised.

'No. She passed away just after her Mum and Dad arrived yesterday evening. So they were with her.'

Daniel turned abruptly and pushed himself blindly out of the ward, his head bowed. The pain he felt was not the physical pain he was coming to know, but an agonizing new pain in his heart. He hadn't really known the little girl, but she had stayed in his imagination as he played to the other children, believing that she would get better and dance around again in her pink dressing gown.

12.   A HELPFUL NEIGHBOUR

UNDER MAGDA'S instruction, the gloomy Kensington mansion flat was being altered and redecorated for the first time in fifty years or more. It had been left jointly to her and her brother when their parents died, but, since her marriage to Nathan, Magda had lived in North London and it made sense for Daniel to stay on there. It enabled him to keep the big piano and teach his classes, as well as welcoming visiting musicians who enjoyed staying with him next door to the Albert Hall.

Daniel grudgingly agreed to go and see what the builders were doing. He saw that the gloomy Edwardian fussiness with its dated Central European overtones, was giving way to a more modern look. Not being a visual man, he had given Magda free rein, only insisting that the austere family portraits and photographs should be re-hung. They were, he felt, all that remained, of his own origins; these and his collection of musical instruments had to go back onto the music room walls, exactly as before. Magda had learned from the rehab department that what a person in a wheelchair needed more than anything else was uncluttered space. In the kitchen, the old dresser, the free-standing gas cooker and noisy fridge had gone and in their place Daniel saw a series of unforgiving new worktops and built-in cupboards. He had enjoyed cooking in the dated, inconvenient kitchen with his mother who'd taught him old Czech dishes and traditional Jewish ones, watching anxiously that he did not burn his precious pianist's hands. The new cooking arrangements had been designed with his wheelchair in mind and nothing would be out of his reach, but he looked around and felt that this was no longer his home.

'So what do you think?' Magda said, excitedly as he pushed himself about, hoping he wouldn't get a puncture from the builders rubbish that crunched under his wheels. 'Looks like an old folks' home,' he muttered as he peered into his bathroom, which had a new, wide door from his bedroom. Gone were the roll-topped bath with the elaborate Edwardian shower fitments at one end and the blue-patterned washbasin and the lavatory with the mahogany seat and pull-up flush handle. He scarcely took in the expensive Italian tiles, for he was gazing at the grab-rails. There was a seat that folded down from the wall under the shower and an odd stool with armrests in front of the washbasin. These were the ugly and embarrassing impedimenta of disability which he had become accustomed to use in hospital, but he felt sick and depressed that they should have followed him home.

Arriving in London from Prague with their two children in 1970, Anna and Dragan Danuczek were overwhelmed at first by the grandeur of their surroundings. The Kensington flat had been let to them at a low rent after the death of a fellow Czech musician who had spent nothing on its upkeep for the forty years he and his wife had lived there. The plumbing was erratic, but there was always a ready supply of hot water from the big, verdigris-encrusted brass taps and it circulated noisily through the fat, rusting radiators. The children were excited to have so much space and bedrooms of their own, so the new arrivals were happy, feeling secure in the shadow of the Albert Hall and the musical community that had welcomed them in London.

The Danuczeks had very few possessions with them,

but were able to buy some of the furniture in the flat – the huge mahogany side board and break-fronted bookcase, the kitchen dresser and all the metal-sprung bedsteads. They concentrated then on finding a piano – they were both musicians and their son was learning to play.

The main room of the flat had French windows opening onto a balcony, which they shared with their neighbour, an elderly widow called Olive Beck. 'Ollie', as she was to her friends, was the author of romantic novels. She wore embroidered silk kaftans and was never seen without an exotic turban, so that the children next door fantasized that her hair must be a strange colour, such as green, or that she was totally bald. Much made up, her face could once have been beautiful. Now it sagged along the jawline but her heavy-lidded eyes were still fine and their expression both shrewd and kind. She told her friends about the interesting new neighbours, who would surely give her – as a student of human nature – plenty of material for her writing.

The Danuczeks bought a piano and Olive watched it being carried upstairs as it was too big to go in the lift. She was surprised that they had thought it necessary to buy so large an instrument for their little boy, when clearly money was short. The next day, she heard the piano being tuned, and then, almost immediately, someone began to play and she stopped typing for a moment to listen. She knew the parents were both musicians, she a singer and he a conductor, but clearly one of them was also an excellent pianist. She went out onto the balcony. It was a summer's day, and the park opposite was full of flowers and the scent from its great stretches of mown grass wafted over the main road, fresh and enticing. She peered in through the French windows of the neighbouring flat. The grand piano stood just inside what had been the drawing room and was now the music room, but it was not Dragan or Anna at the keyboard. Daniel sat with his legs dangling from the stool, his small arms in his grey school shirt moving backwards and forwards, the cuffs slightly too long, so that only his fingers protruded from them, and those fingers raced up and down the keys. He was a beautiful child, tall for his age, rather skinny with a lot of black curls, his knees showing below grey flannel shorts and socks that had fallen down over his black school shoes. His face was rosy, his big blue eyes wide with the excitement of the music. Olive now understood why the piano had been such a high priority for this family. Daniel was supremely gifted. She never forgot her first sight of him.

As the months went by Olive saw more and more of her neighbours. Anna a tall, thin woman, whose face wore a perpetual expression of anxiety, had trouble learning English. At first she shied away from her exotically-dressed and loud-voiced neighbour, but eventually the two women managed to communicate, laughing at the many misunderstandings that their lack of a common language led them into. Olive was sometimes asked to keep an eye on Daniel when his parents were out and Magda was late at school. She would make cakes for him and loved the look of excitement on his face when he saw the plate she'd hand him at the door; she'd never seen such an appetite. Daniel would sit cross-legged in the untidy music room while she helped him with his English, laughing a great deal as he ate. He was a charming boy, but she suspected he didn't see very well and it wasn't until he started at Westminster School that her suspicions were proved right – he appeared at her door one day, looking rather sheepish and wearing a large pair of spectacles.

'Ollie!' he cried, 'You were correct. I have terrible eyes – but do you think I can get a girlfriend now?,' he asked anxiously, and she thought that, with his delicious smile, Daniel would surely never be without admirers. Olive accepted gladly when her new neighbour knocked on her door and thrust a ticket into her hand, saying diffidently – 'please, thank you.' It was for a concert in the Wigmore Hall; one that Daniel's distinguished piano teacher arranged every year to show off her most talented pupils. Arriving there, a familiar place to her, as many of her friends were musicians, she read the programme, and saw that Daniel was amongst the performers. When it was his turn, he came onto the stage and looked around the auditorium, curious and apparently unfazed by the faces staring up at him. Then he smiled a wide smile, bowed low and climbed onto the piano stool. All the children who played that day under the critical eye of their famous teacher were very talented, but the most tumultuous applause was for Daniel. His parents were justly proud, while hoping that the adulation would not go to the boy's head.

Anna had always been pale and thin, but four years after her arrival in London she had begun to look very ill. Tests were run and Magda and Daniel learnt that their mother was dying. Her husband watched in horror and disbelief as she faded away before his eyes. Nothing could be done for her and she died at home just before Daniel's fourteenth birthday. Even in her last days, Daniel's mother had loved to hear him play the piano and had insisted he continue his daily practice, but he now played the pieces he knew she loved, especially her beloved Dvorak. *A Walk in a Bohemian Forest* accompanied her last dreams.

Magda was old enough to keep house and she did so, gradually subordinating her own grief into the re-ordering of the flat and looking after her father and brother. But Dragan's heart, which had never been strong, was beginning to fail, as his own father's had before him.

In his mid-teens, Daniel had already become a celebrity and was enjoying the fame and excitement of the new world that was opening for him. Studio portraits of him graced the covers of his recordings and he was constantly interviewed, first in the musical press and then in glamour magazines. Weak and withdrawn and refusing to see a doctor, his father listened to his playing and noticed the change in his son's choice of repertoire, now seeming to lean towards the much-played romantic pieces beloved of the greater part of the public.

'Come here, Danny. I want to talk to you.' His father's voice was feeble but there was still something ominous in the summons. Daniel had been trying on a Prussian blue coat which had just arrived from his tailor; ordered because he had been told it matched his eyes. He followed his father into the music room and sat down opposite him. Dragan Danuczek looked at his son in silence for a moment and Daniel began to feel uncomfortable.

'What's that you're wearing?'

'It's new – I thought it would be better than a dull old tail coat – you know, when I play at QEH next week. What do you think, Papy?'

'You look like a tart. What are you playing next week?' Daniel reached for the programme he had propped up on the piano and handed it to his father, suspecting as he did so that his choice of repertoire would not please him.

'Well. I suppose this is the sort of thing that goes with a coat like that.' Dragan tossed the programme aside. 'Daniel. I'm thankful your mother never heard you play this rubbish. I shan't live forever. You can do as you like with your life, of course. But your gifts are great. There are plenty of mediocre pianists who can strut around playing to the audience and looking pretty for the girls. I had hoped you would use your talents better than this. That's all I have to say.'

Daniel sat looking down at the floor. He felt as if his father had struck him, but his voice had been very quiet and his words gentle as he reprimanded his son.

'Go, please,' said Dragan.

Daniel went into his room and looked at himself in the glass over his chest of drawers. An hour ago the image had pleased him, but now he took off the gaudy coat and threw it into the corner of the room.

The following week, Daniel stood in front of the audience in the Queen Elizabeth Hall and announced that he had altered the programme. He would now be playing Bach, Britten and Dvorak. He gave no excuse, nor did he apologize, as he went towards the piano. Sitting down, he scanned the audience for his father and Magda, but they were not in their seats.

Dragan Danuczek crept into the concert hall late. The old conductor had heard his son play since the boy had first reached up to the keys and begun to explore them. By Daniel's sixth birthday, he had already learnt a wide repertoire. Neither parent wanted him labelled as a child prodigy and they shielded him from publicity until they no longer could. Then he had his own agent, the irascible Leo Haskell, and more fame than his family found comfortable. But Daniel had revelled in the adulation, the invitations to play all over the world and gladly made himself available to the journalists who clamoured to interview him. His looks and charm combined happily with his huge talent; he was well on the way to being a musical superstar.

Leo was watching with some surprise as Daniel came onto the stage that evening and bowed briefly. Normally he would have taken time to acknowledge this moment of recognition from the audience, but tonight he was impatient to get to the piano. He announced the changes to his programme and a hush fell on the audience, partly because he always held their attention with his particular magnetism, but also because tonight he seemed to be different. He went to the piano, pushed up the frayed cuffs of his father's old dress shirt and rubbed his hands together for a moment. Then he started to play the first of the Bach *Chaconnes* that he knew his father loved, pausing between each one, bowing his head and moving on to the next. Dragan heard the change in his son's playing and saw his modest acknowledgment of the applause that greeted him at the end of his performance. Daniel played two encores and made his last bow to his admirers, who were still calling for more as he left the stage.

In the Green Room, father and son embraced, Daniel expressing, without words, how sorry he was. Dragan had no need of an apology; he died peacefully a few weeks later, happy in the certainty that his son would fulfil the hopes that Anna and he had cherished for so many years.

Magda had rung Olive and told her that Daniel was in hospital, that he was very ill and would possibly not survive. She did not say that her brother had been shot – it seemed so unlikely and so melodramatic – there had been an accident in Yugoslavia, she said. Over the following days, she did her best to keep her neighbour up to date from Daniel's bedside. And then came the news that he was out of danger and conscious. Olive longed for more detailed reports, frustrated only to be told every time that Daniel was making a slow recovery, but would not be coming home just yet. Magda's voice sounded strained and full of anxiety, so her neighbour felt it best to cease her questioning for the time being. Instead, she would go and see the patient herself.

Carrying a homemade orange Genoese sponge, one of Daniel's favourites, Olive took a bus to the hospital and found her way to his ward. Outside his room she looked through the porthole in the door. Unshaven, pale and apparently immobile, the man lying in the bed did not resemble the Daniel she knew. Several plastic tubes still ran into the back of one of his hands and a green screen was monitoring his vital signs; he resembled someone from one of the television programmes about emergency wards that she sometimes found herself watching. A young nurse came up to her and asked if she wanted to go in. Olive shook her head, pushed the dented cake tin into the girl's hands and fled as fast as her arthritic legs would take her.

A week later, Daniel had improved enough to write:

> Dearest Ollie,
>
> Thank you for the delicious cake. You will be entirely responsible for my swift recovery. It was the best medicine ever. Sadly I had to share it out …
>
> Love Daniel.

She knew she should visit him properly, but she wanted to remember the long-legged boy who would climb over the partition between the two balconies to see her. As he got older his life became more hectic, but he was never too busy to put his head round her door on his way to Japan or the USA, invariably full of funny stories about his fellow musicians and the grand hotels he stayed in. And immensely kind too, making time to sit with her after her Douglas had died, just holding her hand over her kitchen table. Ollie had met Felicity, of course, but didn't take to her, and was not surprised when Daniel came back from a concert tour to find her farewell note.

Several weeks passed and Magda seemed reluctant to talk about Daniel's progress. Builders were in the Danuczek flat now, making a terrible noise and apparently taking the whole place apart. She became friendly with Wojtek, the Polish foreman. She fed him and his team with cake and brought them freshly-brewed coffee. They invited her in to see the finished work and she wandered round the flat feeling both admiration and sadness. It was all completely unrecognisable. On her way out, she saw the lift coming up to the landing and the doors opening. Magda stepped out.

'Oh Ollie ... Here's Daniel. He's come to see the flat.' She sounded anxious and then Olive saw the young student, Sam Gore, struggling out of the lift, pulling a wheelchair. He turned the chair onto the landing and its occupant sat looking up at her.

Later that day, Olive and Daniel faced each other over her kitchen table. She had burst into tears when she saw him outside the lift and Magda, horrified by the unplanned encounter, had swiftly pushed him through the front door which she closed behind them with a bang. But Daniel had refused to go back to hospital without seeing his neighbour again and trying to comfort her.

'I'm so sorry you had to find out like that – that I can't walk. I thought Magda would have told you?'

'No, she didn't. I expect she's had a lot of people to tell.'

'Yes. She said it's like breaking the news to your family that someone has died.' And he reached over for the old woman's hand. 'Well, I'm alive, anyway. Please don't look so sad. Aren't you pleased to see me, just a little?'

'Oh course I am. I've missed you terribly. And your piano.'

'Well, as I told you, the cake did the trick – and here I am. They tell me you get used to getting around in a wheelchair. At the moment I just feel like a very old man. But you know me, Ollie ... practice makes perfect.'

'That's my Daniel. Brave as a lion.'

Daniel bared his teeth, tossed his curly mane and pretended to roar. He didn't feel at all brave that day, but was learning how to help people over their first sight of him in a wheelchair. He hoped that, if he could get them to believe he was making a good fist of his new life, maybe he'd be able to convince himself at the same time.

Before he left, he told her about Irena. Olive had known of his fruitless quests for the girl and that it was during one of these forays that his 'accident' had taken place.

'Best news ever. She's alive and living in America.'

'So you could be in touch with her again?'

'Perhaps. But the main thing is she's alive …'

Olive said goodbye and watched Daniel manoeuvre himself onto the landing. He waved at her, looking cheerful, though frighteningly pale and gaunt, but that was being indoors too much. He needed a nice walk in the park. She'd make a picnic and push him over one day. She went back to her typewriter and stared at the blank sheet of paper. Then tears overcame her again.

13. HEDI COMES TO CALL

As IRENA PRACTISED for the UK trip, her mood veered from excitement to a sickening dread. Going to London to perform and leaving the comfort and security of her American life was going to be an ordeal and she wasn't sure how she would manage. Hedija had volunteered to go with her and stay for the first week or two, but the rest of the quartet were unaware of Irena's anxiety; they were far too excited. To be asked to play at the Wigmore Hall as part of their Young Artists scheme was a great honour. They had been heard by one of the scouts the Hall sent out when they played at a small New York venue.

They would mainly play Haydn in London. He was a composer Irena loved: it was his music which had finally broken through her pain and reminded her of the existence of joy. Playing the *Sunrise Quartet* had been a revelation to her and her co-players had been surprised to see her become so animated. They had been thrilled to find a violist who not only played with extraordinary sensitivity and technical skill, but who would from time to make a comment of such maturity and insight that they were taken aback.

'Where did that come from? Is that your idea?' They asked once when she remembered something that Maestro Daniel had taught her. She shook her head. 'No. I had a terrific teacher once. He told me that and I've never forgotten it.' And, she recalled also what Daniel had told her about the Wigmore Hall, joking about his first concert there, when his legs were so short he couldn't reach the pedals. She wondered whether Hedi would manage to find his address and if she herself would ever have the courage to look him up when she got to London. Perhaps it would be better just to treasure her memories of him. He had probably forgotten her and her parents long ago.

Irena shared the Manhattan flat with the quartet's first and second violinists, twins from the Bronx called Bella and Sasha. She had a good life, she thought. Very quiet, just her music and a few girlfriends; she never went out alone with boys and never explained to anyone why she did not. Inside herself, her fear of men and her revulsion from anything to do with sex or any physical contact remained something she had come to accept. Her flat mates, who were fiercely protective of her – she was so quiet and her eyes were so sad – knew better than to question her.

Hedija was on her way to see Irena on a bitter March day, numbingly cold as the early spring can be in New York. On every side, the glowing windows of shops beckoned towards a promised warmth, but she kept to the sidewalks, still slushy from the morning's snow. She had been to Irena's downtown apartment before, but it was not an area she knew well and the cab had dropped her off two blocks too soon. She walked with her head lowered to keep the sleety rain off her face, her hat and gloves already soaked.

Irena was waiting for her aunt and fell into the embrace of her ample arms once they had shed their many layers of sodden clothing. They held each other for a moment, Irena feeling how lucky she was to have this surrogate mother now that she was so thoroughly orphaned. Hedija's warm brown eyes seemed to see her as others didn't, seemed to understand her fears and her fragility.

'Lovely to see you, sweetheart. How are things?'

'Pretty good, really. Lots of rehearsing, but all going well, I think.'

She wondered what this visit was for – there had been something concealed and urgent in Hedija's request to come and see her on this filthy day. They sat down opposite each other, warming their hands on mugs of tea. The heating in the apartment was not working well and, anyway, Irena and her flatmates kept it turned down to economize. Hedija had taken an envelope out of her bag and was opening it.

'Darling. There's something we need to talk about before you're off to London.'

'But that's still six weeks away – you didn't need to come all the way over here – I could have got the bus over to Long Island.'

'I know, but I wanted to be sure we'd be alone and now that Bahro's in the house all day since his stroke I never know when he's going to call me.'

'How is he?' asked Irena dutifully

'He's doing OK, thanks. But he gets very sad sometimes. He misses Sarajevo, of course. Now he can't even play golf he has time to brood. But, Irena, listen. I want to talk about Daniel Danuczek – Maestro Daniel.'

Irena's eyes brightened for an instant. Then a guarded look came over her face.

'I know you'd thought of looking him up in London, didn't you?'

Irena nodded, and her aunt continued, 'I've managed to be in touch with him through his agent.'

Hedija was unfolding the newspaper cuttings she'd taken out of the envelope and smoothing them out on her knee. 'He went back to Sarajevo to look for you and your family – several times, you know. He knew you might have died with Mama and Tata, but he kept on hoping to find you.'

'He went to look for us – for me?

'Yes he did – and he was in Sarajevo again eighteen months ago, playing in some concerts and visiting friends – the ones who are left – at the Conservatory. Something awful happened – it was all over the papers.' Irena put her hand over her mouth.

'He isn't dead – is he?' But no, he couldn't be; Hedi had said she'd been in touch with him.

'No. He's alive and longing to see you. I'll show you his letter in a minute. But be strong now darling. There is something you need to know …'

Irena crossed the room and sat down next to her aunt. She took the cuttings and read the newspaper story first and then, her hand frequently touching the photograph of Daniel, she read the interview from *Music Monthly*. She said nothing and her aunt was suddenly afraid that the shock of what she was reading might send her back into the frozen, silent state to which she would still from time to time return. But then Irena spoke again, strangely not seeming as shocked as her aunt had thought she would be, as she held the precious pieces of paper, her eyes fixed on the photograph of the man sitting in a wheelchair: a man she would have known anywhere, although his curls were cropped short and he was wearing rimless glasses. 'Oh poor Maestro Daniel – he did love running around and jumping on to his bike – Tata's bike. And he was always dancing. Can I see his letter?'

Hedija handed an envelope to Irena. It was addressed to *Mme Hedija Tanović* and she knew Daniel's writing at once. He had always used a fountain pen and his writing sloped steeply as he was left-handed. He'd seemed to write a lot of letters, and she had often watched him scribbling away with his hand curved awkwardly over the top of the line.

Albert Mansions 14th November 1997

Dear Dear Aunt Hedi, May I call you this again? It

was so very wonderful to hear from you and to know
that both you and Uncle Bahro are safe and well
and that Irena is alive. That was the best news ever.
I tried fruitlessly to find her on my various trips
back to Bosnia. The last time I heard such terrible
things from my research that I thought she could not
possibly have survived. I can hardly bear to think of
what she has been through and thank God she was
able to find a new home with you.

You say you know what happened to me on my last
trip and that I'm not quite the man I used to be.
After several months in hospital and rehab I was
able to go home and get used to life in a wheelchair.
Luckily I have a career that I can still pursue –
although in a more limited way now – and the joy of
a life in music.

As you can imagine, the thought of seeing little
Irena again – and I'm sure she's still quite little? – is
marvellous, but please tell her what has happened
to me so that she can get used to the idea. Thank
you for giving me her address. I'm not sure how to
approach her after so long, but please would you give
her this note, so she knows I would love to see her
as soon as possible when she and her friends get to
London.

Your affectionate friend

Daniel Danuczek

Hedija watched Irena read the letter slowly and, as she
came to the end, her aunt saw that the girl was smiling.

'He sounds just the same, doesn't he?'

She read the letter again and then put out her hand to take
the other envelope, which had her name on it. She needed to
be alone to read this precious thing and Hedija, sensing this,
excused herself, went into the bathroom and closed the door.

Hello Little Wren

How wonderful to know you are still flying around.
Of course you must come and see me when you get
to London with your friends. As soon as you can.

I'm rather an old crock now, as you will have been
told, and my hair is going grey, I'm afraid. So don't
be too shocked when you see me.

Until then, DD

PS I found these photos and thought you might like
to have them.

Hedija spent as long as she reasonably could, sitting in the
icy bathroom, renewing her lipstick and combing her hair
several times. Then she opened the door noisily and went
back into the living room. Irena was holding her letter against
her breast with both hands and tears were falling onto it, but
she smiled up at her aunt and pointed to the two photographs
she had propped up on the table. One was of Irena with her
parents and Amela in the garden at Vila Dolena. Behind them
was the blue studio. They were all smiling and Irena, who was
holding a small black dog in her arms, had the widest smile of
all. The other picture was of Maestro Daniel with Irena. They
were sitting on their bicycles and waving at the photographer.
Daniel was wearing dark glasses, so it was not the best picture
to have of him, but Hedija looked at the long-limbed young
man with his white teeth and black curls and remembered
thinking then that Irena had a crush on him. But wouldn't
any young girl? And Irena sat gazing at the photographs, a
smile beginning to spread over her face.

'He was so cute, wasn't he?' and she reached out and
stroked the picture. The other one she turned over suddenly,
picture side down, banging her hand down on it. Was it too
painful? Hedija suspected it was.

Irena said goodbye to her aunt, clinging to her neck and

kissing her again and again. Hedija released herself, laughing anxiously.

'Take care, darling. Call me soon. Now, you're not too upset, are you?' Irena shook her head, hugging herself against the cold air that lay dankly on the concrete landing outside the flat. 'I'll be OK. It's lovely to have heard from Maestro Daniel. Thanks for coming.' She was smiling as Hedija turned towards the lift, waited until the doors had closed behind her, and went back into the flat.

The cuttings were still on the table and she picked them up. Then, sitting down, she read them through again.

In the hours that followed Irena wondered why she had been so slow to take on board the awfulness of what had happened to Daniel. Perhaps, she thought, it was because of the joy she'd felt after so many years of imagining she would never see him again. His letter and the two precious photographs had filled her with a new happiness and excitement while Hedija and she had been together that afternoon. Then she unfolded the newspaper cutting and spread it out on her knees. The shiny steel wheels of his chair seemed very big and she remembered how long his legs were, how he had towered over her. Now he would never stand up again, never run or jump on a bike and chase down through the woods, laughing and singing. Irena lay on the sofa rocking to and fro in her grief.

14. MEZZO PIANO

For the two months before he finally went home to Prince Albert Mansions, Daniel found himself facing rehabilitation at Stoke Mandeville. Everyone kept telling him how fortunate he was to be going to the most famous spinal injury hospital in the world, but this was little comfort; all he wanted was to go home.

In his new environment, he saw many people there who were very much worse off than he was. He saw the floppy, uncontrolled hands that had once wielded tools, the lolling bodies of men and women who were learning simply to sit up unaided in their new wheelchairs, chairs which would become part of their lives, as his already had, and without which they were going nowhere. However, cheerfulness was the order of the day and it was only in the evenings, as they drank together, that he saw the haunted eyes of his fellow patients as they described the agony of marriages that could no longer be what they had been and the new revulsion in the eyes of those with whom they had once shared their beds.

Ross and the physio team had been aware that Daniel was resisting the programme that was planned for him, protesting that he'd manage perfectly well when he got home and that there was nothing he needed to learn about his new condition. It was a shock to him when he began to see how difficult life as a paraplegic was going to be if he didn't at least get himself physically fit and then learn how to be a disabled man reliant on his wheelchair to get around and – the hardest lesson of all – to accept help when he needed it. Internally, he fought every inch of the way, frantic to find some way of escaping the sentence that life seemed to have passed on him. But there was no escape.

The week before his homecoming, Magda told Daniel that she and her husband, Nathan, had parted. Daniel said he was sorry and wished there was something he could do to help. He had never liked his brother-in-law and thought Magda deserved a better deal in life. But when she said: 'Let me come and look after you just until we know how much help you're going to need,' he shook his head adamantly.

'I won't need any help, thanks. I'll manage fine.'

Magda knew that this wasn't so, but she also knew better than to contradict him.

Then Daniel put out his hand to her. 'Listen – the flat's your home too. Yes, come and keep me company for a bit. That'd be great.' It had been an effort to say it, but Daniel felt better when he had.

Magda and Sam brought Daniel back from the hospital and he could hear them in the kitchen, as he wheeled himself straight to the end of the passage, to the double doors which still had their original coloured glass depicting birds and flowers. This was the music room and had been for as long as he had known this flat as home. There his parents had made music with their friends and he had practised the piano hour after hour throughout his childhood. And there stood his piano still, the piano his parents had scrimped and saved to buy for him.

He loved the instrument and it seemed to have been his destiny to play and play, to fill his days with its sound. Harmony, composition and the written notation which he had committed to memory when he was so young that he could not have written his own name, had become the most important things in his life. Even as a teenager, he would get up early enough to play for his own pleasure before the family had left their beds, and the piano was the lure, the bright *shangri la* at the end of the passage.

When he went back to the flat with Magda to see what the builders had been doing, he hated what he saw. Not a person with strong visual taste, Daniel lived happily in the flat as his parents had left it, shabby and old-fashioned, but a comforting place to come home to. Returning from concert trips he had always opened the front door with a feeling of relief and pleasure. He would fling his bags down in the hall. Then he would go into the kitchen and scour the fridge for something to eat and drink and take his trophies down the passage, and the music room was his again.

The lovely Broadwood gleamed as it always had. Gleamed and seemed to beckon to him. He sat in the doorway and did not go over to it. He could, of course, wheel himself over and play a few scales, some arpeggios, a few exercises. Then he could maybe play a Scarlatti sonata, or some Boccherini – there was plenty of early music, after all, that he had been listing for himself over the last few weeks – music that could be played without using the pedals. But he longed then for Schubert, as if no other composer existed. But he knew he could not play the pieces that were jostling each other on his inner ear. That he would never play them again. No matter how much he tried to find new ways to reach the sound he had once been able to produce, that road was now closed to him. For the rest of his life.

He went over to the piano. Magda had opened the keyboard and propped the lid up a few inches, the way he used to prepare the instrument himself. He picked up the piano stool and sat for a moment with it in his hands. Part of him wanted to throw it across the room. He wanted to distance himself from a past he could never reclaim. He had sat on that stool since he was old enough to climb onto it, his little boy's legs dangling down. He put it down now, carefully but with shaking hands, behind the new sofa.

Magda was saying goodbye to Sam who had stayed to see if there was anything he could do to help. They listened for the opening exercises of Daniel's practice routine. But there was silence. Then their eyes met as they heard the lid fall noisily onto the keyboard, setting off a resonant buzzing in the whole instrument. The door to the music room opened and closed and they heard the squeak of rubber tyres on the polished wood of the corridor. Daniel scarcely paused by the kitchen door, as he said, without looking in their direction. 'Don't wait for me. I'm going to bed. Bit tired ...' and he was gone into his own room, shutting the door.

Daniel slept for a while – a deep dreamless sleep – but then he woke with a start. He sensed that someone was in the room with him and felt for his bedside lamp. As light filled the room, Daniel thought he saw someone standing at the foot of his bed.

'Irena,' he said, his voice breaking. 'Stay with me. Don't go.'

The ever-busy road outside his window threw up crooked shadows across the walls of his room, shadows and pools of moving light. There was no-one there.

There was no-one there but he felt the trace of a presence, of Irena, as if she had been in the room with him. But that could only be fancy. He lay and thought about her, fantasising about their meeting, but everything he imagined stalled as he remembered that he was a cripple now with little to offer a young woman who would need to be cared for and protected from the world.

Magda moved in with Daniel. Nathan had gone off to make himself a new life in Cape Town, but Daniel's new state gave her life a purpose again and she needed to be needed. Daniel, however, battling to regain a semblance of the independence he had known, resented his sister's presence and was frequently impatient and sometimes unkind. Magda had attended sessions at Stoke Mandeville for 'carers' of paraplegic patients and thought she was prepared for Daniel to show and voice his frustration, but all the same it was a shock to find him behaving like a spoilt child. She buttoned her lip and simply got out of his way when he was at his worst. Leo gave Daniel a week to settle in. Then he made an appointment with Magda to come to the flat. He wanted to hear Daniel play again and to discuss his future as a performer. Dates had been pencilled into the large new diary he had with him. Programmes would be suggested and, no doubt, rejected. It was natural that Daniel would be unsure of himself now, but surely longing to play in public again?

Magda motioned him into the kitchen and he put out his hands to take the coffee tray from her. But she went behind him and shut the door. 'Leo. Daniel hasn't opened the piano since he's been home. He won't discuss it – says he isn't ready or doesn't answer at all.'

'It's bound to take him time, you know, to accept his new limitations at the keyboard. I expect he isn't there quite yet. We mustn't expect too much of him.' He picked up the tray. 'I'll see what's going on in that head of his. If I can!'

In the music room, the visitor put the coffee tray down and the two men embraced, awkwardly now that Daniel's wheelchair got in the way. Leo went to the piano to see if there was anything on the music rest. But the lid of the instrument was closed and a dirty wine glass stood on the dusty keyboard cover. So Magda wasn't allowed in here now. Daniel had picked up a mug and was spooning sugar into his coffee. 'You're not playing?'

'No.'

'I'd like to hear you. It's been a long time. A bit of Bach, perhaps.'

'No. Sorry.' There was a silence.

'Your feet – the pedals?'

'What do you think?' Daniel spun his chair and went to the window. 'Look Leo, you've been a terrific agent all these years, but you know very well I have no career in music now. You don't really need to be told that, do you? And you don't need to pretend to make things easier for me.'

'Things won't be the same, of course. But there's a large repertoire of early stuff – you have a lot still to offer there. And the harpsichord, of course.'

Daniel shook his head, his eyes still fixed on the traffic below his window. How hard would it be to get himself onto the balcony, pull himself over the balustrade and drop down under a lorry, or a bus?

'I've got some literature for you – remember I sent you some in hospital? German firm makes this gismo for paraplegic pianists. You put it in your mouth and work the pedals that way. Need to have some work done on the piano, of course.'

'You leave my bloody piano alone – and you know where you can stuff that thing, too. Please leave me alone, Leo. Just let me be. Please.' His anger subsided even as he spoke. He was permanently exhausted these days. Tired out and in a good deal of pain.

'Right. I'll go in a minute but there's still your booking to take part in *Desert Island Discs*? I haven't cancelled it. This would be an excellent way to re-establish yourself, you know. No-one looking at you, no comparisons with your old image. It would be good to talk publicly about music again and the programme can be recorded over a couple of days.'

Daniel was not really surprised that Leo remained so persistent. This was the old Leo who'd always managed him, no matter how hard Daniel had fought to get his own way. He turned back to him, speaking quietly now.

'Look. I know you want to help. That's great, but let's face it – a man in a wheelchair probably wouldn't last very long on a desert island.'

Leo became impatient. 'For God's sake, Daniel – Sue Lawley probably has an answer to all that or she wouldn't still have been so keen to use you as her castaway. You don't have to be sparkling or witty. Just do it. Anyway, you need the money, don't you?'

Daniel snorted – the sort of money the BBC paid would compare unfavourably with his usual concert fees. But he looked at Leo, whose fading brown eyes, narrowed in the sagging red face as he sucked on his cigar, had a look in them he'd not seen before. He shrugged his shoulders. 'OK. As the great Lehrer said "self-indulgence is better than no indulgence at all …"'

Remembering what Magda had told him on the phone, Leo stopped by the door as he was leaving. 'I hear the girl from Sarajevo is coming to London this summer. What's her name?' He knew perfectly well, as Daniel had called that name out time after time when he was unconscious in hospital.

'You mean Irena?' Daniel's voice was guarded.

15. A SERPENT'S TONGUE

MAGDA LET Felicity in. She'd forgotten how beautiful she was; her golden fairness seemed to envelope her, so that she appeared to light up the flat as she tittupped in on her very high heels, bringing with her a waft of Chanel No. 5. Her hostess looked nervously at her shoes, hoping they wouldn't mark the hall floor – the old Turkey rugs had been taken up so that Daniel's wheelchair could run smoothly on the newly-sanded parquet.

Felicity walked down the corridor, noticing how bright and new everything looked now and remembering how she had hated the dark paintwork and the faded photographs of Daniel's forebears who looked down from the walls, disapprovingly she was sure, as she had wondered if this gloomy flat could ever feel like home. She would have thought it greatly improved now, had her guts not been churning with the anticipation of seeing Daniel. She could not hear any music, but he would be at the piano, of course – always the piano.

Magda opened the music room door and Felicity saw that the piano lid was shut and he was doing something to one of his old instruments. And she walked towards the man in the wheelchair, the cripple who still looked like Daniel.

'Danny!'

He looked up, his face expressionless, as if he had not recognised her. She forced herself to go up to him, to bend and peck him swiftly on each cheek. He did not respond to her and she backed away from him as he suddenly turned his chair and faced her.

'Well,' he said. 'Here I am. Take a good look. That's what you came for, I imagine.' His voice was unchanged and Felicity wanted to cry. But they had always teased one another and she knew that being serious with him wouldn't work, even at a time like this, and she forced a smile as she said, 'Danny – you're going grey.'

'You're not, of course.' Felicity's hair was always the same pale gold. 'Well, you've seen me now. That's the hardest bit – for both of us.'

'What do you mean?'

'Everyone hates this first session with me. They look so scared – you did when you came in. But now you know I'm not that different – I don't smell horrible, I'm not dreadfully disfigured, am I?'

'No, Danny. You look great. You're still the best looking boy on the block.' And she wondered what would have happened had Daniel become disabled while they were together. He had wondered this too, particularly when he was in rehab. He suspected that she would have found it even harder to be married to a man who sat in a wheelchair than one who was always at the piano. Felicity stood up and went over to him. She wanted to put her arms around him, but wasn't sure how and Daniel, knowing he would not have been able to endure her touch, let his chair roll back a little, away from her, uncomfortably aware of her scent.

'Don't, Flic. Please don't. Let's have a drink shall we?' He picked up the bottle of champagne from the ice bucket Magda had put out for them.

Always Belle Epoque with Danny, she remembered: it was his favourite drink. She noticed how he handled his wheelchair, seeming elegant again in his movements, spinning the gleaming steel wheels as if they were already a natural part of him. So he was no pathetic invalid, this man who wheeled himself around with such dexterity. She wondered if he could still make love. Of course, she thought, music was really the love of his life. Sex was just another thing he was good at. That he had once been good at.

Felicity watched Daniel open the champagne. He knew she was looking at him and his hands started to shake, so that, as the cork flew across the room, the wine gushed out and splashed up at him. He took his glasses off to wipe them and Felicity looked at his naked face: the face she had seen on the pillow every morning as he woke up and nuzzled into her, before her loneliness had begun to embitter her and destroy the desire she had for him.

'Danny ... I'm so sorry,' she said softly, taking the bottle from him.

'It's OK, Flic ... I'm fine. I really am.'

'I mean – I'm sorry I left like that – it was cruel of me.'

Daniel shook his head. 'Listen – I was at fault too – I was very selfish. You deserved someone who'd take much more notice of you. You were – you still are – so beautiful and such fun. I'm married to my music – you discovered that, didn't you? And you made me see it too. Are you happy now, with Carl?'

Felicity wondered whether to tell the whole truth or the half-truth she told everyone else. That was the easiest way, the least complicated way: 'Yes. He's sweet. And Josh is wonderful. I didn't think I'd be much of a mother, but he's the centre of my life now.'

Felicity left the flat. She would tell everyone that Daniel was fine, that he was managing amazingly well.

Daniel shut the front door, his face distorted as the pain of seeing her again hit him suddenly like a pitchfork in the stomach.

'How did it go?' asked Magda, coming out of her room when she heard him wheeling himself back down the corridor. He stopped abruptly and turned towards her shouting, 'Don't you do that to me again. I'm still perfectly capable of deciding who I want to see and when. It's my legs that don't work – not my bloody head.'

An hour later, Magda came out of her bedroom, opened the music room door and let it shut noisily behind her. Daniel was writing on a score, his pen digging into the manuscript paper, his face still angry. He didn't look up.

'Isn't it a bit early for dinner? I need to work this out first.'

'I want to talk to you, Daniel,'

'Won't it wait?' He asked, still not looking towards her.

'No it won't.'

Daniel, surprised by the tone of her voice, spun himself towards her.

'I'm afraid I can't go on like this. I think it's time I went home,' she said, holding his gaze defiantly.

'What do you mean 'go on like this'?'

'I'm fed up with your rudeness and bad temper. I know things aren't easy for you, but I'm not your slave and I'm certainly not used to being spoken to the way you speak to me.'

Daniel stared at Magda. 'But Blossom …' he began.

'No Daniel. Don't try to sweet-talk me. I've done my best over the last months and I was glad to help when you were so ill. But you're better now and you need to make yourself a new life. I admire your efforts, but I don't want to be on the receiving end of your waspish tongue anymore.' Magda turned towards the door.

'So when are you off?' Daniel, presuming that she was just letting off steam and would soon change her mind, thought he'd go along with her for the moment.

'Now,' she said. 'I've packed my things and I'll get a taxi home.' There's food for this evening, but you'll need to shop tomorrow. Your diary's on the table and Leo's coming on

Wednesday morning so you'll need to be up in good time. Goodbye Daniel. I'm sorry it's worked out like this.'

A few minutes later he heard her open the front door and shut it again. He went back to his work, shrugging his shoulders. If she was going to behave like that, he was better off without her, wasn't he?

On Wednesday, Leo arrived on time and rang the bell of the flat. The porter had let him in at the street door, as no one had answered the entryphone, and now he stood in front of the flat and waited. Magda usually opened the door to him, but no-one came and he rang again. Finally, Daniel answered the door, and going through the front door, Leo became aware of an odd smell in the flat and that it seemed darker than usual. They went together to the kitchen and Leo looked around. The sink was full of dishes and pans. Daniel himself didn't look too clean; his shirt was certainly in need of a wash, but he made some coffee, rinsing two dirty mugs first as there didn't seem to be any clean ones in the cupboard. He sniffed the milk and poured it down the drain.

'Have to be black, I'm afraid. I haven't been shopping lately.' He handed the tray to Leo and set off towards the music room. Leo saw that Daniel's bedroom door was open and the curtains hadn't been drawn or the bed made. In the music room, the sofa and armchairs were heaped with scores which spilled over onto the floor. Daniel picked up a pile from one of the chairs, threw them onto the floor and gestured to Leo to sit while he made room on the low table for the tray amongst the clutter of cups and glasses. Dust hung in the air like a veil, where the sun streamed in through the French window.

'Where's Magda?' Leo asked.

'She pushed off last week – I'm on my own now. Quite a

relief,' and Daniel laughed, but he didn't look amused.

'Getting in a bit of a mess, by the look of things. How long has this been going on?'

Daniel avoided his eyes and began to be annoyed. 'Oh shit, Leo. Don't you start on me. Magda said I was impossible to live with – but *she* is, actually. So bloody bossy. I couldn't stand it anymore. Life's more peaceful without all that nagging. She had no idea how difficult it's been learning to play without my feet. I want you to hear something.'

Daniel picked up a score and put it on the piano. He pushed himself up to the keyboard and began to play a Schubert Sonata. His hands stroked the keys, his long fingers holding down notes that he would normally have sustained with the right pedal, until he came to the end of the movement. Then he turned towards Leo, closed the lid over the dusty keys and said quietly,

'See? I'm finished. Kaput.'

Later, Leo phoned Magda.

'He's in a mess, Mags. The flat's a health hazard and he doesn't even seem to notice. Isn't there anyone who'd help him?'

'I've found someone I think, but he's such a rat these days and he won't be easy to work for. I know what a strain he's under learning his new techniques and having to get off his behind every couple of hours, but he's behaving like a spoilt child and I'm fed up with it.' She paused and went on. 'Is the flat really chaotic?'

'Pretty ghastly. But maybe you're right. Perhaps he'll get fed up when the smell gets too bad.'

Magda laughed, but she was miserable now. 'Can you get him out for a bit, Leo? I want to go and have a look. That girl won't want to come if it's too frightful.'

'Ok. I want him to try out a fortepiano – I've got an idea. I'll pick him up.'

Magda arrived at the flat and ran round opening the windows. She worked for two hours, then bundled up Daniel's dirty clothes to take home with her. She had unpacked fresh food into the fridge and larder and laid the table for one in the kitchen, putting a casserole into the oven and the timer on. Outside the front door she hesitated. Then she went along the landing and rang Olive's bell.

Daniel got out of the taxi and said goodbye to Leo. He wheeled himself up the ramp that had been made for him by the tradesmen's entrance at the back of the block. Making his way to the lift he realised how hungry he was and remembered that there was nothing in the fridge. Perhaps it was time he got a grip on things if he was to live on his own. He needed to get the housework done and, in spite of his training at Stoke Mandeville where he had caused chaos in the domestic department – the instructors had never before met a man who didn't know one end of a hoover from the other or how to load a washing machine. All his life he'd lived with women who'd seemed happy to do those things for him, so he'd never imagined a time when it would be his job to keep his surroundings tidy and clean.

He turned his key wearily in the lock. Maybe he'd send out for a pizza later. He saw his mail in a neat pile on the hall table – he didn't think it had come before he left that morning. Something else had changed. He wasn't sure what it was and opened his bedroom door, thinking he'd lie down for a bit. The window was slightly open, a light breeze lifting the curtains. His bed had been made and, looking through to the bathroom, the heap of wet towels had disappeared. He went around the flat and ended up in the kitchen. It, too, was very different from the way he'd left it earlier that day. On the table was a note in Magda's handwriting.

> There's a girl called Jovanka coming to see you in the morning. She needs work to support her child and herself. She's got your washing. There's a pasta dish in the fridge, milk etc. Eat the casserole (in oven) tonight. It will be ready by 8.
>
> M

Daniel put the note down and opened the fridge. Neatly arranged were fresh milk, vegetables and cheese. Feeling a bit strange, he headed for Magda's old bedroom and knocked but there was no answer. He opened the door and saw that the bed was covered with a dust sheet and there were none of his sister's possessions to be seen. Next, he hurried to the music room, hoping his scores had not been moved; he alone, knew exactly where everything was. The piles of music had not been touched, though the air was fresher and the piano had been dusted, the dirty glasses and mugs were gone and the coffee table wiped clean of the sticky rings that had witnessed their accumulation. He went to the keyboard. He didn't play but sat with his head in his hands.

Magda had gone back to Muswell Hill, but there was no husband there. She had made her mind up to move to something smaller and she had planned to search in a part of London closer to Daniel. Now she wasn't sure what to do. So used, over the last year, to caring for Daniel and looking constantly to his needs, she had ignored her own. She stared at herself in the mirror and wondered how she'd got herself into such a state – her grey-streaked hair long and straggly, her face without make up, her clothes ill-assorted. But she could not find the energy to take herself in hand.

A week had gone by and she was unpacking her shopping and had put a "ready meal" in the microwave, but she was not hungry. She opened a bottle of wine and turned on the television.

The doorbell rang when she had nodded off in front of the news. It was dark and she wondered who on earth it could be. Stiffly, she got up and smoothed her skirt. Through the spyhole in the front door she could see no-one; she hoped it wasn't someone playing a joke on her. She put the chain across and opened the door the few inches it allowed. Daniel was sitting on the pavement, looking up at her. On his lap was an enormous bunch of lilies. He had asked a passer-by to ring the bell for him as he couldn't get up the front steps.

'Mags. Come down, won't you? I need to talk to you. Put these in the house. Let's go to the pub.' She didn't move and he added, 'Please.'

She went down the front steps and took the flowers from him, half of her thinking she would throw them into the dustbin, shut the door and let him stew in his own juice. But she took the lilies, went back to the door, put them on the hall table, picked up her key and went down to join Daniel.

The pub was a few doors away in the High Street and Daniel was able to heave himself up the single step and someone moved a stool so he could get to a table near the door. He ordered two glasses of wine and they sat, not looking at each other, until it came. Magda lifted hers, but did not raise it to him as she began to drink. Finally, she asked him, her voice cold and distant. 'What do you want to talk about?'

'Well, you must know that – I need to say sorry, to start with.'

'You're always saying sorry. It never changes anything. You just go back to treating me like dirt again, don't you? I know you've been through a lot ...'

Daniel shook his head. 'That's no excuse. I know it isn't.

It's just that you've been there. All the time. And it's been marvellous. But I get so angry – with this chair, with myself and my stupid dead legs. And then …'

'I understand all that. I know how frustrated you get. Of course I do. But you don't seem to think I exist as a person. I'm just there for you to use as a sort of punchball when you need something to hurt. Danny darling,' and her voice was softer now, 'you've got to accept that you're stuck in a wheel-chair and, yes, you can't walk or ride a bike or do lots of the things you used to enjoy. But somehow you've got to learn to accept that's the way things are now – and they could be a lot worse. Leo tells me he's got all sorts of ideas – you've still got a life in music. You'll always have that. *And* you're still a good-looking guy and I often see women looking at you – see that one over there?' and they both looked across the pub at a blonde woman who was gazing at Daniel. He put his hand out to Magda across the table. She did not respond to his gesture, but nor did she move her hand away.

Daniel spoke again. 'That girl you sent – Jovanka – came to see me and I'll be fine with her to keep the place clean and do my washing and stuff. But you do matter to me, Blossom, you really do. You must know that. And you're right. It's time I accepted the way things are and just got on with it. I've just been feeling sorry for myself – it's unforgivable …' For a few minutes they both drank and avoided one another's eyes. Then Daniel spoke again, his voice rather faint. He sounded frightened, she thought, defeated almost.

'I'm worried about Irena's visit. She'll be here in three weeks now. Thing is – you invited her and her aunt to stay with us – they think you live with me. Her aunt isn't staying the whole time and I'm sure wouldn't expect Irena to stay in the flat alone with me when she goes back to the States. Not at all suitable. I'm not asking you to come back to the flat permanently, but I don't think I could cope with them on my own. I'm longing to see her again, but ...'

'Her aunt says you'll see a big change in her.' Magda said, quietly. 'The poor girl's been through the mill, too. Don't hope for too much. And you're both five years older – she could have changed a lot in that time.'

But Daniel was smiling to himself, 'She's great fun. I'm sure that won't have changed. She'll cheer us all up, I know.'

Magda tried to smile too, but she knew that, for all his excitement at the thought of Irena's arrival in London, Daniel also dreaded it. In her letter to Hedija, Magda, touched by the girl's tragic story, had asked if Irena wouldn't be better staying with a family, and offered her a room in the flat she shared with Daniel. It was the little room he'd slept in as a child. Daniel had said the quartet could rehearse in the flat whenever they liked; the place needed to be full of music. Hedija wrote back ecstatically. Yes, of course, it would be a great relief for her to know that Irena was comfortable and well cared for. She had decided to travel over with her niece and they would stay for a few days with friends in North Kensington. She hoped to visit Scotland before returning to the States – if Irena seemed to be getting on all right.

'The poor girl still has nightmares and flash-backs
from time to time, which was why I thought I would
go with her to London. If this is happening when
I have to go home, she could move in with her two
friends, Sasha and Bella – the two violinists from the
quartet. They know how to handle things, but I hope
Irena will be too busy and tired to have bad nights.'

Magda had not read out this part of Hedija's letter, not wanting to worry Daniel further, but she already realised that the visit could be difficult in all sorts of ways. She knew he loathed the thought of greeting her from a wheelchair, that he would be looking up at her as he looked up at everyone now, and unable to take her around London except in the laborious way that was forced on him. His life now was bounded by ramps and the helping hands of others.

'So you want me to move back in, is that what you're saying? As a chaperone?'

'Maybe you could stay just while she's over here?'

'Let's leave things as they are for the moment. I don't want to let you down, but it really is time I put my life together again. I must sell up here – the house is only half mine anyway – and I'd like to make a fresh start somewhere.'

Daniel nodded.

'Yes, I can see that. You probably should face up to being on your own now. It's tough for you though. I wish I could help. Are you OK for money?' Magda had looked less well-dressed than he remembered her and never seemed to get her hair done these days.

'Please ask me if you need anything, won't you? And don't get all lonely and miserable.' He was looking anxious now. This was the Daniel she had always known and she found herself laughing.

'Oh Danny. You are a chump. Look, I just need some time to myself now. I'd got in the way of being so miserable about you that it's been taking up all my waking hours. You think you can manage with a bit of help from Jovanka, do you?'

'Trouble is you've spoilt me rotten and I've done nothing for myself since I got home. But, yes. Yes, I'm sure I can. High time I got a grip really. Forgive me, Blossom, please forgive me. Do you think you can?' and he pulled one of her hands to his lips and kissed it.

'No, I won't forgive you until you repay me by getting back onto that stage and being the silly old genius I used to know and love. I'm not hanging around while you work out your frustration. Get your act together before that poor girl turns up and I'll see if I can spare the time to make your set-up look respectable.' She stood up, taking her hand out of Daniel's and leant to kiss his forehead. Then she left the pub and he pushed himself up to the bar to pay for the wine and wheeled himself into the street to find a taxi.

'Leo? Hi – it's Daniel.' Leo laughed to himself – as if he could mistake that voice for anyone else's. 'I need your help.'

'What can I do for you, sir?'

Daniel didn't answer at once. Then he spoke fast. 'Thing is, I need to get that fortepiano – as soon as I can. You're right – that's the answer now. There's a lot of repertoire I can tackle and the harpsichord's never really …'

Leo was looking at the brochure he'd just had from a piano showroom. 'Might not be able to get you anything very remarkable right away … how about a modern one?'

'I'd need to try it out, of course. I can't wait to get back to Beethoven – I want to play the Pathétique – that slow movement – no need for pedals – in fact they mess the whole thing up … and yes, Haydn is full of joy – I was thrilled to find recently that I could make quite a good fist of the F minor Variations. Almost his last – written before 1790 – when he began to use pedal markings and its infinitely better and sweeter without.'

Daniel rattled on for a few minutes and Leo listened, wondering what had happened to renew the frenetic enthusiasm he had once taken for granted but come to fear he would never witness again. He opened his diary and scored out that afternoon's entries. 'OK. I'll pick you up at three. Oh, by the way – are you thinking of getting rid of your Broadwood – I mean where the hell are you going to put another grand?'

Daniel laughed. 'Dining room, I thought. We don't use it often these days and anyway I loathe that mahogany table – we'll get rid of that.'

Leo wondered what Magda would think of this idea, but he said goodbye and set about cancelling his afternoon's appointments, his heart lighter than it had been for a very long time.

16. EXPECTATIONS

A S THE DAY of Irena's arrival drew near, Daniel waited with increasingly mixed feelings. He longed to see her again, but this would be a very public reunion; he wasn't sure he'd be able to hide his feelings. He and Irena had both imagined their meeting again during the years since they said goodbye at the gates of the Vila Dolena. How they would greet each other, what they would say. When he was still an able-bodied man, Daniel had envisaged a cheerful, if tearful, coming together, filled with laughter, both of them shy at first and then becoming exactly as they had been at her parents' table, wandering together through the streets of Sarajevo, cycling in the woods. Now, sitting in a wheelchair, feeling old and pessimistic about his future, Daniel wished the visit could be cancelled. The ways in which Irena might – must – have changed, were hard for him to imagine, but he had read enough about the treatment of captive women during the Bosnian conflict to be very afraid for both her mind and her body.

Magda, wondered how he would react to the reality of the girl after all the years that had passed since she had posed for her photograph in Sarajevo just before her world was torn apart.

It was arranged that Hedija and Irena would come straight to Albert Hall Mansions from the airport and the other musicians would open up their rented house and come on to the flat for supper. It might be easier that first evening if other people were at the table with Irena and Daniel, Magda decided. She had brought her things back to the flat and moved into the maid's room behind the kitchen two days before the girl's arrival, leaving her old room for Hedija. If only, she thought, Irena could have come at a different time. Daniel and Sam were going to Bosnia in a month's time and this was causing her sleepless nights. It would be Daniel's first long journey as a disabled man, his first master-class for over a year followed by a couple of recitals and meetings of his new charity for wounded musicians. He longed to be in Sarajevo again and to tell his friends there the good news about Irena. Sam was delighted to have been asked to go with Daniel, but Magda suspected that her brother had not taken his preparations seriously enough, although they had been warned about awkward buildings and difficult access to concert venues. She hoped the younger man would be able to cope.

Daniel went to inspect Irena's room, the room he'd slept in as a boy. It looked across to the park and the window had recently been doubled-glazed so it was no longer noisy as it had been. He had frequently imagined her sleeping in the little bed that had once been his. Magda, too, looked in to see if there was anything else to do – Daniel had put a large bunch of spring flowers on the chest of drawers, their scent slightly overpowering in the tiny room, she thought. The rest of the flat was full of flowers, too, vases and vases of them.

Daniel couldn't keep still that day. Even that morning, as he practised, he would keep stopping to look at his watch.

At six o'clock he shaved carefully for the second time that day, changed his shirt and put on a jacket and tie. In his hand-kerchief drawer lay a spectacle case that held the glasses Irena had called his Buddy Holly ones, and he toyed with the idea of wearing them again; but the image in the mirror told him that it was not just the wire-rimmed spectacles he now wore, but his thin face and grey–streaked hair that made him look middle-aged and professorial. He took his tie off, pulled his collar open and took off his jacket. That was a more relaxed look, but not as much improved as he had hoped.

Irena had been to London with her parents as a child, but had little memory of it, except that the food had been almost uneatable and, although it was mid-summer, the sky was grey. Now the sun shone brightly as she and Hedi stood for a moment, the taxi paid for, and looked across the road at the Albert Memorial and the green stretches of the park, newly planted with drifts of tulips and irises. Then they went up the white stone steps with the bright brass handrail and rang the bell to Daniel's flat. Over the intercom Magda told them to take the lift to the third floor.

The entrance hall was gloomy and old-fashioned; lots of places in Sarajevo had looked like this, thought Irena, and then she saw the lift. It was a gilded cage enclosed in a black and gold metal shaft and suddenly Irena remembered her father's office building after it had been bombed. Nothing had remained of the old music publishing house but some vestiges of stone wall and great heaps of rubble. In its midst, the ornate, turn-of-the-century lift-shaft was left undamaged. It seemed to point upwards, accusingly, Irena had thought, as it stood glittering against the dust-filled sky.

They piled Hedija's luggage into the lift and she went up first, instructing Irena to follow with her own things.

Magda met the lift, greeted Hedija and they went together into the flat where Daniel was waiting just inside the front door. Their guest had been prepared for the wheelchair, but she hadn't imagined that the Maestro Daniel she had known could have changed so much since she last saw him at her brother's table. But he smiled and then she knew him again and bent down and embraced him and he put his arms up around her neck. Magda asked him to help take Hedija's luggage to her room, and, as he was putting her dressing case on the bed, she called out, 'Oh there's the lift again. That'll be Irena. Will you go and help her, Danny?'

He didn't answer at once and then he said, his voice sounding strangled, 'I can't … I'm sorry, I just can't.'

Hedija put her hand on his shoulder and they heard Magda's hurried steps as she returned to the lift just as the doors opened.

The young woman who walked into the flat, pulling a large suitcase and holding her viola case close to her, was as small and slight as the young Irena had been. She had the same long chestnut hair, wisps of which fell over her eyes, but her eyes were downcast and she only looked up when Magda called to Daniel to join them. He pushed himself into the hall and looked up at her. The bold, mischievous look he remembered was no longer in those eyes; they were veiled and guarded and she did not come close, but seemed almost to be cowering away, to be afraid of him. Her whole presence and aura were so changed that he wondered for a moment if it was really her.

'Irena – is it really you?'

The young woman finally looked at the man who should have been Maestro Daniel. She wanted him to smile that broad smile that showed big white teeth between bewitching, curly lips, but his expression was anxious, strained and he clutched the guide wheels of his chair as if he was about to move – closer to her, or away, she could not tell which. Neither of them moved and it was a moment before Irena whispered, 'Maestro Daniel.' It was not a question. It was a statement of recognition and he reached out to her, wanting in that moment to catch her tiny hands between his two large ones as he would have cradled a bird who had flown in through his open window in the days when he could run around the room after the terrified creature until he finally caught it. He

would fold its wings against its sides and whisper to it, his lips
close to the silken head, feeling the wild fluttering of its heart
before going to the window which overlooked the back court-
yard and, leaning out, slowly opening his hand and watching
the bird drop for a split second before it spread its wings and
swooped away in ecstatic, parabolic flight.

The moment passed and Daniel knew he was in no position
to hold Irena in any way at all, but at last she was looking at
him, although the expression on her face gave no hint of what
she might be thinking or feeling. She had taken a step backwards, her arms wrapped around her viola, which she held
against her breast, still looking at Daniel. He saw then that it
was fear preventing her from speaking. She was afraid of him
now and he was bewildered, wondering if it was because he
was sitting there in front of her in a wheelchair. Perhaps it was
not fear but disgust.

Magda, who had been watching and wondering about
this reunion, saw that Irena had not taken Daniel's outstretched hands and, trying to sound cheerful and normal,
she exclaimed, 'You haven't seen your room yet. Come on –
I'll show you.'

Irena hesitated a moment before she followed her hostess
down the corridor and went past her as she opened a bedroom
door. She looked around her curiously. A single bed had been
pushed to one side to make room for a painted harpsichord
and from the window she could just see the Albert Memorial
glittering in the green oasis of the park. She turned back to
Magda who was saying:

'I hope there's everything you need here. Oh, I'm afraid
those freesias have a very strong smell ... Daniel bought them
for you.'

'They're lovely,' Irena said, and then. 'Does he play the
harpsichord?'

'Yes. Quite a lot these days.' Irena sensed there was something unsaid in Magda's answer, but her hostess was already leaving the room.

Irena looked curiously around her and wondered about the young Daniel. She examined the chest of drawers with its swing mirror, the glass badly foxed, and the fading posters advertising his concerts. One showed a curly-headed teen-ager playing at Carnegie Hall. She reached up and touched the picture, following the lines of his face with her forefinger. There were other posters, too – Manet's *Olympia*, Rodin's *Kiss*, and the bare footed Sandie Shaw.

Irena squeezed in behind the harpsichord to examine the bookcase which was crammed with scores and books about music and musicians. She saw that that there were other books, too: children's books in Czech and a well-thumbed copy of *Lady Chatterley's Lover* shared the shelves with *The Seven Pillars of Wisdom*.

Opposite the bed was a small painted wardrobe. It was like the ones she had known so well as a child, its door was hung on a long steel hinge and bore the date 1768 under the some-what primitive painting of a rustic scene, harvesters with straw hats and scythes, and demure wenches giggling behind a haystack. She turned the big key and looked inside. It was full of suits in plastic covers, several of which were tail coats; these must be Daniel's concert clothes and she lifted one of the covers and pressed her face into the dark fabric of the jacket, but it smelled only of dry-cleaning fluid.

She washed hurriedly in the small shower room, anxious to make an appearance in the music room before someone came to look for her. She pulled a crumpled shirt out of her case and rummaged to find the Hermes scarf with blue butterflies that Hedija, watching Irena pack her few, rather dull clothes, had given her. As she undid her hair and brushed it down onto her shoulders, she heard the front door open again and an inrush of movement and voices. Mark, Bella and Sasha had arrived, relaxed and noisy, and she heard Daniel laughing with them and wondered if she and he would ever laugh again together as once they had. She waited for them to go into the music room and then she walked nervously down the passage. She felt rather sick and wished she had not come to London.

Daniel heard Irena enter the music room but continued his conversation with Mark. Magda stood up and gave her guest a seat next to her on the sofa and Irena remembered how Daniel had told her about his stern Jewish forebears with their beards and hats and shawls. There they were, hung amongst a collection of musical instruments, some modern and many which looked as if they had not been played for a long while: sakbuts and flutes and recorders, viols and harps of several kinds and battered brass instruments, too. Fascinated, she didn't at once hear what was being said to her and Magda tried again: 'He can never resist an instrument.' She sighed. 'This is only a sample, you know – there's a whole lot more in his bedroom.'

Daniel looked across the room at the two women and as his eyes met Irena's for a moment he wanted to grin at her and crack a joke as once he would have done. But everything had changed between them and would not ever be the same again. He turned back to Mark, who had asked him a question about the Ravel quartet they were to play the following day.

'Terrific viola part,' Mark said, ' And Irena gives it her own magic. Have you ever heard her play?'

'Yes. A long time ago. I expect she's even better now.' He didn't add that it was he who had introduced Irena to the Ravel piece.

17.   ANOTHER POINT OF VIEW

SAM'S DIARY, 1997

*O*ver the weeks since he left hospital, I had slipped into
the role of Daniel's 'gofer'. I was at the flat almost every
day, helping him when he needed to go anywhere and, it
seemed, accepted by Magda as part of their family life. She
talked often and anxiously about Irena's arrival and, as the
day neared, asked me to join them at dinner that night. I was
curious, very curious. Now I was to meet the girl whose name
Daniel had called out so often as consciousness returned to
him in hospital, sometimes out loud, sometimes pleadingly
under his breath as he begged her to wait for him. I had never
dared to ask him about her, not knowing if he realised I'd
even heard her name. Then he'd said, casually, a few weeks
before her arrival in London, as he was marking some fingering on a Scarlatti piece he would play in a few weeks' time
in Sarajevo, that an American string quartet was coming
over to the UK. One of them would be staying with Magda
and Daniel. He'd known her some years ago. A viola player.
'Was she one of your students in Sarajevo Conservatory?' I
thought this was a question that gave nothing away.

'No.' Daniel pushed himself away from the piano, putting
his pencil in his breast pocket with the other bits and pieces
that poked out over the top. 'No. She was still at school – I
lived with her family for several months just before the Siege
began.'

Then Daniel told me about the blue studio with its huge

piano, how he helped Irena with her music, went on bike rides with her and danced with her mother, who ... there he paused. 'Irena was terrific fun – still very young and inno-cent. She always saw the funny side of life – like I did then. Anyway, things were brewing up in Yugoslavia and I had to bring the UK students back to this country while it was still possible to travel. I hated leaving.'

I saw that his hands were shaking. I didn't look at his face. He was an emotional man at the best of times and since he'd been stuck in that wheelchair he'd been completely unpre-dictable – tears one moment, hysterical laughter the next.

He was speaking again, his voice low, strained. 'A few weeks after I left, her parents died, killed in their own garden along with their old cook. I didn't know this until my first trip out there to search for them and to see old friends at the Conservatory. But no mention of Irena. 'I went out a few more times and got shot up, as you know. By then the journalist who'd been taking me around whenever he could, had told me that Irena had been captured and imprisoned by some vile Serb war-lord, but he didn't know if she was still alive. Well, I was in no position to search any more, just then. But, when I'd been in hospital for three months or so I had a letter from Irena's aunt, Hedi – Hedija Tanović – who was living in the States. I remembered her from family parties with the Vidakovićs. She told me Irena had escaped from Bosnia and arrived in Long Island – in a dreadful state – three years ago now. Hedi got her back to health and well enough to take up her music again. She found her a viola and Irena joined a string quartet and moved into an apart-ment in Manhattan with the two violinists – twin sisters. When the quartet were coming to play in London, her aunt wrote to me via Leo.' Daniel went on.

'She was worried about how Irena would cope in strange surroundings. Seems she's still very nervous and has bad

dreams. Not surprising – I expect you read some of the Bosnian war trial reports … Anyway, Mags suggested they both stay here with us while they're playing at the Wigmore. So there you are. Irena and I are to meet again – she having been through God knows what and me in this chair, like Humpty Dumpty …!'

The girl who walked into the music room and sat down next to her aunt was not at all what I had expected. A small, delicately built woman, slow and hesitant in her movements, her head kept low. When we were introduced, her eyes flickered to mine, but only for a second before they were lowered again. Great big eyes – I just had time to take in their colour, an unusual, flecked grey and fringed with very long lashes. Her rather round face looked like a little girl's in the way it was held on a slim neck. Her smile, when finally we were given a glimpse of it, caused two deep dimples to form in her cheeks. Her hair was her real claim to beauty. Very thick, and that sort of reddish brown that reminds you of a bright chestnut thoroughbred. That evening she wore it loose on her shoulders, the top bit tied up with an elastic band. Her clothes – well this girl is no fashionista. She wore jeans that were too big – shame as her figure seems to be good – and a shirt with an outdated pointed collar. Slung round her shoulders in no particular way was a silk scarf – a very good quality one, I'd say – covered with blue butterflies.

Dinner was painful that evening. The aunt, tired out by the journey was not hungry and went to her room. Now that Daniel's fortepiano had pride of place in the dining room, space was very limited, as his sister had refused to replace the massive Victorian table with something smaller. After trying out almost every instrument London had to offer, he had finally splashed out on a rare and beautiful Arnold

Dolmetsch − I always associated that family firm with recorders, which we played painfully at school, but apparently they made the best fortepianos.

Little Irena sat, her eyes downcast, squeezed in between the two violinists, Bella and Sasha. Nice Bronx girls, and a good deal better behaved than the cellist, Mark. From the first, I could see that Daniel was not enjoying his company. To start with, the goon referred to his host as 'Irena's uncle' and I saw his host's eyes flash with anger behind his glasses. Clearly this was not the role he intended for himself vis-à-vis Irena. Though what else he had in mind, I had no idea. She never looked in his direction, ate very little, chewing slowly as if she was about to throw up, and only spoke when addressed.

Back in the music room, Irena drank a cup of herb tea, seeming to find it hard not to spill it − her hands were shaking now. Magda took the cup from her and suggested that she should go to bed. Mark complained, 'But aren't you going to play this evening?' Magda replied for her, 'Poor girl's exhausted and you must be too?'

'Oh no, not us.'

Before she left the room, Irena had whispered 'good night' to everyone and aimed an even fainter, 'and thank you' in the direction of Daniel. Then she fled, and the other musicians picked up their instruments and Mark asked Daniel if he'd do them the honour of playing with them. I sensed by the way that he kept shifting in his chair that he was in pain − but he smiled as he shook his head. 'No. Not tonight − I want to hear all of you − so how about rehearsing here tomorrow morning and we'll give you lunch before you go over to the Wigmore?'

Mark was clearly disappointed but Sasha and Bella looked relieved as they picked up their things and muttered that they would like to get to bed as well. But Mark lingered, talking noisily for a further half hour before he could be persuaded to make his way to the front door. 'What a selfish bugger, but Danny's his own worst enemy – he'll never admit to being tired. So bloody proud ...' Magda muttered as she and I filled the dishwasher.

Irena changed into the black skirt and top that she wore for concerts.

'Won't be a minute,' she called out to Bella and left the door open as she brushed her hair and was pinning it up when she saw Daniel's reflection behind her. He was sitting in the open doorway.

'You look wonderful!' Her hands, as she tried to catch up the last wayward strands while Daniel watched, would not obey her and the hurriedly placed hairpins started to fall out of her heavy chignon, and as she bent down to retrieve them, the rest of her hair fell in a thick curtain about her face. Daniel came into the room and picked up the pins that had scattered within his reach.

'I can never get it to stay up.' she said, beginning to panic.

'Can't you wear it loose?' But Irena shook her head as she started to twist her rebellious mane into a ponytail and pull it through a rubber band. Daniel came closer. He had sometimes helped Felicity put her hair up and remembered the feel of it – very fine and light, like golden candy floss. 'Let me help?'

Irena, taken aback, stood still while he came up behind her. He reached up, wound the hair around his hand and secured the coil he'd fashioned. The smooth weight of the sleek stuff he was handling aroused him and he hurriedly positioned the last few pins. Irena looked in the mirror while he worked, discomforted to see his image and hers so close together and to feel his hands touching her neck. He turned away abruptly,

'Taxi'll be here soon.' He picked up her viola and she took it from him, avoiding his eyes.

'I dreamt once that I got on stage and found there were no strings on my viola. It was awful.'

He reached across, clicked open the fastenings on the case, folded back the silk scarf covering the instrument and said, 'Strings all present and correct.' Irena was smiling to herself as she closed the case again. He waited for a moment, seeming to be pondering, then he took something out of his pocket.

'In case your hair comes down again.' He handed her a piece of black ribbon.

She turned it over. 'I used to wear this kind of ribbon.' then she saw the frayed edges. 'It isn't new.'

'It was yours – I picked it up when we got back from our last cycle trip and forgot to give it back to you. I've kept it with me. Please take it to bring you luck.'

Irena held the ribbon against her cheek for a moment before she put it in her bag.

'Where will you be sitting?'

'Sitting? I won't be coming, I'm afraid. I thought you knew that.' Irena shook her head, turned away and started to walk towards the front door as Magda came out of her room. Daniel tried to catch her arm as she passed him, saying, under his breath, 'Magda, help me,' but she brushed his hand away and hurried to join Irena. The taxi turned against the traffic in front of the flats and joined the queue for the lights at the entrance to the park. Irena leant against the window and stared out, unseeing.

'Are you all right?' Magda asked, but there was no answer and when Irena turned to her, her cheeks were streaked with tears.

'Didn't he want to hear us tonight?'

'Daniel, you mean?'

Irena turned her head away and wiped her eyes on her sleeve. 'I just thought he'd be coming.'

'Oh, sweetheart … he would have loved to come – longed to hear you play in his favourite hall, but you must understand that he was one of their biggest stars. Used to be mobbed in the street. But he hasn't been there since he was hurt and he thought people might recognise him and he wanted tonight to be yours and the quartet's … but he's very sad not to hear you play.'

Irena, searching for a tissue to blow her nose, felt the ribbon at the bottom of her pocket. Her fingers closed on it and she smiled at Magda, thinking, 'He kept it all this time. He must care a bit about me. He must.' And, content for then with that thought, she sat back in her seat as the cab turned into Wigmore Street.

[SAM]

Well, the days passed. The quartet played their first concert, at the Wigmore Hall. Quite a success – they're good, if a little raw still. I looked at Irena as she played. Gone was the terror, the anguish, her eyes had held the night before. As I accustomed myself to picking out the viola part from the rest of the strings, I realised that she did find joy and peace in that instrument of hers. Perhaps the only joy and peace in her whole life now.

The next day I found Daniel in the kitchen, listening to Radio 3. I went in, thinking I'd tell him about the concert, but, as I began to speak, his hand went up to silence me. I recognised then the quartet's performance of the previous evening. Daniel's face was enigmatic. With his students, I have always believed he listened like two people – the professional musician and teacher, of course, but also with an almost tender and paternal understanding of the performer. He knew what it was to live simply in order to interpret great music. It was his life, after all, and he knew that, without musicians like him, the composer had no other means of speaking to the world. Without performance, Beethoven, Schubert, Bach and all those whose work must be amongst the very highest of man's achievements, would be dumb. So Daniel listened always to hear this commitment in a musician, the commitment of interpretation, and searched amongst the aspiring pianists who came to him, hoping to hear that commitment sing out with a new voice, a new insight, a new passion. Not the ego of a virtuoso, of a glamorous star of the classical stage, who wooed the public with eye-catching CD covers and designer concert dresses; but that magical bridge-making between composer and the playing of an instrument – which is, after all, simply a contraption made of wood and steel, of gut and ivory and, now probably, plastic – this was what he lived to create himself, and sought in his followers.

The first time I met Daniel I was seventeen, a piano student at the Royal Academy of Music and wondering what the hell I was going to do with my life. I'd seen Maestro Danuczek about the college and been to a couple of his recitals, which had blown me away. I was in awe of him, and would stand aside, almost tugging at my forelock, as he passed. It was a Friday afternoon when he stopped by me, his fat music case in one hand and a plastic shopping bag in the other.

'Gore, isn't it? Sam Gore?'

'Yes,' I gasped, looking up at him.

'I hear you're having some problems with performance – audiences and all that ...?'

'It's just that I get in a state and everything goes out of my head. I can't bear being on stage.'

'It happens to a lot of people, you know. With some, it provides the adrenalin that makes a good performance. With *others … How about joining my master class next week?'*

I stared at him. 'Me?'

'Yes, you!' I must have looked ridiculous, standing there with my mouth open.

'Look forward to seeing you, then?' It wasn't a question; it was almost an order and I nodded my head, still unable to speak. He touched me on the shoulder and strode off in the direction of the lecture theatre.

My first master class with Daniel was a disaster. I could not play even in front of the small audience of students I knew and, try as he might, Daniel could not calm my nerves. However, I started attending the composition class he held every week in his flat. To say these evening were a revelation is no exaggeration. Not only did he have an extraordinary gift for teaching, he was an eccentric and very amusing person. Often the class would begin with a short piano performance from him, Bach usually, broken off in the middle by his leaping up and tap-dancing around the piano, as he talked about contrapuntal rhythm.

The summer term was almost over when I heard that he was in hospital; I went to visit him. Seeing him coming and going from consciousness horrified me, but I continued to go most days and fetched and carried stuff from his flat or the shops as he got better. Orderly by nature, I found myself tidying his chaotic bookcases and one thing led to another. When he finally went home in his wheelchair it seemed natural to become something of a personal assistant. He insisted on paying me then because I could see it would otherwise have made him feel unable to accept my help. I accepted, relieved not to have to take my usual holiday job playing in a piano bar. I had driven him around in his big black Saab when he had a broken leg a few years before, and became his willing but nervous passenger when the car was converted to be driven without pedals.

Although he was cheerful in adversity, at least in public, I soon became aware of how nervous and jumpy he had become since he was flown home. When a car backfired or a helicopter flew low overhead, his eyes would widen and I'd see him look wildly around, as he began to shake and sweat broke out on his brow and upper lip. The horrors of the Balkan war continued to haunt him. He spoke of the Siege of Sarajevo quite often and showed me articles, some about the appalling treatment of women during the conflict – by both sides. I had to file these away from his music, in the bottom of his bookcase. Something seemed to be eating at him and now I know that it was the fate of Irena. And here she was, still a frightened girl who should by then have become a self-possessed young woman.

I would hear her practising in her room, making use of Daniel's harpsichord to tune her viola. She was good. Very good. But she was frightened of her own shadow and when, as happened almost every day, the flat was filled with musicians and hurried meals and bottles of beer and wine, she never ventured to join them. Instead, she would put on her coat and leave the flat and I would see her every time I looked out of the window, sitting on the steps of the Albert Memorial.

Preparing for Irena's arrival, Daniel had asked me to put his Bosnian files on a high shelf, out of her reach, but I had forgotten and, one morning, I found her sitting on the floor of the music room, reading a pile of press cuttings.

'Take it away and read it in your room,' I said, knowing that Daniel would soon be home. He'd been at the hospital gym and would be tired and probably short-tempered when he got back.

❀

Magda and I had been thrown together a lot of the time since Daniel's long stay in hospital and our shared duties at the side of her brother and our feelings for him, drew us together. She would show me, from time to time, a lighter, more frivolous side of her, which I would never have suspected. And in her big, bony frame I saw the handsome, original young girl she must have been, or would have been had life not thrown her constantly into the role of 'carer'. First, as her mother became ill, she was responsible for Daniel. Already spending many hours each day at the piano, he was not as much trouble as many boys of his age might have been, but he had his stubborn, insubordinate side and, once fame had lured him into her lair, he became almost impossible to handle; it was always Magda who had to hide his excesses from their grieving father, or make excuses for his frequent absence from the flat.

Magda had a few brief years for her own life when Daniel had grown up and his concerts took him around the world. But she chose unwisely in her husband, Nathan; he was not the man to give her the nurture under which her warm, kind nature and sharp wit would have been able to blossom. Instead, she became a domestic drudge, reared two stolid boys and battled on until her husband tired of her. And by then Daniel had met his own tragedy. Magda came to his side, comforted and cherished him and probably saved his life. Maybe she saved mine, too, but that was later.

I'd been getting rather impatient with the uncomfortable atmosphere that pervaded the flat when Daniel and Irena were in the same room. I supposed he just wasn't ready to approach her as he once would have done with any other girl – I'd seen him in action and he was clearly irresistible to women. I consoled myself by looking forward to going to Bosnia with him, when I hoped he'd be too busy to think about Irena.

❄

Daniel and Irena saw each other every day, but they were seldom alone together and neither of them recognised the person that the other had become over the years. Irena, Daniel saw, was a polite girl, her upbringing still evident in the way she greeted people or answered their questions. But she gave nothing away. Her head was bowed most of the time, her eyes lowered and when she raised them there was a frightening blankness in her gaze, as if she inhabited another world. If she did, there was no invitation to join her there. She was listening, however, to every word that was said and when she did speak, because it would have been rude not to respond to remarks clearly addressed to her, each softly enunciated word – she had a slight American accent – was considered and well chosen. All the time she was observing the changes in Daniel since she had first known him and fallen under the spell of his constant good humour, light-heartedness and energy. Her heart ached as she watched him getting around in his big shiny wheelchair and her breath would catch painfully when a swift movement of his arms reminded her of the man he had once been. He still laughed a good deal and made jokes, but she noticed that, when people offered unwanted help, his voice would take on a sharp edge that she did not remember from former days. She watched him closely then and thought she detected pain in his eyes and a deep weariness.

Daniel looked at Irena far more often then she would have suspected. He saw that she had not grown in height since he'd first known her, but always wore a series of baggy sweatshirts over torn jeans, so her figure remained a mystery to him. Clearly she was not fat and she moved gracefully, her narrow hips swinging, her shoulders square under the drooping head. If she had breasts, it was impossible to guess their size or even where they were under the hotchpotch of unbecoming garments. In his presence, her eyes, which were of such a light grey they seemed to be silver in some lights, remained downcast, and she skilfully avoided catching his glance. After Sam had discovered her reading the Bosnian file, Irena put it under her cardigan and carried if off into her room. There she lay on the bed and read the contents. On top were programmes and notes for Daniel's concerts, recitals and meetings, mainly at the Conservatory. There was a large clip with cuttings about some of the war trials. One was of Milosović and the case of a thirteen-year-old girl who had been captured in circumstances that reminded her of her own imprisonment. The child had been raped many times and suffered other humiliations at the hands of her captors. Irena felt cold. Daniel had read these descriptions and thought them worth keeping; he must know, then, what she could have been through during her own captivity. Far from forgetting her and her family, scribbled notes and faded newspaper cuttings documented the time and effort he had spent in his search for her and her parents.

She put the cuttings back, her hands shaking and her stomach heaving. As she was about to close the file she saw an envelope that had been under the cuttings. In it was a bundle of letters and notes. A few were from a famous war correspondent, Martin Bell, and then many more from someone called Peter Henderson. Hurriedly written, it seemed, they all had the same theme – Daniel's search for the Vidaković family and then, once it seemed he knew of her parents' fate, for her. This man seemed to have been frequently in Bosnia. Irena, looking at the heading of some of the letters, thought he must have worked for the BBC. So not a soldier. A reporter, perhaps. He'd been trying to find her. For Daniel. And for years.

Then there were a few notes of a later date, the tone quite different. She read a short letter with the address of a hotel in Prague:

Dear Daniel,

At last you're beginning to look more like yourself.
I can't tell you how glad I am. I can't stop blaming
myself for your being shot – the bullets were, of
course, meant for me. I'll be over in London next
month and I wonder if you'll be out of hospital by
then and starting to stagger around again. No doubt
you're already being a thorough nuisance to everyone
– don't make passes at the nurses – we don't want an
irate husband finishing off the sniper's work.

All the best, Peter

PS Sandy sends his best – he's making a great
nuisance of himself trying to get back to work
with me – I do miss him. He is a bloody good
photojournalist.

Irena closed the file, thinking she must return it as soon as she
could. Daniel must still be out; she saw that his coat and beret
were not on the pegs near the front door. Then she walked
down to the music room. Sam was standing at the bookcase,
re-arranging some scores in alphabetical order.

She couldn't quite fathom Sam. He was, she had gathered,
a gifted pianist and Daniel's protégé, but she had never heard
him play. He seemed to do all sorts of jobs for his mentor
and spent a good deal of time in the kitchen with Magda or
writing in what looked like a big dairy, which he would hurriedly put away when anyone came close. He scarcely spoke
to anyone but Daniel, she noticed, but watched the quartet
closely and Irena felt that he resented them – and her, too.

'Daniel has asked me to go to Bosnia with him next month,
you know.' Sam said, taking the file from her.

'Have you been before?'

'No, but Daniel used to talk about Sarajevo a lot. And your
family.' He looked at the folder he was holding. 'Did you find

anything interesting?'

She did not look at him as she replied. 'Yes, thank you. But it's all very painful still.'

Sam nodded and went to the piano. To her surprise, he began to play. Delibes's *Valse Lente*. How could he have known what that piece was, would always be, to her? Her legs suddenly weak, she sat down on the sofa and listened. He did indeed play well and she thought she heard in his interpretation an echo of Daniel's own phrasing and touch. As she listened, the music room door opened and she heard the squeak of rubber tyres on the floorboards. Daniel stopped still when he saw Sam playing for Irena, and he did not meet her eyes. She rose hurriedly, smiled briefly at him and fled to her room.

A few days later, Irena again waited for Daniel to leave the flat, heard the lift going down and went into the music room. First, she collected a pile of sheet music from the bookshelves, then she threw a cushion onto the floor behind the piano and sat down on it, the scores in her lap. The sun shone through the French windows and the warmth on her back began to make her drowsy. She nodded off and dreamed vividly of the forests around Sarajevo and saw herself and Maestro Daniel on their bicycles. They were singing and, when Daniel jumped off his bike and propped it up against a tree, he started to dance, round and round and she found herself dancing too – dancing and laughing – but there was no sound as they spun around each other on the pine-scented forest floor.

She woke with a start. She heard voices and she could see Magda's legs and Daniel's wheels from where she sat, pressing herself against the window and wondering whether to jump up and excuse herself for surprising them, but then she heard her name:

'But Danny, Irena's been here over a week now and you haven't once made any effort to take her anywhere. Hedi and I are delighted to spend time with her, but I really must do some house-hunting. You could take her out in the car, couldn't you, or to a museum or something?'

Daniel had his back to her and she could see now that Magda was sitting on the sofa facing him. 'I don't understand why you're ignoring her – you barely speak to her except when the quartet come over and then it's about music. After all that time searching for her and now she's here you ignore her at meals *when* you deign to eat with us. Hedi's wondering if bringing Irena here was such a good idea – she doesn't understand and nor do I.'

Daniel didn't answer at once and when he did speak, it was slowly and diffidently, 'I know it must seem unfriendly, and I'd planned all sorts of things, but now ... well I'm just not the person she remembers. For years I imagined I'd find her again and bring her back here and try to help her over the horrible things she's been through. I imagined biking with her in Richmond Park, but I'm stuck in this chair and I just feel helpless again – like I did in hospital. Not like someone she'd find fun or interesting. I can't be anything to her now.' He paused and Irena thought there was a catch in his voice as he went on, 'Anyway, she'll be going away again soon and maybe I'll never see her again.'

Magda said nothing for a few minutes and then asked, her voice hesitant, gentler now, 'Are you in love with her – is that the problem?'

Crouched behind the piano, Irena didn't want to hear any more. Her own feelings crowded in on her until she thought she would suffocate.

Daniel was speaking again, very softly now. 'I suppose I've always loved her, but she was so young. And now she's a woman and so lovely and delicate. I just wish I could look after her and protect her.'

'So why don't you tell her that?'

'Oh don't be so stupid. She thinks of me as a decrepit old music teacher – if she ever gives me a thought at all. She was pretty keen on me when I was staying with her family, I think – you know, a schoolgirl crush. We had fun together, but I had all my letters to her family returned, so she probably had no idea I was looking for her all that time. And now she has her own life in Manhattan and that great little quartet who all think she's marvellous – maybe she'll end up with Mark.'

'Perhaps you're wrong about Irena's feelings. They'll be going back to the States in a couple of weeks and you're going to Bosnia. You'll kick yourself if you don't make the effort to reach out to her.'

'Not too good at kicking myself, these days …' replied Daniel.

Magda got up. 'I'm sorry – I must go now, I want to look at a house in Queen's Park. I've made some soup and it wouldn't hurt you to have lunch with Irena for once. I haven't heard her go out this morning.' Magda left the room and her hurried footsteps resounded down the passage.

Irena, still crouched behind the piano, watched Daniel go over to the sofa and transfer himself onto it. He pushed his chair out of the way and bent down to lift his legs up, so that he was looking straight into her face.

'Is there someone under my piano?'

Irena stood up clumsily, rubbing her numb leg.

'I'm sorry. I was looking at some Primrose scores. Then you and Magda came in and I didn't know what to do. I'm so sorry.'

'So you heard all of that?'

'Yes – you were already talking when you came in. I'm really sorry.'

'We're a fine pair, aren't we?'

Irena didn't answer and Daniel was about to reach out to take her hand when they heard the front door open and Mark's voice.

'Is it OK if we do a bit of *répétition*, Magda? Is Daniel in?'

'*Prdele!* – is there no peace now?' Daniel looked furious. Irena got up and pushed his chair closer to him. She knew he'd want to be sitting in it when Mark and the girls came in.

'Thanks.' His voice was gentle now. 'Can you hold them off for a few minutes? Take them into the kitchen and open some beers or something.'

She left the room, closing the door quietly, just in time to steer Mark and the girls towards the kitchen.

'Hey, Sweetheart,' said Bella, hugging her. 'You look bright today. Doesn't she look good, guys?'

Irena laughed and opened the fridge, glad of the blast of cold air on her flushed cheeks.

Later, Irena found Daniel outside the dining room pinning a scull-cap onto his springy curls.

'This is so nice of you. The girls are really thrilled.'

'Don't thank me – Magda's been cooking all afternoon. Have you witnessed this caper before?'

'Yes, Bella's parents used to ask me over most Fridays.'

'I see,' said Daniel dryly and followed her to the table.

Everyone seated, Sam turned out the lights and Magda lit the candles. Leaning towards the flames, she seemed to gather their glimmering light to her eyes with graceful movements of hands that were golden in the glow of the flames. After she had poured wine, she whispered something to Daniel, who had been sitting with his head bowed, frowning. He shrugged his shoulders and began to intone the blessing prayer, pausing frequently to dredge up the Hebrew words he had all but forgotten. '*Shalom aleichem*,' everyone sang before they drank, reaching out to grasp their neighbours' hands. Sasha and Bella hugged Magda, who was tearing the bread she had made that afternoon and sprinkling it with salt and herbs. Daniel saw the girls' pleasure and his face softened. Then he sang the songs his parents had sung at Friday supper, slapping the table with the flat of his hand, relaxed now and beginning to enjoy the familiar dishes and the warm glow of the guests. Mark, who had never invested in the proper headgear, had a napkin on his head, as he always did at the girls' house. His parents were Mormons and he did not tell them that he frequently took part in these rituals. Dinner over, Daniel was unpinning his skull cap when Irena same to his side. 'You enjoyed that?' he asked.

'Oh yes. It reminds me of my own family – do you remember those endless weekend lunches at the Vila Dolena?'

'Of course I do. Particularly that first one when we'd just met.'

'Me too.' And they both laughed.

About to walk down to the music room, she turned back to him. 'Is Sam Jewish? He was wearing a ... What do you call that? I'm never sure.'

'In theory, Kippah is Yiddish, and Yarmulka's Hebrew. Sam's mother is Jewish, so officially he is, too, but he doesn't seem to practise his religion.'

'You don't either?' She never remembered Daniel attending Synagogue in Sarajevo.

'No. I don't.'

Later that evening, Irena was waiting for the rehearsal to begin, sitting on the floor as she often did. 'Daniel,' Sam said, 'Do you remember that fiddle I found in the Prague junk shop?'

'Yes, but you never showed it to me. Where is it?'

'I've got it with me – I thought the girls ought to have a look at it. It's a big instrument compared with theirs, but I don't know much about strings. I was wondering whether to sell it. It's a bit beat up but I think it might be worth doing up first.' He left the room and Daniel continued to watch Irena, who was stroking a block of rosin onto the hairs of her bow. The sun had set outside the window and her delicate profile was silhouetted against the rose-coloured sky.

Sam came back carrying a very battered black case.

'Certainly looks a bit worse for wear – has it been through a war?' Mark asked.

'They said it came from somewhere in Bosnia.'

Daniel looked up sharply and Irena rose to her feet. Bella opened the case and took the instrument out. Sasha, peering over her shoulder, said.

'That's not a violin – it's a viola. Small one ...' and she twanged the one remaining string.

Irena walked over to where her friends stood. Daniel saw that she was trembling and wheeled himself behind her as she took the instrument from Bella and turned it over. Then he caught her as she staggered back against his legs, tears pouring down her cheeks and making bright rivulets on the dusty, figured wood of the little viola. His hands holding her by the waist, he whispered to her, 'Just like a tabby cat?' and she nodded, starting slowly to smile first and then to laugh. Sam and the others, confused at first by Irena's behaviour, now gathered round the couple and Daniel told them how Irena's father had given her this viola. Six years ago. In Yugo-slavia, which was still at peace. Irena got to her feet and put her arms around Sam.

'Oh thank you, thank you, thank you! You've made me so happy'. And Sam bowed to her, wondering at the avalanche of feeling his purchase had unleashed. Bella and Sasha were examining the battered instrument.

'The scroll's a bit broken and those pegs don't belong to it – can you get it fixed?'

'Surely' said Daniel. 'We'll take it to Luke tomorrow. He's the best luthier in London. Always very busy, but he'll make time for this treasure – Irena's papa thought it might be a Guarneri … or at least from his workshop.'

Irena smiled at him, and her face was the face of the girl he had once known but had feared he would never see again. She was dancing from foot to foot as she tuned up and only stopped when Mark rapped with his bow on the edge of his cello. He was impatient to start going through the piece the quartet would play in their final concert in London.

Daniel watched Irena intently while she played that evening and she looked at him from time to time, smiling as their eyes met. How strange life was – one moment taking everything away and leaving you raw and desperate, and then presenting you with a gift of joy and renewed courage.

18. REPAIRING THE DAMAGE

DANIEL, unable to get up the steep steps to the luthier's cluttered workshop, was amusing himself with the finished instruments hanging in the shop below. Luke shouted down at him, 'Leave that lute alone – Julian's coming for it this afternoon. I left it in tune.'

Daniel returned the lute to its place and took down a viol, put his ear to the sounding board and stroked the strings with the pads of his finger.

'Bloody hell – he's at it again. Can't leave anything alone.' Luke turned his attention back to Irena and the viola on the workbench between them. 'Nicest viola I've seen in a long time. Wait till you see it finished. Wait till you hear it … ah …' And the luthier escorted Irena down the steps.

'So?' asked Daniel.

'No problem. I'll get this fixed and your young friend can collect it in, say, six weeks.'

'Oh dear,' said Irena. 'I'm going back to the States – can you send it to me?'

'Send it? Don't be ridiculous. This is a beautiful instrument and it'll be tailored to your playing when I've finished with it. You'll have to come yourself.'

'Don't worry,' said Daniel. 'We'll sort something out. Join us for lunch, Luke? I've booked a table at Franco's.'

'No thanks – but let's have a tune before you go.' And he took a viola down from the wall, brought it to his piano and tuned it for Irena. She looked over at Daniel as she played a few bars of the Schubert violin sonata that he had transposed for the viola. She had found it on her music stand when he'd left the Vila Dolena, with a note that said: *'Please learn this and next time I see you we can play it together'* As she finished playing, he looked up but she could not read his face as she gave the instrument back to Luke. Luke clapped his hands. 'Fabulous. The maestro told me you were a worthy owner of that little pet upstairs. He was right, as usual.'

They sat opposite each other at Franco's and Irena looked around her.

'This is a great place. Sad Luke couldn't join us.'

'I knew he wouldn't – he never has time, but I wanted to ask him anyway. He'll do well with your little fiddle, you know. He's a real artist – a poet in wood.'

'You come here a lot?'

'Quite often. It's one of the few places around here with no steps.'

Franco was hovering by the table and he and Daniel chatted in Italian. Without looking at the menu Daniel ordered 'the usual' and, seeing that Irena was about to protest, said, 'I'm having the day's special, but I know you don't eat much, I've just ordered you two puddings – Franco's famous Mont Blanc and a passion fruit ice.'

'I'm not fussy … it's just that a lot of food worries me. It sounds silly, but you see we had so little to eat – then – and I can't forget what it's like to be hungry. I'm sorry …'

'No, no. Don't ever say that. But I know you still have a sweet tooth, so you'll be OK won't you?' Irena nodded and took a mouthful of the wine he had poured for her. He watched her empty the glass, smiling to himself. 'So. Now we have to work out when you can get over again to fetch your fiddle.'

Irena began to enjoy the fuzzy, unreal feeling that the wine gave her. Alone with Daniel for the first time since she'd arrived in London, she needed courage, too, and she drained the second glass that the waiter poured for her. 'I've been thinking …' she began, and then stopped; she needed to choose her words carefully. Daniel was watching her, aware that she was a bit drunk. He thought she probably wasn't used to wine.

'What were you thinking?'

'That I'd like to come back to work in London – to live here maybe …'

'Really? You like London, then?'

'Yes, I absolutely do. I love it.' She paused. 'I sound like an American now, so people sometimes they ask me where I'm from – they know I'm not English. Do you feel foreign here? I mean, would you like to go back to Czechoslovakia?'

'No, not really. Prague was a pretty gloomy place when my parents defected. And I've lived in London for so long now and I move in the musical world mostly – a lot of musicians are wandering Jews, like me. When you're part of a minority – even in a country as accepting as this one – you'll always feel slightly out of things …'

Irena was surprised at his words, but he went on, hurriedly, 'You could get a work permit and see how you like living here – I mean without your quartet and Aunt Hedi – you don't know many people, do you?'

Irena had exasperated Magda by refusing the many invitations she'd had to visit people as she travelled with the quartet. It was a profound change in her, Daniel thought, as he remembered the gregarious teenager he had once known. He saw that she now had a very real fear of people she did not know – and especially of men.

'I know you.'

'Yes, you do. And of course I'd love it if you came back – but where would you live?'

'Couldn't I live with you? As your lodger, I mean?'

Daniel didn't answer for a minute, then he leant towards her. 'Of course I'd love that – but Magda is moving out of the flat quite soon – when she's found a new house – so ... But we'll talk about this later, shall we, and ...'

Daniel's first course and Irena's Mont Blanc had arrived and he picked up his fork.

'*Buon appetito!*' he said and Irena took a mouthful of chestnut and cream, half shutting her eyes with ecstasy.

'I think you're secretly still a greedy little girl, aren't you?'

'And you're always hungry – I remember that. Oh poor, poor Amela.' and Irena put her spoon down and reached again for her glass.

'Hey, slow down. I can't carry you home, you know.' And Daniel took her glass away and filled another with water.

Mark and the girls returned to New York. Irena, who was to stay on for a fortnight to start looking for a job in London, was helping Daniel get his music ready for Sarajevo. It fascinated her to see how he thought out each performance, master class and lecture; but he wanted to talk to her of other things and took every opportunity of distracting her. After a while, seeing that Daniel's brow was furrowed with anxiety, she went over to him. He reached for her hand and sat for a moment, looking down at it. How tiny it was, cradled in his.

'Are you sure you want to leave the quartet and come to London? It's a big decision.'

'I know, but I feel ready to leave New York now. I'm sure I'll find a job in London that I could do – anything to do with music, really.' Irena had wondered whether he would ask her to go with Sam and him to Bosnia. Although she would have done almost anything for Daniel, she knew she could not face seeing her homeland again. Not yet – perhaps not ever.

'I'm glad I'm going away too – I'll miss having you around.'

'I'll write, shall I? There are things I ought to tell you and I think I could write them down. Where are you staying?'

Daniel went to his bureau and opened one of the long drawers. He brought out a string-tied package, which he tucked down the side of his cushion. Then he scribbled a few words on a scrap of paper. '*Evo naše adrese!*' he said as he handed it to Irena.

'Goodness – are you learning Serbo-Croat again?'

'Well, a few phrases. And hoping I don't come out with any of the words you taught me! But, yes, please write. And I'll write to you.'

'Proper letters – not emails – I still can't work that horrible computer.'

Daniel laughed and then, his face serious again, he held the package out to her, 'These letters were returned to me – I wrote constantly to your parents after I left, but never had an answer. Then I was told the post wasn't working any more. Read this one first …'

He untied the string and took out a letter, still sealed in its grimy envelope and bearing, in black, the words: VRATITE PRŠALJIOUS – Return to Sender. Irena slit the envelope and took out the words it had held, unread. for over five years.

Prince Albert Mansions

15th July 1992

Dear Finola and Adam

The papers are full of the horrors you are going through in Sarajevo – I'm so desperately worried about you and your family.

I beg you to leave if you possibly can. My sister, Magda, and I would happily welcome you here in London for as long as necessary. But if you feel you cannot abandon your home town, would you at least send Irena to us? Magda would look after her

and see to her schooling and I would supervise her
music, with huge pleasure, of course. Please, please
consider this –

Your affectionate friend,

Daniel D

Irena was trembling as she gave the letter back to Daniel
and it was a while before she could speak. 'I couldn't really
believe you didn't care – but Mama and Tata were already
dead when you wrote this.' Daniel held the package out to her,
but she shook her head, saying, 'Get rid of them now, please.
I know all I need to know.'

Daniel replaced the package in his bureau and turned,
anxiously, to Irena. He sat for a moment and then reached
out and touched one of her cheeks where a dimple formed as
she smiled at him. 'Look after these for me. I'll inspect them
when I get back.'

'Yes, Maestro Daniel!' And their laughter seemed to echo
in their shared memory round the little garden behind the
Vila Dolena where the sunlight, dappled by the great acacia
tree, shone on the roof of a blue studio.

My dearest Ireniskaya,

I'm writing this on the plane – I can't wait until I
get to Sarajevo before I tell you what it has meant
to me to see you again. Just three weeks ago I was
struggling along, managing perfectly well but not too
excited about each day and life in general. All that
has changed now that I know for sure you're alive
and just the same Little Wren.

You'll laugh when I tell you they got me up into the
plane with a fork lift … But here I am in my seat
and drinking a glass of champagne to toast you with,

precious girl.

I'll write properly when I'm installed in our hotel. Here comes our cardboard 'meal'.

Love, lots of it,

Daniel

Prince Albert Mansions

Dearest Maestro Daniel

I should stop calling you that, but it has such happy memories for me. When we'd said goodbye I cried and cried, but also felt happier than I have for ages. It was so wonderful to be with you again, something I thought would never happen. Just being with you and looking at you and hearing your voice. And your wonderful laugh.

But we talked of sad things too, and soon I am going to try to write down the things I've never been able to talk about – what happened to me after you left Sarajevo. I know I've got to face up to my past some time. People do learn to heal themselves by bringing things into the open and maybe that can happen to me, even after so long … Friends have suggested I go to a therapist or a counsellor – but I have learnt to shut all the doors in my head which lead to things I can't bear to think about. Telling you will be hard, because you will find it shocking and perhaps see me differently when you know the whole story. But I <u>will</u> write it all down because I think you're the only person who could understand.

I don't know that I envy you being in Bosnia again. Of course, I still long for Sarajevo, but I know nothing would be the same. To be honest, I'm not sure I'll ever have the courage to go back. They tell me our forests have gone. So the wolves must have gone, too. Do you remember the first day you were with us and you said you'd protect me from the wolves? You looked so great with your big glasses and your long hair – and we were all expecting another grisly old man ...

I hope you're managing OK and that the hotel is helpful. It must be quite alarming to travel for the first time in a wheelchair – the cobbled streets were good fun on a bike, but you must hate them now.

We're playing Haydn – Sunrise quartet – this week, and I'll be playing specially for you, dearest Maestro Daniel, and trying not to make all the 'offal' mistakes you used to notice – always so kindly. There's no-one to tell me these things now, but maybe you will again some time? I'd love that. But now I must start my packing and get ready to go back to New York. Kind Magda is taking me to the airport and seems really sad that I'm going.

Please keep well and tell me how the concert goes and who you've seen that I might remember.

Lots of love, your Little Wren

Darling Little Wren,

Well, we're here – settled in the hotel and more or less over the journey, which had its moments ... Thank God for Sam. Our rooms are great – newly decorated since the war knocked the hotel about a lot. But I can't get into the bathroom – the door's too narrow for my chair, and poor Sam has been having to help me bath and stuff, which is a bit embarrassing – for him – I'm afraid I got past caring about that sort of thing in hospital. With any luck they'll move me into another room.

I won't describe the town to you. I'm sure you know what it looked like when the Siege ended, but it's a shock now to see the less than harmonious rebuilding everywhere. Strange coincidence – Peter Henderson, the journalist who took me round when I came back here to look for your family, (and who was with me when I got shot) is staying here. We're going to meet for a drink tomorrow. Peter's a special guy, very intelligent and well-read (unlike me!). Doesn't know much about music, which is quite refreshing – remember how at the Conservatory it's all they talked about – all the time? There's no way I can get into the music school now – six flights of marble steps. Some of the students and staff have offered to carry me but I don't want to be responsible for hernias and heart attacks, so we'll use any building that hasn't more than four steps up to it.

I'm off there this p.m. for a rehearsal. Access and getting around is – well, not easy is an understatement. Cobbles, broken kerbs, potholes, you name it … No wonder I've hardly seen another disabled person since I arrived – there were thousands of people really badly hurt in the war – where are they? I shall have to find out.

Guess what – they're lending me a room in your old school so I can practise – it has a rather awful piano, which must have been there when you were a pupil. It's so nostalgic remembering how I used to wait for you after school sometimes so we could go and buy cakes. Dr Solomon is rather bent now and has a hearing aid, poor chap. He's just as crusty as ever but I get the feeling he's really pleased to see me, but finds the chair alarming. Oh well, don't we all to start with …?

The music school carpenter is making me a beautiful ramp up to the stage for my masterclass in the Military Hall – thank God, as being man-handled this afternoon was uncomfortable and rather embarrassing. We've worked out a programme for my recital tomorrow – all early stuff, so no pedals indicated. I'd have liked to include some of the moderns – composers born here, particularly. But I'm not happy that I can ever get enough legato and I really should just accept that.

Sad, sad gaps in the orchestra – the students tend to go abroad when they graduate, as things are hard here for a professional musician. How lucky we are in the UK.

Well, I'd better get tidied up for dinner – a get-together with some old students, only 6 around now. Bogdan is terribly scarred but still plays the flute beautifully. Do you remember him?

Needless to say, I'm thinking of you a lot and wish, in a selfish way, that you could be here with us, but you'll be back in New York by now. Please don't let Manhattan seduce you into wanting to stay.

Oh and yes, Haydn is full of joy – I was thrilled to find recently that I am really enjoying playing the F minor Variations. One of his last – written before 1790 when he began to use pedal markings. This needs no pedals – infinitely better without.

Keep your beautiful dimples polished for me,

Love, lots, Daniel

Daniel was getting ready to go out for his last day in Sarajevo, a day that was crammed with engagements, and he was still eating his breakfast as he got dressed. Sam knocked and came in. He looked worried.

Neither of them had anticipated the toll this trip would take on Daniel. As a newly disabled man, he had been nowhere that was not equipped for his needs. In hospital, as at Stoke Mandeville, no eventuality had been overlooked, and at home Magda's careful arrangements had made life equally easy for him. But, partly because he had no experience of travelling as a disabled person, and partly because his thoughts had been elsewhere, he had not anticipated how difficult staying in an old-fashioned hotel might be.

The manager had allocated Daniel their largest room with its own bathroom which was beautifully tiled in the art deco manner. Actually using it, as he had cheerfully told Irena in his letter, was not easy. Sam did his best to help, but he was a small man and Daniel well over six feet tall. Added to this, although his upper body and arms were strong and muscular, his paralysed legs were a dead weight and he had already pulled down the shower curtain and broken the paper-holder as Sam struggled to drag him in and out of the bath and on and off the lavatory with Daniel slipping this way and that, jarring his fragile back. In spite of Sam's protestations that he could manage and his own reluctance to have to admit to his difficulties, Daniel went to see the hotel manager, who was horrified to think that his illustrious guest should have been suffering such indignities under his roof. He would see what could be done.

That morning Daniel taught a masterclass in the temporary City Library, (the fine old building of which the city had been so proud had been bombed). Daniel circled the group of specially selected 'students', several of whom were already well into careers as performing pianists and watched Maestro Danuczek anxiously as he spun his gleaming chair and stopped by the piano.

'*Dobra dan* – good morning,' he said. 'Now, first of all, I apologise for getting you up so early – I know that at least one of you gave a recital last night some distance from here and was probably looking forward to a well-earned lie-in.' He knew that one of his old Conservatory students had travelled from Vienna to be there that morning. 'Tamaś! How good to see you. I seem to remember you thought Chopin should be left in the drawing room?'

The young man he was addressing had been prepared for Daniel's wheelchair, but he remembered his teacher's habit of executing little dances around the lecture hall piano and did not know what to say. Daniel, seeing his discomfiture, stretched out a hand to him, 'Come, Tamaś. Give us some revolutionary Chopin.'

A taxi took Daniel and Sam back to the hotel. Opening the door, they thought for a moment they must be in the wrong room, for a curtain hung where the bathroom door had been and, pulling it away, they saw that the whole frame had been removed, leaving a raw brick edge through which Daniel, whooping with joy, glided with ease. Seeing that a variety of grab rails now adorned the tiled walls, he started to run the shower, shouting to Sam that he was no longer needed.

Although Daniel now enjoyed a greater independence, the long list of invitations he had accepted nearly all necessitated journeys by taxi across the city, and the inevitable jolts and shocks that came with getting in and out of his chair. Disabled access was almost unheard of in the public buildings of Sarajevo and Daniel usually had to be lifted, chair and all, onto the stage. This was tackled with great merriment by those lifting him, and their charge's cheerful smile encouraged them to indulge in a good deal of horse play – dumping him hard on the stage, tipping him sideways or putting him down so that he slid forwards or backwards in his chair before he was sure he was on a level surface. His back was beginning to complain bitterly. He stuffed himself regularly with painkillers but they seemed to do little good. Sam saw him on several occasions arrive in front of the piano, his hands shaking and his eyes wide in an ashen face.

'Are you OK?' he'd ask, anxiously, and Daniel would grin ruefully, 'Can't complain. At least they didn't tip me into the orchestra – I thought I was heading that way.' And he'd start to play, gradually regaining colour as the music eased the pain and he was in control again. But Sam didn't like any of it. He was making notes of the things they should have brought with them, the enquiries they should have made of the hotel and the aids they should have insisted on having installed before their arrival. He would be very sure none of this happened again.

It was nearly the end of their stay when Daniel announced, 'Listen, I'm going to cancel this morning. I'll do the master class this afternoon and give them a bit of Dvorák this evening at the Military Hall, but I want to hit the shops. Hand me the phone, will you, and I'll deal with the committee. I'll tell them I haven't yet had time to see the beauties of Sarajevo. And my girlfriend needs a present.' He could feel Irena's letter in his coat pocket – he'd get himself a beer and re-read it. Sam was relieved not to have to go out again. All he wanted to do was to sleep. His only prayer now was that he would get Daniel home in one piece and hand him back safely to Magda.

Irena's letter had been the nearest thing to a love letter Daniel had had for some time and the memory of her words buoyed him up as he set off into the town, where he wanted to shop for presents – for Magda, of course, and Ollie, but something very special for Irena. What on earth, though, brought from this beleaguered city, would give her any joy? He passed a bookshop, not far from the hotel, one he remembered. Its stock was depleted and much of it bore the signs of plaster fall and damp storage. Unable to get up the steps into the shop itself and loath to ask for help, Daniel stationed himself by the table outside and picked through the battered books. There, amongst all the Serbo-Croat, much of it in Cyrillic script, Daniel saw a faded cover that seemed somehow familiar to him. The book was in English; he opened it and read the dedication on the fly-leaf. Then he rapped on the smeared window to attract the shop owner's attention.

Although he looked forward to getting home, Daniel was dreading the journey. He had suspected for several days that he was beginning to develop a pressure sore from spending too long in his wheelchair without contriving a change of position from time to time. The painful burning sensation under his left buttock told him he would have to pay for his lack of planning, but, in spite of the initial intimacy of Sam's ministrations in the bathroom, he had recoiled from asking the young man to confirm his fears. On the last evening, he padded out his cushion with a pillow from the bed and cheerfully conducted his last Master class.

19.   UNRAVELLED

[IRENA]

I HAD RETURNED that summer to New York to fulfil my outstanding concert engagements with the quartet and to clear my flat. I spent as much time as I could with Hedi. I had told her soon after my arrival that I wanted to go back to London – to live with Daniel. Brave, kind woman that she is, I dreaded saying goodbye to her. 'Forgive me, Aunt. You've done so much for me – and here I am deserting you. I just wish you could come too …'

'Darling girl,' she said, stroking my hair. 'I know you'll be in good hands. And I shall see you again very soon. Daniel has already sent me a ticket to come and see you at Christmas; he's so kind and generous.'

'Yes, he is. But he must have some faults. I'm terrified of finding he's not nearly as perfect as he seems. He can't be, can he?'

'Perfect? No man is. And Daniel's much too good at saying "yes" to everyone, to start with!' Hedi and I sat in silence for a while.

'Don't toy with him, will you…'

'What do you mean – toy with him?' I said, offended, but suspecting uncomfortably that I knew what she meant.

'He's a man. He doesn't see you as a niece, that's for sure. You must make up your mind. If Daniel's the man you want – then you must become a woman for him.'

'I don't think I'll ever know how to be a woman. And he

would find out all the awful things I've done ...'

'The things you were made to do? Haven't you told him yet – I mean so that he knows the details, not just what we all read in the papers – what other girls went through?'

'Don't Aunt. Please don't. I can't talk about it. I just can't.'

'I know you have dreadful things in your memory that you feel will always be connected to any physical contact you have with a man, to sex itself. But maybe something else could replace those painful memories. With the right man ...?'

'I don't think that can happen for me. I had one of my nightmares once when Magda was away – I told you, didn't I? Well, he came in to comfort me and I was half dreaming and thought he was one of Milić's awful friends, so I offered to ... satisfy him. I threw myself at him. He was very kind and put me back on the bed and went to get me some water. But, Aunt, he wanted me. I know he did.'

'I'm not surprised at all and I'm glad he still has these feelings. But you could try looking at it from his point of view?'

'His point of view?'

'He's been very damaged too. His body will never be whole again and, even if he's still – well, virile – I suspect he feels a great deal of uncertainty about being with a woman now – and maybe even shame. Had you thought of that?'

'I should have, but I try not to think about that side of things ... And he's still so handsome and gets so much admiration – I've seen girls looking at him and his pupils think he's dreamy. I've heard them talking about him.'

Hedija laughed and shook her head, 'Well, there you are.'

She went on, anxious now. 'Forgive me, I've never asked you this – you do love Daniel, don't you?'

'Yes. More than ever. You see I've loved him since the day we met. He's always been, well ... he's my ideal man.'

'Even now? He must be very different ...'

'Yes, but so am I. And you know, he has his music and that

matters to him more than anything else. He's still a spectacu-
lar pianist. He's working very hard to make sure his playing is
as little changed as possible. It's wonderful to listen to him – a
huge privilege.'

'But you must try to imagine what it would be like day after
day having your own life restricted by Daniel's disability –
because it would be. You need to be sure that you wouldn't
begin to find it something you can't manage – some women
think they won't mind, but can't live up to their ideals when
all the everyday things get on top of them.'

'Yes, I know. Daniel's told me about the Stoke Mandeville
patients and how a lot of relationships and marriages came to
an end. I see some people are quite uncomfortable when they
first meet him, but he's very good at putting them at their
ease. Doesn't mind me teasing him either. I think it makes
him feel normal again. And I can talk to him about Mama
and Tata without getting upset because we share memories of
happy times with them.'

Bahro came shuffling onto the terrace and Hedi got up
to help him into his armchair. She smiled at me and I knew
our conversation was over, but she'd left me resolved to tell
Daniel about my imprisonment, to tell him all the details I
could remember. I was terrified of reliving the past that I had
tried so hard to erase from my memory and shut into rooms
there whose doors remained locked. Now, for Daniel, I would
force myself to open all the doors and show him what lay
behind them.

That night I sat down at the table in my room and re-read
the two letters I'd had from Daniel. Then I started to write,
intently, late into the night.

20. INTERLUDE

MAGDA met Daniel and Sam at the airport, relieved and delighted to see her brother home again, though looking very tired and even thinner than when he had left. Then she saw him wince with pain as he transferred himself into the front seat of her car. Once home, she inspected Daniel's back-side with her experienced eye and then, furious, she drove him to hospital and left him there. The pressure sore was not deep, but he would need a week or more off his seat before he could carry on with his life.

She went home and looked sadly at the dinner she had pre-pared with a great deal of care. She was about to open a bottle of wine, when there was a ring at the door. Sam stood there, holding a bunch of roses.

'May I come in?'

She was pleased to see him and ushered him into the kitchen. His visit gave her an excuse to open the bottle but he surprised her by producing another out of the music case he was carrying. They sat opposite each other at the kitchen table and she saw how distressed he looked.

'For goodness sake. It wasn't your fault. How could you have known if he didn't bother to tell you he had a sore coming on.'

'I don't think he'd have wanted to ask me to look at his bum. As it was, he was black embarrassed at first when he had to ask me to help him. Giving him a shower and getting him onto the loo wasn't exactly in my job description and it was not a way I'd seen my tutor before, but I was glad to be able to help if I could. He never took anything for granted – always thanked me and we laughed a lot. It was quite a special time in many ways.

'I think you did amazingly well and at least he's learnt to take it all more seriously for another time. He's furious about going into hospital, but he knows it's his fault. Luckily Irena is still away and he should be home by the time she gets back here. But, mind you, if she's going to be part of his life, she'll need to know about these things too, won't she?'

'She's learnt a lot already. And makes light of things, which is good for him. She's nuts about him, of course.'

Sam was rather envious of Daniel, having someone to care so much for him. He was feeling very unsure of his future. 'And he's pretty keen on her, isn't he?'

'Oh yes. He certainly is, but I don't think he knows what to do.'

'In what way?' Sam asked.

'Well, for one thing, I'm sure they haven't slept together. I don't know what Danny can do in that department now. His specialist said he could probably be a father. But it takes two to tango and she's got a lot of problems if you ask me. She was very badly treated by the Serbs for a long time, as you've probably guessed. Raped and mistreated for months on end. I don't suppose she'll ever get over that. People don't.'

Sam nodded.

'If anyone could heal someone who was miserable, it used to be Daniel.' Magda went on. 'But perhaps he's got too many problems himself now to take on someone so needy. I'd wish him a girl who didn't have so much baggage of her own. Time will tell, I suppose. But do you remember how he told us she'd cheer us all up, and was always laughing?'

Sam, beginning to be bored with the endless speculation about Irena, picked up the corkscrew and opened the second bottle.

They had drunk a lot already, but she allowed him to refill her glass. As they ate and drank together, Sam began to see the young Magda in the middle-aged woman beside him, her strong features softened by the flickering candle-light. She had always been there, a mother figure in a way, but tonight he saw her for the first time as a woman, a woman with her own needs. He reached across the table and touched her cheek, following the line of her jaw down to her neck and pulling aside the collar of her shirt. Then he saw the lean, almost masculine line of her shoulder and upper arm, which gleamed golden in the light of the candle she'd lit for them.

Looking back, Magda remembered how surprised she'd been. Sam was much younger than her and over the last few months she'd bossed him around and teased him as if he'd been her child. And there he was leading her along to the spare room, where he knew the bed was always made up. Afterwards, Sam brought their wine through to the bedroom and sat Magda up next to him, pulling the bedclothes over her naked breasts.

'I wasn't expecting this tonight,' she said 'Have you been wanting to do this for a long time – or did it just come over you with all this wine?' Sam heard Daniel's humour in her voice. It was the sort of thing he'd have said. Or so Sam imagined. 'I just suddenly wanted you. You're wonderful, Mags. You really are. But I'm not – well …'

He picked up his glass, wondering how to finish what he had been about to say. Magda, suspecting she knew why he hesitated, asked him bluntly.

'Are you gay, Sam?'

This was a thought she'd had from time to time. She'd suspected that Sam felt more than a student's respect and affection for Daniel by the way he looked at him, unable to hide his own palpable misery when he was aware that Daniel was suffering.

'Yes. Well, a bit of both really. It did for my relationship with my last girlfriend – Holly – when she guessed why I spent so much time with Daniel. She was very jealous. I suppose you'd realized I'm mad about your brother?'

'It had crossed my mind. But I'm afraid there's not much doubt about Daniel's sexual orientation. He used to be a serial lady-killer! But he's very fond of you and thinks you're a wonderful musician.'

'Thanks! But I can't help feeling it's my fault he got into this state – I really thought I could help him and bring him back safely.'

'Oh Sam don't go over that again. Yes, it was all a bit too much for him so soon after he was home, but it's also a great achievement. And he couldn't have done it without you, sweetheart.' The endearment was spoken before Magda had time to reflect, but he laughed, wanting her again. What future they could possibly have together? None, of course, but for now they were warm and comfortable and full of a fierce new desire. And Magda was grateful, as older women are, for the attentions of a young, attractive man. Tomorrow would be tomorrow.

In the days that followed, Magda supposed that Sam might perhaps be suffering from remorse or regret, for she heard nothing from him. He had gone home and immersed himself in his music. And Magda took to visiting her brother every day and concentrating, as she had always done when Daniel needed her, on him and him alone. Sam the other side of London, had found some relief seated at the shiny Yamaha with its dazzling keys. Its tone was so true that he almost longed for a false note or careless tuning to make the perfect instrument come down to the level of his own messy, far from perfect, life.

A troubling image would not leave Sam – an image of Daniel. The week before their trip to Bosnia, Sam had been getting ready to go with him to the photographer's accompanied by Leo. This was not something that Daniel was going to enjoy, and his mind was full of other things than the picture of him that was to appear on the programme of the concert that would mark his return to the London concert circuit.

That day, Sam, looking anxiously at his watch and wondering if Daniel had remembered his appointment, knocked on the bedroom door, but there was no reply and he opened it tentatively. Daniel was sitting in the middle of the room, a towel on his lap, but otherwise naked apart from the headphones over his ears. He was conducting, Sam presumed, to the music he alone could hear. His arms rose and fell, his gestures restrained and delicate, his hands fluttering like leaves. The dark diamond of hair on his chest and the smaller patches under his arms were wet, glistening from the shower; as he moved his head to the rhythm he was hearing, his dripping curls sending out a halo of translucent droplets into the room. Then, just as Sam was about to attract his attention, Daniel's hand caught the flex from the headphones and pulled it away from the sound system. The room was suddenly filled with pounding, soaring music and Daniel, apparently then oblivious to all else, lifted his arms high and wide above the broad expanse of his chest and seemed, Sam thought, to have become a great bird, a swan, whose immense wings beat again and again as if, any moment, they would lift him out of his chair, lift him into the soaring flight for which he fought with every new down-beat of the music, the flight for which his longing became palpable as the music grew ever louder and the flailing of his arms more and more frantic while the final chords sounded and the music ended. Daniel's eyes, which had been closed, opened wide as the sound died away, staring upwards with an expression of agonised supplication as he

dropped his arms to his sides. Then he saw his visitor standing in the doorway. For a moment, he and Sam stared at each
other.

'Just having a good stretch ... exercise, you know.' Daniel
started to rub his head vigorously with the towel, only then
realising that he had removed his one vestige of modesty
and was now stark naked. He dropped the towel into his lap
again, as Sam dragged his eyes away from Daniel and found
his voice; 'Sorry, Daniel, but we're going to be late. I'd better
ring Leo.' and he fled, shutting the door and leaning against
the wall outside while he sought to regain composure. 'Oh
God ... Oh Daniel!'

He had thought a lot about Magda as he drove to and from
the hospital to visit Daniel, but he did not try to speak to her.
He felt confused and guilty at first and then another feeling
overcame him one day as he rattled automatically through
the Bach piece Daniel had suggested he study; he remembered her sleeping face and how she had nuzzled into him
on waking, blindly almost, like a new-born kitten groping for
its mother. He paused in his playing, then stopped altogether
and fetched his coat.

PART TWO

21.   REVELATIONS

I saw pale knights and princes too,
Pale warriors, death pale they all:
They cried, 'La belle Dame sans Merci
Hath thee in her thrall.'

John Keats (1795–1821). From 'La Belle Dame Sans Merci'

[IRENA]

1260 Riverside Avenue, New York.

Dearest Maestro Daniel,

I love your letters and they bring back so many memories – the Conservatory and Dr Solomon and Bogdan – poor things, they've really suffered. But it's good to hear they're still around and still making wonderful music.

You will be in London soon, so I'll send this to you there. I promised I would tell you what happened to me after you left Sarajevo, but I can only write it very factually, because I have spent years trying to shut my mind and my memory to what I am about to tell you and you will be the only person who knows that I have not forgotten it but remember every horrible moment.

I'll begin in July 1992 after the Serbs had murdered my parents – I've told you about that and how I was waiting to be killed too when Colonel Milić threw me into his Jeep.

I don't remember much about the drive. It seemed a long way but I must have been in deep shock I suppose. The Colonel hit me every time he heard me crying, as the images of what had just happened to Tata and Mama and Amela came back and back. Surely they couldn't be dead – it must be a nightmare and I would soon wake up.

We got to a village when it was almost dark and I was taken down to a cellar and into a room with a small window high up on the wall, at street level – I could see people's feet scurrying past. My bladder was bursting and I asked the soldier where the lavatory was. He roared with laughter and kissed me on the mouth – it was disgusting – and he said he'd see me later and went out, locking the door. There was no furniture in the room – just a wooden bedframe and a grey blanket which smelled awful. I sat down on the bed and waited but was desperate to pee and eventually squatted down in the corner. The urine spread across the floor. Later a woman came in and gave me a piece of bread and a tin cup of watery soup, and put a bucket in the corner of the room, pointing at the puddle of pee and shouting at me. I couldn't eat and lay down and cried. There didn't seem to be anyone else nearby.

It was getting dark and the only light came through the dirty window when a passing car lit the room for a moment. The soldiers must have been drinking before they all burst into the room, laughing and cat-calling. Colonel Milić, who had taken me there, pulled off my clothes and raped me. He took a long time and it hurt a lot. Then the others all raped me, one after another, but they were quicker. They stank of beer and vodka and garlic sausage. And sweat, too, and dirty clothes. I can't remember if I slept, but I must have done. In the morning I was very sore and there was dried blood on the bed. From then on, almost every evening a kind woman called Chesna, took me to wash and would give me a dress to wear – always a horrible, tarty dress. Then she took me up to eat with the soldiers in one of the upstairs rooms where there was a bar and other men drinking and smoking. I was so hungry that I did eat, though it made me ashamed. Sometimes, I was made to dance with the soldiers and they roared with laughter to see me waltzing with the older men in the bar to the music which came from an old phonograph. Vienna Woods, the label said and there was a picture on it of woods that looked like our Sarajevo forest where you and I used to cycle. I tried to hold the picture in my mind when I was taken back to my cellar and made to … I just can't tell you the sort of things I had to do for them.

I had been there for a few weeks when the Colonel told me I was to come with him and bring my things. Chesna had smuggled in to me a wooden toothbrush, a piece of towel and a few bits of clothing. So I bundled these up in a sheet of newspaper she'd given me to read and followed him. I thought he was taking me home. Excitement and grief flooded over me. But he took me to a small house in a side street, which I learnt was where he lived. He had a wife, Lidija, and there were other people and children in the house – I could hear their voices. I was put in a room with a proper bed in it and there was an outside WC in the yard, so my life should have become better. But Vukašin Milić was a cruel man. He beat his wife when he was drunk and that was almost every night. I could hear her cries. He beat me too – when I wouldn't do the awful things he liked. During the day I cleaned their house and prepared their food. Luckily Amela had taught me to cook a few things and I was not punished too often for my efforts in the kitchen. The Milić family seemed to have more food than most people at that time, but I was only given scraps when they'd finished eating.

I had begun to be very sick and was afraid I had caught something in the filthy cellar. I had stopped having periods, too, but that was a relief at the time. The sickness passed and then I noticed I was getting fatter – which seemed odd, as I was constantly hungry. One day Lidija asked me some questions. I wasn't meant to talk to her but I was aware that she had been watching me and I felt she wanted to help me. She couldn't believe I'd never thought I might be pregnant. I screamed at her and said it wasn't true, but I finally had accepted that she must be right. Milić was often away fighting, but soon there was no longer any doubt about my condition and, watching me undress one night, he said: 'Who's is it?'

'Yours of course, Sir.' I had to call him 'sir', which he loved, particularly when I was doing filthy things.

'Ach, a fine Serb child – he'll fight on our side one day.' I learnt later that the raping and impregnating of enemy women was symbolic of the pollution and control of Bosnian and Croatian blood and was relished by men such as Milić.

When the baby began to move and the bulge of my belly moved upwards until it was high under my breasts, I started to imagine what it might be like to have a child to love. After all, I had no family left that I knew of. I fantasized about a future shared with a little, curly headed toddler. In a funny way, this gave me some sort of hope and when Milić was away I took to singing to Lidija's nieces and nephews (she had no children of her own) – all of them huddled together on one side of the bed they shared with their parents. This was the only joy I knew in that terrible part of my life. Early in March, Lidija told me her husband would be away supervising the building of a prison camp. He wouldn't be back for at least a month. She knew I was near my time and told me she had a plan and I must trust her.

I went into labour on the first day of spring and the pains went on for thirty-six hours. Lidija's mother and sister took turns to be with me. The baby came with a rush of blood and blackish yellow liquid – and I instinctively held out my arms for it. It didn't cry and the Babushka took it and wrapped a cloth around it, telling me to go to sleep and I'd see the baby later. But I never did see it – him. They told me he'd died – but I was sure I could hear a baby crying somewhere in the house, a very young baby and the sound of it made my womb contract painfully and thick yellow milk oozed from my nipples making my straw mattress smell sour and buttery. Lidija held a hot cloth to my swollen breasts and tried to comfort me.

I cannot remember those next few days. I was very weak and had lost a lot of blood. At first Lidija thought I might be dying. But, once I was able to stand, she and her mother led me away from the house to a truck which stood in a side street and I was driven away from the village. They got me to a field hospital amongst terribly wounded people from the city and countryside. When I was a bit better I started to work, washing the patients and emptying their slops. They were grateful and liked to talk, particularly when they were in pain at night – or dying.

I don't know exactly how long I was in the hospital,

but it was late summer when one of the doctors
managed to get me over the border and I went by
train to Vienna. There the American Embassy took
me in and questioned me kindly, but I couldn't
answer them. I was again amongst living, well fed
people and I couldn't speak. Talking to the dying
had been easier. Eventually I told them my name
and where I had been brought up. I seemed to be
on a list of missing people and learnt that my aunt,
Hedija Tanović, was living in America. She and my
uncle had thought I must have been killed when
my parents were, and could hardly believe it when
they heard that I was still alive. Aunt Hedi met me
at Kennedy Airport and burst into tears. She and
Uncle Bahro kept asking me to tell them where I'd
been and what had happened to me. I said I couldn't
remember anything. My aunt has been with me when
I have flashbacks and nightmares and she no longer
asks me questions.

Hedi has done all she could to be a mother to me.
Her own daughter – do you remember Lati, who was
always giggling? Well, she took up with a Serb soldier
and was still living with him in Belgrade, I think.
Her parents never mention her, but there is a photo
of her by her mother's bed.

It was a couple of years before I had the strength
to leave Long Island. I had met up with some
musicians and, as they were looking for a viola
player, I joined them and we formed a quartet. The
two fiddlers, Bella and Sasha, let me rent a room
in their Manhattan apartment. I was quite happy
there, as I was making music again, but I didn't try
to have any social life of my own. I have never had a
boyfriend as I cannot overcome my fear and disgust
when I am alone with a man I don't know. So you
see, I'm not the nice pure girl I was when you first

knew me. I disgust myself as I must now disgust
you. I'm so sorry to have such horrible things to tell
you, but it would not be fair not to tell you the truth
about my past and the things I've done. Imagining
that I might go back to be with you in London was
a wonderful dream – I used to think about you so
much and wonder what you were doing. Sometimes,
when you were staying with us in Sarajevo, I had
imagined meeting you when I was grown up and
that maybe you wouldn't be married and might …
but now I know that could never be anything but a
dream. I shall go back to my life in New York now,
but I won't ever, ever, forget you and our happy times
together. And I hope your life becomes easier with
the difficulties you now have to bear. I expect it won't
be long before you find someone to share your life
and go on making more and more wonderful music.

It's better that you should just try to remember the
girl I was at fifteen and not what I became later.

My love, which you will always have, and goodbye,

Irena

Irena finished writing, folded the sheaf of paper, stuffed it
into an envelope and walked to the post box.

As the days passed, Irena wondered when Daniel would get
her letter. And how he would take the horrible things she had
dredged up from her past – and whether, having been left
in no doubt about the degradation she had known, he would
be relieved that she had changed her mind about going to
London. She had been strangely buoyed up by the activity
of writing and the sense of catharsis it had brought; but now
began to wish she had not written the letter or, most of all,
committed it to the post.

In New York, she had begun to put together her few possessions, telling the girls she was going to live in London when their present concert season was over. They would need to find a new viola player and that could take time. Sacha and Bella were sad; they would miss her and admitted to being very envious. She decided not to tell Mark until she was about to set off for London.

Not long before what was to have been the date of her departure, the quartet played at a local school and then met up at the local pizza joint. Mark sat down beside her and she saw at once that he was upset – or angry. How stupid she'd been to trust in the girls' discretion.

Mark had often noticed Irena's eyes on her host in the flat and Daniel's glances in her direction too, but worst of all was when their eyes seemed to lock and both of them would smile. He hated those smiles and he'd felt a rush of disgust as his mind filled in the details of an imagined love-making between the two of them. And now Irena, for whom he still had dreams, both musically and for his own personal life, was risking all to go and stay – or did she mean live? – with a crippled man who could not possibly fulfil her needs. The idea was repugnant to him and, sitting beside her, he found himself blurting out: 'I honestly thought you'd have more sense, Babe – going off to London just because a middle-aged pianist flatters you. He's far too old for you and you'll end up being his nursemaid …'

Irena put her hand on his arm to stop the flow of his speech. 'Mark, please. Don't go on – you don't need to say any of this. You see, I've decided not to go back to London. I'm going back to live with Aunt Hedi on Long Island – she could do with some help these days.' And she got up, leaving her three companions staring up at her, said goodnight and went out into the street to find a cab.

❋

Almost as soon as she had posted her letter to Daniel, Irena had begun to realise the enormity of what she had done. She wondered how she could go back now to the comparative peace of the Manhattan life she'd made before seeing Daniel again had turned everything upside down. When she returned to her apartment, and looked at the half-packed suitcase on her bed, she sat down beside it and slumped forwards, weeping. That afternoon she had called Hedija to ask herself to stay, saying her departure had been delayed. Her aunt, delighted, ran upstairs to find the bedlinen she kept especially for Irena – the old linen from the castle in Moravia that held such happy memories for both of them of another life, another world.

22.   MAROONED

HEDIJA looked at Irena with concern.
Her niece had turned up the previous day on their door-step and her aunt had welcomed her warmly, but clearly the girl hadn't slept and, with her unbrushed hair and haggard face, was beginning to look frighteningly as she had at Kennedy Airport, three years before.

'What's wrong, darling? You look awful. I hope you're well enough to travel …'

Irena sat down heavily, her arms wrapped around her own waist, hugging herself.

'Please may I stay here a bit – until I've found another apartment?'

'Another apartment? But surely you're flying back to London in two weeks' time?'

'No. I'm not. I'm not going back to London.'

Hedija started to speak, but Irena stopped her. 'I was wrong. I can't possibly make a life with Daniel. I shouldn't have let things get this far.'

'But what has made you change your mind? You seemed so happy to be going back – and being with Daniel.'

Irena looked out of the window. She was very tired and thought she would not be able to express the tortuous feel-ings that had kept her awake all night. But she looked up at Hedija and said very quietly, 'I wrote to him last week – that's why I needed to borrow your typewriter. He'd asked me to tell him about Colonel Milić and what happened after Mama and Tata were killed. But as I wrote it all down I realised that he couldn't possibly want me any more when he's read that. No-one could.'

'But it can't have been news to him – he knows perfectly well what you have been through. He wants to care for you and help you to forget.'

'I shan't ever forget. How could I? and I don't want ever to have to pretend to want to ... to sleep with a man. It's all so revolting what men do, and Daniel will want to do all that when we're together. Of course he will and I won't be able to stand it. I'll hurt him even more and he'll feel rejected and ashamed ... Or else, he'll find it all rather titillating – he might, you know. He probably won't be any different from them. He'll want me to suck him and blow him and he'll want to put his penis into all sorts of places ...'

Hedija recoiled, shocked by the images that Irena's tirade was calling up, but her niece had begun to falter and was wringing her hands together, as if, Hedija thought, to wash them clean.

'Oh, my darling,' she said and sat down next to Irena.

Daniel was lying on his side in the hospital bed, held in position with wedges so he wouldn't roll onto his back. He was listening to music through his headphones, as reading was uncomfortable. This was how he had passed his days since his return from Bosnia, and he was bored and frustrated, but determined to behave himself if that would mean his wound would heal and he'd be able to sit in his chair again. He was amused to find himself longing for the once-hated wheel-chair – it seemed like a dream of freedom now. Magda came in bearing a carrier bag of clean clothes, fruit and chocolate, and a thick bundle of post. Most of the letters could wait, she thought, but one had a US postmark and she put it into his hand. Magda slit the envelope for him and handed him his glasses, curious to know what Irena had written, but, as Daniel started to read, the troubled expression on his face told her to go.

Sam had been staying with his parents in Suffolk while Daniel was in hospital. Now the patient was back in his wheelchair, sitting on what he called a 'very embarrassing' cushion while the sore healed enough for him to be allowed home. Sam was shocked at his appearance. His face was still pale, thin and haggard and now there was a desperate look in his eyes.

'Sam. Oh thank God you're back. Sit down. I need to ask you something.'

'Ask away.'

Daniel turned his head, looked out of the window for a moment, turned back and began to speak very fast. 'Sam come to New York with me? I need to go as soon as I get out of here – next week I hope. Please come with me.'

'New York? But surely you'll have to take it easy for a while?'

'Bugger that. I'll be perfectly OK once I'm out of here. I must go over to the States. I've got to see Irena.'

'But isn't she about to come back? I thought she'd be here again in a couple of weeks ...'

Daniel looked out of the window again. Since reading the letter, he had told no-one of Irena's decision not to come back. He'd rung Luke to see if Irena had arranged to collect her newly restored viola, but was told that the luthier had unwillingly agreed to send it to her in New York.

Daniel began to rock in his chair, as if he were in pain. 'She's not coming. She's decided not to come. I've got to go and get her. I must.'

Sam was imagining his conversation with Magda if he gave in to Daniel's request. She would be furious, incandescent –

he'd seen her like that when her brother behaved in a way she couldn't support, but he also knew that gainsaying Daniel was well- nigh impossible. He might as well give in and take whatever Magda doled out to him. Better her wrath than Daniel's.

'Shall I see about tickets, then?'

Daniel was amazed at the lack of opposition from the young man. 'You're sure? It's a big ask.'

'Always good to see the Big Apple. Where do you want to stay – I'll check out the bathroom doors this time. Wide doors should be OK in the States – everyone's obese there!'

Irena hadn't been out of her tiny new apartment for several days. Nor had she practised for the forthcoming concert. She lay on the sofa most of the time watching television. She didn't really take any of it in, but would turn the sound off when the relentlessly raised voices of the presenters and their victims began to offend her ears. She hadn't eaten either, but had a large bar of chocolate next to her and a bottle of cheap white wine. So, when the doorbell chimed, she was not best pleased, particularly when she heard a babble of voices outside, which she recognised as those of her upstairs neighbours. She suspected that they were drug dealers, which was not uncommon in that run-down area, but they were helpful and cheerful, if noisy and prone to drop litter on the stairs.

She peered through the spyhole, which was too high for her to get a good view of the landing. All she could see was Rio and another boy laughing outside her door, their big white teeth the only part of their faces visible by the light of the grimy bulb outside. She pushed her hands through her unbrushed hair and slid the chain from the door.

'I'm afraid the girls aren't here …' Bella and Sasha had been to see her a few days ago and the boys had chaperoned them to the subway – with Rio and his gang there was no fear of being mugged. She looked at the group as they divided their ranks, laughing uproariously.

'Brung yo a nice surprise – all the way from good ol' Lunnon town ...'

Irena stood, an expression of disbelief on her face as Daniel appeared between the two boys who were still holding onto his chair. They had carried him up three floors, laughing and whooping as they did so, but putting him down gently at his destination. Daniel turned to his companions but they were already running up the remaining eight flights of steps to their own front door. 'Thanks!' he shouted after them and Rio stuck his head over the banister,

'One hour – then we've gotta be 'way, so don' get settled in that bed!'

'Can I come in?' Daniel asked; Irena seemed rooted to the spot. She stood aside while he propelled himself through the door.

'There's not much room, I'm afraid.' she said, pushing aside a box which was blocking Daniel's progress into the small, cramped sitting room. He swivelled himself into the space made for him between the packing cases.

'What are you doing in New York? Are you playing in a concert?'

'No. No concert. ' He paused. 'I've come to take you back to London.'

'Didn't you get my letter?'

'I did. And you didn't tell me anything I didn't know – or hadn't guessed. But, if it's me you can't face and all this', and he touched the wheels of his chair, 'please be honest and tell me now, because I have to know.'

She didn't answer but moved the bar of chocolate away and sat down on the far end of the sofa, her hands clasped in her lap.

Then something snapped in Daniel. All the weeks of anticipation, the uncertainty, the lurching from joy to despair, seemed to overcome him. He'd held his feelings in check for a long time, but now he had nothing to lose.

'Irena, my darling, come home with me, please. I can't live without you now ... Please don't leave me. I've waited so long to be with you again – so, so long. And I love you more than anything in the world.' Tears began to run down his cheeks, but he made no effort to stop them.

'Please don't cry,' she whispered, but Daniel's sobs continued to shake him. She hesitated and then moved up close to his chair and put her arms around him.

Later, Irena went to look for another wineglass and finally unearthed a pink plastic toothmug.

'Mmm,' said Daniel after his first mouthful of the drugstore wine. 'Do you know I've never tasted anything quite like this – maybe it's the plastic – or the toothpaste ...'

She looked at his laughing face. 'You came all this way and got up those stairs – I can't believe it.'

'Now you know I'd do anything for you. Even as grubby as you are now.'

'Shall I take a shower?'

'No. No, don't waste time and, anyway ...' He wanted to tell her he loved the ripe, womanly smell of her, but sensed that she was not ready to hear this sort of thing. Instead, he asked: 'How soon can you get to London – this week?'

Irena didn't answer at once, but she was smiling still and hugging herself in disbelief that a horrible day had turned into this extraordinary evening, when a cacophony of voices outside the flat door announced the return of Daniel's chair-bearers.

Sam had parked the hired goods van round the corner and was climbing the badly lit stairs, wondering if he'd come to the right address. From the landing below, he saw Irena come out of her flat with a hooded youth who pushed past him, carrying a wheelchair as if it were a feather. Two other boys appeared with its owner, for whom they'd made a seat out of their hands and carried Daniel down, his arms around their shoulders.

Sam met them on the stairs and Daniel, seeing his expression of astonishment, grinned. 'Oh, hi Sam. There you are!'

As he lifted Daniel into his chair outside the apartment block, Rio was curious suddenly about the crippled Englishman.

'You a vet?'

Daniel laughed and shook his head. 'Not exactly, but I *was* shot.'

Rio nodded. This was something he could understand. 'We got the gun scene here, too,' and was about to join his friends when Daniel, feeling he couldn't leave them unrewarded for so big a favour, called him back. 'I don't know how to thank you – I haven't any money on me, but I could get some tomorrow.'

'Don't need no money. Business is good jes now.' They seemed about to go, so Daniel took off his watch, the platinum Jaeger-leCoultre that he'd bought with his first concert fees.

'You could sell this.'

Rio took the watch and turned it over in his hands. 'Not gold. Waterproof?'

'I've never taken it swimming – maybe not, but it's worth quite a lot, I think.'

'No dials or nothin'. Kid's watch?' His teeth flashed in the lamplight, as Rio handed the watch back to Daniel. 'You keep this mister. We'll get you a new one when you's back – a real man's watch.' And they were gone down the street, their laughter echoing off the warehouses on either side. Irena was laughing too. Everything seemed funny now, and she bent down and put her arms around Daniel's neck.

Sam opened the side door of the van and let down the ramp, muttering to himself. 'Thank God. Now we can all go home.'

23.   JOURNEY'S END

[IRENA]

THAT SUMMER I went to live with Daniel next door to London's Royal Albert Hall. Magda had not yet moved, but was out most of the time seeing to the new house she had bought and would return late with paint in her hair and under her nails.

At first, I woke every day convinced I was a fifteen-year-old girl again, at home with my parents in Sarajevo. For in the distance – surely drifting in from the blue studio opposite my bedroom window – I could hear a piano being played. It was the same pianist, playing with the touch that I had come to know so well after the arrival of the long-legged, bespectacled musician who had become such an important part of my life.

It was a time of joy and pain in equal measure. I wished that I could be a better companion to Daniel, but there were still days when I found it hard to speak. At first I would lie on my bed, half of me dreading his knock on my door when he had finished practising. But I soon found that he had an instinctive understanding of my changeable moods and would never try to cheer me up or ask me questions. Sometimes he would just sit next to me and talk quietly about music. He knew I loved the park and when he had time we would go there together and watch the ducks on the Serpentine, Daniel feeding them with the remains of one of his exotic cooking experiments.

It was during those weeks that I began to understand

how difficult life was for Daniel. He never complained and did his best to be a cheerful companion, but I soon began to see through the smiling exterior, to understand the twin struggles that he faced each day. The first was the battle he fought with his physical limitations. I watched him closely, wishing he would let me help him, but soon became aware that what he needed most was the space and time to work things out for himself; but the day did come when he shouted down the passage: 'Irenita – are you busy? I'm a bit stuck ... and I went to his aid. After that, things were easier and I was secretly proud that he came to rely on me for a few daily tasks that made his life easier. But with the second struggle – the search for new ways to approach his career in music and the bitter acceptance when he had to accept defeat – neither I nor anyone else could help him.

Magda had hired a cleaner for Daniel shortly before I'd originally come to London and he was living on his own. Her name was Jovanka and I would see her vacuuming and mopping, her hair tied back in a scarf, wearing embroidered slippers. I should have approached her and introduced myself, but I had heard her speaking on her mobile and knew at once where she was from. Magda, seeing me abandon my uneaten toast and leave the kitchen as Jovanka came in one morning, said later: 'She comes from your part of the world – Montenegro I think. Have you talked to her?'

I turned my head away, feeling a mixture of shame and revulsion. 'We don't actually speak the same language.'

Daniel had come into the kitchen and looked from Magda to me. 'It's rather a difficult situation, Mags. I should have warned you – and Irena.'

I got up and left the room, wondering what he would say to his sister and hoping they would get rid of Jovanka somehow.

Later that morning Daniel and I went to the Park and I sat down on a bench by the Serpentine. He shifted himself out of his chair and slid across to sit beside me, his arm around my shoulders. It was a few minutes before he spoke, looking away from me at the water.

'Darling, listen. Jovanka is not your enemy and you are not hers. She suffered as much as you in that war. Put into a camp, made to be a sex-slave – just a victim of the horrors of that war which were suffered by women on both sides. You know that, my darling, if you let yourself think about it. Don't punish the poor girl for something she could not control. She needs your understanding. 'And,' he added, as I did not reply, 'She has a daughter to look after on her own. The baby was conceived in terrible circumstances ...' I got up and looked at the scum that had collected at the edge of the black lake water. Daniel was still speaking, 'You should feel sympathy for her, darling. Surely you can.'

'Should I feel sympathy for the man who shot you, too?' My voice was raised and a woman who was feeding the ducks close by, with two small children, moved away.

'Yes, of course you should. I do. Think about it – we fight on the side we were born on, don't we? All sides are the victims of conflict and, in war, all sides commit acts they would normally find repellent.'

I knew he was right, but I was not ready to forgive anyone who had done harm to my family, my country – let alone my Daniel. He was getting back into his chair and we made our way up the path past the Serpentine Café. We didn't stop for coffee, but went home in silence and Daniel disappeared into the music room.

I found Jovanka cleaning my bedroom window. Seeing me, she excused herself and began to gather up her things.

'*Dobar dan*,' I greeted her and went on in Bosnian, 'The Maestro tells me you have a little girl – what's her name?'

Jovanka's eyes filled with tears. I took the duster out of her hand and motioned her to sit beside me on the bed.

'Marika – she's called Marika.'

'Where's she at school?'

Jovanka turned away. After a moment she said, her voice almost inaudible. 'She goes to school in Peterborough.'

'Peterborough? But that's a long way away, isnt' it?'

'There are lots of Serbs up there now. She's living with a family.'

'And you go up to see them when you can? Or do they come to London?'

Jovanka looked away from Irena. 'I haven't seen Marika for four years.'

'Four years! But why …?'

'My boyfriend – Haris – doesn't want her,' and Jovanka stood up. 'I was a prostitute in our town during the war – I don't know who her father is. Haris doesn't want her around. And I don't earn enough to look after her on my own.'

Of course I understood her shame and self-loathing, but I thought of Daniel and how he would comfort me when nightmares took me back to my own sordid past.

'I'm sorry,' I said, and added rather lamely. 'If there's ever anything I can do to help …'

Jovanka shook her head and left the room. It had been an awkward conversation, but it cleared the air between us and I came to be fond of the young woman, who was immensely loyal over the years to come; whether because she felt responsible for Daniel's well-being after the months she had spent keeping his surroundings in order, or because he was charming and attentive to her. I could not guess.

Every morning I practised my viola, standing by the window which looked out onto the park and knowing that Daniel was down the corridor in the music room. I would play for two hours and then, impatient to see him, make a pot of Bosnian coffee and sit next to him while I opened the post and he worked on a score or at his computer. I began to be happy and my dreams were no longer fearful. Living with Daniel, I began to feel safe at last, safe and complete.

Then, as the weeks went by, I felt something begin to change.

One day, he said 'I've had an email from Mark. Did you know they were all coming over to give a chamber concert at St John's, Smith Square before Christmas?'

'Yes. I meant to tell you. They haven't found a violist yet and have asked me to play with them while they're here. What do you think?'

Daniel shut down his screen and sat looking at his hands for a moment. Finally he said, 'My darling, I think you should.'

He didn't meet my eyes as he went on, speaking very fast. 'And maybe then you should go back with them to New York.'

'Go back with them? But why?'

Still avoiding my eyes, he said, 'I've been thinking for a while that you need a life of your own.'

'But you said you wanted me with you – you needed me and wanted to look after me ...' I felt tears prickling in my eyes.

'Yes, I said all those things and I meant them. But I've been very selfish – you must see now that you need someone who can look after you better than I can. You must have found life with me and my wheelchair very difficult sometimes. I know I do!'

Daniel looked up at me then and held out his hands to take mine, but I couldn't move.

I whispered,' I always thought ...'

'You always thought what?'

'It doesn't matter.'

'I think it does. I want to know what you've been thinking.'

I couldn't answer him – if he didn't know anything of my thoughts, what was the point? I picked up the coffee tray and left the room.

I have no idea what time it was or how long I'd been sitting on my bed and wondering what to do. Should I rejoin the quartet and go back to Manhattan? I tried to imagine what my state of mind would be as I packed up my things and left the little room with the harpsichord.

Daniel knocked softly on my door and pushed himself in. As he came close to where I was sitting, I saw that his eyes were red. His voice was hoarse as he said, 'I've hurt you, haven't I?'

'I'm so stupid – should have seen it coming. I'm not much of a companion. And we aren't a proper couple …'

'What do you mean – not a proper couple?'

'Well – we don't share a bed. Now I see that I've been cruel to you and expected you to put up with someone who's no use as a woman.'

'Irena, my darling. Don't say that … You know, surely, that I understand how hard things are. And I love you exactly as you are.'

'But you want me to go away.'

'I don't want you to – that's the last thing I want. But you're much better than you were, much stronger. And …' Daniel paused and his voice broke when he said, 'You must want to get married one day – and have children – don't you? I mean if you find the right man …'

How could he ask me that?

I found myself shouting then: 'Yes. Yes, I do want to get married and I've already found the right man. You must know that by now …'

I did not look in Daniel's direction after my outburst and was surprised to hear him begin to laugh. 'Oh darling, darling Little Wren. Are you proposing to me?'

'No. That's your job.' I said and found that I was laughing too.

'I can't kneel – you'll have to do that for me.' And I knelt down beside his chair and he took my hands in his and, pronouncing the words slowly and carefully, he asked me: '*hoćeš li se udate za menet?* Will you marry me?'

And I replied, '*Da, da naravno. Hoću.* Yes, yes of course I will.'

Then I began to dance around the room whirling Daniel in his chair with me.

When I started to write these memories of my life, I had no idea who, if anyone, might ever come to read my hastily scribbled words. Then the need to write became more urgent and I re-wrote almost as much as I wrote in the effort to make the words express what I wanted them to say, for I realised I was no longer writing only for myself. When it came to trying to describe the way in which Daniel and I finally became lovers, I made several attempts and each time moved the cursor almost at once to obliterate the passage. The occasion was far too private for any eyes but Daniel's and my own, but often over the years, as I fell asleep at his side, I would think of how he had rescued me from the dark place from which there had seemed to be no escape.

'No, please don't look …' I said one morning. He was caressing my stomach and I pulled the duvet back up to my chin.

'Why? You're so lovely and I've wanted to see your body for so long. I've got scars too, and not such pretty ones. Your baby marks are like little silver fish …' He looked serious for a moment and then asked, 'Have you never had any news – of your child? Do you know anything at all?'

I sat up then, remembering the brief moment of motherhood I had known. 'No. Nothing. But I know I heard a baby cry the next day somewhere in the house – a newborn baby. It was such a terrible time and people were starving – I don't suppose he survived ... but I can't help hoping he's still alive.'

'Will you let me ask Peter to do some more research. He has so many contacts. Now that peace has come, maybe he can go out into the country and find out what happened to – Lidija, was it?'

'Yes, Lidija. If he found her, you could go and thank her for me.'

'But why me? Would you still not be able to face going back? You must one day, you know and I have to go and play there, soon. Come with me, won't you?'

I didn't answer, but tried to imagine what it would be like to be with Daniel again in my beloved city, which I knew had been all but destroyed.

24. PASSION AND PAVLOVA

Olive, bearing a larger than usual cake tin, let herself in and sat down at the kitchen table. Magda was standing by the window, craning her neck to see the pavement below.

Olive was opening her tin.

'I saw the lovebirds getting into the lift just now. Just when I'd made him a passion fruit Pavlova as I missed his birthday. Where are they going – do you know?' She could never contain her curiosity about Daniel, whom she adored.

'They're off to the Albert Hall,' Magda said, 'to hear his beloved St Matthew Passion. Daniel never misses a year, though he can't sit through the whole thing now – they've gone to hear the second half.'

'Is that Irena's cup of tea?'

'She's going for his sake, I expect. She won't discuss religion – ever. I suppose that if you've been the subject of genocide and all that horror … But Bach – well, I think few people are unmoved by those Passions. I used to sing in the Matthew with the choir I belonged to – oh, ages ago, when my parents were still alive. It was a wonderful experience. And I could boast that Danny wasn't the only person in the family who'd performed in the Albert Hall!'

'And Daniel – I don't think I've ever heard him talk about religion – is he a believer?'

'He certainly doesn't practise Judaism, but Bach and church music have always been important to him. He used to play the organ at school and got bitten then. I think religion in general interests him a lot, but what he believes … who knows what Danny thinks about anything – except music! And he always makes a joke of everything.'

'He told me that he'd stopped playing the Romantics – so I was surprised to hear some lovely Schubert last week when my window was open – it sounded marvellous – very rich …'

'Ah'. Magda said, laughing. 'That would have been him duetting with Sam.'

'Oh, so it was four hands – I see. Who's idea was that?'

'Irena's – she'd once seen Marta Argerich and Daniel Barenboim playing a duet together – apparently they grew up knowing each other in Argentina. Anyway, Irena noticed that Marta, who was playing Segundo – you know, the bass part – was doing all the pedalling. So she thought this would be a way Danny could enjoy his beloved Schubert again. He plays Primo and digs Sam with his elbow when he's late with the pedal – it's very funny watching them. It's been such a success that the students have asked for a course on piano four hands. Irena has lots of good ideas and he actually listens to her suggestions – remarkable.'

'She certainly looks more cheerful these days. I was worried when she first got here.'

'Well so was I – it was fairly tricky at first. I have to say I'd hoped Danny might find someone a bit stronger than Irena, someone without so much baggage of her own, but he looked for her for such a long time that I think she became a sort of an obsession. Now they're so wrapped up in other and she clearly makes him happy, but whether she'll ever be able to put her past behind her and be all that he really needs – who knows. There's still something very childish about her …'

'Helping Irena could be his salvation, don't you think? Optimism is a great healer. And so is altruism. I have good vibes about this – I think they'll be very happy.' And Ollie straightened her scarlet turban, tucking in the wisps of white hair which had escaped. She took out her compact mirror and applied a vivid lipstick, wishing there was a way to stop it creeping out along her wrinkles like the legs of a Schiaparelli Pink spider.

The last notes died away and no one moved for a few moments before they began to applaud. Daniel, whose head had been bowed during the last chorus, *Hocht vergmügt schlummern da die Augen ein*, turned to Irena.

'Thank you for coming with me. I know you didn't really want to ... but now you know why I have to hear it every year. That *Erbarme Dich* – what a sublime, heart-rending aria – and the final chorus, ending in one of the most beautiful cadences in the whole of music, surely ... If I knew I were going to die, I would want to hear this when the end was near. This would be a most joyful way of saying goodbye to the world. The highest form of art – music, words, voices, instruments all in the service of something unfathomable, incomprehensible. One could lay one's soul bare in front of this music, and be absolved by its clarity, its purity. What did you think? Did you hate it as you thought you might?'

Daniel wanted to hear her say that she, too, had been moved. When he had looked at her during the performance her face had told him nothing.

'You're such a maudlin old thing! I wish you wouldn't keep talking about death – it's horrible. Of course I don't hate that wonderful music ... but I'm uncomfortable about religion, as you know ...'

Although the Passion had indeed touched the musician in her, Irena could only feel an impatient repugnance as the familiar story had reached its terrible, inevitable end. For the symbol of the cross itself seemed appalling to her – to see nuns and young girls and old ladies displaying around their necks reminders of a hideous torture depicted in gold and even precious stones, an incomprehensible obscenity. But she did not say this to people – any more than she spoke of the body of a girl nailed to the door of a Sarajevo church.

25.   VARIATIONS

[IRENA]

DANIEL needed to start planning his first public appearance in London for three years. He feared his audience would be watching and listening for the differences in his performance and, anyway, he could not decide what to play.

The concert was a few weeks away when I threw myself into a kitchen chair with a heavy sigh. Magda turned from the stove, 'You sound fed up.'

'I almost wish Daniel wasn't giving this concert – he's working so hard and looks exhausted and …'

'He's giving you a hard time, I suppose.' Magda pushed a cup of coffee over to me.

'I'm not a pianist and it took me a while to understand fully how awful it is for him not to be able to use the pedals. He pretends to me that he really loves the early stuff best. And he plays it marvellously, but I know he still longs to play the pieces that made his career for him, doesn't he?'

'Of course he does – but that's not what's bugging him now – it's the indecision. Once he's settled on a programme for the Wigmore, he'll be fine – always has been like this. Shall we go and see a girly flick?'

Daniel and I seldom went to the cinema together and in his current mood he would probably be glad to have the flat to himself for an evening.

He was sitting at the fortepiano, a pencil between his teeth. Gone was the anxious, irresolute expression he'd worn that morning and he looked up, removed the pencil and held out his hand. 'Sorry. I've been a rat, I know. Forgive me?'

I kissed his cheek, wondering what had happened to make him suddenly so cheerful.

'I've cracked it. For the Wigmore. I know what I'm going to play.'

'Great!' I said. 'What?'

He put his finger to his lips. 'Can't tell you yet. You'll have to wait. But I will tell you that this old girl will be going with me.'

He meant his Dolmetsch fortepiano. He had worked on adapting his playing to the lovely instrument, the gentler, more refined performance needed on a handmade instrument built entirely of wood without steel bracing, The clarity of the straight-stringing and parallel grain of the wood gave his playing a new freshness and his joy was transparent as he found a hitherto unknown repertoire. The quasi-Elizabethan pieces of Herbert Howells and the Wadenhoe Clavichord Book by Trevor Hold and Gordon Jacob's Suite for virginals gave him hours of pleasure, as did the two-part inventions for piano which lent themselves to an instrument without pedals. So, to his joy, did a Beethoven sonata which he now loved to play.

I went out that evening with Magda, relieved and excited.

Tickets for Daniel's concert were sold out the day after the box office opened.

The Wigmore Hall is more than a concert hall; it is an institution and much loved by Londoners, but I wonder how many people know about its complications for anyone who cannot manage stairs. As the building is listed, no changes can be made to the steep staircases and winding corridors that are to be found backstage. Daniel could not possibly get up to the dressing rooms, which are on an upper floor, and he needed to be lifted up a short flight of steps to the Green Room, where a corner had been screened off for him. Once there, two doors lead straight onto the stage under the glittering half dome of turquoise mosaic. Daniel appeared, pushing himself through one of the curved mahogany doors. He skirted along the side of the fortepiano before turning to bow to the audience. Only then did he see that they were standing, quietly at first and then shouting and clapping and stamping their feet. I watched from my seat on the balcony – the seat I have always liked best – and saw him look up at me. I knew, although he was smiling as he sat acknowledging his ecstatic admirers, that he was on the brink of tears. He cried so easily and I used to tease him that it was time he became more English and developed a stiff upper lip. He lifted both his arms above his head, clasping his hands together in a gesture of victory, smiling broadly now. Many performers would have waited for the applause to die down, but Daniel gave one last bow, his right hand on his heart, and pushed himself to the piano, turned his chair to face the keyboard of an instrument that would have been very familiar to Bach – and, looking towards the auditorium, raised his hand in the authoritative gesture I knew so well. A hush descended. Everyone sat down and Daniel, when all was quiet, stretched his hands over the keys and began to play. He had never been a pianist to throw himself about, but used, I remembered, to sway slightly backwards and forwards. Now he sat very still and upright to maintain his balance. His body remained motionless while his graceful hands mastered the keyboard again, as they had so often in the past. He felt at home and was smiling as he began to play.

I went down early to the Green Room while Daniel was playing his final encore and found Leo already waiting there. He embraced me.

'Well,' he said, and I saw that his eyes were red and filled with unshed tears. 'Our boy needn't worry any more about pleasing the public. He's still a star – and what a bright one.'

How few people, I have often thought, have the privilege to see the work and anguish that goes into a performance of great music. As I watched Daniel thanking the staff who were also clapping him as he left the stage, I felt very humble and wondered how to greet the person who had inspired all this fervour. I shared most of my waking and sleeping hours with him, but now he inhabited a different plain, elevated above normal life and far beyond my reach.

I stood by the dressing table in the Green Room and Daniel came through the stage door still followed by a billowing cloud of applause. He was smiling as I went to meet him.

'Noisy lot, aren't they'

'Clever old thing,' was all I managed to say and he pulled me onto his lap.

'Darling, darling Irena – it went OK didn't it? I think I played quite well ...' but I didn't answer. I picked up his hands and kissed them, one finger at a time.

'Clever old hands ...' I said and then I busied myself wiping the make-up off his face before he went out to meet yet more adulation.

Magda and Sam were there, of course, already lined up with Leo and, pushing to the front of the throng was a shaven-headed man there I'd not seen before. His left sleeve was empty, I noticed, as he threw himself at Daniel almost before he was through the door.

'My God – Sandy!' Daniel was embracing him. 'Surely this isn't your sort of gig?'

'Pete asked me to stand in for him. He's in Helmand again. Christ, it's lucky it was me who lost the hand and you your legs. Otherwise we'd both be out of a job!' And the two men laughed together for a few moments before Daniel had to move on. He was exhausted, but also elated. Only the way he rocked backwards and forwards in his chair told me that he was in pain. How he had got through the second half of the concert and three encores I have no idea. The applause still ringing in his ears, he went home that night with the assurance that he would resume his career, and he fell asleep a deeply contented man.

Irena got out of bed carefully, so as not to disturb Daniel who was still asleep. She took the newspaper out of the brass cage inside the front door and went into the kitchen to make herself a cup of coffee. Then she searched the pages for Edward Waterstone's promised review of Daniel's concert. It was there on the arts page and surprisingly long. She read it nervously.

Wigmore Hall, June 17, 1997

Piano Recital

DANIEL DANUCZEK Fortepiano

J S Bach. The Goldberg Variations

HE'S BACK!

Daniel Danuczek looked understandably nervous as he appeared on stage at the Wigmore Hall last night. This was his first public performance since after playing a series of benefit concerts two years ago, in Sarajevo, he was shot in the back by a sniper on the balcony of his hotel room. He now needs a wheelchair to get about, but has never wavered in his determination to resume his career as a concert pianist.

It is not unusual for a performer to receive a standing ovation at the end of a concert, but last night when Danuczek came onto the stage and turned his wheelchair to bow to the audience, he saw that they were all standing. Clearly moved, the pianist hesitated and then a wide smile spread over the famous face, which is as startlingly handsome as ever. He raised his arms above his head, clasping his hands in a gesture more familiar on the football pitch than the classical concert platform. As he took up his position by the keyboard of his own fortepiano, the audience responded as always to his raised right hand and, when they had resumed their seats, he began to play.

Last month I had the pleasure of an interview with Danuczek at his Kensington flat next to the Albert Hall. The usually suave musician greeted me wearing a track suit, unshaven and with a towel around his neck. Confined to a wheelchair for over two years now, he has to organise his life around rigorous daily sessions of physiotherapy, one of which he had just finished. I saw that he was wearing leg-braces – 'state of the art', he told me wryly – and he explained that these enable him to stand between the parallel exercise bars which have been installed next to the exquisite painted harpsichord in his spare bedroom.

We sat in his music room, alongside his piano, a Broadwood grand, and drank champagne, talking about the changes that being unable to use his legs have made to his pianism.

'Thing is,' he began, reminding me that, although he has now spent most of his life in England, there are still traces of his native Czech in Danuczek's slightly accented speech, 'I have horror of using any of the gadgets that would make it possible for me to use the pedals – particularly the sustaining pedal. And I don't want to rely on a specially adapted piano. I must be able to play wherever I find myself, you see. My hands are large with long fingers, so I was working at first with the 'finger pedalling' technique and achieved a pretty good legato – holding notes down while I am on to the next passage, so to speak. But I have had to accept that this is for myself, for my own pleasure. A public performance demands a greater degree of perfection.'

If this was difficult and painful terrain for him, he gave no sign of it, and even laughed a good deal as he demonstrated his problems for me at the keyboard.

'As you know,' he explained, 'many of the earlier works – those written before, say, 1780 or so – were written for instruments without pedals. So I am wedded these days to a fortepiano – wonderful Austrian instrument. Come and see her – she lives in the dining room. She's very excited as I'm taking her to the Wigmore Hall with me ... ' Danuczek was laughing as I followed him into the dining room.

Before I left, my host showed me a picture of his fiancée, the Bosnian violist Irena Vidaković. 'I can never resist a viola – my second favourite instrument. Oh, and she's very lovely too!' The couple first met in Sarajevo when he was teaching there at the Conservatory. Happily reunited, they are to be married next week.

In choosing to play the Goldberg Variations for the first half of the concert, Danuczek was wearing his heart on his sleeve. He has twice recorded this iconic and enigmatic work, once when he was still in his teens and the second time not long before his last ill-fated tour of Bosnia, where he played it at the Sarajevo Conservatory, following it with three works by the Croatian composer, Lysinski. There, the audience recognised in his playing the musician's personal tribute to their constancy and courage throughout the unimaginable horrors they were still enduring, and there was scarcely a dry eye amongst those who thronged afterwards around his tall, energetic figure.

To play the Goldberg was a courageous choice then, as indeed it was last night, and one in which to demonstrate that not only was he still possessed of the same unshowy virtuosity; his delicate voicing and very personal articulation are as refined as ever. The signature clarity of the immaculate fingering – perhaps even helped by the complete absence of the pedalling that can often blur and obscure a performance – brought a heart-breaking tenderness to his interpretation of the beloved Bach. More remarkable yet, the 'third voice' that Glen Gould called the part played by the organ pedals and which he missed so much when he abandoned that instrument for the piano, was subtly implied throughout.

There must inevitably have been some members of the audience waiting to see whether his physical trauma had affected this artist's abilities and whether they were to witness an embarrassing diminution of his former musicianship. Perhaps some expected a programme chosen to give the performer as little anguish as possible on this auspicious occasion. If they did, they would not have waited long for confirmation that, although Daniel Danuczek may not be able to walk, his fingers are still able to dance and they bring from the keys a song that is as sweet as ever.

26. PETER HAS NEWS

DANIEL was dressed and ready to leave for the Register Office when the telephone rang. It was Peter.

'Just thought I'd wish you luck. And happiness and all that.' He was calling from Paris, unable to make time to come over for the wedding. 'I've got some news for you – I may as well tell you now and you can choose your time to tell Irena.'

'About the child? You've heard something?'

'Yes, and I suppose it's good news. He's alive. Milić's mother-in-law took him away from Irena at birth – Irena was in a very bad way and the baby didn't look as though he would live either. But he did and the widow – Vukašin Milić was killed shortly after Irena's escape – brought the child up. She has no children of her own and this must have been the baby she was nursing when I went to see her that time. Anyway, this isn't the moment to go into it all. I hope this will be happy news for Irena. Not without difficulties, of course ...'

Daniel hardly knew how to reply, but he thanked Peter and made some jokes about the wedding. Then he hung up and went down to the cab where Sam and Magda were waiting for him.

A few weeks earlier, Peter had been in London on a flying visit and checked in at his club. Depressed by the situation in Afghanistan, his next assignment, he was glad to see that Daniel had left a message with the porter. Would there be time for them to meet before Peter went off again? He needed to talk about something – rather urgently.

'Great. Come to lunch? Tomorrow?' Daniel turned up, wearing a dark suit and a cheerful tie. The men greeted each other with an embrace.

'My God, you do look smart. It's years since I've seen you in anything except joggers or a hospital gown ...' Daniel did look markedly better than Peter remembered seeing him, and not just because of his newly trimmed hair and the very superior cut and cloth of his suit; there was something else.

'Magda told me I look very scruffy these days and I should smarten up. Actually I had to go to my tailor to get all my suits altered. Nothing seems to fit me now – I've got the shoulders of a prize bull and the legs of a heron. And I need zips now in very odd places – but a visit to Savile Row can make anyone look normal.'

'So it seems – no one would guess how deformed you are,' Peter said, shaking his head with amusement as he looked down at his own well-worn grey pin-striped suit, whose trousers had been pressed under his mattress.

Daniel looked at his friend and wondered if he was attractive to women. His manners were good, but he seemed to have no gloss, and probably no vanity. His thin, narrow face, topped with thick brown hair that grew up from his forehead in a cow-lick, was rather austere, but his hazel eyes were lively and humorous. Daniel had learnt to respect him from their first moments together in Bosnia. Maybe because Daniel was so used to the company of other musicians, the journalist opened a window on another world altogether. Daniel found himself fascinated by the breadth of the other man's experience, and enjoyed being given a new and wider vision of the trouble spots of the world, constantly revising his own rather lazily formed opinions, usually based on the last newspaper he'd read.

Their friendship had been forged out in Bosnia and the

traumatic circumstances of his shooting had brought them closer together as Daniel's progress from helpless patient to resentful paraplegic had wrung his friend's heart. To see Daniel now, elegant and cheerful, even lending a certain glamour to the gleaming metal chair in which he moved skilfully and with great energy, was something he could not have predicted in those early days. Added to which, he hugely enjoyed Daniel's company, his refreshing enthusiasm and sense of the ridiculous.

The two sat in the club's Morning Room and Peter ordered a bottle of champagne. 'Not as grand as you're used to, but it's not bad this house champagne.'

'Tastes great, and here's to your next trip. How lovely Kandahar used to be. What a tragedy ...'

'So' said Peter, 'Spill the beans. What's up that can't wait a few weeks?'

'Have a guess.'

'No idea. With you it could be anything, let's face it. But tell me first about Irena. She must have been back in London for a while now. How's she getting on?'

Daniel took another sip of champagne before he answered. 'Playing in a new quartet, doing well ...'

'And how is she in herself? Still very low?'

'No. She's pretty cheerful actually.' Daniel put his drink down and paused, his face inscrutable now. 'So cheerful she's agreed to marry me.'

'Good God – now that is a surprise. And I haven't even met her yet to see if she's suitable. Poor girl. Does she know what she's in for?'

'You are a bastard. What about congratulations and things?'

'Tell me more first. When did this all happen? When we last spoke things were a bit gloomy – she was having nightmares and you were worried about her.'

'Yes, I was. Very. And it was quite a responsibility bringing her back here. But we got on so well, just as we used to, in spite of everything that had happened to us both ... I can't imagine life without her now.'

'And how does she feel about your disability?'

'Seems she's known other short-sighted people ...' Seeing Peter's face, Daniel became serious, 'Ok, you mean the chair? I was worried about that of course. To begin with I felt she would always compare me with how I was when she first knew me – all that dancing and rushing around we used to do. I hated getting in and out of the car and so on in front of her – got really embarrassed. But she's extraordinary – very quickly learnt how I do things now and she teases me a lot. I think I've been able to help her too. She said once that my damage shows and hers doesn't. A good way to look at it. But she is still very delicate emotionally. I suppose she always will be and I want to make sure nothing ever hurts her again. She's the best thing that's ever happened to me.'

'So you popped the question? How did she react?'

'She danced around the room and she grabbed hold of my chair and danced me around. She was laughing and crying at the same time.'

'But you were very worried about the physical thing?'

Peter's frankness didn't surprise Daniel – as a journalist he always told it as it was, but Daniel didn't answer at once. He thought of Irena when they had parted that morning. She had interrupted his practising to say goodbye before she went off for a rehearsal and sat down on his lap, turned herself round and wound her legs around him, her mouth against his, her hand busy lower down. Daniel smiled at the memory and Peter saw his friend's colour deepen.

'Ah, I see you *are* getting your oats. Fantastic. So, when do you get hitched?'

'Two weeks' time. I've got my first Wigmore concert on the 17th. Wedding on the 24th. Kensington Register Office.

I wish you could be there. Don't get yourself into trouble in Afghanistan, will you? Luck can run out, you know.'

The two men went into the dining room, Peter exchanging the odd word with other members as he passed their tables. A few people recognised Daniel, but Peter sensed that he was embarrassed by their sympathetic curiosity. Lunch was ordered and the men began to talk and laugh. The wine arrived, the cork was drawn and Peter raised his glass.

'Right. Congratulations. I really mean it. You deserve a good woman and she sounds as if she fits the bill.'

Daniel bowed his head, suddenly overcome with emotion. When he looked up again his eyes were filled with tears. 'I would never have found her again without you. I might even have given up looking ...' But Peter was remembering that Daniel would not have been shot had he not been mistaken for him. They looked at each other, their thoughts back in Sarajevo.

'Come over when you get back. You must meet Irena – we'll be married by then. She's very curious about you.'

Peter turned up in Prince Albert Mansions a month later to find an apologetic Daniel. Magda was not well and Irena had gone over to see her. She'd be back as soon as she could, but Peter couldn't wait, so she didn't meet him that evening and they were both disappointed. The two men drank for a while and then Daniel brought out some photographs of his year in Sarajevo. Peter held a picture in his hand, a photograph of a young girl on a bicycle. Her appearance moved him for some reason but he only said, 'Far too good for you, I should think. How's her cooking?'

27. TYING NEW KNOTS

I RENA SPENT the night before their wedding with Ollie and was sitting with Magda and her hostess eating their supper, when there was a knock at the front door. She heard Daniel's voice, but, as Irena was superstitious about their wedding eve, he did not come in. He had left her a small parcel and the two women watched curiously as she opened it. Seeing that it was a book, she remembered him saying excitedly on his return from Sarajevo:

'You know that second-hand book shop we used to go to – down by the Latin Bridge – well, he's opened up again. Full of stuff looted from empty houses, I suppose. Anyway, I was looking for something to get for you, but I wasn't sure what. Then I found this. I've been bursting to give it to you, but now it can be your wedding present.'

Irena, her face as excited as a small child's on Christmas Day, pulled the string off and tore away the paper, revealing a well-worn copy of *Middlemarch*. She turned the book over and then, her hands trembling, opened it and read the dedication on the flyleaf:

> *To Darling Irena, on her tenth birthday, from her loving aunt Kristina, This is my favourite English novel – for you to read when you are older. 5th September, 1985.*

Below was written, in neat, childish writing:

> *This book belongs to:*
> *Irena Kasimira Finola Vidaković,*

Vila Dolena
Nevinosti Street
Sarajevo
Yugoslavia
The World
The Milky Way
The Universe

Leo tapped his glass with his spoon. The room fell silent and he moved over to stand next to Daniel and Irena. The groom tugged at his sleeve in the attempt to stop him speaking, but Leo ignored him and refilled his glass and Daniel's.

'I haven't been asked to speak, but I'm going to anyway. This is a very special occasion for me. Daniel was one of my first artists. As a teenager he was already sending all the women swooning and he played the piano like a dream. So I thought I had it made. But he wasn't a soft touch, this Daniel of fifteen – I won't go into his tantrums and bad language – you'd all be far too shocked.'

'Now, eighteen months ago I went to see him in hospital.'

Daniel, who had been hanging his head in mock shame, shifted in his chair – this was surely something no-one wanted to hear – least of all him.

'He was as weak as a kitten and as miserable as hell. All of us who knew him wondered how he was going to cope with the rotten trick that life had played on him. Well, just look at him now. I'm thankful to say that one of my most lucrative artists is back on form – he plays just as well as ever, he looks terrific and I shan't be bankrupt after all. He's been going around for weeks now looking revoltingly like the cat that's stolen the cream. And I know whom we have to thank for that. No, Irena, don't hide over there. Come here – yes, this is the girl who has put our Daniel back, not only sitting extremely pretty again, but even briefly on his feet this afternoon – I hear he refused to be married looking up at his bride. I'd forgotten how tall you are, Danny – always made me feel very inferior, so your chair has been something of a relief to my ego. Anyway, we were treated to a few minutes of his former, towering self, which left the lady Registrar all of a dither, I noticed.

'Daniel and Irena first met in Sarajevo at her family home. The events they lived through over the next few years could have destroyed them both, but not these two. Then Fate brought them together again a year ago … It's clear they were made for each other. So, please raise your glasses to Daniel and Irena, and wish them every happiness – much of which I suspect they've already found'

Amidst applause, laughter and cat-calls, a group detached themselves from the crowd. Daniel's long guest list had been made up of musicians from all over the world. Now Jean-Yves, Steven, and Izak took over the piano and music stands and began to play. Some of the other guests threw themselves into their national dances then, others jived or waltzed or polkaed until Magda began to fear for the strength of the floor.

Irena, sitting now on Daniel's lap, had laughed at Leo's speech, but some of the words stirred up her painful recurrent conviction that the rotten trick that fate had played on her husband was her fault and if he had not been looking for her, he would not have been the target of that sniper; he would be dancing at his wedding.

'My darling wife, what is it? Don't be sad, not now. Don't you like your wedding?'

'It's been lovely, really lovely, but …'

'I think we could go home now if you want to. I know you can't wait to make love to me.'

They had decided to postpone their honeymoon as they were soon to head out to Bosnia together. But, as Sam drove them home, Daniel wished painfully that he could take Irena off to somewhere romantic and far away.

They found the flat filled with flowers whose scent greeted them as they came through the door, Irena on her husband's knee, and Daniel took his wife to their room, and there were flowers there too, everywhere.

'You can't wear a tee-shirt on your wedding night,' Daniel had said the week before. Spread out on the bed was a creamy lace and satin nightdress. A pair of swan's-down slippers lay on the floor beneath. Irena pulled the nightdress on over her head and looked down at her shimmering body. Then she jumped off the bed and ran around the room with tiny dancing steps amongst the lilies and roses, her little hands imitating the fluttering wings of a delicate bird, as she laughed and pirouetted, her arms outstretched. Finally, she kicked the slippers off across the room, leapt onto the bed and flopped down beside her husband, rosy and panting. Daniel caressed the satiny whiteness of his wife's body in the moonlight before he slid the nightdress over her head and sent it sailing and drifting into the silvery darkness.

28. RETURN TO SARAJEVO

I RENA was lying in the hotel's cavernous, old-fashioned bath, her eyes shut, and Daniel was at the wash basin, shaving. He wiped his face and pushed himself alongside her, his hand feeling for her through the scented bubbles. She opened her eyes, caught his fingers and kissed them. 'That looks very inviting,' said Daniel. 'If I got in with you do you think I'd ever get out again?'

'I don't think now's the time to try – it might take a while to get the fire engine and we'd be late for the concert.'

'Shame. Maybe tomorrow.'

Irena stood up in the bath and Daniel held out a towel to receive her as she stepped out. She was so slight, so little, he thought. So fragile. For all he had tried to prepare her, the shock of seeing Sarajevo after so long and the city so changed, had been worse than he'd anticipated. And the next day was also going to be a hideous one for her. He wished he could go with her, but she had insisted on going alone and he had acquiesced, remembering the rugged mountain roads and unreliable taxis; he would simply be one more burden.

Daniel and Irena had been married for three days when he told her Peter's news. He had watched her carefully as he spoke and Irena, who had been looking at him, turned away and said nothing for a few minutes. She seemed not to have heard. Then she put her coffee cup down and dropped her head into her hands.

'His mother knows you are alive and has asked you to come and see them,' said Daniel quietly. 'She sounds like a very brave woman.'

'Oh yes. Yes, she is – I remember her so well. She saved me from despair.'

They dressed for the concert, Daniel wearing a dark blue Nehru jacket Irena had bought him. He'd laughed as he tried it on and told her about his father's reaction to the flashy blue coat he had ordered when he was seventeen and how, to please him, he had gone back to wearing a tail suit and white tie. Thus formally dressed for his first concert in Sarajevo, he had seemed to Irena the acme of glamour.

That evening, Daniel would have loved to play again at the Conservatory, to see the concert hall again where he had spent so many days teaching on the Bösendorfer piano that he had come to love. He had heard that the builders who had restored the school after the war had insisted on leaving the hole made by a mortar bomb in the wall, covering it with a sheet of glass so that it remained as a painful reminder of a terrible time in the history of the old building. It would have been wonderful to be playing there again, but the music school was at the top of six flights of marble steps. The concert was to take place, instead, in the school on the ground floor at the far end of the building. Those of his old friends and fellow musicians who had survived the war and stayed on in the city would be there to greet him. The programme had been chosen from the Baroque repertoire with compositions from Serbia, Croatia and Bosnia. Daniel had finally finished the school anthem he had been composing, and would conduct the orchestra and choir in its first performance to finish the concert. It was based on Psalm 84, with the line from the King James version which had inspired him: *'Blessed is he who, going through the valley of pain, maketh it a well'*.

[IRENA]

The lights dimmed and Sam pushed Daniel up the ramp and onto the stage. He propelled himself along the side of the piano, turned to the audience and bowed from the waist. The wave of applause that rose from the auditorium took him by surprise; it swelled to a deafening roar and people stood by their seats shouting: 'Maestro, Maestro! Welcome back to Sarajevo.'

Daniel bowed again, his hand on his heart this time Then he went to the keyboard. A hush descended, almost magically, as though his presence alone gave him total command of this vast gathering. I had heard Daniel play many, many times, but it was always an extraordinary experience. Even now that I was his wife and knew him so well, I never ceased to marvel at the depths of the man in his musicianship, at the rich variety of his skills. He opened the concert with a series of Bach Chaconnes, and that evening he seemed to surpass himself. As he ended the first suite there was again a hush, just for a minute or two, before the audience again exploded in a great cacophony of applause. He was to play again at the end of the concert and would not normally have provided an encore after his first appearance, but there was no possibility of his escaping now without one; the audience would not let him go and, when he did leave the stage, they clamoured for him to return. After a few minutes, he shrugged his shoulders, laughed and asked to be pushed back onto the stage. He played a Scarlatti sonata which, though so different from the Bach, had a simplicity and clarity that stayed within the mood he had created. Then he left the stage and the orchestra played Smetena's *Ma Vlast* and I heard in it a hymn to my own beloved land, its wounded pride and ruined beauty.

In the Green Room during the interval, Daniel was again surrounded by the orchestra, whose musicians brought with them reminders of a happier time. A few original members of the orchestra had come back to play, some wounded, like the young flautist who now had only one eye and a dreadfully disfigured face. Those who remembered Daniel personally – they all knew of his reputation – were also pained to see the graceful, loping Adonis now sitting in a wheelchair. But his smile reassured them as he wrung their hands, accepted their embraces and laughed at the ridiculous misunderstandings that the multi-tongued conversation led them into as they reminisced about the time when Sarajevo was innocent of blood and a lovely cosmopolitan city.

During all that long evening, I tried hard to keep smiling. We had gone to a restaurant Daniel had often frequented before the Siege. The owner shook his head and there were tears in his eyes when he saw his former client so changed. The heavy, spicy food, dish after dish made me feel very sick and I longed for bed as yet another course was served, I knew I had to get out into the fresh air. Daniel had been sitting at another table, but, as I struggled to stand up, I heard his voice behind me and felt his hand on my shoulder.

'Darling, you aren't looking at all well. We could go now if you like …' I wasn't able to answer him, as the smoke-laden atmosphere in the room overcame me and I felt myself falling into darkness, as I slumped back into my chair and passed out.

I awoke in our hotel bedroom, where Daniel had undressed me and was sitting beside the bed.

'Oh Danny. I was sick, wasn't I? Oh God, I'm so …'

'Do you think you'll be well enough to go to Kureć tomorrow?'

'I have to go. I can't wait any longer. I have to see Lidija – and Stefan.'

❄

Trying to navigate the once-familiar streets of Sarajevo, Daniel still held an image of how beautiful the city had been when he had first known it. He didn't just mourn the gentle refinement of the Vila Dolena and the twisting alleys down to the Old Town, but the City Library and the elegant buildings that had lined the main street when he had first arrived there, many of which were missing, or mere shells; all were pocked with bullet holes. Mosques and churches were screened by shoring and fences. Entering the old market, he saw for the first time the painted red discs – Sarajevo roses – which marked the pools of blood where civilians had been gunned down as they went about their daily activities. His head again filled with their screams as he wheeled himself around between the stalls, almost overcome by the memories of the horrors he'd witnessed there.

That morning Daniel felt conspicuous in a way he had not expected, and mortified when a passer-by pressed coins into his hands as he sat in his wheelchair, trying to get his bearings. At first he had wondered why there were no other disabled war victims on the streets, but the truth slowly dawned on him as he struggled to push himself about. It was not just the cobbled areas that made progress difficult but potholes, missing kerb stones and sudden changes of surface.

Everything looked different. Only the shallow, brown river was the same as it flowed under the newly restored Latin Bridge. He saw, on the far side, a café he had once known well. He would go there for a beer and for a few moments he felt confident and independent again. He stopped by a crossing, waiting for the lights to change. A young man, also in a wheelchair, pulled up beside him. He had no legs from the knees down. Daniel looked away and studiously watched the lights, hoping they would change soon so that he could escape this disturbing sight. But the young man called to him, 'Aren't you Maestro Danuczek, who used to live with the Vidaković family?'

They reached the café and took over a table under the lime trees; most of the city's trees had been cut down for firewood, but these had been protected, Daniel later learnt, in a determined and dangerous act of civic pride. The young man, whose name was Kasimir, turned out to be a first cousin of Irena's. Daniel remembered him as a little boy who had loved playing card tricks after Sunday lunch at the Vila Dolena.

'I never even got the chance to fight,' he said bitterly. He was seventeen and had been working in his uncle's office when the bomb had gone off. He'd been in hospital for two weeks when they had told him they could not save his legs. He'd married one of the nurses and now worked in an IT department, but he dreamed that one day he'd be able to go to the States or Japan for some state-of-the-art prosthetics so he could walk again and play with his children.

'Didn't the West know what we were going through?' he asked bitterly.

'We did, though no one really understood – or what we should have been doing to help …'

Daniel told Kasimir of his attempts to bring music to the city and his fruitless search for the missing family.

'I was told pretty soon about Adam and Finola's terrible end, but no one knew where Irena was – I came out here three times and each time I drew a blank. Then, the evening before I left for London the last time I forgot about the blackout.'

'We heard what happened to you – it was all over town. What a shameful thing when you've done so much for the city.'

The two men were silent as they drank their beer. 'Did you know that Irena did survive and managed to get to America?'

'Yes – Hedija Tanović – she must be your aunt too – wrote to me more than a year ago. It was like a miracle, but Irena had been through a lot – she was very traumatized … Her aunt saved her reason, I think.'

Kazimir smiled then. 'Oh, dear Aunt Hedi! Is Irena OK now? She was always good fun – very naughty sometimes. She was mad about you, I remember. We all used to tease her.'

Daniel laughed, 'Yes, she's still fun ... And I hope she's still mad about me – we were married last month.'

'Not really? That's fantastic. Wait till I tell everyone. Is she in Sarajevo now?

Daniel thought how excited Irena would be to know her cousin was still alive; she would certainly want to see him and his family. 'We go back to London at the end of the week and I've got a few more engagements. Are you busy on ... ?' And he took out his diary.

They said goodbye, and, as he crossed the river and paused again to watch the turgid water between the frothy weirs, Daniel wondered how Irena was coping with the pilgrimage into the countryside which held such terrible memories for her.

29. IRENA'S QUEST

ONCE SHE had been convinced that her child had lived and she could soon see him, Irena never mentioned him to Daniel. It was as though she held the thought of her son in some quiet, private place and imagined things she could not share even with him. Understanding how hard it must be for her, Daniel never brought the subject up. Legally, he thought to himself, this must be a mare's nest. Goodness knows how the child's parentage could be proved, one way or another.

Then, to his surprise, Irena said to him the week before they set out for Sarajevo: 'Please don't be shocked darling, but I don't think I could bear to have Milić's child living with us. I need to say thank you to Lidija – she was such a special person and so terribly brave. But his father was – well, you know what he did to me. And the boy would always remind me of him. Oh Danny, I feel so wicked and heartless.'

Daniel had held her in his arms and kissed her bowed head. When he finally spoke, his voice was quiet. 'We're going out there next week. You can see the boy, anyway. You don't have to make any decisions yet. And I'm with you – whatever you want to do then.'

He hoped this was the right thing to say. He couldn't tell her not to visit her son. But he could see little joy in the addition of a Serbian boy to their household. That she, too, was unsure of the wisdom of such a move, surprised and heartened him. But he suspected that talking about this in London and actually seeing her child in her own homeland were two different things; her emotions when she saw him would then be the natural feelings of a mother; he must be prepared to accept her decision if she found it impossible to leave the child again.

[IRENA]

Early next day I got into the battered car which would take me to Kureć, the village where Lidija still lived and where I would see my child. The drive took us out of Sarajevo on the road that Daniel and I used to take at the start of our bike rides into the dark and magical forest; very little was left of the trees now, just stumps, jagged and broken; the ground, churned up as if badly ploughed, was still littered with shell cases and the occasional blackened carcass of a car or tank. The sky, though, was a transparent blue, so that the shadows were also blue and brought beauty to a landscape that would otherwise have had none.

We found the village with difficulty; I could recognize nothing of the road or the buildings along its verges. The quaint, crumbling houses with their jutting tiled roofs, each property fronted by a vegetable patch, were gone. In their place were ugly, squat, newly-built houses and blocks of flats, totally without feature or charm. The bombing had obliterated so much that even churches and town halls had gone and nothing remained to give character to the hamlets and villages. But there were signs of rural activity again. The newly-cut hay had been heaped onto lopsided hay-cocks and some of the enclosures held a few sheep or goats.

I had to ask to find Lidija's house, reluctantly using her married name which stuck in my craw as I said it. Eventually, an old peasant, whose face was creased and furrowed by sun and work, gestured towards a low house at the end of the village street. I stood outside it for a minute, afraid to knock on the door. Then I saw a face peering from a window and the door was opened. A few minutes later a woman came out. She wore a bright woollen headscarf, tied at the back of her head. Her ample form was accentuated by an apron which bound her below her globular breasts and above a bulging stomach, against which she was clasping a large loaf, the breadknife held somewhat threateningly in her other hand.

'*Tragim Gda Milić – Lidija,*' I said. The woman smiled then, showing yellow teeth. She gestured me into the house, the interior of which was so dark that I stood as if blind until my eyes became accustomed to the gloom. Another woman came forward and threw her arms around me, crying loudly to all around her that she had found me again. Lidija smelled strongly of a mixture of things, not unpleasant but earthy and spicy, and her face, though aged and weathered by working all the year in the fields, was the same, her eyes the kind, humorous eyes that had given me courage to stay alive. Around her stood and sat a roomful of women and children.

I scanned the faces in the row of children, boys and girls of all ages and all looking curiously at me. Then I saw the little boy who had moved to stand next to Lidija. His eyes were not black like the others and nor was his hair dark. He had grey eyes and red-brown hair. His skin was darker than mine, tanned by the sun, but the rest was me. Terrified that this should be as obvious to the others as it was to me, I turned away from the line of children and implored Lidija with my eyes to go outside with me. We went out of the dark little house into the sunshine and she motioned me to sit down on a bench by the haycock in the vegetable patch.

'You knew your son? His eyes are the same as yours. I named him Stefan.' And then she said. 'My husband died, thank God – Vukašin was a terrible man.'

✳

Lidija smiled at the thought of the summer days the whole village made hay together. All women now, since their men had been taken away and none had come back, they threw themselves into the work, sweating and laughing and, finally, sitting together around a fire and roasting a rabbit or two, drinking beer and thinking the world not a bad place now that peace had come. No one in that village could forget, could ever forget, the terror of that warfare. The terror of never knowing who would disappear next or which village would be burnt to the ground or which female relative raped until she could no longer stand, Now, at peace, they were poor, but they had a bit of land and they had each other and, at the moment, God be praised, they were all in good health. She was still speaking when the old woman came out with two small beakers of thick, sweet coffee and, for a few minutes they drank in silence.

Then Irena spoke, 'Does Stefan like school?'

'Oh yes – he works very hard and he can read well already. I hope he'll go to college if we can afford for him to go away from the farm ... I've been saving up ... Otherwise he'd serve an apprenticeship. But now ...'

Lidija's voice tailed off as she remembered that she was not Stefan's mother, that his real mother was sitting opposite her in that lovely coat and expensive boots, clean and refined and undoubtedly wanting to take the boy with her. She felt a sharp pain in her heart, but she had known so much suffering that it had been an extraordinary thing to have lived so happily and peacefully of late. She could not expect it to last. She bowed her head and said, very quietly: 'When will you take him back to England with you?'

Irena took Lidija's roughened hands in her own smooth ones. Irena asked, speaking slowly so as to be understood with her Sarajevan accent, foreign in those parts.

'Does he know you are not his natural mother?'

'No' said Lidija vehemently. 'No he knows nothing of his birth. I never thought I'd see you again. He did not need to know and has been a happy boy.'

'Then he must remain a happy boy,' said Irena quietly. 'You saved my life and Stefan's. I've thought about you so often and wondered what happened to my baby. I so badly needed to see him, but he is your child now, Lidija. I cannot give him what you have given him. Our lives are so different. Stefan wouldn't be happy without you. Please don't ever tell him that you aren't his mother. This will be our secret for always.'

Lidija's face cleared and she burst into tears throwing herself on Irena's neck and kissing her over and over again. Irena's last view of the house was of all the children standing outside and waving to them, smiling and waving. Lidija stood a little apart and Stefan pressed himself against her skirts. As the taxi drew alongside them, and Irena wound down the window, she just heard the whispered words, '*Hvala ti za mog sina*. Thank you for my son.'

Arriving back in Sarajevo at the hotel, Irena, knowing that Daniel would be back late, crept into bed, pulling the covers over her face. The nausea had returned and she wanted only to sleep.

Daniel had to wait until morning before she woke in his arms and he could ask her diffidently about her day. For a moment she was silent, then she burst out, breathlessly, 'I saw Lidija – she hasn't changed.'

'And you saw the boy?'

She nodded.

'And?'

'Well – he's just a little boy, but he looks like me – he's got my eyes, anyway.' Gradually and far from fluently Irena related the sequence of the day, pausing often in her account of the journey to Kureć, of her search for the house and, finally, of seeing Lidija and Stefan. Then, after a long pause, she told Daniel, haltingly and tearfully, of her decision. 'Oh Danny,' she sobbed, 'before I saw Stefan, I was afraid I'd long to take him away to live with us – that I'd feel all stirred up and maternal – but all I could think about yesterday was that he is Lidija's life – they are so close and happy. It would be a terrible thing to do. He doesn't know the story of his birth.'

Irena went to the window. Sarajevo lay spread out in the sparkling morning light, so beloved and so mortally damaged. After a few moments she turned back and sat down beside Daniel. 'He doesn't need to know, does he? Have I made the right decision?' She seemed uncertain now.

'If that's what you really want and don't think you'll come to regret it, then you have made absolutely the right decision. I wish I'd been able to be there … I felt so useless.'

'No. I had to go there on my own.'

Though secretly relieved for himself, Daniel knew Irena well. He knew that she would chastise herself for what she would view as cowardice in her rejection of her child. That was the way she was. He wondered if the birth of another child, one that they shared, would perhaps lessen her tortured guilt.

Irena was silent at first when Daniel told her about his meeting Kasimir. Then she said, 'I'm not sure I could bear to see him like that – I mean with no legs. He was so sporty as a boy. Have you got his number – I could just call him and have a chat?'

They were sitting up in bed and Daniel put his arms round her. 'He's still a handsome chap … and you've got used to me like this, haven't you?'

Irena still remembered her turbulent feelings in the days after Hedija had told her that Daniel would never walk again, and agreed to join the lunch party. But, overcome with the emotion of meeting her cousins and their entourage of old friends, and feeling desperately sick, she excused herself early and went back to the hotel. Daniel returned an hour later and felt her forehead, saying, 'I think we should call a doctor.'

He reached for the telephone, but Irena took the receiver out of his hand. 'I'm just still upset about being back here again – and seeing Stefan. And poor Kasimir. And driving through our forest – what's left of it. It's all been too much …Please don't worry, though – I won't starve and you'll be cooking the things I like when we get home.' She smiled for a moment, thinking how good it would be to get back to her life in London and to put Sarajevo and its new ugliness away at the back of her mind. Then she looked up at Daniel. 'Will you really get Kasimir over to the States and have him fitted with new legs?'

'Yes, of course I will. We'll get him fixed up and then he can enjoy his kids and even do some sport again. Prosthetics are amazing now.'

'You're such a star, darling…'

'No, I'm not. But I was lucky – I'd earned enough to be able to buy the kit that wasn't on the NHS – state-of-the-art wheelchairs and stuff. It makes a tremendous difference to how you feel about yourself – especially when you're young like Kasimir.'

Daniel had one more engagement before he went home, a Scarlatti recital at the Military Hall. He told Irena to stay in bed but she tried not to sleep, knowing that her dreams would be full of ugly spectres of suffering and broken lives.

They hired a taxi on their last day and drove to the road they used to take to the woods with their bikes. Everything had changed and it took them a while to guide the driver towards the once familiar path. The great dark forest outside the city walls had been decimated, thousands of trees cut down, so that the meandering tracks where he had bicycled with Irena had vanished and nothing but blackened tree stumps and the courageous sprouting of new saplings littered the naked hills amongst craters and areas marked out with red tape. 'Let's get out and go a little way, shall we? The ground's quite hard.' Irena and the driver took Daniel's chair out of the boot and unfolded it. Daniel was not as enthusiastic about this venture as she was, wondering how far he'd get before his wheels stuck in the rutted clay. He was better at judging this than Irena, but she was so longing to go that he slid into his chair and followed her. She ran ahead a little and he wished he'd brought with him the wide outdoor wheels that would have made this trip easier. But he pushed himself hard and caught her up, out of breath with the exertion. Irena, looked around her, frowning: 'What are those red ribbons over there – the ones marking off that area up the hill?'

'They're uncleared landmines – thousands were laid here during the war. They're trying to get them all out, but it will take years.'

Irena closed her eyes for a moment. 'Everything's spoilt. Absolutely everything.'

She walked on in silence until she saw what she was looking for. 'Look darling – see the river? This *is* the right path. That's where we used to picnic, isn't it?'

They stopped and looked between the charred tree stumps down the shell-pocked slope to the river bank.

'Let's go down,' said Irena, 'Can you make it, do you think?'

'I could probably get down all right, but you'd never get me back up that slope. Why don't you go on your own? I'll wait here.'

Irena shook her head. 'No. It wouldn't be the same.' She

shuddered. 'It's horrible here now. I wish we hadn't come.'

Daniel pulled her to him and put his arms round her. 'We're still alive, darling. That's what matters. We're alive and we're together. I'm a bit battered, like our taxi, but I'm still on the road, too.'

She laughed. 'Oh Danny – we never could have imagined we'd come back as husband and wife, could we?'

'It's extraordinary, isn't it? Though I sometimes found myself wishing then I could kiss you without breaking the law.'

She bent and put her lips on his, sliding her tongue between his teeth. Coming up for air, he gasped 'That would certainly have put me in prison!'

They found the café and Daniel was helped up the two steps by the owner. They went straight to the table where they'd sat before and the menu was the same. They studied it, trying to remember what they'd eaten that day. But Irena wasn't hungry and Daniel reached across the table and took her hand. This trip had been a terrible one for her: to see what remained of her beloved Sarajevo, to find old friends terribly changed and to hear news of those who were no longer alive. Then the journey through the once resplendent countryside, now laid bare, to find her child. How many women, let alone someone as fragile as he knew his wife to be, would have found the courage to face all this.

Irena, knew that she had been changed by the last two weeks and wondered if she had taken on adult womanhood at last.

'Maestro Daniel,' she said quietly.

'Yes?'

'I just wanted to tell you how much I love you and please don't leave me ever.'

'Why on earth should I leave you? You're my whole life. You must know that.'

Irena didn't answer. Then Daniel said, 'Why don't we go back to the hotel and not do the shops this afternoon. I rather think I need to lie down.' And Irena stood up briskly and followed him out of the café and across the square. Turning his chair, Daniel looked back at a hotel across the road and up at the balcony where once he'd stood, smoking a Turkish cigarette.

30. SECRET SORROW

[IRENA]

As soon as we were back in London, Daniel began to prepare for his next recital and was teaching regularly again. Busy though he was, I became aware that he was watching me more than usual, telling me to sit down and urging me not to walk too far in the park. My encounter with Lidija and Stefan had profoundly shaken me. I had known before I actually saw him that I could not ever be a mother to Milić's child and, when I had finally seen him, there was something in the boy that made my flesh creep. I knew that, even had Lidija begged me to take Stefan with me, I would have struggled to give a home to someone who had in him the genes of my torturer. It had, in the end, been made easy for me. I had even appeared brave and self-sacrificing. Daniel who knew better, woke me gently from my re-occurring nightmares, comforted me and did his best to keep me busy at his side.

I wondered if he had guessed the secret I had been keeping from him. Carrying Stefan at so young an age had damaged my stomach muscles and left my skin permanently marked and Daniel was fascinated by the silver striations on the sides of my belly and above my breasts. He was tracing them one morning with his delicate fingers.

'Lovely silver fish …'

'I hate them. Oh please let's have the light out.'

'You should be proud. You're a real woman. Look at your lovely tits – I think they're getting bigger, aren't they?'

I tried to cover my breasts with my hands but he took them away, an amused expression on his face.

'Have you got something to tell me?'

I couldn't answer him and he put his hand onto my belly, where I had recently become aware of a fluttering movement, like an imprisoned bird. I could feel it then.

'I was beginning to wonder how much longer I would have to pretend to be even more stupid that usual. Why didn't you tell me sooner?'

'I've rejected one child. What makes me fit to have another?'

Daniel stared at me, seeming bewildered. 'Couldn't you have talked to me about it? You make me feel as if I was nothing to do with this – our – baby? You haven't been thinking of having an abortion, have you?'

'Yes. But I was frightened ...'

I had pulled my dressing gown around me and sat on the edge of the bed, facing away from Daniel. 'I wasn't going to tell you ...'

'You weren't going to tell me? You were going to get rid of my baby and not even discuss it with me? I thought you'd like us to have children – we could have talked about it – and used something if you weren't sure. How could you be so cruel – get yourself pregnant with my child and then decide to kill it – without telling me.' Daniel was shouting as he swung himself off the bed into his chair and wheeled himself towards the bathroom. I ran round to him but he went in, slamming the door behind him.

Daniel and I didn't speak all that day and, although I'd heard him moving about, he hadn't played the piano. Each time I tried the music room door, it was locked.

Then, at last, I heard the key turn and he was sitting there looking up at me.

'Please, can't we talk?' I pleaded.

'Why now? You could have talked to me weeks ago. You'd

better go off and do whatever you want to do, since I have no say in this.' And he turned away.

'It's much too late for that now. I couldn't have gone ahead with it, anyway. It's your baby, too.'

'Oh really? I was beginning to wonder.' I had never seen Daniel so angry. I had never seen him angry at all, except when he was frustrated by something he couldn't do.

'Please try to understand – I just couldn't come to terms with being pregnant again. And all that pain … I'm frightened and I feel so alone.'

Daniel turned towards me.

'Alone? Oh darling, you aren't alone. You never will be alone again. As long as I'm alive. Come here.'

I went to him and knelt beside his chair. He took my shoulders and held me, looking into my face, and now his voice was very soft. 'I want to understand how difficult this is for you but darling, I'm only human. And I have worries about being a parent, too – look at me – I'm not exactly an ideal father, am I? Maybe neither of us is up to bringing up a family. We should have talked about this before. But, I'd love to have children – our children – and I really thought you would too.'

'Danny darling …' I reached out to touch his face and he caught my hand and held it.

'What?' he asked and I took both of his hands and held them to my belly. 'Please forgive me. We're having a baby and it's yours and mine and it's wonderful to have a bit of you growing inside me …'

It had never occurred to me that Daniel would ever want to live anywhere but the big mansion flat that had been his home since he was a boy. I was getting to know our part of London, but I hated the constant roaring of traffic along Kensington Gore and having to run the gauntlet with other residents and the porter, so our comings and goings seemed to be everyone else's business. And the whole scale of the area was so big, so grand that I secretly envied the people we visited in little terraced houses. So, when Daniel told me that he thought we should move to a house with a garden, where our child could play, the thought of finding somewhere that we'd chosen together thrilled me.

'Magda will be delighted if we sell this – it's half hers you know.' Daniel was saying, 'Why don't you go house-hunting and, when you find something you like, I'll come and have a look. But just remember how much space I need for my pianos – and my harpsichord – and me, too!'

I started my search just north of the park, cruising around in Daniel's Saab, which he had taught me to drive. I didn't like the big white mansions of the Pembrokes and being too near Portobello market would be a mistake. But then I found a little road with houses all painted different colours. I loved them at once; they were so unlike anything I'd known as a child. Sadly, they were very small, but then I saw two side by side, one painted pink, the other green. Both had *For Sale* signs and the twin houses seemed to beckon to me. They had long, narrow gardens, one with a big apple tree; the other had a large shed at the far end. I rang Daniel excitedly on my mobile, begging him to come and look. As I waited for him to arrive, a house martin flew in under the eves of the pink house and, peering up, I saw the nest and knew I had found our new home.

Daniel arrived in a taxi and the driver pushed his wheelchair down the ramp to where I stood in front of the pink house. He could see how excited I was, but looked puzzled as I showed him into the narrow hall and, as he followed me out into the garden, he said gently: 'It's charming – I do see that. And only one step up, but isn't it far too small for me and my wheels?'

'But look – that one's for sale, too. The green one. And see the shed – it would make a great practice studio for you. We could paint it blue.'

'Well, a studio – *ça c'est beaucoup dire …*' but he knew then why I wanted to live there – it reminded me of my home, of Vila Dolena and the garden with the fruit trees and the blue studio at the end. There, within sight of my bedroom window, Daniel had lived and made music when we were both young and life seemed to promise to be good to us.

The agent showed us the second house and I explained to Daniel how we could knock down some walls and make enough space for him and a growing family. He wasn't really listening, but looked at me with that kind, laughing look I knew so well. He didn't care what the house looked like or what had to be done to make it livable for him. He was simply delighted that I had found something I liked so much.

Daniel came into the music room when Irena was practising and listened for a few minutes. Then he handed her a sheaf of manuscript paper thick with notation in his hurried and accomplished writing. It was a piece he had been working on the last few days and the title was *Little Wren*. It was set for viola and piano, equal parts. Irena studied it and Daniel said:

'Let's have a go, together, when you've had time to look at it.'

Irena spread out the score on the kitchen table and began to study the piece. He was not going to let her off lightly she saw. All the things he had worked on with her all those years ago were there, the things she had been lazy over, practised sloppily, were there. But above all this, she saw the line of the melody, a lovely simple line and she knew it was for her, it was a portrait of her in sound and she wept, her tears spreading the ink on the manuscript paper making it illegible in places.

'Oh dear,' she thought, panicking now, 'He'll be furious. He's been working on this for days. She went back into the music room with the spoiled manuscript in her hand, looking sad and feeling a little frightened. 'You'll be cross, I know ...'

Daniel looked up, 'What is it? Don't you like my piece? Is it too easy for you?'

'No, it's lovely, but it made me cry – and look...' she held out to him the splattered page and he looked at it closely. Then he put it to his mouth and kissed the tear blots, one by one.

'You've made it much, much better, darling.' He was laughing now and pulled his old piano stool up beside his chair and sat her down on it.

'Let's just tidy it up a bit. Oh dear, it's very wet. I'll make another page. And Daniel put a clean sheet of manuscript paper on the music stand and began to write on it. He played a few notes of the piano part and then started to write Irena's viola part again, swiftly and without hesitation.

When he'd finished, Irena held out her hand for the wet copy, meaning to put it in the bin, but he shook his head and held onto it.

'I'll keep this in a safe place,' he said. The next day Irena came to the music room and they started to play together. Playing with him always reminded her painfully as well as joyfully of the long-gone Sarajevo days when he had inspired her with his gentle suggestions and almost uncanny insight into the problems the music posed for her. She marvelled that Daniel, for all his greater knowledge of music, would listen attentively when she queried an interval or disliked a bowing he had written for her, rewriting the passage sometimes at once, at other times after making her play several ways, his head cocked and his extraordinary sense of hearing picking up sounds and textures surely hidden from ordinary mortals.

For Daniel, writing music was the most natural thing in the world and he had no idea that most people viewed his facility with amazement. They had invited two friends over, artists both of them, called Eleanor and Franky. Franky wanted to paint Daniel's portrait and had spent much of the meal trying to persuade him to sit. Irena thought she'd love to have a portrait of Daniel – if it did him justice. Daniel was adamant.

'I'm not sitting still for hours while you fill the studio with turpentine fumes. And, anyway, there are plenty of photographs – and they make me look really good – very flashy, some of them, aren't they darling?'

Lunch went on longer than expected and Daniel excused himself half way through the afternoon; he had some work to finish.

'Are you writing something of you own – composing?' asked Eleanor.

'Oh no I just need a little cadenza for something I'm playing next week.'

Sam snorted with laughter.

'This man writes cadenzas as we write shopping lists.'

'*Ma che dici! È cadenze* – ees a lady word.' Daniel scolded, imitating the Italian stall-holder in Portobello Road. '*Cadenze! Cadenze! Due al prezzo di uno. Freschissime! Bellissime!*'

'Cheaper by the dozen?' Sam joined in, '*Non dire schiocchezze, tre per due! È facilissimo scrivere cadenze – lascia fare a me, non c'è problema.*' and Daniel disappeared into his studio, followed by our laughter.

As she neared the end of her pregnancy, Irena supervised the conversion of the houses. The flat had been sold and the furniture put into store while Daniel and she moved into a nearby hotel and he hired a practice room at Steinways. The studio, now sound-proofed and doubled in size, straddled the ends of the two gardens. Irena wanted to paint it herself, choosing exactly the blue she remembered so well. Daniel offered to help with the lower part, as she was having trouble bending, but he had never held a paintbrush before and Irena, convulsed with laughter, watched the rivulets of azure gloss that streamed down the walls and pooled on the paving. Daniel played at a recital the evening after his valiant efforts, the bright blue paint around his finger nails surprising the admirers who asked for his autograph.

The baby was due in a matter of weeks and Irena felt the urge to get things straight. Daniel had let her go through his bureau drawers while he stacked scores on top of the piano and Sam put them into neatly labelled boxes. She came across an envelope of photographs and looked through them, curiously.

'Where did you get this one of Mama? I've never seen it before. Did you take it?'

He took the picture from her and looked at it intently. He had indeed taken it and remembered the occasion vividly. Finola and he had gone for a walk together shortly before he left Sarajevo. She was relaxed and happy as they had walked through the back streets to a little grassy area with a seat and there he had taken a photograph of her wearing a soft yellow silk dress. He had first unpinned her golden hair and let it fall, as he liked it best, down onto her shoulders. In the picture Finola was looking up at Daniel, a half smile on her pretty lips and her hands were smoothing her hair down, as a slight wind was lifting it. He had been screwing up the courage to tell her that he had been summoned back to London by the Foreign Office to take his students and himself away from the increasing danger in Sarajevo; he knew that soon she would be in floods of tears and that there would be nothing he could do to help her. They had gone back to the studio and there he had held her in his arms until the first violent paroxysm of grief had subsided. Then she had run from him across the garden.

'Yes, I did.' Daniel knew the moment he had dreaded had finally come, as Irena put the picture back where she had found it and turned to him again.

'She was in love with you, wasn't she?' As she said the words, she wondered for a moment where his answer could lead them. If her mother *had* loved Daniel, perhaps it would be better not to know. But she had asked the question and Daniel did not avoid her gaze. Nor did he speak at once, and looking into his anxious, guilt-ridden eyes, Irena found that she was laughing.

'Oh darling – you were such a stud, weren't you?'

He was shocked by her words and pushed himself away from her. She followed him and knelt down beside his chair.

'Don't say anything, please. I don't need to know the details. She died so soon after you took that photo and she looks happy. She looks as I feel now.'

Daniel had dropped his head down in shame and confusion. He had to tell her that he had behaved badly, that he had been her mother's lover, that he had deceived his host, her father, Adam, who had been so good to him. She would have every reason to be disgusted, to find it impossible to forgive him.

For a vivid moment he remembered the knock on the studio door in the early hours of a morning not long before he had been obliged to leave Sarajevo. Half asleep, he'd called out, 'Who is it?' and he'd sat up, feeling for his glasses, but then become aware that Finola was standing by his bed, wearing a silk wrap and, taking his glasses out of his hand, she sat down beside him and took him in her arms. She had smelled wonderful – the warm, womanly smell that he loved. He did not resist her, but slipped the sheer covering from her shoulders and kissed the delicate line of her neck as his hands discovered the soft weight of her breasts.

Daniel knew that he would never have brought Finola to his bed had she not come to him that night. He'd have continued to admire and desire her across the dining table and to flirt gently as he accompanied her delicious singing. But when temptation had come, the young man had yielded to it, gathering the lovely woman to him and entering her soft body with a sigh they seemed to share. After that, she'd come to him most nights and he'd been surprised at how inexperienced she was in love-making. Then he'd taken pleasure in teaching her things she did not know about her own body and about his. She had come to him almost innocent and, after a few ecstatic weeks, had become a subtle and imaginative lover. Her passion for him began to dominate her days and nights so that a future that was not centred around the young musician seemed impossible. Daniel, however, had begun to regret his easy compliance. He tried to reason with her, but Finola would not listen. She begged him to take her away back to London with him and he was riven with guilt, knowing that they could not possibly plan a future together.

'And Irena?' He'd question, horrified by her suggestion.

'Oh lots of her friends have divorced parents. And she adores you – she'll be thrilled to have you as a step-father.'

Daniel felt wretched. He had betrayed two people who were now like family to him – enchanting, innocent Irena and her generous, hospitable father. And Finola was forcing him to make a choice that was no real choice for him. Half of him was in love with her – the passionate, spoilt young man for whom winning women had always been so easy – and the other half was horrified to see the damage he might be about to inflict. Then the summons had come from London and he saw a way out of the complicated foolishness into which his desire had led him.

Now Irena looked at him. She knew him well by now, but this was an expression she had never seen before on his face.

'Darling' she said, forcing him to meet her eyes again 'Have you been feeling guilty about this for a long time?'

Daniel nodded and turned away. 'I'm afraid I've kept pushing it to the back of my mind. I love you so much, my darling, and I was afraid of losing you. I should have confessed long, long ago. I'm despicable. And I'm ashamed. Pleased try to forgive me if you can ... I'll understand if you can't ...' Not knowing what to expect, he backed away from Irena, but she followed him and put her arms around him, laughing again.

'Sweet, darling Daniel. I know what you have given up for me. All that glamour and those frantic fans and beautiful women throwing themselves at you. And all I have to give you is my sad old self and I'm not even the good musician you thought I'd become.' She kissed the side of his neck before she spoke again. ' I suppose I knew really. You weren't all that discreet! But I didn't want to believe it. And now you've told me and I think of poor sweet Mama, I'm glad – I really am, that you were able to give her some happiness before she died that awful death. Can you understand that?'

'I can, but it's amazingly generous of you. I should have told you ages ago, but I couldn't bear the thought that you'd not want any more to do with me.'

'But you love *me* now and we're having a baby together. It's like a wonderful dream. You've told me now, so is there anything else I ought to know?' Irena was playful now as she continued to caress his neck.

'Well, as I'm in confession mode, I'd better tell you ...'

'Oh Lord, who else have you seduced under my nose?'

'No. Nothing like that. Do you remember me taking your

fiddle from you and playing the Walton piece and how surprised you were that I made it sound rather good?'

'Yes of course. Don't tell me there was a recording playing and you were miming to it?'

Daniel laughed. 'No. Not quite so ingenious. The Sunday before you'd gone off to a family party and left your viola and music in the studio. So I started seeing how much I could remember – it was ages since I'd played a stringed instrument. I ended up learning your piece pretty thoroughly. I meant to tell you when I played to you and your parents, but it was such fun seeing how impressed you all were!'

Irena considered this second confession in silence, her head still tucked under Daniel's chin.

'What a very bad person I've married. And I thought you might be perfect. Hedi said she thought it unlikely and now I know you're a rat and a liar, too. And a show-off.'

'Help! Please don't go on. Wait till I catch you out.'

Although bookcases and shelves and cupboards had been built for him in the new studio, Daniel continued to survey the stacks of unopened archive boxes with increasing dismay. Unused to organizing his own surroundings, he sat there, gingerly taking the lid off each box and promptly putting it back again. Irena watched him with amusement, unaware of quite how traumatic the process was and how it had disrupted his working life. Too pregnant now to lift the heavy boxes, she was showing him where everything should go, when Daniel erupted: 'For God's sake, why the hell are we doing this? You might be enjoying playing at houses, but I'm not. Let's see if they'll sell the flat back to us. I really can't live like this ... I'm weeks behind with my work.'

'Danny, it was you who suggested moving. You know you did. All that about a sandpit in the garden for the baby – that was your idea. I don't think you've ever done anything for yourself, have you? Always your mother or Magda picking up the pieces so their precious boy doesn't hurt his lovely hands …'

Irena stopped and sat down. Very pregnant now, she was hot and out of breath and getting so angry sent her blood pressure soaring. She wondered if she was going to faint. Daniel, who had been staring at her as she blew her top, her face getting redder and redder, steered her over to his daybed.

'Sweetheart. Calm down, you'll start the baby off.' He put a cushion behind her head and pulled himself up next to her.

'I'm sorry,' she began, but he touched her lips with his fingers to stop her talking.

'No, it's I who should be sorry. You're right. I have never done any of these things before and I'm no help to you at all.' He started to laugh. 'Do you really think I'm spoilt? How appalling. And I thought you liked me.' He was kissing her now and stroking her great belly.

'The trouble with Daniel,' Irena thought, closing her eyes the better to enjoy his caresses, 'is that he's totally irresistible and he always gets away with everything.' She was too tired to carry on abusing him and couldn't think of anything else to say to stir him into action. He was far too good at deflecting her anger, but she didn't resent that: it was just one of his many talents, she had decided long ago, looking up into his laughing eyes, so magically blue and fringed with dark lashes. Irresistible.

Daniel did take Irena's tirade to heart and wished he knew what to do. It was true that he had never done the practical things other men do. He'd used his left-handedness as an excuse; he could never quite understand how things were put together. Also his mother had indeed taken care he should never endanger his hands with any activity that could harm them.

The next day, Sam, carrying a toolbox, turned up at the Pink and Green House – the new owners never changed the colour of the stucco and the two houses were always referred to that way now. He threw himself into the task of unpacking for Daniel and the two men talked and laughed as homes were found for the mountain of scores and manuscripts and books. Irena was relieved; now the studio would become somewhere where music could be made and Daniel would be happy in their new home. He'd spent a fortune on a new piano – a golden walnut Fazzioli, which stood in the middle of the studio, shrouded still with dust-sheets. He longed to get down to work on it, and with one more meticulous tuning it would be ready for him.

31. ARRIVALS

IRENA HAD BEEN to the garden centre and come back with the car loaded with fruit trees and flowers, which Sam was helping her to plant. Watching him through the open studio window, Daniel shouted: 'Hey, Sam you really are a dark horse. I had no idea you were a gardener as well as everything else.'

Irena, who was almost full-term, sat back on her heels, her face red with the exertion of filling in the holes. 'Oh, didn't you know – he's a great odd-job man – can do anything and everything – absolutely wasted on the piano.'

Sam grinned and wiped his hands down the side of his jeans before he extended one to Irena to help her up. She stood for a moment, an odd expression on her face as she looked down at the stream of liquid which was pouring out of her and onto the paving stones between her feet.

Sam yelled at Daniel, 'I think her waters have broken. Ring the hospital, will you.' He helped Irena to stagger towards the kitchen, clutching her stomach, an expression of terror on her face.

Moving house had been a help to Irena in the weeks that preceded her confinement, for, being busy and physically exhausted, she had managed to keep her mind off the terrors that the imminent birth held for her. Daniel and she talked about their child, he so excited sometimes that she wondered if all men were like this before the birth of their first baby.

Milić had not, of course, been anything but his usual cruel and insulting self while he had watched her belly increase in size, but there had also been triumph in his attitude to the young girl who was soon to bear his child. He was her captor, her violator. His offspring would be Serbian, a symbol of the dilution and oppression of a despised people. Daniel had listened as she wept beside him in their bed and told him about those agonised last days before her labour had begun. He felt helpless and quite unable to cope with the intensity of Irena's emotions and her constant re-living of the darkest experience he supposed a woman could know. 'My darling, nothing will ever be like that again. Look how happy we are together and soon you'll have a little person to care for – for us both to care for, because I'm not going to let you have all the fun.' And Daniel would smooth her hair away from her tear-stained face and cover it with kisses.

Irena was filled with apprehension although she had known for some time that she was to have a caesarean; she had been damaged giving birth so young. At the hospital, a large midwife shut herself in with the mother-to-be and prepared her for the operation.

Daniel was waiting in the corridor when he was summoned into the delivery room.

'My name's Monika,' the midwife introduced herself, handing him a gown and some other articles which he surveyed with alarm. 'You put these on now. Mr Goodbody's waiting for you. Your lady's pretty well dilated now, so we need to get our skates on. Come on, I'll help you.'

Daniel allowed himself to be attired in green scrubs, a theatre hat and mask and followed Monika to the delivery room. There, he wheeled himself up close to Irena's bed, hoping he wouldn't show any intimation of disgust and fear –

or faint, perhaps – as a low curtain was positioned over Irena's chest so that she would not witness the procedure, for she had asked to have an epidural so she could be conscious throughout. Mr Goodbody, the obstetrician, who, in Daniel's opinion, was too young and far too glamorous for such an occupation, explained what was about to happen. Irena looked up at Daniel's terrified eyes which were all that showed above the mask. 'Don't be scared, darling. It's not you having the baby,' she said, taking his shaking hand. She could not, however, see what he saw as he looked down the bed over the curtain that shielded Irena's view of the surgeon as he drew his scalpel across her stomach. A thin string of scarlet beads followed his knife and he cut deeper. Daniel wanted to look away but could not and watched in fascinated horror as the long wound was parted and the surgeon's gloved hands reached inside his wife's body.

Irena felt an odd tugging sensation and heard a sloshing sound from behind the curtain. Daniel looked down at her face, unable to believe that she could feel nothing of the violence that was being perpetrated on her little body.

'Here we are!' Mr Goodbody's voice was triumphant as, grinning, he lifted his arm high in the air, his bloody hand grasping the feet of a new baby, which hung, pink and glistening above the bed. It twisted in his hand, its red mouth opened and they heard its first spluttering, anguished cry as it tasted air for the first time. The sound caught Irena unawares and she felt pain then, a sharp pain in her breasts. She shut her eyes and turned her head away. Daniel pulled the mask from his ashen face and whispered.

'Darling, we've got a little girl and she's got a very loud voice.' Monika relieved the surgeon of the baby, wrapped her in a cloth, and brought her to the new parents, her broad face split in an enormous smile.

'Here's one beautiful little baby girl – aren't you going

to hold her?' Irena, her face still averted, did not move and Daniel held out his arms.

'I'll take her.' And he took his new daughter, who was still wailing her frantic, broken, new-born cry, and, weeping himself now, he laid her carefully on Irena's breast and the crying ceased as the baby seemed to sense the nearness of her mother. Irena still did not move or open her eyes. Monika was watching and Daniel felt he owed her an explanation and said, softly, 'She lost her first child ...'

Monika took the baby and left the delivery room with Daniel while the surgeon finished closing up Irena's wound.

'You OK?' she asked Daniel. 'Yes, I'm fine. Won't be long,' and he headed down the corridor to wash his tear-stained face.

Monika was waiting for him when he returned and Irena was back in her room, the baby in the plastic cot at her side. He peered at the tiny, crumpled face. He wanted to share this moment with Irena, but she seemed to be asleep.

'Could I hold her?' he asked. Monika hesitated and then fetched a pillow which she put on Daniel's lap before she lifted the baby and laid her there. She watched the new father lift the shawl away from his daughter's face and bend to kiss her.

'May I ask – have you always been disabled?'

Daniel looked up, accustomed to this sort of question but suddenly aware that he maybe didn't strike her as good father material. 'No. I damaged my back about eight years ago now. Actually I was shot.'

'You were a soldier?' Monika was surprised – he didn't look military although a uniform would have suited him very well, she thought.

'No, not at all. I'm a musician – a music teacher now mostly. I teach the piano. Irena's a musician too.' And at that moment, hearing her name, Irena opened her eyes and looked at Daniel. Then at the baby lying in his lap, who had begun to whimper. She held out her arms as Daniel laid the baby on her naked breast, where it buried its nose in the scent of her skin. Monika reached over to help Irena and the baby latched onto her nipple with a contented grunt. Daniel leant forwards so that his head was close to Irena's and his arm enclosed his two girls.

Monika smiled and shook her head. 'This one won't go hungry,' she said, as the child sucked noisily.

'Greedy – just like her father,' Irena said, laughing up at Daniel. The baby did not feed for long and Irena had fallen asleep again, when Monika lifted her and went towards the cot, but Daniel held out his arms. Infinitely gently, she laid the sleeping infant on her father's knee again and Daniel kept his daughter there until Irena woke again, not trusting the regulation plastic cot to be comfortable enough for someone so precious.

[IRENA]

We called our daughter Klara and, when she lost her dark baby down, I saw that she had my mother's red-gold hair and my own grey eyes.

It was the beginning of Klara's life and for me it was a new beginning too. I think that only being with Daniel again could equal the feeling of joy and rebirth that my little daughter gave to me. From that day, he and I shared something even more precious than our love for each other and with her arrival I began to look forward as I had not done since the days of my childhood.

I was weak when I returned from the hospital and Jovanka moved in to help me in the early days. Daniel embraced parenthood with an enthusiasm which I had only seen before when he discovered a new piece of music. He carried Klara around in a blanket nest on his knees. He took her to the

corner shop and showed her off when she was scarcely a week
old, watching with pride as Mrs Bhakta gathered the child to
her ample bosom and cooed to her in Gujarati. Sam however,
kept his distance and would only take on the duty of rocking
Klara's pram when her cries outside the studio disturbed the
musicians; he was not prepared to let Daniel leave the keyboard when he had finally managed to snatch a few minutes
of his teacher's attention from fatherhood.

Klara lay between us in bed and Daniel was looking at her
hands, so pale and tiny on his own, which were long and sun-
tanned, their backs lightly covered with dark hair.

'I wonder if she'll be a pianist,' he mused '– or a viola
player?'

'Yes, of course. That would be lovely, too.' He gently moved
Klara's right arm back and forth as if she were holding a bow.

'Would it mean a lot to you if you think she is musical?'

'Of course. But then there are other things she might like
better ... brick-laying or hay-making.'

'You're so silly.' I was looking at Daniel's profile as he
admired his daughter. 'And you play with her all the time –
I'm getting rather jealous.' Daniel seeing that the baby had
fallen asleep, put her back in the crib beside our bed. Then
he turned to me, took me in his arms and pulled me on top
of him.

Two years later, their son was born, a week early, while Daniel
was in Edinburgh performing at the Usher Hall. He flew back,
mortified, to find Irena sitting up in their bed with Klara in
one arm and the new baby in the other. Though still recovering from her caesarian, Irena was feeling well and strong. The
child was as dark as Klara was fair, olive skinned and with a

thick crop of black curls. They called him Johannes, but soon he was known as Jo-Jo.

'See – he's the image of you darling. Look at that hair. And his eyes.' Daniel examined his son, counting his toes and admiring his little clenched fists. The child looked back at him with serious, misty eyes that were already the blue of cornflowers and Irena said.

'They're just the same colour as yours.'

'Let's hope they see better than mine.'

Irena was changing the baby's nappy and Daniel looked at the little bowed legs, which kicked strongly. 'Just think – in a year or so he'll be walking ... That'll be marvellous.'

Irena was suddenly pensive. 'I suppose we have to book the rabbi quite soon, don't we?'

'The rabbi – what on earth for?'

'Don't you want him circumcised, like you were?'

Daniel thought for a moment.

'You like mine a lot, don't you?'

Irena giggled. 'Of course I do, but it seems such a cruel thing to do to a little boy. I'd hate to see it being done.'

'You wouldn't of course. Only chaps allowed to be present. But come on darling, I'm not a practising Jew and you're a complete mongrel, so why can't he hang on to the bits that our various gods provided him with?'

'You wouldn't mind?' Daniel was leaning over the naked Jo-Jo when an arc of golden liquid spurted out into his face from the organ they had just been discussing. Wiping his laughing face, Daniel observed: 'Well, that's what Jo-Jo thinks – and that's that.'

When Klara took her first steps Daniel held her hands as she tottered around his feet. Irena had watched him, wondering what he was thinking. The little girl, and then Jo-Jo in his turn, learnt to crawl around his chair and under the piano. When he had finished playing he would bend down and lift them onto his lap. As they learnt to sit, they would hold their arms up, entreating him to give them a ride; Irena watched them, knowing that Daniel had found a new release and joy in their acceptance of him that he felt with no-one else, not even her.

Irena's garden flourished under her care. The fruit trees were covered with blossom in spring and, if the birds and a late frost allowed, a few apples and quinces and plums would swell on the branches. She would take out her basket and harvest the little crop, remembering her mother doing the same, so many years ago. In summer, she checked every day through the broken window of the shed to see if the house martin mother and father had returned to their nest.

When he had finished working, Daniel would take Klara onto his knee at the piano and sing and play nursery rhymes, placing her little fingers on the keys as he sang. Klara knew quite a lot of the words of songs, although she didn't often speak, having discovered that her smile usually worked as well as words in obtaining whatever it was she wanted. And so it was that Irena heard his joyful shout one afternoon as she was weeding outside the studio.

'Darling, come here, hurry.' She stood up, wiping her hands on her jeans, and joined him, wondering what had caused his urgent cry. 'Listen,' said Daniel and began to play 'Frère Jacques'. On the second phrase he played a wrong note and Klara, who had been watching his fingers, cried.

'No, Daddy.' And she sang the rest of the line as it should have been, pressing her little fingers onto the keys as she did so.

'That's very good, Klary,' said Irena, encouragingly, but Daniel was shaking his head.

'No. Listen.' And he played a line from a nursery rhyme. The little girl joined in and again corrected him when he seemed to have made a mistake, her pure, high voice sailing up to the note he should have played.

'See,' said Daniel. 'Perfect pitch. Isn't that amazing.'

'Really? Can you tell already?'

'Yes, yes. Wrong notes really annoy her. I can change key and she still follows exactly. I think she's very musical.'

'But she's only three – you won't drive her to be a prodigy will you?' Irena sat down on the piano stool next to Daniel and took Klara from him. She was half joking, but she knew that, to him, the piano was the thing that drove him to wake every day and she often thought that, should something prevent his being able to play, he would not know how to live.

Klara and Jo-Jo had started to go to the local kindergarten, which the little boy enjoyed, relishing the companionship of other boys, often coming home cheerfully with cut knees and torn clothes. Klara, however, was frightened by the boisterous children who surrounded her. Irena and Daniel decided to try to educate her at home with them, in the early years at least.

Jo-Jo's escapades and injuries began to worry Irena. He seemed to fall over too often and to bump into things. She went to see the head teacher, nervously, as she was rather alarmed by the school and thought that Klara was really very sensible not wanting to go there. Sam had rigged up a basketball net on the side of the house and Daniel enjoyed taking exercise in the garden, at first alone or with him, then when the children were running around, with them. Little Jo-Jo seemed bemused by the catching of the ball and Irena was afraid there was something wrong with him.

Irena arranged to meet the boy's Head teacher and school doctor the following day to discuss Jo-Jo's difficulties.

'I expect he's just a big clumsy boy,' Daniel said distractedly over the telephone from Birmingham, where he and Sam were running a week's workshop on duetting. 'He seems perfectly normal to me. Maybe he just hates ball games – I always did ...' Home again and feeling guilty, he asked, almost as soon as he got through the door. 'What did Miss Squeers say?'

Irena didn't answer but called up the stairs and the children rushed down to greet their father. Klara climbed onto her father's lap but Jo-Jo stood in front of him. He was wearing a pair of tiny round glasses.

'He's just very short-sighted like you. He's been longing to show you his glasses. He's amazed at how much he can see.'

Daniel pulled Jo-Jo to his side and examined the new acquisitions with enthusiasm.

Later he said to Irena, 'Poor kid. Specs for the rest of his life. Such a pain at school.'

He went on, 'I was so worried on my way back from Brum – you thought Jo-Jo might have something serious wrong with him, didn't you?'

'Yes, I did. Sometimes I think our life is so happy and perfect that something bad has to happen ...' Irena had begun to undress and Daniel watched her for a minute.

'We are very lucky – but life is full of uncertainties. Perhaps we have no right to bring children into this terrible world ...'

Irena did not reply, thinking of how Daniel had come to live with his disability so that most people imagined that he never mourned the man he used to be. Her own rehabilitation, under Daniel's ministry, from a frightened, gloomy girl to a young woman who went through life confidently, engaging in family life and making music, was born through acceptance too, for it was only by finding stratagems of self-protection that she managed to present this outwardly normal appearance. She had locked away her past in a dark room down a passage of the mind she seldom visited.

❄

[IRENA]

Daniel was reading about the Bosnian war trials.

He had spread *The Observer* all over the floor around him, as he always did. I still couldn't look at the papers when there was anything about my homeland. It was far too painful for me, but he had become something of an expert on the war that had wrecked the former Yugoslavia.

'Oh God …!' he exclaimed, 'Oh no …!'

'What is it?' I said, seeing that he had gone very pale.

'It's Peter – Peter Henderson. He's been blown up – in Afghanistan.'

'Your journalist friend? How awful … is he …?'

'He's alive, but hurt. He's being shipped back to Edinburgh for plastic surgery.'

Daniel made some telephone calls and discovered that Peter would be in London for a few days before he headed north. As his family lived in Scotland, he had chosen to go and stay with his brother in Edinburgh and be treated there. Daniel went to meet him and came home looking more cheerful.

'His flat's on the first floor and no lift, so he suggested the Kensington Hilton. Ghastly place and poor Peter, his face is really messed up and his eardrums have been damaged. We got quite hysterical when he misheard things I said. He's really great and wants to meet you, but not until he's a bit prettier again. I told him he never had been pretty and he completely misunderstood. It should have been difficult, but it was really funny. Mind you, he's never let me feel sorry for myself, so I wasn't going to let him either.' Daniel was laughing, but I could see he had been touched and saddened by his friend's condition. I suppose I'll meet the man some time, but I'll probably hate him; Daniel does like some very odd people.

To Daniel's surprise, Leo and I became good friends. Since his speech at our wedding I had had a soft spot for him, unattractive as he was with his fat tummy and shaking jowls and the smell of cigar smoke in his clothes. After a while I began to work with him organising Daniel's concerts and tours and broadcasts. We had been complaining together one day about my husband's inability to keep his paperwork in order, when Leo put his pen down.

'He's not been himself lately, has he?'

'What do you mean?' I asked, but I knew what he meant; I'd been trying to deny to myself that anything was wrong. Daniel had always taken painkillers, quite a lot of them, but I knew that the relatively pain-free days were becoming less frequent. I noticed that he was spending less time at the piano and struggling upstairs every few hours to lie on our bed. Sam suggested that we put a daybed in the studio, so he could rest when he needed to. Seeing the bed had been installed, Daniel complained that it took up too much space, but the following afternoon I saw him stretched out on it, fast asleep.

Leo was saying, 'He couldn't concentrate this morning when I tried to go through that Edinburgh Master class with him. I had to pretend I was short of time and we'd finish it off another day. He's always driven himself pretty hard. Perhaps I should suggest he slackens his schedule a bit ...'

'Oh no, Leo. Don't say anything to him, please.'

'Hmm.' Leo went over to the window. 'He's done so well. He doesn't deserve this.'

'No. But I don't think life works that way. If it did it would be easier to know who were good people by their lovely, easy lives. Danny's a very good man, so this isn't anything about having what he deserves. It's just sod's law or bad luck ...'

'It was pretty good luck finding you, sweet angel.'

I shook my head and went on looking through Daniel's diary, remembering the morning two days before when I had found him slumped forward over the keyboard, breathing hard. Going to his side, I raised his head and looked into his eyes.

'Hurting?' I asked.

'Just missing you.' He put his arm round me and I held him until his breathing quietened.

Daniel's back specialist, Aziz Hussein, had become a close friend and quite often came round to hear his patient play. He was also one of Klara's godfathers and took a great interest in the child, mesmerised by her growing skill at the piano.

'I think Danny's having a lot more pain. Aziz. I don't know what to do. He takes his pills as usual, but by mid-morning I can tell he's in agony.'

'Wouldn't come and see me, I suppose?'

'No. I think he's in denial.'

'I told him last month that it's time we got that last bullet out – last X-ray shows that it's moved … and several of his vertebrae are in a bad way.'

'He hasn't told me you want to operate, of course. Would it really make a difference to the pain?

'It's not quite as simple as that. Yes, I can make him more comfortable, but all that work is very near the spinal cord and his remaining mobility might be affected …'

Irena had sat down, feeling sick now.

'In the meantime,' Hussein went on, 'More painkillers aren't the answer. He's on a big dose of everything now – I've let him have a stock of morphine – so that he can get some rest at night, really. But it's addictive as you know. I'm sorry you're so worried – I'd pop in, but I'm off to the States tomorrow. I'll give you a call when I get back. I wish I could be more helpful, but without Daniel's co-operation …'

Daniel was nearing the end of his forty-eighth year and Leo was determined that his fiftieth birthday should be fêted with a concert at his beloved Wigmore Hall. This was something many musicians did, filling the stage with their friends and frequently playing the fool with their instruments and including their families in the occasion. But Daniel was not sure he wanted the publicity the concert would entail or that he was up to the bonhomie and cheerfulness that would be demanded of him. However, to please Irena and Leo, he sketched out a few ideas and put them into a new file. Then he put his mind towards Christmas and tried to forget the feeling of fear that had once again become his constant companion.

32. PLAY IT AGAIN DAN

IT WAS the end of December and they were back in the ancient stone house near Agen, which they borrowed from time to time from a musician friend. Hearing that it had an excellent piano, they had first taken it one June and it was in the dark green bathing pool among the waterlilies that Klara and Jo-Jo had learnt to swim. It had remained a favourite place for summer holidays but Daniel, the dedicated gourmet, wanted to show Irena and the children gastronomic glories of Christmas and New Year in France. At the local Christmas Eve market, he fell with delight on the oysters, fat ducks and geese, lobsters, truffles and ceps, and spent hours preparing complicated Perigordian dishes which scented the whole house with garlic and herbs and the sauces he made with the local wine, deep and fragrant.

Sam, taking a break from his concert tour, had been invited to join them and leapt at the opportunity to forgo Christmas with his family and his mother's insistent curiosity about his love life. Magda and he laughed together, knowing that a large part of their holiday would be spent at the kitchen sink. Good cook though Daniel was, his *batterie de cuisine* always included every implement he could reach. Washing up, he said, was very bad for a pianist's hands. Irena, who was uncomfortable in the presence of so much rich food, preferred to read her book or play with the children and ignore the colourful accusations that accompanied the noisy culinary activity down the corridor.

The view towards the hill opposite Les Coquillages seemed

to Irena to be one of which she would never tire. It was mid-winter and a low mist still lay in the valley which was suffused with a rosy glow, the dormant buds on the rows of the old vines, stretching in curved lines away from her to the horizon caught like little bright flames on the hillside below her. All was soft, she thought; no sharp outlines picked out the features of the landscape and even the darkness of the yew tree that stood on the garden's boundary was softened by this gentle winter light.

On Boxing Day Magda had said, 'Go on you two – it's almost the last night of the year. Have a romantic night in a château hotel – look here's a leaflet about a fabulous one – Château de Trellissac.'

Magda and Sam said they would keep the children happy and finally Daniel and Irena agreed to take off together – just one night and then they'd all celebrate the New Year back at Les Coquillages with fireworks and a *pièce montée* that the baker had made as a surprise for Klara and Jo-Jo.

Arriving in Sagoulême, Daniel drove into the square by the edge of the Charente and parked in front of the church. The sun was high now and beginning to warm the winter land-scape. Daniel got into his chair and sat for a moment staring into the ink-dark, green river. Irena looked at him, smiling. He was wearing a beret Basque, as he often did in England, but she was amused to see how very French he looked.

'Shall we look around the church?'

'Yes let's. I think I've been here before.' Daniel tried to remember, but he'd travelled a lot round France 'doing' the music festivals for a few years in his early twenties, and he wasn't sure if this place had been one of his stops.

They entered the church by the Western portal under the lozenge-shaped Christ in Majesty that crowned the main door, the damned trailing away on one side towards their nameless and eternal torture, the godly on the other, their heads held high. Irena held the heavy doors back, straining against their strong springs as Daniel pushed himself through. The interior seemed pitch black to him before his eyes accustomed themselves to the gloom, and they both waited until they could see whether there were any steps to negotiate. Relieved there were none, Irena found the light switch with its slot for a coin and all the brass chandeliers lit up at once. She half expected piped organ music or Gregorian chant to come on at the same time, but it was not until they were half way down the side aisle and looking at the Stations of the Cross, that the music began.

'That's a better disc than usual' said Irena, but Daniel had turned to look up at the organ loft which dominated the main door where they'd come in under a dazzling rose window which cast its multi-coloured pattern down onto the tiled floor of the nave. Irena looked up and saw then that there was a light high up in the organ loft and a figure at the console. The organist was playing a Bach voluntary. As the music filled the church, Daniel sat very still and the dust, stirred up by their progress, swirled in the light that illuminated their figures. Irena sat down in a chair, thinking she'd listen to the music for a while. The organist was very good, first class, and Daniel would enjoy that. He'd be unable to climb the steps up to the organ console, which was sad; she knew how important playing the organ had been to him when he was a boy.

A group of tourists entered the church and were starting to spread out as the music rose up to the ancient vaulting and seemed to set them in movement with the fierce vibrations of the great pipes and the dancing of the spangled light. The upper registers trilled above the dancing line of the musician's feet, the great instrument's third voice. The loft and carved figures around the pipes must be earlier than the much newer instrument, she mused, looking at the ranks of ecstatic, instrument-playing cherubim and seraphim. She looked around for Daniel but he was nowhere to be seen.

He had left the church soon after the organist had begun to play. Even had he been able to climb into the organ loft, he'd never again be able to master the instrument, to dance along the pedals as once he had, and the realization hit him painfully. He'd loved the organ and had played in Westminster Abbey as a schoolboy. He was the best piano student the music master had heard in many years, and his teacher had delighted in taking the boy up into the loft to meet the organist and show him the complexities of the pipes and stops. Daniel's eyes had lit up, his hands and feet itching to make music then and there. Finally, he'd been allowed to come from his practice in St John's, Smith Square and climb into the organ loft of the Abbey, and he'd played what was to be the first of the great organs he had come to know and love.

The day had come, however, when he'd had to make a choice for his future and he had chosen the piano as his first instrument. But the organ had remained a great joy.

The Charente ran swiftly below its stone parapet, its dark green water mirroring the leafless trees and the silver stone of the buildings on the opposite embankment. Daniel could still hear the music through the church doors and spun his chair away across the little square. There was a steep camber and the surface was cobbled, so his progress was slower than usual as he propelled himself towards the terrace of a small café on the far side of the square. There, a few metal tables and plastic chairs were grouped optimistically outside and Daniel installed himself alongside one of the tables. A waiter came out and looked doubtfully at the man in the wheelchair, who wore a beret Basque. He enquired as to whether Monsieur wouldn't be warmer inside. Daniel shook his head and ordered a Cognac, which he drank down in one, the spirit scorching the back of his throat. His back to the church and the river, he watched the wind collect up a few bits of Christmas decoration from the gutter by the café and blow them into a loose ball which made its slow way past the house next door and disappeared up a narrow alley.

Wondering why Daniel had gone out without her, Irena came out of the church and stood in the biting wind, clutching her coat around her. She looked in the car but he was not there. Worried, she was turning back towards the church, when she saw him sitting with his back to her outside the café opposite.

'Hello darling.' She sat down beside him and he nodded, but didn't smile. She took hold of one of his icy hands and rubbed it between hers, but he still did not respond. She said, 'It's freezing out here. Let's go inside.'

As they found room for Daniel's chair by a table in the window, two old men sitting at the bar muttered: *''Sieur, 'Dame ...'*

Irena looked at Daniel. 'What is it darling?'

The memory of the organ music still with him, he just shook his head.

Irena ordered coffee and they began to thaw out in the warm nicotine-thick atmosphere, Daniel still looked strained. He could not yet explain to Irena what it was that had sent him out of the church without her, but, finally, he forced himself to smile. 'Look' he said, and slid his eyes sideways to the two old men by the bar. 'Same hat as me;' and they both started to giggle. Daniel shared Irena's coffee and ate some croissants. It seemed a while since breakfast.

Irena looked at her watch under the table. 'Danny, we should go. We have a table for lunch at the Château and you know they won't serve late lunch in France.'

Irena came out of the malodorous toilette and found Daniel chatting in his fluent but inexact French to the patron, who was giving him directions to their hotel. It would be wasted information: Daniel would not retain it and would look in bewilderment at the map Irena unfolded in the car. Finding a destination was not his forte, but he drove well and only occasionally forgot which side of the road he should be on. Irena waited for him to get into the car, stowed his chair away in the boot and got in beside him, putting her head on his shoulder. He put his arms around her and told her in some detail what he had in mind to do with her that afternoon. He saw with amused delight the big smile that spread over her little face and the deep dimples that appeared in her round cheeks.

Irena laughed then. 'That was wonderful music in the church – but there's only one organ that interests me just now …'

Daniel had to concentrate hard to stay on the road.

They checked into the hotel and Irena went up to their room reflecting sadly that she would have loved to sleep in one of the towers which ornamented each corner of the chateau – slate-capped pepper pots and reached by steep, spiral stairs – but wherever they went now Daniel was dependent on a lift. She looked out of the window as she brushed her hair. The wind was getting up and the beech tree just outside their window was tossing about, its lichen-encrusted branches which still bore the dark, desiccated leaves of last summer, twisting this way and that and scraping against the great stained glass window of the hall below their room.

After a long and delicious lunch they had been heading back to the lift, across the cavernous entrance hall of the hotel which was part of the old abbey and had a tall gothic window at the far end, when Daniel noticed a glistening white grand piano pushed back against the tapestry covered wall.

'Oh no,' thought Irena, hoping he wouldn't decide to play. Monsieur Polliot, the manager, came up to them. 'Unfortunately our pianist is not well. So sad – we have a full restaurant every night with the approach of the New Year.'

Daniel opened the lid of the piano and the manager Monsieur Polliot asked, nervously, '*Monsieur sait jouer? Plus tard peut-être ...*'

Perhaps his unfortunate guest would like to tinkle away that afternoon, he thought. After the lunchers had left.

Daniel hesitated a moment, noticing the look on the Manager's face, and, unable to resist showing that he could indeed play, launched into the Minute Waltz, dashing through the immortal piece, his hands lifting and dropping as he made the ugly instrument sing at the top of its voice. He never played Chopin in public, as pedal marks were on all that composer's scores, but he hoped there were no musicians there to judge his performance.

Monsieur Polliot, turned slowly back towards the hall, noticing as he did that the buzz of conversation amongst the guests had ceased and everyone's eyes were on Daniel. The pianist stopped playing and closed the lid over the keyboard as the guests, who had left the dining room when they heard the music, started to applaud enthusiastically. Out of habit, he gave a little bow and looked around for Irena. She was standing by the lift, which had just arrived and, without turning to Daniel, she got in and the doors closed behind her. 'Oh God' thought Daniel. 'I'm for it now. How stupid I am.' He was waiting for it to come down again when he saw that the Manager was at his side.

'Monsieur le Maître, please may I have a word?' Daniel hesitated but a couple with a pushchair had just got into the lift and he turned politely and followed the Manager into his office. He must hurry, though. Irena was going to give him a hard time.

Lying together in their ornate four-poster bed at last, Irena had tried to forgive Daniel at first and then it had come easily to do so. He was so delicious, so cross with himself, so understanding and apologetic. They made love and he forgot about the organ and the organist and Irena forgot about the white piano. Lunch had gone on a long time and soon it would be time for that champagne. Daniel ordered it over the telephone, choosing one that was very expensive, and some *amuse-gueules* to eat with it. 'No foie gras', he reassured her.

Irena had a new dress and was about to put it on in the bathroom as she wanted to surprise Daniel. She hated shopping and almost never bought new clothes, but she had seen this one in a window and Magda had persuaded her to buy it.

'It's not really me...'

'Oh come on,' her sister-in-law found Irena's refusal to make the best of herself exasperating. 'Daniel will love it. It's your colour and very sexy.' Irena had looked down at her cleavage and pulled at the short skirt that was open at the side, but then she saw what Magda meant – Daniel seemed to accept her nondescript, oversized clothes but she had seen him looking appreciatively at other women, women in low-cut tops, wearing make-up and high-heeled shoes. She wanted Daniel to look at her like that. As she laid out the make-up Magda had chosen for her, she heard a knock on the bedroom door and Daniel speaking to someone. He sounded rather uncertain and she put her dressing gown on over her dress and went back into the room. M. Polliot greeted her apologetically. He was holding up a plastic suit cover.

'*Peut-être Monsieur le Maître voudrait bien mettre ce smoking – pour la réception ce soir?*'

Daniel looked guiltily towards Irena. 'I'm sorry darling. They've asked me to play a bit this evening. You know – because their pianist can't and they've got a lot of people in tonight. Just a little bit – not a concert.' Irena stared at him. 'Oh, and Monsieur Polliot thinks I might like to wear this – as I haven't brought a tux,' the manager had unveiled from its bag a shiny white dinner jacket. A frilly-fronted white shirt and made-up bow tie were already laid out on the bed.

Irena went back into the bathroom, not trusting herself to be polite to either of them. She went to the window and looked down into the writhing limbs of the tree below her. There was a storm brewing, she thought, and picked up her mobile to ring the children before they went to bed. Magda answered and Irena asked what the weather was like at Les Coquillages.

'Quite exciting here – the children are scared of the lightning, so we've made a nest under the kitchen table and we're all going to sleep there. Well, not Sam. He's watching some DVD and cursing because the power keeps going on and off.'

'The sleeves are too short,' Irena said as Daniel got into the shirt and began to put the jacket on. His eyes did not meet hers. He knew she was angry again, but he wasn't sure that he deserved to be castigated just because he'd been asked to play the piano. After all, he did that all the time at home and she didn't complain. And – though she did not know this – the hotel would give them their board and lodging free in exchange for Daniel's services that evening. He pulled the cuffs down as far as he could on his long wrists and fiddled with the bow tie, not quite sure how to attach it and hoping that Irena would come to his rescue. Putting on his glasses so as to have a better attempt at the tie, he noticed that she was wearing something he hadn't seen before and perched on very pretty high-heeled shoes. She'd piled her hair up and made up her face and he was about to tell her she looked very sexy, but he hesitated as he saw the expression on her face. He held his arms out to her, but she didn't move.

'*Blago tebi!* Sometimes I don't like you at all. You're a sort of Guy Pringle – always keen to please everyone. Everyone except me.' Daniel had not read any Olivia Manning, so the reference to her tiresome hero was lost on him. 'Darling. I'm sorry. I really am. But I felt so sorry for the guy – the hotel's been advertising this evening for ages and their piano player's got flu. I promise I won't play for long. And we can have a lovely dinner. Look – we can start with this really special fizz now. And just look at those little goat's cheese tarts. You know you love them. You love me a little bit, too. Or you did this afternoon.' Daniel was looking his most beguiling, in spite of the vulgarity of what he was wearing and the way they fitted him so badly, the shirt front gaping open, revealing the black hair on his chest, the tie hanging around his neck and acres of wrist showing from the sleeves of the dinner jacket. And Irena, to hide her sudden desire to laugh, bent over him, and pulled the tie tightly round his neck.

'Next time I'll strangle you properly, you louse,' she said and he fondled her through her pretty dress, making little loving noises.

They sat by the window and finished their champagne. The tie was now in place and the shirt front buttoned up, Daniel's hair was immaculately brushed back from his forehead and his spectacles shone. Irena looked at him and thought how lucky she was. She pulled her grey cashmere shawl around her shoulders – the noise from the buffeting of the trees around the hotel was giving her goose flesh.

33. CRESCENDO

DANIEL had been at the piano a long time, it seemed to Irena. They'd eaten the first course of their dinner and he played for a while. Then, after the fish course, he'd gone back to the piano. By the time the main course arrived, she was no longer hungry, but she watched Daniel polishing off his own plateful and then, hardly hesitating a moment, hers as well. Then he went back to the piano and began to take requests from the guests. Irena got up and left the table, annoyed by the interruptions of their long, romantic dinner. He would want cheese, no doubt, and an elaborate pudding of some sort when he rejoined her. But let him wait.

She went over to sit under the big window at the end of the hall. It was two storeys high, a remnant of the 16th-century gothic abbey, glazed with grisaille glass and emblazoned with the arms of the former owners of the château. Fantastic beasts and the ubiquitous ermine and phoenix cavorted between delicate stone tracery. She was unnerved by the writhing of the beech tree as it kept scraping across the window, sinister and threatening now. The wind was howling louder and louder like the bellowing of a great beast.

As the storm gathered outside, Daniel, tired of the demands for *Milord* and *La Vie en Rose*, started to play some Duke Ellington. He pretended not to be much of a jazz pianist, but threw himself into the mood of the blues, swaying in his chair, his hands jabbing at the chords. The guests were, for the most part, French, and loved his unexpected playing, his versatility and – for the female guests – his looks and charm.

Distracted by a woman who had draped herself over the end of the piano, the better to display her deep décolletage, he took off his glasses and put them in his pocket.

Suddenly the lights went out and, for a few moments, the guests clutched at each other in the dark, too afraid to move, but then the emergency lighting came on. Daniel had not even paused in his playing; he knew the keyboard as a blind pianist would, but then there was a deafening crash and he felt the piano jump under his hands. He looked towards the window where Irena had been sitting, just as a gigantic branch fell through it, taking glass and stone with it and reaching half way across the floor. Dust and debris billowed up and the guests were milling about, screaming. Daniel stared at the chaos around him and, as if in a dream, propelled himself away from the piano and towards the remains of the window.

'*Non, Monsieur. Reculez-vous. N'avencez pas.*' The staff rushed at him as he pushed himself into the jumble of branches, glass and stone which lay all around him. He could see Irena's shawl hanging now over the part of the tree nearest the huge hole in the window where it had forced itself through, the light woollen material blowing around in the gale that gusted through past the devastation it had brought. She must be lying under all that. Daniel had no thought for anything else and pushed aside the waiter who was trying to stop him and began to pull at the branches, breaking them off and tossing them aside in the effort to find a way through to Irena. The emergency lighting was faint and greenish and the whole scene was like something dreamt, as the thundering of the storm, no longer muffled by the window, drowned the voices behind him as he struggled to pull the broken branches out of his way. Other trees could be heard falling in the park and another trunk-like branch from the beech came suddenly through the already gaping hole in the window.

He fought to free himself, calling; 'Irena! Irena! I'm

coming,' but, no matter how he tried to push aside the broken branches, he could get no further. He tore at them with his hands, breaking and bending them as they sprang back into his face and chest.

'*Monsieur. Non. Non. Non. Reculez-vous* ...' One of the guests had reached him and was pulling at the back of his chair. A waiter one joined him and together they got Daniel free. He was covered in twigs and bark and some of the brown leaves that had still clung to the trees canopy. His face was scratched and his hands torn and bleeding. He fought to gain control of his chair but was pulled backwards and then turned towards the room, though he twisted himself around, vainly trying to see the window seat where Irena had been sitting. Her shawl, blowing wildly still in the wind, came loose and flew across the room towards him and he caught it as it went past, staring with unbelieving eyes at the shredded dove-grey woollen stuff he held.

Irena had made several visits to the ladies' room, taking her hair down, coiling it and pinning it up again. She half wished she had the courage to call a taxi and go back to the children at *Les Coquillages*. Daniel had surpassed himself, seeming to give no thought to her and the precious evening they were to have spent together.

She put on some lipstick, made a face at herself and wiped it off again. Even in the windowless cloakroom of the hotel, she was aware of the storm outside as it seemed to reach a crescendo. Then there was an enormous crash in the foyer and the lights went out. Suddenly anxious, she groped for the door. The emergency lighting was on within a few seconds and she went out into the hall, looking around at the scene of chaos that greeted her, unable to understand what had happened. People were screaming and the air was full of dust. And all over the floor, as she tried to walk towards where Daniel had been playing the piano, were shards of glass and pieces of stone. Beyond, towards the window, tangled branches filled the space where it had been, heaped up ceiling-high around where the great tree had burst through taking everything with it. The wind, unimpeded now, swept through the ground floor of the hotel and found its way out the other side, tearing the kitchen door off its hinges as it went and forming a wind-tunnel through the ground floor of the hotel.

In the centre of all this, Daniel was sitting facing her, the hall porter and two guests holding onto his chair. He was twisting around and shouting at them as he tried to wrestle himself free. His hands were streaming with blood. It was all over the white dinner jacket and smeared on his cheeks.

'*Ma femme. Elle est en dessous … Laissez-moi passer. Je vous en prie. Lâchez-moi …*' He looked as if he'd been under the tree himself, she thought, covered in bits of branch, lichen and bark and yet the piano looked unscathed at the other side of the room. Then she looked again at the hole through which the great branches had come. Minutes earlier she herself had been at that end of the room, sitting on the window seat, until she'd slipped away. But why was he covered in sticks and dead leaves? She went towards him, staring at the blood-stained face. Without his glasses, it was a moment before he recognized her.

'*Regardez Monsieur. C'est Madame. Elle est saine et sauve!*' The men let go of his chair as Irena bent over him and held him in her arms.

'I thought you were under it. I thought you were dead …' Daniel was starting to shake. A few guests and members of the hotel staff were grouped around him and a young man who had been dining at the next table came forward, saying in good English: 'I am a doctor. May I look at Monsieur?' Irena stood up and watched as the doctor examined the scratches on

Daniel's face and the damage to his hands. He took his pulse and then put his ear against Daniel's chest. He beckoned to Irena: 'He seems to be in shock – quite bad – take him to your room and I'll follow you when I have my bag. There are some deep cuts – he should have an anti-tetanus *piqûre*.'

Daniel was still staring at Irena and seemed not to understand what was happening. The hall porter again took command of his chair, as Daniel fighting to regain control, realized that his tyres had been punctured by the fallen glass and his hands didn't seem to work as he tried to turn the wheels. Daniel craned his head round to Irena, who was trying to help, 'Don't go away. Stay with me,' he begged and she stood close to him in the lift and walked beside him to the bedroom.

The porter helped to lift Daniel onto the bed and left them together. He held his arms out and Irena lay down beside him; he was still shaking like one of the leaves still clinging to the beech tree. A chamber maid had been enlisted to help and arrived with the doctor, carrying towels and a bowl of warm water. Irena cleaned Daniel's face and the doctor inspected the cuts on his hands.

'I must give these wounds a few stitches. I think there's a small bone broken in your right hand. Have it x-rayed when you can get to a hospital.'

Daniel gritted his teeth while he was given a local anaesthetic and submitted to the stitching across the back of his left hand. The doctor took Irena's arm and led her away from the bed, speaking softly, 'He seems badly shocked – does he often react like this?' Irena shook her head.

'No. I don't think so.'

The doctor turned back to Daniel, took out his stethoscope and listened to his chest. He helped him to turn over so he could listen to his back. Daniel asked Irena to pull his shirt up, and there was a sharp intake of breath from the doctor.

'These are bullet wounds, I think? You were shot?'

'Yes. Six bullets. I was in Bosnia ... ten years now.'

'You've been *handicappé* since then?'

'Yes.' Daniel wanted to end the conversation. He needed to be alone with Irena and kept looking round at her, willing her to come to his aid. The doctor continued to question him: 'You are well now, normally?'

'I'm very well, thank you,' said Daniel. The doctor listened again to Daniel's chest and then hung his stethoscope back around his neck.

'I will give you a letter for your GP. You should have an electrocardiogram as soon as you get home. I don't like the sound of your heart.' Irena had gone into the bathroom to add the dirty towels to the heap in the bath and did not hear the doctor's words.

'Please don't mention this to my wife – she will worry unnecessarily.'

'I don't think it's unnecessary – You're sure you've had no problems before?'

Daniel shook his head. He thought of his recent breathlessness and the tightness in his chest that came and went. Perhaps he'd see Dr Middleton when he got home. Irena had rejoined them and looked from one to the other. 'What's wrong?' she asked, but Daniel said, lightly,

'Nothing – but look at that tux – the pianist will think there's been a murder.' He tried to hold the jacket up but was having trouble doing anything with his bandaged hands. Irena felt suddenly sick – what if he'd damaged them permanently? That didn't bear thinking about.

'Fortunately our local nurse, Benedicte, lives in the gatehouse. I shall ask her to help you in the morning,' the doctor said as he bade them goodnight. Daniel and Irena exchanged glances as he headed for the door.

Alone at last, Irena helped Daniel to undress. Lying beside

him, she smoothed his hair away from the scratches on his face. 'Do you feel a bit better now?'

'Yes, thanks. But I can't seem to stop shaking …'

Irena looked out of the window, but there were no lights in the park and her reflection looked back at her.

'I'm worried about Magda and the children. I keep trying to ring them, but all the telephones seem to be dead …' She went towards the bathroom, but he called her back.

'Please don't go away. Please stay with me.'

The following morning the sky was blue again, and streaked, high in the stratosphere, with mares' tails of cloud. Irena got up quietly and looked out of the window at the devastation outside. Fallen trees littered the grounds and the ornamental *parterre* and topiary garden had been torn up and thrown around.

She saw that Daniel was awake. He looked around the room, dazed and still half asleep. Then he saw his hands.

'My God,' he said. 'What happened?'

'You were so brave, darling. You tried to rescue me from under the tree. And I was in the loo all along.' She tried to speak lightly, but Daniel was looking at her now, fully awake.

'I thought you were dead.' He tried to sit up, but his shoulders and neck were very stiff and there wasn't much he could do to help himself with his bandaged hands, which hurt now, too.

'It'd take more than that to kill me, darling. Do you think I'd let you loose with all those fans longing to look after you?'

Daniel didn't laugh. 'How the hell am I going to get around? We need to get these bandages off – I'm not going to be pushed. And how am I going to get back to work?'

'You'll have to be sensible, Danny. You've got some horrible cuts – and a broken a bone in your right hand. You must take that seriously. The doctor said you should stay in bed today. He's sending a really glamorous nurse to wash you – and you know what France is like – I should think there's an enema in it for you.'

Daniel rolled his eyes, but was smiling. 'Come here. You're very badly behaved considering how terribly injured I am. You should be speaking in a quiet voice and soothing me. Can you see my specs anywhere or did they get left in the tree?'

Irena brought them to him and helped him put them on. 'Darling old Four Eyes, I do love you. Even when you're as horrible as you were yesterday.'

'Even though I spoilt our lovely evening together? Will you forgive me?'

'I probably will, but just now I'm worried about the children. The telephone lines are all down.'

A waiter came in with their breakfast and told them that the whole area was in chaos. The hotel had its own generator, but the houses around were without heat or light – all the electricity cables had been brought down with the falling trees, taking the telephone lines down with them. Thousands of square hectares of forest had been flattened. Several people had been killed. It was a catastrophe.

Irena was becoming increasingly frantic now about Magda, Sam and the children; Les Coquillages was surrounded by trees. They ate their breakfast in silence, Daniel holding a croissant between his bandaged hands and dipping it into his coffee, feeling miserable and frustrated when he had to ask Irena to wipe his mouth. She leant towards him, her eyes half closed, and licked the coffee and crumbs from his lips until she managed to make him smile. Then she ran downstairs to see if there was any way of getting to Les Coquillages. The receptionist shook her head; it was only five kilometers away, but there were many trees across all the roads. No-one was going anywhere.

Desperate now, she went up again to the bedroom and sat by Daniel until the promised nurse appeared. She was plump and pretty and smiled tenderly at Daniel as she laid out the tools of her trade. He submitted to her ministrations with a good grace and Irena left them to it. A note from Monsieur Polliot had been sent up; he was full of apologies, as if it had been his fault that a hurricane had visited his hotel. And please could she come down as there was something that might be of help to them both. The patient was sitting up in bed and having his teeth brushed, looking rather sheepish, but not unhappy, so she left the room and went down to the foyer again.

Daniel's chair had been taken away for the tyres to be mended by the handyman. However, the nurse promised to find some strong men to lift him later, so that he could sit in the armchair by the window. He lay back and started to work his way through the brochures about châteaux and tourist sites and canoeing which was all the reading matter the room had to offer. He thought the river trips looked inviting and, for a few minutes, felt sad that such a thing was probably impossible for him now. He rarely indulged in self-pity, but that morning he was beginning to feel very sorry for himself indeed. Then the door burst open and the children ran into the room, Jo-Jo exclaiming as he jumped up onto the bed next to his father: 'We came by bulldozer, Dad. It pushed the trees off the road and a tractor with an enormous saw cut them up.'

Klara sat down carefully beside the bed, too, scolding her brother: 'Daddy's hands are very sore. Be careful.'

'Monsieur Polliot has been wonderful,' Irena told Daniel. 'He arranged it all – they're trying to clear the roads as fast as they can.'

The two tractor drivers came in, without their boots so as not to dirty the floors, lifted Daniel out of bed and carried him to a gilded armchair by the window. He wanted them to stay and talk, but they excused themselves. They had weeks of work ahead and the neighbourhood was in mourning for the colleagues who had perished in the storm.

'There's still no power anywhere,' said Irena two days later. 'No-one knows when it'll be on again. The hotel's got its own generator, but we can't stay here indefinitely.'

Secretly, she didn't dislike this idea and her family were enjoying themselves, having discovered the swimming pool. For the first few days, Daniel had eaten his way through the hotel menu, read to the children and listened to France Musique on the radio, but Irena began to worry about him when he stopped doing these things and she found him sleeping in the armchair or staring gloomily out of the window.

Things were not going to be easy wherever he was until his hands had healed, but she knew he longed to be home. At least in London he'd have his own things around him.

'I'll die of boredom if we stay here much longer.' said Daniel. 'Now I know what it feels like to be a tet.' Daniel meant a tetraplegic. He'd watched them in rehab and, now that he couldn't use his hands, he saw what his life might have been had those bullets hit his back a few inches higher.

'Why don't we fly home with the children? Sam and Magda can bring the car and our stuff with them.' And Daniel brightened visibly and remained palpably more positive until the day of their departure.

34. UNRAVELLING

DANIEL had looked forward to being home again. Even if he could not play the piano for a while, he would have scores to work on and a composition that was showing its first signs of growth. His hands were now strapped up so he could at least push himself around slowly within the house and studio. Refusing to let Irena see to his personal care, they had hired a nurse to come morning and evening; he hated this, but there was no choice for the time being and he did not allow himself to think too far ahead.

Irena, too, had imagined that Daniel would be happier when they got home to London. But he would seldom go across to the studio, and followed her from room to room as she dealt with her chores, shouting anxiously to her when she was upstairs. The cooking she so disliked now fell to her and she had imagined that Daniel would enjoy instructing her in the preparation of their food. But he didn't seem interested in anything.

'Darling, I've got to go out' she would say, picking up her coat and bag. 'Can you keep an eye on Klara for an hour? I've got to do some shopping and you need some more pills. Jo-Jo's having tea with Marcus, but I'll bring him back.'

Daniel would beg her to stay with him. 'You'll get run over. Or there'll be a bomb. Please, don't go out. We can get Jovanka to do the shopping.'

Irena longed to get out of the house. She could hardly bear now to be alone with Daniel who gazed mournfully at her, refused to work at anything he could do without his hands and seemed to find endless ways of stopping her from pursuing her own activities; her own music was certainly on the back burner for now, she thought ruefully.

'But Danny I can't stay with you all the time. I'll be fine. You can't keep thinking about that tree. You must put that behind you.' And Daniel would wheel himself over to the front door and bar her way, his pale face frantic. She gave in each time, and then eventually rang Dr Middleton.

'I want to see him anyway.' The doctor was looking at an email from France which he'd brought up onto his computer screen. 'I'll drop in tomorrow and we'll see if he needs a sedative. Shock can take many forms.'

'Who was that you were speaking to?' Daniel was at the kitchen door.

'Oh, just the school. I couldn't remember when Jo-Jo breaks up ...' but Daniel shook his head at her.

'Why are you lying to me?'

'All right. I rang Dr Middleton – I'm worried about you, darling ...'

'Bloody hell. I don't need a doctor. I just need you to stay with me. Don't you care about me any more?' He reached his bandaged hands out to her. He looked miserable and she sat down next to him, trying not to feel impatient. He was behaving like a child, she thought, and could see no reason for his getting into such a state.

'I want to be with you, too. Of course I care about you. It's just that I can't stop doing all the things I normally do and sit with you all day long. There's lots of work you can do without your hands. Write me a lovely piece for my viola, couldn't you.'

Daniel exploded, his voice hysterical. '*Write me a lovely piece for my viola.*' He imitated her voice. 'Who the hell do you think I am?'

Mortified, Irena walked towards him, holding out her

hands. 'Please don't be so angry. I do understand ...'

But he exploded again, 'No you don't. You have no idea what it's like being in this thing, have you? Well, it's a living hell being disabled, I can tell you. It doesn't get easier – it gets worse. You all think I've got used to it, and everyone thinks I manage so marvellously, don't they? Well, I haven't got used to it. I want to be free again – and you and Magda clucking over me – do you think that helps? I'm tired of your sympathy.' He turned his chair away from Irena, who stood frozen to the spot. As Daniel wrenched the garden door open, they saw that Klara was standing in the passage outside the kitchen.

'Why's Daddy so cross?' She had never heard him shout like that and she looked out into the dark after him. Illuminated only by the light from the kitchen window they could see him making his way painfully down the path between the bare fruit trees. He pushed the studio door open with his elbow and went in, reached clumsily for the light switch and they saw his outline silhouetted against the brightness within.

'He's just fed up not being able to play the piano for so long.'

'I'll go and play him my new piece, shall I?' Without waiting for an answer, the girl went out of the kitchen door, and Irena went with her for a few steps, watched her gain the studio and saw Daniel turn as she went in. Irena returned to the house, shut the door and sat down at the table, clutching her cardigan round her, her hands still trembling.

When she next looked out of the window, she saw that Klara was sitting at the piano, playing, and Daniel was close to her. The telephone rang; it was the mother of the boy with whom Jo-Jo was having supper. Her husband would drive him home, but was still in the office, so they'd be late. Irena was relieved; the boy was very sensitive: once he had heard Daniel shouting at her and remained upset for several days. She saw that Klara was on her way back and opened the door for her.

'Daddy needs his pills. Will you take them?'

Dreading how she would find him, Irena took Daniel's pills from the dresser and went out to the studio. She found him trying to make sense of the heating controls, a task he normally left to others. She wanted to suggest they go back to the house, at least until the studio had warmed up. She wondered then if she knew this man at all. Looking back on her marriage, the time now seemed to her to have been sunlit years, warmed by her own personal sun, her beloved husband. Now he had become a stranger to her, a bitter, angry stranger and she began to question herself. Had she taken his resilience and courage for granted?

Daniel took the pills between his bandaged hands, swallowed them without water and thanked her politely, as he would thank someone he barely knew.

'Where's Jo-Jo?' he asked. 'Shouldn't he be back by now?' Irena explained and he nodded. 'It's bloody cold in here. Let's go back to the house. I want to talk to you.'

In the kitchen, Irena turned on the oven and Daniel sat shivering by its open door. She poured him a glass of wine and pulled a chair over beside him. Now he'd apologise and she would too and all would be well again. He didn't look at her and she, with a cup of coffee between her hands, willed him to meet her eyes, to be someone she recognised again. He had only to make a joke if he couldn't bring himself to explain or to apologise. But for what, she asked herself – for being honest at long last, for telling it like it was?

When he did speak, he did not look at her. 'I think we should part – for a while anyway.'

'Part?' she said, faintly. 'But why? Don't you love me any more?'

'Love! Is that all you think about? You're so childish with your romantic ideas of life, aren't you? I really don't think you've grown up yet.' He emptied his glass and took hold of the bottle clumsily between his bandaged hands and filled it again, almost to the brim. Irena had recoiled against the back of her chair and the coffee slopped onto her lap. He had never spoken to her like that before and she felt as if he had struck her. If he wanted her out of his life there was not anything worse that could happen to her – other than death, and that was beyond her imagining.

Perhaps Daniel had expected an impassioned plea or floods of tears, but Irena merely waited a moment to form a sentence in her mind. When she spoke, her voice was calm and toneless. 'All right. If that's how you see me. I'll go away. I'll find somewhere tomorrow where I can take Klara and Jo-Jo.' She tried to think practically: 'But you'll need some help until your hands are better.'

'There you go again,' this time Daniel knew he was being unfair, but Irena, just raised her eyebrows. She said, 'Well, you make whatever arrangements you like.'

The doorbell rang as she spoke and she went out into the hall, shutting the door behind her. Daniel sat where he was. He tried to turn the oven off and, unable to turn the control with his clumsy hands, began to tear at his dressings, pulling with his teeth at the sticking plaster that held them in place. The bandages and lint fell to the floor. The broken middle finger of his right hand was still strapped to its neighbour and he was about to tear that plaster off, too, when he thought better of it. He left the dirty bandages where they had fallen and listened to Irena greeting Jo-Jo and saying goodbye to whoever had brought him home.

'Where's Dad? I want to show him the game I've been playing with Marcus. He burst into the kitchen and saw at once that his father's hands were no longer bandaged. He was standing with his arm around Daniel's shoulders, looking with interest at the half-healed wounds, when Irena came in.

'Look – Dad's hands are nearly better!' His mother stayed

just inside the door and told him to come upstairs. He was looking from one parent to the other when Klara squeezed past them and went up to Daniel.

'He's bleeding again. I think he should have new bandages, Mummy.' Irena went to the dresser drawer. She opened it, took out a package of lint and a reel of sticking plaster, put the dressings between Daniel's knees and added the kitchen scissors from the pot by the cooker. Then she left the room, pushing the reluctant Jo-Jo in front of her.

Klara needed to be called several times and, leaving Jo-Jo finishing his homework, Irena went downstairs to find her. She was standing beside Daniel, winding a long strip of sticking plaster around one of his hands, a look of intense concentration on her freckled face. The plaster kept sticking to itself and, as they were both left-handed, they were having trouble using Irena's scissors. Irena watched them for a moment and then Klara started to laugh her high, piping laugh, hugged her father and reached up to put her other arm around Irena. As she disentangled the dressings, Irena did not look at Daniel; they both wanted to laugh, too – she knew they did. But, instead, Irena dressed the wounds in silence and, without looking back at him, took Klara upstairs with her.

Finally Irena slept and, forgetting that Daniel was downstairs, reached over to his side of the bed and found he was not there. She sniffed the slight scent of him that still remained on his pillows. Should she go down to him? But then she remembered what he had said to her and was wondering what she was going to do on her own, if that was what he really wanted, when she heard Klara calling out to her. She jumped out of bed and went to the weeping girl.

'What is it, darling? Was it a bad dream?' but the child had already forgotten the reason for her tears and, comforted by Irena's presence, drifted off to sleep in her arms. Irena waited a few minutes and was about to return to her bed when she became aware of a familiar noise on the stairs. It was the bumping sound of Daniel lifting himself up step by step on his behind. She waited, wondering if he was coming to her or if he had heard Klara crying. He got to the top step where his upstairs chair stood and Irena thought of his hands and that he would reopen the wounds if he tried to get into it. She went out onto the landing and sat down on the top step next to him.

'I heard Klara,' he said, not looking at her.

'She's all right now. I expect we upset her shouting at each other.'

'It upset me, too.'

He shifted uncomfortably and regarded his wheelchair, feeling foolish on the floor and wishing he could get himself into it.

'You are an idiot – where did you think you were going from here?'

'I hadn't really got that far. I can't sleep down there.'

Irena knew he wouldn't be able to use his swing bar to get onto their bed from the floor; she thought a moment: 'I know!' She ran down the stairs and Daniel heard her rummaging in the under-stairs cupboard, coming up again carrying a blow-up mattress and a foot pump.

'I'll have the bed. You can sleep on this,' she said, spreading the mattress out on the floor, and beginning to pump with one foot, her bottom in the air. Daniel watched her for a few minutes and then started to shuffle himself along on his behind until he was in their bedroom. He put his arms round Irena's legs and she stopped pumping, off-balance, as he continued to hold on to her, so that she sat down heavily on the half-inflated bed next to him and they looked at each other. The only thing to do then was to laugh and they did, holding onto each other and then rolling together onto the half-inflated mattress.

When they woke the children were staring down at them.

'Why are you camping in the bedroom?'

'Daddy got lonely downstairs and he can't use his monkey swing to get onto our proper bed, so I thought of this. It's very comfortable. It's time we went camping again.'

Daniel made a face – it was not his favourite sort of holiday, though they had once tried it out in a very up-market French camp site.

Jo-Jo whooped with joy and climbed in under the duvet, between his parents, who rolled apart to make room for him. Klara saw that everyone was behaving normally again, and crawled over Irena to squeeze in beside her brother.

'Please try to be patient with me. I know I get things wrong,' Irena said when they finally felt able to talk about their quarrel. 'And I can't help thinking about love and having romantic thoughts about you. You're my whole world.'

'And you are mine. But it's frightening to be so bound up with one person. When I thought you had died under that tree I felt as if my life was over. There would have been no way of carrying on without you. I feel so helpless now – when we got home these hands made me feel so vulnerable somehow, as though I was something you and Magda – and even Sam – could just do what you wanted with – pushing me around and helping me with everything. And needing a nurse to get me up and put me to bed. It's been terrifying. Almost as if I'd been shot again. This is the longest I've ever been without touching a piano – except when I was really ill in hospital. I don't know that I could live if I couldn't play. And I know I couldn't live without you. Will you be able to forgive me for saying all those things?'

'The trouble is I think you meant them. I do understand, really I do, how hard things are for you. I don't belittle your difficulties. I live with them, too, but I think I've been unrealistic, because I saw my own acceptance of you like this as being something that would heal you in a sense. By sharing your pain it would be less bad for you. Do you understand what I mean?'

'Yes, I think so. And of course it has been amazing that a lovely girl like you could go on loving me. Maybe I've taken you for granted?'

'Perhaps we're just both rubbish!' Irena bent to kiss him and he moved his head so that his mouth and hers met.

Irena gave up trying to get on with her own activities. She spent her days at Daniel's side and, in the evenings, made him instruct her in the art of cooking. His laughter returned and their time together became precious to them both, he waiting impatiently for the day when he could get to his piano again; neither of them voicing the fear that his wounds and broken bone would leave his playing permanently impaired.

Sam brought in a box of music written for the left-handed pianist. Daniel struggled at first – it was too long since he had touched his piano, but he was soon playing fluently again and enjoying the novelty of the pieces which made great demands on his one useful hand.

'Poor old Wittgenstein – how awful to lose an arm, but he ignited a terrific wave of inspiration amongst the composers of his time. And he was rich enough to commission them himself. This Ravel is a pig at first, but what a joy in the end. I think I read that Herr W never played it in public – or was that the Saint-Saëns ... Hey, Sam be my pedal foot, will you. I think this needs warming up.' And Irena watched the two pianists, joshing and jostling by the piano, and hoped that normal life was starting again.

35. PERFECT PITCH

DANIEL had written a duet to play with Klara, and Irena heard his laughter through the open window as he pretended to play wrong notes and the girl's stern little voice reprimanded him.

Irena went into the kitchen to fetch coffee for Daniel and drinks for the children. Looking out into the garden, she felt a great rush of happiness. She thought of the day she had flown to London to meet him again ten years ago, when she found it impossible to believe that the glamorous Maestro Daniel would want to share his life with her, changed and damaged as she was. She thought, too, as she often did, of Stefan; she had learnt to live with the memory of her imprisonment and seldom had the fear-filled dreams that had once tormented her nights. The boy was to come to London soon, with his mother. He would meet Daniel and Klara and Jo-Jo, but would have no idea that Irena was anyone but a kind British benefactress.

She carried the tray across to the studio, admiring on her way Jo-Jo's athletic figure as he stretched and leapt with the ball.

Daniel had Klara on his knee now, but she jumped off.

'Can I go now Daddy?'

He gave her a gentle push towards the door. 'Very good work, Miss Danuczekova,' he said and made a quick mark on the music he had written for her.

He joined Irena by the low table where she'd put the coffee. The light-hearted mood of the morning had changed; Daniel now looked pensive and anxious. 'God, darling, what a responsibility. That child's very gifted, you know.'

'Aren't you pleased?'

'Of course. It's wonderful to see glimpses of an artist in the making in such a small person.' Irena remembered something he'd said to her father: 'It's a privilege to see an artist in the making'. He'd said it about her.

Daniel went on, 'but I know what hard work lies ahead if that's the way we take her. And it must be our duty to nurture her gift. We owe it to her and she'd be right to resent us if we didn't ... but it's a long, hard road she faces. And she's just a child, like any other little girl ...'

'Did you question the way your parents made you work at your music when you were a child?'

Daniel smiled as he shook his head.

'It was a no-brainer really. I adored playing the piano. In fact if we were somewhere without one I was miserable – I'd even pretend to play on the table if I was taken out to lunch. But you'll have to watch her – to be sure she's happy at the instrument.'

'Why me? Surely you'll have a better idea of how she's getting on than I would?'

It was the sort of thing that Daniel had started to say. He would say 'you' instead of 'we' or 'us' when talking about the future.

'Well, you're a woman so you pick up these emotional things. I might be so focused on her music that I wouldn't notice how she's feeling in herself.'

Irena knew this was nonsense. One of the reasons he was so valued as a teacher was that he was intuitive about a pupil's inner connection to music. Daniel would watch his students closely, and not just for their technical progress. Sam had often spoken to her about this, admitting that he had once actually wept on Daniel's shoulder and knew of others in the college who felt it was to him they owed their ability to see clearly as far as their musical future was concerned. He had a rare understanding both of the infinite variety of musicians and of the human spirit. He knew that musical ability was only one aspect of the complicated make-up of an artist. He also knew intimately the stresses and difficulties of a performer's life and that not everyone was cut out for it.

But now Daniel was having to think as a father. And, though he did not share this fear with Irena, a father who might not be in a position to oversee his daughter's musical formation; he felt that he had lost, or almost lost, the strength to endure any more pain. He longed to rest, to be in a place where his body was no longer his enemy, a torturer from whom there was no escape. He was not sure where that pain-free place might be, but he feared that it was somewhere very lonely.

36. PORTRAIT

MIRANDA THESIGER drove to an area she didn't know well, north of the park, oppressed by the misty nakedness of the trees and the dark greasy surface of the road which reflected a wan winter sun. Hardly the best day to be thinking about painting, she thought, with the dim half-light that would make even the laying out of her palette difficult. This was the lightless gloom, she reflected, that has sent painters abroad for centuries in their quest for colour and light.

A small, slight woman came out to greet her. She had thick brown hair, piled into an untidy chignon from which wayward strands were constantly escaping. This must be Irena Danuczekova whose husband's portrait she had come to paint.

Irena had seen one of Miranda's pictures in a friend's house and liked it very much. Sitting opposite the canvas over lunch, she'd been fascinated by its luminosity and freedom, as well as the likeness to the subject, whom she knew well. She had hesitated for a week or more and then rung the artist. Miranda had explained that she was not well known; the famous people she had painted had none of them, in the end, bought their portraits. This had made Irena laugh. She told the artist that she hoped that a portrait would not involve a great many sittings; her husband had agreed to sit, but unwillingly, and only because it was to be commissioned by the Sarajevo Conservatory, a place he loved dearly.

❋

On entering the house, Miranda looked around at the musical instruments and family photographs which covered the walls. The room was large as it extended the entire depth of the house, but there was very little furniture and the stripped wooden floor was streaked with tyre marks. A long-case clock ticked between an antique viol and a framed photograph of a man in a tall black hat with side curls.

'Daniel's practising – he'll be finished soon. He works over there in the studio. ' Irena said, as she took the folding easel and portfolio from Miranda and showed her into the kitchen. Pointing out of the window, she added with a laugh, 'Oh, there he is – amazing, he's usually late.' And Miranda saw a man in a wheelchair propelling himself swiftly across the paved garden. This must be Daniel Danuczek. Irena opened the garden door and her husband pulled himself up the step into the room. Miranda's first impression was of a man who would have been tall, had he been standing, with broad shoulders and long arms, but, lit from behind by the feeble winter sun, Miranda couldn't make out his face. He moved his chair briskly across the floor and looked up at her, smiling and holding out his hand.

'So this is the woman who's come to torment me?' He was laughing as he wheeled himself up to the table.

Sitting opposite him, Miranda's practised eye quickly took in the face of her subject: his eyes were bright blue behind rimless glasses which gave his strong features a vulnerable delicacy. His nose long and slightly curved, his lips finely modelled, his dark eyebrows echoing the upper curve of his large, thickly-lashed eyes in a golden olive complexion. His hair was almost white now, but still thick and curly and long enough to be tucked behind his ears. This will be a challenge, she thought. Physical perfection is seldom interesting to portray. Whereas Irena – she'd like to paint her unusual little face.

'It's too late for coffee,' Daniel said. 'Let's take a drink over to the studio.' He opened the kitchen door and started back across the little garden, which, Miranda saw had originally been two gardens, but the wall between had been taken down. Traces of autumn colour still remained in the flowerbeds under the bare fruit trees, and the fences on either side were thick with climbing roses and ivy. The blue-painted pavilion at the end must be the musician's studio, Miranda thought, as she saw her host pull himself up the ramp and through the double doors.

Irena took a bottle of Belle Époque from the kitchen fridge. 'I hope you drink champagne – that's what Danny means by a drink.'

'Oh goodness, how lovely – but I have to drive home.'

'But not just yet. You can have a look round the studio and talk to Daniel about the commission. I hope he'll be cooperative – he's rather embarrassed about being painted, but he'd do anything for the Sarajevo Conservatory. Then you must stay to lunch and meet the children.'

'How long has your husband been …' Miranda began to ask.

'In a wheelchair?' Irena finished her question for her, 'About twelve years now. He was shot in the back and his spine was badly damaged. Out in Bosnia – Sarajevo, where I was born and we first met.' Irena knew that people usually thought Daniel must have been in a motor accident, or hurt himself playing rugby. Being shot was not something they expected and Miranda's face registered shock and then concern.

'How awful … but he seems to manage very well.'

'Yes, he's terrific, really. It affected his career – people don't realize how much a pianist needs his feet – you know, the pedals are really important. So there are things he can't play now, but music is still his life and he does a lot of teaching.'

Miranda had with her a small sketch pad and a soft lead

pencil so she could make a quick drawing if there was time. In the studio, she looked around her with interest and walked over to the piano.

'What a lovely instrument!' She touched the golden case of the Fazzioli. Daniel was delighted: 'Yes, my pride and joy. I'd always wanted one and this came up for sale just when we were moving here. It seemed meant.'

'It seemed very expensive ...' Irena muttered as she completed the job of clearing the sofa and armchair. The two women sat down.

Miranda took a sip of her champagne. 'How delicious!'

'Another of Daniel's extravagances!'

The couple seemed very comfortable together, their eyes constantly meeting. Miranda felt a stab of envy. Clearly their lives couldn't be easy, but they did seem very fond of each other. There were sounds from the house and Irena got up: 'That's Jovanka, our au pair, with the children. They've got a half day, but I'll keep them over in the house while you sort out your sittings and everything.' And she went back across the garden, fielded the two children who were on their way over to the studio and steered them back to the house.

'I won't stay long,' said Miranda, feeling self-conscious and uncomfortable at being alone with this new sitter. 'Can I just work out with you how you want to be painted?'

Daniel pulled a face; 'I'm afraid this is something I know absolutely nothing about. The general idea seems to be me playing the piano – shall I go over there and you can have a look?'

Daniel pushed himself over to the piano, and began to play, looking up at her. Miranda listened. Music seemed to fill the air as she walked around the studio, looking at the angles of the construction of the roof, at the shape made by the curves of the piano, and only then at her subject as he played. And suddenly she was excited and wished she had a canvas and could make a start straight away. Daniel stopped playing and Miranda asked him:

'Just to the waist? I must paint your hands, of course.'

'Yes, I imagine so – they're a bit scarred now – I had a fight with a fallen tree and they're not ... well, as pretty as they used to be! And I'm afraid this has to go in too' and he indicated his wheelchair. 'No-one will recognize me without it.' He laughed, but Miranda was a bit taken aback. A big canvas, then, and there was a lot of geometry which needed to be right.

'I've never seen such a smart wheelchair' she ventured and Daniel grinned broadly.

'It's good, isn't it? Weighs almost nothing and I can race Irena round the park to stop her getting fat.' He turned away from the keyboard and spun his chair round, inviting Miranda to look at it. She was embarrassed, at first, but he was smiling as he pointed out the sporty, angled wheels, the low back and lack of arm rests.

Returning to the piano, he asked her what she'd like him to play. She hesitated and pushed back a bit of her faded blonde hair which had come out of the comb holding it back from her face.

'*La Fille aux Cheveux de Lin*?' she asked, uncertainly. He wondered, as he played, if she knew enough about music to be aware of the inadequacies of his performance. She sat looking out of the window, and seemed to be a long way away. She had a stillness about her that he found intriguing. Even though she was no longer young, she was still a very beautiful woman.

As they returned to the house, the children came to meet them: Jo-Jo a dark-haired boy with glasses, walked beside his father's wheelchair as they returned to the kitchen, and golden-haired Klara, two years older than her brother, shook hands solemnly with Miranda.

'Daddy – you were playing Debussy, weren't you?' Daniel laughed.

'She's got a very good ear, this young lady. But it can't possibly be this one,' he said, lifting aside the girl's hair, 'it's far too grubby.'

'We've sorted the sittings – 16th and 17th and 18th, 19th if she needs it,' said Daniel when Miranda had taken the chair opposite him. 'So the paint won't dry between. I'm off to Paris after that, aren't I, if it's not finished we'll have to have another session when I'm back.'

After the first sitting, Miranda left her paints and easel in Daniel's studio. She'd come by bus this time as Daniel had a hospital appointment and could drive her home; he wanted to look at her work, and Miranda accepted the lift with pleasure. The first sitting, followed by family lunch, had been a joyful affair filled with magical music which stayed in her head. Daniel had to lie down regularly these days – his pain had reached a point when spending more than an hour sitting at the keyboard was impossible, and he would roll himself thankfully onto the daybed in his studio. Miranda had been prepared for this and spent that time working on the background and the wheelchair while Daniel rested. He fell asleep and lay like a beautiful knight on a tomb, she thought, his hands crossed on his chest. And she mourned the fact that she had never known the love of such a man. He seemed to her heroic in some way. And yet he was so human, so funny and down-to-earth. Except when he played the piano, and then she felt as though she was drifting into another world. There was no way she could follow him there and she wondered if Irena could, if another musician could join him in those extraordinary journeys of sound.

At lunch, Daniel had cooked omelettes for Miranda and

himself. The children and Irena had eaten sausages, over-cooked by Irena. She and the children hated the *baveuses* omelettes which their father loved and burnt sausages were not to Daniel's taste. He sat breaking the eggs with Jo-Jo, Klara helping her mother at their side. There was a lot of banter and jostling of Daniel's wheelchair in front of the cooker. Miranda made a salad and then they all ate.

'Can we see the picture?' asked Klara.

'Well, not yet. I'm afraid,' said Miranda. 'You can see it when I've finished.'

'Is Daddy nice to paint?'

'Yes,' said Miranda, 'and he plays lovely music. I haven't ever painted a musician before.'

'And there are so many similarities between music and painting, you know,' said Daniel. 'I didn't realise that the palette is laid out the same way each time – it's the painter's keyboard, just like the piano, and she knows without looking where her brush should go.'

'The studio has a wonderful quality of light.' Miranda said. 'Why the blue paintwork?'

'Ah …' Irena and Daniel said simultaneously and then laughed.

'My grandfather was a painter who had this lovely studio in the garden of my family home in Sarajevo.' Irena spoke quietly and then stopped. Daniel took over, putting down his fork and reaching out for her hand.

'When I first met Irena I was teaching in Sarajevo and stayed as her parents' lodger. The studio was painted just this blue. Anyway, when we bought this house, she was determined to make me a studio that would be the same. And you're right. The light is superb. It's a wonderful place to work …'

Since meeting the Danuczeks, Miranda had become ashamed of her ignorance about music and began to taking out library books and buying music magazines in the hope of enlarging her knowledge. 'I know that you are known for the colour you put into your playing. What does that mean, exactly – are you synesthetic?'

'Ah no – many musicians and writers are, I believe. Messiaen the most famous I suppose. But what you artists interpret as colour, I hear as a variety of richness of tone, I think. Music – movement, dancing, singing and all the instrumental sounds, rhythm, tonality, these are my palette. However, I do enjoy going to exhibitions and Irena has taught me how to look at paintings. Perhaps because I have rotten eyesight, sculpture is almost more a language I can understand, because touch is such a huge part of my own art. Touch and form, light and shade ...' Then Daniel shook his head, 'Forgive me. I'm rambling on. Back we go – when you're ready, Miranda. And you two – are you swimming this afternoon?'

'Yes with Tetka.' The children called Magda this – it was Serbo-Croatian for 'aunt'.

'She looks very floppy in her swimsuit.' Jo-Jo said and Daniel spluttered into his coffee.

Daniel drove Miranda home after the sitting on his way to hospital, and promised to drop in before he went home to look at her studio and some of her work. When he returned, she brought some paintings down from her first floor studio for him to see and he wheeled himself round, looking intently at the canvases and drawings. Miranda answered his questions about the sitters and the paintings. Daniel seemed in no hurry to leave so she got out a bottle of wine. He drew the cork for her, rather slowly, seeming to be deep in thought.

'Miranda, I need your advice,' he said abruptly.

She was taken aback, but Daniel had turned his chair and she saw that he looked tired and his face had taken on an unhealthy pallor.

'What is it?' she was suddenly afraid of what he might be about to say.

'You know I was at Charing Cross Hospital this afternoon? Well, they've confirmed that I've got heart trouble – a quite serious thing apparently – arrhythmia it's called.'

'You didn't know before today?

'I had a mild heart attack a while ago. They kept me in for a couple of nights and I was OK. Irena was away and I never told her. But I had another turn in France last winter – the doctor out there wanted me to have some tests done. I left it a while – I'm very good at putting my head in the sand and I don't go anywhere near hospitals if I can help it. But I've been having chest pains and – well, I finally got round to having the tests and the French quack was right. I am on the waiting list for a heart operation.'

'You haven't told Irena? Surely she'd want to know.'

'Her emotions are so fragile – I try to protect her from anything upsetting. Do you know what happened to her during the Bosnian war?'

'No. I don't know anything about that. I've sometimes thought there was a great well of unhappiness in her – yet she is superficially very happy. It's hard to understand.'

'I'll tell you.' And Daniel told Miranda how Irena had witnessed her parent's deaths and his voice rose until he was almost shouting as he went on to describe Irena's subsequent ordeal in captivity. 'Constantly raped and abused by whoever happened to be around – just used as a sex object. She was only fifteen – grew up in a very old-fashioned family – had known nothing but kindness and happiness. The brute got her pregnant and when the baby was born the village women told her it had died. She was ill but eventually she was helped to escape while her captor was visiting his concentration camps – you'll have read about them. After a while in hospital they managed to contact an aunt in America. It was some time before she could lead anything like a normal life. But we met again – after I'd been shot – and yes, we've been very happy together.'

Miranda's hand was covering her mouth and she said nothing for a moment. Then she went over to Daniel, whose head was turned away from her, and touched his shoulder; after a moment, he put his hand on hers.

'I'm sorry,' he said eventually, his voice hoarse, and she went back to her chair facing him. Then he blew his nose and tried to remember what he had been saying before he had allowed himself to reveal something he had always kept to himself. But he was not sorry to have taken this woman into his confidence. Finally, he went on,

'You know my back was pretty badly messed up when I was shot, and a couple of years ago it began to hurt like hell – most of the time. Hussein – he's my orthopaedic surgeon – had left one of the bullets in because it was very near the spinal cord, but it's moved and he's afraid the paralysis will extend to my arms and hands; he wants to cut me open and try to get it out.'

Miranda was horrified. She gripped the arms of her chair, determined not to allow herself to cry. 'So you'll have the operation soon?

'In theory, yes, and if it helps with the pain, I'm all for it, but there's nothing to say it'll succeed. I could well be worse off than I am now.'

Oh God, thought Miranda, why is he telling me all this? 'And Irena – what does she think you should do?'

'She can't seem to take it on board, really. I think she just can't face the truth.'

'Yes. I can understand that. What can they do about your heart?'

'Quite a lot nowadays, I think. But it's a question of priorities. If I go for the back op first, there's the anaesthetic to think about … I'm too much of a coward to let them chop me up under a local.'

Miranda knew she should say something. Anything.

'You must tell Irena about your heart.'

He nodded. 'I know. I know. And she'll be very hurt that I've kept it secret from her. We don't have secrets from each other …'

Miranda made to refill his glass, but he shook his head and looked at his watch. 'You've been much too kind. I'm sorry – it's unfair to tell you all this – and you're right – I must talk to Irena and we'll work something out together. But, you see, I can't live if I can't play the piano. It's always been my life.' He wheeled himself out into the road and Miranda followed him to his car. He unlocked the door and then turned back to her.

'So you'll come again when I'm back?' He reached towards her and took her hand, put it to his lips and held it there for a moment. She watched him slide across into the driver's seat, dismantle his wheelchair and stow the pieces behind him. Then he wound down the window, thanked her again and drove away.

He was gone into the night leaving only the echo of his voice. Miranda went back to the studio, her hand against her lips where Daniel's had been. She lay awake that night, anxious and wishing he had not been so frank with her. And she felt the familiar urgency she had known too often in her complicated life. She was in love and there was nothing she could do about it.

37. TO HAVE AND TO HOLD

SAM had found a poster of the film *Casablanca* and had superimposed Daniel's face on Bogart's. *Play it Again Dan* graced the kitchen wall for some time before it began to annoy Daniel and one day he tore it down angrily. Klara stared at him as he screwed it up and threw it across the kitchen into the bin.

'But Daddy – I love it. Why are you so cross?'

Daniel was angry with himself – normal day-to-day tasks and even the gentle banter of family life had begun to get on his nerves. Everything seemed an effort now and the pain in his back was often unbearable, so his temper was short. He wanted more and more to be left alone.

'Sorry, sweetest' Daniel reached out to the girl and held her face between his hands: 'Daddy's a bad-tempered old bear sometimes.' He and her mother were the pivot and linchpin of Klara's world and Irena was usually the stricter of the two parents, but she had recently sensed that the balance was changing. Irena, seeing the child's distress, now too frequent to be an aberration, tried to reason with Daniel.

'Darling – she tries so hard to please you. Don't snap at her. You're hurting her.'

Daniel was filled with remorse. But it wasn't just his close family who fell victim to his shortness of temper; from time to time, Sam and Magda had been shocked by the violent impatience of his response to them. Poor Daniel, he was constantly ashamed of his own behaviour. Irena took him in her arms one night in bed to kiss him goodnight.

They seldom made love now – he was too tired. Irena desperately missed their laughter-filled passion. Instead, she made it her business to get him comfortable for the night and woke herself at intervals to lift his lifeless legs so he could turn over. Sometimes he would remain asleep and grunt a little as she moved his limbs. At other times, already wide awake, he would hold her against his body and murmur to her or sometimes sing in her ear. And Irena, whose heart was aching now for the energy and strength that had once been Daniel's, would nestle into him. Sometimes she took him in her hand and moved her fingers slowly up and down until his prick stood like a great dark tulip. The flood of white, life-filled emission semen always surprised her as he came into her hand or over her stomach. The scent of it reminded her of their early days together, when she was always changing their sheets in case Magda should guess how often they made love. As her fear of being touched retreated, Daniel's whole being had become godlike to her, beautiful and potent and strongly scented. He had been surprised, again and again, by her appetite for his body. Delighted, too, that, feeling himself to be less than a whole man, he'd never failed her in her desires. His own appetites satisfied too, he had marvelled at his luck. And she, finally revealing her violated body to his gaze, had fully known this man, her husband, her lover, her life's sweet fulfilment.

Aziz Hussein examined Daniel while Irena sat in the car with the children. In the consulting room Daniel gave his reluctant and hesitant account of the pain and fatigue that were now dominating his life. They looked together at the X-rays which showed some changes that worried his surgeon; Hussein had not foreseen such serious deterioration of his patient's vertebrae.

'Daniel. I'm not going to bullshit. These bones could collapse at any time now. We'd better plan an op. – and soon.'

'And will that stop the pain?' was all Daniel could think to ask.

'The answer is I don't know. I don't even know if I can get that bullet out and patch things up without doing further damage – and you know what that could mean?'

Daniel said nothing and Hussein took a letter out of Daniel's file.

'And then there's your heart. That's not going to make my job any easier ...'

'Jock MacDonald wants to have a go at fixing it, doesn't he?'

'Yes. And you'd better have it done. It's hard on your heart shoving yourself about in that chair – particularly the way you carry on. Can't you take it a bit easier? You're coming up for fifty, aren't you? That's middle age, you know ...'

'Oh bloody hell. I don't want to spend any more time thinking about all of this.'

'Daniel. Listen. You're facing cardiac failure and your back's giving way. Don't you think you could consider your family for once and not just yourself?'

Daniel dropped his head. 'I know you're right. But Irena doesn't know about my heart. I haven't known how to tell her.'

'She must have realised something was wrong out in France.'

'There was a lot to worry about with the damage to my hands. And Docteur Lemarquais was very discreet. I was in a bad state when we got home – I found not being able to play the piano absolute hell and I couldn't do much else either. Perhaps I've been unfair on Irena, not coming clean with her. But you see she's been through so much in her life and our marriage has been so extraordinary. I don't want to spoil it before I have to.'

'But surely you want to have as much time together as you can?'

'Yes. Yes, of course. But that depends on what sort of life ... I only know one sort of life and that depends entirely on my hands. Take those away and I might just as well be dead.'

Daniel looked across the room and out of the window to where he could see Irena playing by the car with the children. Cherry trees were shedding blossom over the car park and Klara was leaping about trying to catch the petals. Jo-Jo was picking up handfuls of fallen flowers and throwing them at her.

When Daniel emerged the children came to meet him and ran alongside his chair to where Irena stood, now covered in pink cherry blossom, by the car. He smiled his biggest smile.

'OK?' asked Irena, reassured by the smile.

'Fine,' said Daniel 'and that blossom really suits you. You should always wear pink.'

When he got home that day Daniel went straight to the studio and sat at his table, writing. Seeing Irena come across from the house, he folded the sheet of paper and slid it into an envelope. He didn't seal or address the envelope but put it into the breast pocket of his linen jacket.

'Can I post that for you?' asked Irena.

'No thanks. It's not quite finished.' He had turned away from her as he pocketed the letter, and Irena felt a heaviness in the air. He seemed a long way from her, in some dark place where she could not join him. She looked down at him and felt again as though some profound change were taking place between them – a gulf that widened with the passing of the days.

She knelt down beside him and he saw that she had tears in her eyes. When she spoke, her voice was almost inaudible.

'Come back to me please. I don't know where you've gone. You seem so far away these days.'

It was an odd thing to say and Daniel, knowing very well that she spoke the truth and that they were entering a new phase in their lives, took her hand and kissed it.'

Here I am Little Wren. Don't be sad, I'm not far away at all.' And he tried to comfort her.

He was reading when Irena got into bed that night. He looked up at her, as she said: 'Danny, please tell me what Aziz said. I know it wasn't good, but please don't keep it to yourself. Share it with me.'

Daniel turned towards her and put his book down. He had been reading *Silas Marner*, still trying to understand Irena's fascination with Victorian literature.

'It's just more of the same. My back's in a bad way – we've known that for some time now.'

'Can't he do anything? Surely there must be something ...'

'He says there's a chance that he can make things better – with an operation to take out that last bullet and shore my back up where it's crumbling a bit. He thinks I ought to let him have a go.' The words he chose were always cavalier and Irena frowned, knowing he wasn't giving her the whole picture.

'So, will that help you – will that make you better?'

'Better?' Daniel's voice was unusually shrill. 'It's time you understood, my darling girl, that I'm never going to get better. Don't you understand? I can only get worse now – possibly much worse.' He took off his glasses and threw them onto the bedside table, but they slid off the back and down the wall. 'Shit' he said trying to pull the table away so he could reach down behind it.

Irena got out of bed and went round his side to help him.

'I can do it! For God's sake, leave me alone. Don't always

tell me I can't do things,' he shouted at her. Leaning precariously out of the side of the bed, he retrieved his glasses and was regaining his balance when the table slid away from him and he fell heavily onto the floor, banging his head on the corner of the table. Irena bent down to him.

She knew better than to make a fuss, but was terrified by the way he'd landed so hard on his back. She pulled a pillow down from the bed and put it under his head and knelt on the floor beside him. Daniel lay with his eyes open, watching her.

'Come here.' he said softly. 'We've never done it on the floor, have we?'

'But darling … let's get you back into bed. Then we could.' But he pulled her nightdress over her head, threw it aside and cupped her breasts in his hands. He loved them more than ever now that, having fed her babies, they were very soft and drooped a little, the nipples hard and red. He pulled her down onto him and put his face between them, making little appreciative noises, as he always did.

'Oh Danny …' Irena was astride him. It had been too long and Daniel, try as he would, could not contain himself and came before she did. But then he gave her the lovely caresses she had been missing for too long. He loved all of his wife's body and knew how each part could be aroused.

'You're so randy. And so sexy and I love you so much.' Irena murmured. She had lost count of how many times she had come in the intense multiple climax that Daniel had always loved to give her. Lying with him on the floorboards she wondered what had made him want her so badly that night of all nights. 'Well, at least I can still do something well.' Daniel lifted her off and laid her close beside him, wiping her carefully with his handkerchief.

'Darling, you're getting cold. Your legs are freezing. Can you get up?'

He managed to sit up with his back against the bed, wincing with pain as he did so. Irena brought him his chair. It always amazed her how he could get up off the floor and into it; it was one of the first things he'd been taught at Stoke Mandeville. When he was back in bed, Irena started to massage his feet. She'd put the electric blanket on – his legs were very cold and she wanted to restore his circulation as quickly as she could. 'I love your feet,' she said. 'They're so beautiful. You've got long second toes like a Greek statue.'

'Oh for God's sake, darling. They're like dead fish. I don't know how you can touch them.' She kissed his toes, knowing her kisses were wasted on them, but she loved him so, every part of him. Just as he was.

Daniel woke several times in the night. He had been forced to ask Irena to fetch some morphine soon after he'd got into bed, but he still couldn't get himself into a position that wasn't agonizing. Nothing he did in the way of turning his body this way or that would assuage the stabbing pain which pulsed through the length of his spine. Irena felt sick and helpless as she watched him stab the hypodermic needle into his thigh. She wished she knew how to help him. She knew he believed his condition would worsen if he went under the knife and that he would end up not only unable to play the piano, but impotent and unable to make love to her. The joy they had in each other's bodies was something he could not sacrifice, not even for a pain-free life. There seemed to be no way out and whatever route they took seemed blocked by unknown horrors.

She lay close to Daniel and saw with relief that he had dozed off. He seemed, in the light from the street lamp outside their window, once more the delicious young man of her girlhood. Her fingers traced the familiar lines of his cheeks and brow, then the outline of his smiling lips. Daniel opened his eyes and reached up and took her hand.

'I thought you were asleep'.

'Not yet. Darling, I want to talk – are you awake enough?'

'Yes, what is it?'

'I've decided to do it … I'll let them cut me open and see if they can make things better. It's worth a try, isn't it?'

'Oh thank God. Yes, of course it is. Thank you darling. Thank you, thank you,' and Irena threw her arms around him and was kissing him passionately, when he pulled away from her.

'There's something else.' and Daniel paused, dreading her reaction to what he was about to say. He reached up for his monkey bar and sat up against the pillows.

'You remember that night in France – the tree and everything?'

'Yes. Of course I remember. Why?'

'Well, I should have told you, but you know me – I always think things will go away if I put my head in the sand. Docteur Lemarquais heard something when he listened to my chest.'

'Heard what?'

'My heart didn't sound right – he wanted me to get tested when I got home. They did an electrocardio thing and it seems it's a bit out of rhythm. Not good for a musician.'

Knowing that he was trying to lighten the news he had given her, Irena asked quickly, 'so – what can they do about that?'

'Oh lots of things now. A pacemaker, maybe, or a new valve. It's quite routine nowadays.' Irena said nothing, so he went on.

'Problem is that if – when – I have my back done, I'd be under anesthetic for quite a while and …'

'And that's dangerous for your heart?'

Yes. So I – we – need to decide what to do first. Back's about to collapse and heart's ... we could toss a coin, I suppose.' He was trying to make what he said less momentous, but Irena shouted at him.

'Don't you dare laugh about it. Don't you dare.' And she put her hand over his mouth to stop him speaking any more.

38.   THE MUSICIAN'S DAUGHTER

Wearing the dress that Magda had made to her design and her golden hair tied back with the black ribbon that Irena had worn as a girl, Klara walked onto the stage towards the piano, her head lowered. She made a little bow in the direction of the audience and sat down at the keyboard.

Daniel, sitting in the front of the audience, sensed at once that all was not well. He had coached her and she was note perfect; she always was. But over the last few days she'd become more and more tense until he wondered whether he should have postponed this first public appearance.

Several moments passed and Daniel saw that she was shaking, her hands clenched in her lap. There was a ramp up to the stage and he pushed himself towards it. Sam left his seat and helped him up the steep slope. Klara heard the squeak of her father's wheels and turned her panic-stricken face to him. He tucked himself under the keyboard at her side and whispered something in her ear. Most of the audience had seen Daniel on Sports Day taking part in the egg and spoon race with Irena perched on his knee. Others were aware of his reputation as a musician. All watched intently as he put his own hands alongside Klara's, and they both began to play.

Daniel and their daughter at the keyboard together was a sight that Irena saw most days, but she would remember that image, that afternoon, in the years to come, when Klara learned to overcome her stage-fright with the warm and comforting presence of her father, sitting beside her and impro-

vising a second part for the Chopin murzurka she had chosen
– in spite of his urging her to find something less technically
demanding for her first concert. Daniel played a few phrases
with Klara and then he saw that her face had taken on an
intent and smiling concentration. The little pianist was now
lost in her music and her father backed his wheelchair away.
Careful not to make a sound this time, he turned to go back
down the ramp where Sam was waiting for him. Irena saw
that he was moved and still anxious that the spell should not
be broken before Klara woke to the fact that she was alone on
stage in front of several hundred people. But she finished her
piece and stood to acknowledge the applause, her right hand
on her heart.

The day before Daniel was due to go into hospital, he and
Irena went to hear 'The Dream of Gerontius' at the Albert
Hall. Daniel had been playing CDs of the work for several
weeks, filling the house with Elgar's last masterpiece. As she
listened yet again to the composer's agonized goodbye to the
world, Irena begged him to play something more cheerful.
She was dreading the concert; profound and beautiful though
it was, this was not music she wanted to hear with Daniel at
that particular time.

They had a box to themselves and Irena sat in the back, her
little red chair pulled as close to Daniel's wheelchair as possible. As the final chorale began, Irena saw his hands begin to
move. His fingers fanned out and began the fluttering dance
that he could not control when he longed to be conducting or
playing. When the last cadence died away, he folded his hands
together like the closing of a book and brought them up
towards his face, bowing his head so that his lips touched the
tips of his fingers. To Irena, it seemed that Daniel was closing
not just a piece of music, nor even a chapter of a book, but

something within himself, something very final. He sat still for a moment and then looked up at her.

'So,' his voice was soft. 'There's nothing more to say after that, is there?' and he took her hand and brought it to his lips, where he held it for a moment, before looking out again at the great auditorium, where he had spent so many hours both as performer and as part of an audience, always feeling completely at home under the enormous dome he could see from his bedroom window.

'I've always loved playing here, they've been such great times.'

'You're booked for the Proms next year – that's something to be looking forward to,' Irena said, but he didn't answer.

The orchestra had left the stage and the choirs were filing out. Irena opened the door of the box, but the corridor outside was still full of people and Daniel disliked being hemmed in by a crowd. He patted the chair next to him and they sat looking at each other, the sound of the Angels' Farewell still seeming to envelop them.

The corridor had emptied and Daniel pushed himself towards the lift. The group of waiting people divided as the doors opened, inviting him to go in first and Irena mimed that she'd take the stairs. When she got to the bottom, she found him outside, talking to some of the orchestral players who had been leaving by the stage door. His silver head was caught for a moment in the headlights of a passing car, and she felt an overwhelming cloud of grief and foreboding. And then she was behind Daniel's chair as she and the driver pushed him up the ramp into the cab.

Later that evening Daniel put on his old record of the Lindy Hop. He was twirling round and round in his chair and the children twirled too, putting their hands up to turn under his arm as they came face to face with him.

'Mummy, Mummy!'

Klara's face was scarlet with excitement. 'Daddy's teaching us the Lindy Hop! Come and dance with us!'

Irena, who had been packing Daniel's case for the hospital, watched as he spun Klara around.

'Knees up higher ... faster J-J!' Then Daniel began to cough, his shoulders heaving, his handkerchief over his mouth. Irena knelt down beside him. He seemed to be both laughing and coughing, so the children continued to dance around him and their mother.

'Come on Mummy – please dance with us!' cried Klara clapping her hands and starting to sing, her high voice picking up the tune where Daniel had left off.

'No. No more Lindy Hop. Let's have something slower – what about a waltz, darling? I've got a disc here somewhere – you used to dance this with Mamija, didn't you?'

She sat down on Daniel's knee, putting her head close to his. His coughing had ceased but his breathing was still laboured. Irena knew he didn't want her to tell the children to stop and spoil the joyful mood of the occasion. She began to sing The Blue Danube and Daniel turned his chair slowly with one hand, his other arm around Irena, bending to kiss her ear under the long scented hair.

'That's not dancing. That's kissing,' snorted Jo-Jo and Klara said, in disgust, 'They're snogging.'

Irena had reprimanded the girl for using that word before, but now she giggled and started to sing with the music. Daniel, feeling stronger, joined in with the 'pom poms,' at the end of each line.

'Your heart's beating so fast,' she said, her head against his chest.

'As long as it's still beating ...' he replied as he continued to turn to the rhythm of Irena's voice,

'Da, da, da, DA'

The music stopped and Daniel stopped too. He took Irena's hand, brought it to his lips and kissed it. 'Thank you, Madam. You dance divinely.'

Irena heard the door-bell ring. Magda had come to collect the children; they were to stay with her for the first few days while Daniel was in hospital.

39.   AUTUMN FLIGHT

DANIEL had slept badly. Unable to get comfortable, Irena, awake herself in the early hours, had seen his open eyes glittering in the light of the street lamp outside their window.

'Can't sleep?' she'd asked, as she helped him turn over, so that he was facing away from her.

'I was thinking … it seems a waste of time, to be asleep. There's so much I want to say to you, but I am quite tired and …' but he didn't finish his sentence and she kissed the back of his neck.

Irena woke early and got out of bed quietly so as not to disturb Daniel. She pulled on her clothes and left the room, went downstairs and unlocked the back door.

It was the end of summer and the house martins, who nested every year under the eves of the house, just above the bedroom windows, were circling above in a perfect blue sky. They'll be gone soon, she thought. It was always a sad moment, but that morning she refused to allow herself either regret or anxiety. Instead, she picked flowers to take into the hospital and put beside Daniel's bed: Michaelmas daisies and Japanese anemones and the last of the intense blue crane's bill which matched his eyes. Then she went into the studio, but, that morning, did not open the piano. She touched the golden case of the Fazzioli and then laid her head down on it, enjoying the cool smoothness of the polished wood and wondering how long it would be before Daniel would be back there and playing again. He would play again, of course, but she hated to think of him on the operating table, of the violation of his beloved body. She forced her mind away from that image and looked out at the garden again. She should try to put the garden to bed properly; it was a resolution she made every autumn but each spring found it still a brown forest of seed pods and sodden leaves. She secretly rather liked it that way, but felt that by now she should have become an orderly gardener and housekeeper. She suspected that it was probably too late to mend her ways.

The church clock chimed seven. It was time to wake Daniel; everything was packed and ready and he was 'nil by mouth', so no breakfast for him that day. She bunched the flowers together and ran up the stairs calling, 'Darling. Better get up now ...'

Seeing from the landing that Daniel was still lying as he had been before she'd gone downstairs, she closed the door and knelt down beside him, dropping the flowers on the floor. She took his hands in hers. But they were very cold and, when she tried to gather his body into her arms, he was stiff and unyielding. She picked up the fallen flowers and laid them on his chest. Then she put her head next to his on the pillow.

Later, Irena remembered hearing voices downstairs, but not Magda arriving or who had called the ambulance. She wanted to stay with Daniel, to be alone with him, but suddenly there were other people in the room, speaking in hushed voices. Then someone was lifting her to her feet and she was struggling and looking back at the bed over her shoulder as two men in dark suits went into the bedroom and closed the door behind them.

'Please, please don't take him away,' she begged, 'Don't let them take him away,' but Magda had her arm around Irena and was coaxing her down the stairs. In the kitchen she could hear the kettle hissing and Magda starting to sob as the bottle of milk in her hand spilt over the worktop and onto the floor.

Irena went to the window. The house martins had lined up on the telegraph wire between the studio and the house, ruffling their feathers and calling to each other as they bobbed into the air, circled and then took their places again, waiting. How did they know, she wondered, when the time had come to leave? How would they find their way?

As she watched, the first bird spread his dark, pointed wings and, hesitating no longer, the other birds sailed upwards in a winnowing, swirling blue and white cloud and were gone from sight.

'Please don't go without me, darling. Take me with you,' she whispered, but Daniel was already beyond her reach. She could not follow him because she did not know where he had gone.

PART THREE

40. ASHES AND ICES

Pourait-il d'un feu qui devore
Éprouver deux fois les effets?
Les cendres s'échauffent encore,
Mais ne se rallument jamais

L. Andrieux

IRENA had only one pre-war photograph of herself with Daniel. Hedija had put it in a silver frame and given it to her for her birthday, six months after her arrival in America. It showed the two of them on their bicycles, he wearing a broad-brimmed hat, pulled down to the top of his glasses, so the wind wouldn't blow it off, his guitar slung across his back. And Irena was wearing a beret, as she did again today, crammed onto her small head and down almost to her eyes, hugging her round face and containing most of her abundant chestnut hair. They were both smiling broadly and waving at the photographer, her mother holding her new camera nervously and laughing as she felt for the right button to press, so that the picture was slightly out of focus. It was the autumn of 1991; they were going into the forest outside Sarajevo to look for mushrooms and all was well with their world.

Fearing she would break down, Magda had kept her face averted from Irena's gaze since they had landed in Sarajevo, but, as she was being shown her hotel room, she did look anxiously back at her sister-in-law, who stood in the corridor with the children. The porter opened the doors of the adjacent rooms, carried the luggage in and pocketed his tip.

Klara and Jo-Jo loved hotels and, having stayed in a good many when Daniel was working abroad, considered themselves to be experts on the facilities. Irena opened one of the suitcases and took out a cardboard box which she stuffed into her bag while the children examined the fruit bowl with the manager's welcome card and went on to eat the chocolates that had been put on their pillows. They were walking towards the lift when Magda appeared in the doorway, her eyes red and swollen. She gave Irena and the children a brief hug, shaking her head when they stood back to let her go first into the lift. She blurted out that she would not be coming with them and her eyes met Sam's for a moment, but the young man could not help her. His own feelings were enough to bear and he had a new widow and two fatherless children to care for that afternoon. He wondered how long all this would go on and what Daniel would have had to say about the despair he had left behind him.

All this daily anguish was new to Sam, who had not yet known death in his short life. For his mother, however, he knew that grieving for her family whose lives had ended in Auchwitz and Treblinka remained a constant part of her daily existence.

'Sometimes I think we owe them at least this,' Zdenka would say, 'but where they are now and whether they benefit from all these tears – well, we just don't know. Maybe it's self-indulgence, or just guilt to have been spared their fate. It doesn't get any better, so maybe I've allowed it to become a habit and wouldn't know what to do with myself without the companionship of all those ghosts.'

She had managed to laugh, but she knew her son was suffering and she could not help him in the raw newness of his loss. Her own grief, the gradual piecing together of her family's jigsaw, the acceptance of the many missing pieces, had

seemed to ripen and develop over the years. There was something in her that could not accept the finality of their fate.
In her dreams each still appeared regularly to her, reopening
great wounds that would not heal. Until, at last, she had come
to believe that she owed the recognition that life itself had
been denied them, they who had no graves, no sacred place
where their passing might have been marked by special words
on special days.

So Sam set his jaw, bundled his charges into their hired car
again, and consulted the map he had bought. Irena leant over
to trace with her thin fingers the roads she had once known
so well. He drove confidently at first – he had often served as
driver to Daniel in that city; but now he was heading out into
countryside that was new to him. Irena directed him through
the straggling suburbs onto a road that twisted upwards
into the hills. He pulled onto the verge where a path led off
between some of the few remaining conifers that still stood,
now charred and branchless. There had been attempts to
replant the forest; rows of saplings struggled to take root on
the war-ravaged hillside, amongst them the jagged and blackened stumps of the remaining ancient trees.

Jo-Jo strode ahead, but Sam took Klara's hand as she held
back, overawed and alarmed by the unfamiliar and gaunt
surroundings. Irena walked ahead, clutching her big red bag
against her. 'There's the river – see' and she pointed down
the now bramble-entangled path. 'That's the bank where
Daddy and I used to eat our lunch.' She was smiling in spite
of herself, as she would always eat most of their picnic long
before they arrived at the river bank. Daniel, knowing this,
had refused to release the chocolate bars from his guitar case
until they were sitting side by side with their bare feet in the
icy water.

The last time Irena had been in those devastated woods, just after their marriage, Daniel had been with her in his wheel-chair and they hadn't ventured far. Although they had known that nothing would look the same as it did in their shared memories, the reality of the hideous destruction all around them was more shocking than they had anticipated, and a pall of sadness had overcome them as they turned back. Their taxi driver had been summoned to help Daniel, whose chair had stuck on the muddy track, but it was not the indignity of having to ask the driver for help, that had caused Daniel's silence on the return journey. It was the unbearable sight and stench of the ruined forests. They clung to each other in the back of the taxi and Irena had wept. Now, however, she was prepared for what she was to see. And she had a task to fulfil.

'Sam – take the children down there to the river, would you?' Jo-Jo was already some way down the path, walking determinedly, only stopping now and then to disentangle himself from the brambles that caught at his legs. Klara walked close to Sam hoping that he would protect her from the scary dark shapes that loomed at them from every side. It was hard now to imagine what those woods had been like all those years ago. Irena had only to mention her rides there with the young Daniel to become radiantly girlish again, her normally pale face glowing and her smile once more forming dimples in her cheeks. This had remained a special place for them, imprinted in their shared memories with their laughter and singing, as they had bumped down the well-worn pine-scented paths between huge trees of a thousand greens. They could not have known, as their voices rang out and shafts of sunlight flashed between the branches above them, of either the joy or the pain that would lie ahead on the path that was life itself.

Irena watched Sam and the children until they were almost at the river bank. Then she opened her bag – the red Birkin bag that Daniel had given her, astonishing her with its glamorous chic – now well-worn and rather out of shape. She took out a cardboard box. Soon after the cremation, she'd disposed of the false brass urn that had held Daniel's ashes, and put them under his piano in a box that had once held a metronome. The whole business was both tragic and bizarre – she imagined his amusement at having been so reduced – the big warm man now just a handful of ashes, with nothing else to show for his bright, life-affirming presence.

She walked off the path and stood for a moment, hesitant about her momentous but somewhat ludicrous task as the wind had got up a little, lifting the skirt of her coat. Taking a deep breath, she held the box down close to the ground and let the ashes trickle slowly out, forming a grey pyramid at her feet. Almost at once a gust of wind scooped them up and swirled them away in spiral eddies. Irena shook the final particles, which were disconcertingly large, from the box and then, without knowing why, she picked up the last piece from the pile at her feet and put it in her pocket. The wind did not leave the rest of her offering undisturbed for long, but wafted Daniel's mortal remains into the air again and tossed them here and there, playfully. She watched their progress across the hillside, leaping upwards again now and again, like a willow-the-wisp, as if to dance once more, to twirl with the uninhibited grace of a young and ardent spirit.

Sam stayed for a while on the river bank, showing the children how to skim the flat river stones across the water. Looking back up the path, he had seen Irena's detour and that she was now returning. Jo-Jo scrambled up the path ahead of them, but Klara seemed lost in thought, looking at the river.

Irena had told her many times how she and her father had sat in that spot with their picnics, and she tried to imagine her father as she had never known him – able to run down the hill and perch on the bank of the rocky river bank. She caught up with Sam and the two went back up the path to find her mother standing where they had left her, closing the clasp of her red bag.

Sam looked over to Irena and, as he scanned the hillside, a puff of wind caught and lifted a handful of ashes and sent them upwards into the cold air.

'Goodbye Daniel,' he said under his breath, wondering if his tutor's laughter might sometimes be heard here in years to come. He wanted to believe it would. Irena, too, was whispering something – a farewell or a benediction perhaps – but only one word was audible to him. Klara looked at her mother and then at the young man who had taken her elbow as if to steady her. And she looked away again, accustomed as she now was to all the manifestations of grief that had taken over their family life. They all cried a lot these days. Sometimes she dreamed that her father had come back, rather late as usual, and heard him calling their names, as he pushed himself into the house, his lap filled with little parcels and bunches of flowers. Waking was the most painful thing she had ever known.

The café was still there. Or maybe it was just very like the one Irena remembered from before the war, where Daniel had taken her to lunch, a new and exciting experience for her, as her parents never ate in such places. His glasses had steamed up in the hot atmosphere of the café and he'd taken them off. As Irena looked at him, she became aware again of the new feelings she had begun to have for him, feelings she did not yet understand. He polished his glasses with a big red and white handkerchief, and put them on again, smiling at her. Then he picked up the menu and read it out. Irena had corrected his pronunciation and mis-translated the names of the dishes, laughing as he gave their order to the bewildered waitress.

Sam called Magda from the payphone on the bar, rejoined them and ordered himself a plate of goulash. The café seemed to have much the same menu as before but Irena was not hungry. Sam looked at her anxiously but she betrayed no emotion – she could not have, for she felt nothing – only a great empty numbness. She kept her hand in her coat pocket, holding between her fingers all that was left to her of the earthly presence of Daniel. She did not believe in the soul or the spirits of the departed. The small charred piece of bone comforted her somehow. She left the table and went to the ladies' – much improved since she last visited it. Then it had been necessary to go into the back yard amongst the chickens and into a small shed with a wooden seat over a bucket. Now she looked at her face in the pink-tinted mirror and pushed some hair back under her beret. Returning into the gloom of the café, she seemed to smell Turkish tobacco and saw a figure sitting at the corner table, his back to her, a spiral of pale blue smoke curling above his head. There was a huge choice of ice-creams and the children studied the coloured photographs around the walls. They chose with care and forgot, as they ate, the mission that had brought them to Sarajevo that day.

41. SCISSORS

WHY IS IT, thought Irena, that one can never find a pair of scissors? She rummaged through the drawer in the kitchen dresser where there was to be found an eclectic assortment of objects swept off the table from time to time when it became too cluttered for the family to eat. The children used the kitchen table for their homework, and Daniel had resorted to covering it in sheet music, as he couldn't reach the top of his piano. Amongst the piles of junk mail, boxes of sticking plaster, out-of-date parking permits, takeway menus, pens, pencils and elastic bands, she found what she was looking for. She ran upstairs and sat down at her dressing table.

The mirror was dusty; the room hadn't been cleaned for – oh, how long? Time was hard for her these days. It felt like something thick and sticky through which she was wading, her legs seeming too weak to make any headway. She wiped the glass with the back of her hand but did not look at her reflection. Instead, she pulled the elastic band off her tangled ponytail and ran her fingers through the chestnut mass of her hair. Then she lifted a handful and held it out to the side, opening the scissors with her right hand and closing the blades over it. The scissors made little impression on the thick lock she was holding and she started to cry as she succeeded only in cutting a few strands, pulling at the roots as she did so.

'What are you doing, Mummy?' Klara stood in the doorway. She came towards her mother, hesitantly as she did these days.

'I want to cut my hair. I hate it. I want it short. These scissors don't work ...' Irena went on trying to get the blades to close on the now ragged clump of hair. She was becoming hysterical and Klara wanted to cry too, but she was learning about grief and that the mother she had played and laughed with had gone and she did not know if she would ever return. Her father's playfulness and laughter had been taken away from them too, but she knew that he would never come back. And his music had gone away too, for Irena had locked the studio and only Sam who had started to go through Daniel's papers and scores, was allowed in there. The piano had been silent for three weeks now and Klara had to practise in the school music rooms.

'They won't work for you. They're mine – for lefties. I'll get you Teta's big ones – she left them when she'd finished making my concert dress.' She went off on her errand, trying not to cry herself. When she came back, Irena was sitting at the dressing table, combing her hair with her fingers to get the tangles out. She had not brushed it properly for days.

'Oh, please don't cut your lovely hair. Please don't.' but Irena took the cutting-out scissors from her and started to chop around behind her jaw on one side. Then she pulled the hair down on the other side and sliced through that.

'Do the back for me, darling.' but Klara backed away, crying now.

'No no! Daddy loves your hair. You know he does.'

Irena turned around, threw the scissors down and took hold of her daughter and began to shake her. 'He won't see it! He isn't here!' she shrieked. 'Don't you understand? Why can't you understand?' Then she focused on Klara's terrified face and chattering teeth and pulled the child towards her, so that her tangled brown hair became mixed with her daughter's, which was the pale red-gold that her grandmother Finola's had been.

Later, when they had both cried themselves to the stage

when they were sodden with tears and begun to snivel quietly, they washed their faces and Klara helped her mother to straighten up the ragged back of her bobbed hair. The girl gathered up the long clippings and Irena motioned towards the waste basket. Obediently, the girl dropped the hair in and watched her mother go into the bathroom and shut the door. She bent, then, and quickly gathered the hair up again and took it into her room. There she laid it out on her bed and smoothed it carefully before tying around it an old black hair ribbon of Irena's. Before she tied the bow, she changed her mind and pulled a few strands away from the thick skein. These she wound into a coil and laid in her 'jewel box', where she kept only precious and secret things. The rest she carried back into her parents' room and put away in the top right hand-drawer of the French *commode* amongst Daniel's handkerchiefs and old spectacle cases.

Magda was cooking spaghetti when Klara appeared in the kitchen. She had the the tight, constrained look she always had these days. Jo-Jo was finishing an essay and didn't look at his sister.

'Hurry up, Klara darling. Have you washed your hands?'

Klara nodded. She hadn't washed them, but now she could hear Irena's step in the hall. She watched Magda's expression as the door opened and her mother entered.

Irena's little, round face on its slim neck looked more than ever like a pale flower.

Never a big eater, she'd lost weight over the last three weeks and Magda had found it hard to persuade her to join her children at meals. Now, with her roughly-cropped hair falling like a brass bell around her face, she looked like an urchin and her sister-in-law stood staring at her until Klara went to her mother's side and put her hand through her arm.

'Mummy's got a new haircut. Doesn't she look nice?'

Jo-Jo looked up, his mouth falling open.

'No. It's horrible. Daddy wouldn't like it, would he Teta?'
Magda turned back to her pan of water and did not answer.

The great Fazzioli had gone from the studio and in its place
was an upright piano for Klara to practise on, and two trestle
tables. Sam was back in London; he had cancelled all his
engagements for the autumn and a light could be seen late
into the night as he and Irena tried to make sense of the piles
of papers on Daniel's desk and spread out over the tables.
Somewhere they should be able to find the outline programme for the concert that was to have celebrated Daniel's
50th Birthday. After the shock of his death, the manager
of the Wigmore Hall had asked Leo Haskell whether the
family would consider a memorial concert on that date.
Leo, glad that there was something he could still do for his
favourite client, had contacted the musicians who were originally to have performed with Daniel; all were delighted
to take part. They would accept no fees; the proceeds, after
expenses had been paid, would go to the foundation which
Daniel had set up to look after Sarajevo's musicians after the
war.

Irena knew she must accept the generous offer, although
the thought of such a public airing of grief filled her with
horror. Eventually, they found Daniel's notes for the concert
programme. Tucked in amongst the musicians' details, was
an envelope addressed to Sam. He turned it over. Irena looked
up, wondering why he had suddenly fallen silent. Then she
saw what he was holding and Daniel's unmistakable writing;
she held out her hand for the envelope, her heart leaping with
expectation.

'Is that a letter – Oh, it's for you. Sorry, I didn't realize.'
Irena was embarrassed when she saw Sam's name and turned
back to the file in front of her. She waited for him to finish

reading, a wave of envy enveloping her – she wanted a letter from Daniel. Just something for her alone.

My Dear Sam

I hope you won't need to take any action on this, but it seems sensible, given my present state of health, to make some plans for the possibility that I shan't be able to take part in my birthday concert.

Leo will no doubt try to do something on that date – I know the old rogue, so I suspect there will be a happening of some sort even if I am no longer there to take part.

I originally chose pieces to play with my friends which have had most meaning in my life as you will see when you read the sketch programme. They are all things you play wonderfully well – probably better now than I do! So please would you do me the honour of being host in my place?

You know that I have always thought you a very fine pianist and my only sadness is that you haven't been heard as much as you could have been. I'm more proud than I can say to have been able to teach you over these years, always feeling that you are truly a musician after my own heart. So please don't try to hide your light under a bushel of shyness and modesty.

How to thank you for your years of help? When you appeared at my bedside all those years ago, the shyest of my pupils but the only one who dared to face your very changed teacher, we did not know what a long road we would travel together. I cannot express my gratitude, and can only hope I have never seemed to take for granted the many things you have done for me – and for my family, who all love you as one of them. You have lightened my burden in many,

many ways, not least in encouraging me to embrace
teaching as a calling when I could no longer perform
the music that had hitherto seemed my only goal.

When you read this I shall no longer be with you.
Look after Irena for me. She will not know which
way to go. My own life is fading away, but she must
go on – she and our beloved little ones. Help her
in whatever way you can to find the strength she'll
need.

With all my very best wishes, as ever, your
affectionate friend,

Daniel

Sam remained turned away from Irena, trying to regain his
composure while she watched him, wondering if he was going
to share the letter with her. At last he took a deep breath and
turned to face her. He read aloud the first part of his letter
before he folded it small and put it into his breast pocket,
unable to watch Irena's face as he did so.

After a moment, she whispered, 'How terrible that Danny
seems to have known that he wouldn't be able to play himself.
Did you have any idea about this?'

'No, I didn't. He was a bit embarrassed about the concert
and felt that he was not feeling up to that sort of public expo-
sure. But he never said he might not be well enough to play in
it, or even …' He paused, unable to bring himself to finish his
sentence, before he asked: 'Would you like me to play, Irena?
Do you think I should?'

'But of course, Sam. That's what Danny wanted, so you
must do it for him. Is the concert programme settled otherwise, with the other musicians? I suppose you'd better tell
them and start rehearsals soon.'

Irena and Sam were working in the studio. She stopped what she was doing. 'Sam', she said for the third time that morning and once again couldn't finish her sentence. He waited, seeing that her hand was shaking as she typed something onto her laptop. Then she said, her voice sounding choked: 'Sam … Did you ever think Daniel was tempted to end his life? I know we were told he'd had a massive heart attack, but he'd taken a lot of morphine the night before – I know he had.'

Sam looked up from the manuscript he was copying, but he did not answer immediately. Then he asked, hesitantly, 'Because he couldn't take any more pain, do you mean?

Irena nodded and began to speak rapidly now. 'He kept talking about death. It was often on his mind. He wasn't afraid of dying, but he couldn't bear the thought of parting from the people and things he loved in life. He'd become quite religious – in a universal sort of way. He had never practised as a Jew, though he was proud of being one; it was church music that always transported him and more and more the philosophy of Christianity – loving your neighbour as yourself. He was such a giver, wasn't he? Such a sharer of the things he valued. But a little while ago he woke up saying he'd dreamed of being able to put an end to everything. He said the peace had been so wonderful, the peace of leaving his body behind and not having to struggle any more. Since that time in France he'd become obsessed with the fear of losing the use of his hands permanently. He was sure it was going to happen and he was terrified. But – he loved us all so much – I just can't believe he'd leave us and not even say goodbye. He didn't leave a note for me – or anything.'

'I did wonder if he was stock-piling the morphine.' said Sam wondering, as he said it, how wise it was to pursue this painful speculation, hut he went on, not sure how to change the subject at so intense a moment. 'He used to get me to pick up his prescriptions on my way over to you, sometimes.

I noticed that he already seemed to have a lot of morphine on the shelf when I was putting it away for him …'

They looked at each other and Irena ran over to the house. Sam followed her reluctantly into the bathroom and she opened Daniel's medicine cupboard. They examined the packets and looked at the dates. There still seemed to be a good deal of morphine, but they couldn't judge whether a large dose had been taken the night before Daniel died. Irena turned away and went to her room, shutting the door.

As Sam was leaving the studio later that day, he saw that Daniel's linen jacket was still hanging on the back of the door. He took it off the hook, thinking he'd take it back to the house for Magda to put with the rest of Daniel's clothes. For a moment, he held it against his cheek, stroking the well-worn fabric and wondering if it would still smell of its wearer. He searched the pockets hoping to find something, a handkerchief perhaps, that would still retain a trace of − of what? He wasn't sure but he found himself longing for Daniel, for his strong physical presence, and, overwhelmed with a violent spasm of pain, he shouted, 'Daniel. Daniel where are you, why have you left us?'

Sam thought he had learnt to live with the aching, everyday grief of loss, but now a new wound seemed to have opened and the pain was unbearable. He sat down and sobbed, his tears soaking the jacket he held against his face. Then he remembered Daniel's words about his own mourning − for his young man's body − and that it had been a long time before he saw that it was a self-indulgent grief, which fed on itself and led nowhere.

Sam rubbed the sleeve of the jacket against his face. Something crackled in the breast pocket and he took out a sealed envelope, addressed in Daniel's handwriting to Irena. The ink was smudged as if it had been in the rain. Or spotted by tears.

He stood for a moment watching Irena circling the table where they had been working earlier in the day. She was still as graceful as a young girl, he thought, as she organised the papers in the coloured files she'd allocated to the artists who would be performing in the concert. He placed the envelope on the table in front of her. As she focused on the writing, she seemed confused and looked up at Sam questioningly.

Pushing the letter towards her, he said, 'I found it this morning in his jacket pocket – here on the back of the door.'

Irena continued to stare at the letter, and it was minutes before she was able to pick it up. Then she sat down abruptly, put her thumb through the top of the envelope and ripped it open.

Sam left the studio and closed the door softly. Outside, the autumn garden, fresh from the recent rain, sparkled and rustled. Apples were swelling on the trees that he and Irena had planted – eleven years ago? Yes, about that, as she had been pregnant with Klara. He remembered her pleasure as they called Daniel from the piano – his precious Fazzioli, newly delivered – and showed them the tiny, leafless saplings.

'Apples? Lovely – but where's the fruit? Oh, you've eaten them all!' cried Daniel and leant his head against Irena's great belly, his arm around her waist while Sam dug a hole for the next tree, thinking his own thoughts.

My darling Darling,

I never thought I'd need to write a letter to you, since we are always together. In fact, I don't think that I have even written you a love letter, which is a shame, as you should have had one every single day.

This letter is such a very hard one to write – I don't know if I'll have the courage to finish it and put it in an envelope for you to read. For when you do, I shall no longer be with you. I am writing to say goodbye to you, my darling, adored wife and it's unbearable.

Today Hussein told me that eventually the paralysis is likely to extend to my hands. Then I'd be no good to you as a husband and useless as a pianist. I could not live like that – please try to understand.

You have been so patient, so strong and wonderful. You gave back the meaning and joy to my life when everything seemed broken and dark. I hope – I believe – that we have been able to mend the broken pieces in each other's lives and to bring light into the dark places, too.

I know you will look after Klara and Jo-Jo for me as you are the best of mothers and will know how to stop them from being too sad for too long. They love their old father, but time will help them to forget. And one day, not too soon, Darling you'll find love again, too. I know you will because you are made to love. And when you do, don't hesitate to follow it – I beg you to remember that I want your happiness and have always wanted it. Do not destroy yourself with grief for me. I can't bear to be leaving you, but I believe you _will_ have the strength to make a new life for yourself and for Klara and Jo-Jo. Don't close your mind to the future, I beg of you.

Don't hate me for deserting you. I know you will to start with. But, my darling heart, we both know, have always known, that one of us would have to go first and that the other would be left alone. But with music you will never be truly alone. Play that lovely little viola for me a little every day and think of all those happy times, so many of them, we've had together. More than most people have, I know.

Goodbye my sweet, sweet one and be at peace with me if you can,

Your husband, who adores you, Daniel

Irena felt very cold. Her hands no longer seemed to belong to her as she put the letter back in the envelope. Sam who'd gone to the kitchen, wondered whether to go home or to wait and try to help her. One thing was sure, he would have to talk honestly to her; he'd have to tell her all he knew about Daniel's last days. He made some coffee and found a bottle of brandy, put both on a tray and went out to the studio noticing that the leaves were already leaving the lime tree that spread over the roof and making a blanket of yellow patchwork on the tiles and the paving below.

Irena was sitting with her head on the table pillowed in her arms, her whole body shaken with sobs. Sam put down the tray, poured her some coffee and put some brandy in it.

'Irena, I want to tell you something.'

She tried to stop crying, but continued to sob with great gusts of despair.

Finally, she looked up at him. 'What?' Surely nothing he told her now could bring more pain, more finality into this stifling, claustrophobic grief?

'Do you remember when you went to Amsterdam with Magda to see the Rembrandts?' The two women had gone together as Daniel had a master class and the exhibition they wanted to see was about to finish.

'Yes.' Her voice was hoarse and she sat up, her face swollen and her eyes red. 'Why?'

'Daniel had a heart attack while you were away – quite a minor one I think. He was in hospital for two nights. He made me promise not to tell you.' She stared at him, her mouth ugly and downturned as tears came again.

'Seems he'd probably inherited a weak heart from his father and grandfather and he'd strained it pushing himself around and trying to live a normal life. They had said he might be able to have a pacemaker fitted or an operation, but you know how he hated anything to do with medicine and hospitals – I think he was beginning to feel more disabled than he was prepared to accept.'

Irena picked up the letter and said: 'I don't know if this is a suicide note. I don't know what he means. He says he can't take any more pain. After he wrote that, he did agree to have the back operation – for my sake. But I know he didn't really believe that it would help him.' She was holding the letter out to Sam but he shook his head. If anything was private this surely was.

They drank their coffee and then a good deal of brandy as the day turned into night in the dark studio. Magda had taken Klara and Jo-Jo home with her that night as she often did – she didn't want them to have to go to bed again to the sound of their mother weeping. She took them to the cinema and then back to her own house in Muswell Hill to sleep. And Irena and Sam finished the brandy and fell asleep at either end of the daybed in the studio, innocently like children taking comfort in the other's presence. But not before Irena had torn her letter into tiny pieces, put them into her coffee saucer and set light to them. Flames leapt up for a few seconds and then died to a glowing heap of blackening embers.

42. AN OUTING

[IRENA]

A S DANIEL'S student and then his indispensable helper, Sam had been a part of our lives for most of our marriage; Daniel regarded him as his protegé although the young man's public performances had only consisted of small recitals in little-known halls and churches. Knowing Sam was a pianist of high quality who should be heard, this had frustrated Daniel. There was a delicate, almost feminine quality about Sam's slight figure and the long sandy hair that he wore in a pony tail.

His relationship with Magda remained a mystery to us. Daniel had once surprised them in bed together and I found him pouring himself a glass of brandy in the kitchen – he was a good judge of character and seldom shocked by anything, but this was not something he had expected. He and I speculated about the future of the relationship, but nothing was ever said and Magda refused to discuss the subject with either of us. I think it all tailed off after a few months. But something precious remained of their love, even when it became obvious that it was not going anywhere; we had long suspected that Sam was gay. Magda and he remained good friends and were my own staunchest allies in the years to come.

After Daniel's death, desperate to comfort one another in their own grief, they decided that they would between them relieve me of the burden of my two children until I seemed more able to cope; I was still in such a state of shock that I suffered from loss of memory and an inability to make the smallest of decisions. I regularly forgot what day it was. Once I forgot to collect the children from school and the mother who brought them back found me weeping in the studio. So Magda moved in to the spare room and Sam would arrive after breakfast, do the school run and come and go all day fitting my children's schedule in with his own. Leo muttered to himself about the cancelled recitals and concerts, but he understood that all our lives had been changed when Daniel ceased to be their centre.

I knew that Sam often stayed with his parents in Suffolk, and one Friday he asked me if he could take Klara and Jo-Jo with him.

I had no idea what his family would be like. Not being English, I found it hard to evaluate an accent, which I knew was usually an accurate guide to a person's background and education. The other students came from all over the country and I had found the Northerners particularly incomprehensible, but I never had any trouble understanding Sam. To me he sounded like one of the Radio 3 announcers.

'Could I come too?' I asked, 'I'm sorry, that's very rude, but I miss them so much when they're not here.' It was true, but I knew also that, alone in the house, I would use the day to wallow in grief and that could do me no good.

My suggestion seemed to embarrass Sam and he hesitated for quite a long time before saying more politely than enthusiastically: 'Of course. My parents would love to meet you. I'll pick you all up at 10 o'clock. Don't be smart. Bring your wellies.' And he was off, looking as if this was not a development he welcomed.

The next day Magda got the children ready and cast a despairing eye on my appearance. 'Do wear something pretty, darling. It might make you feel better.'

I always wore the same sort of clothes these days, just anything comfortable and warm. I was constantly cold.

'Sam said not to be smart.'

'As if that's likely …' Magda snorted.

'He lives in Suffolk, you know. But I don't know anything about his family. I've no idea what to expect.' Then I saw in Magda's expression that she did know something about them. She was smiling secretively as I asked her if she had met Sam's family and she admitted she had, but was non-committal and clearly preferred not to say any more.

Sam collected us in an estate car; I remembered that he'd used this car to collect us once, when Daniel had found a home for his harpsichord when we moved from the flat. My memory had become very bad – I couldn't recall where we'd taken it.

This was my first outing for the ten weeks I had been a widow. Of course I had gone to Daniel's cremation and to Sarajevo with his ashes. Now, looming closer and closer, was the memorial concert. I dreaded the occasion and felt sick all the time – another manifestation of grief, I supposed.

The day was bright and sunny, the countryside looked verdant and seductive, but my spirits were so low that I would happily have opened the car door and thrown myself out onto the road. Sam played quiz games with the children as he drove, making up funny answers and feigning indignation when they scored a point. His high spirits reminded me painfully of Daniel when I had first known him. In most other ways they were not at all alike. Sam was usually a very quiet person and had always so admired Daniel that he hung on his every word, offering few of his own. His modesty and diffidence had a certain charm, but sometimes I felt impatient with his too obvious adoration of Daniel. To my great surprise, he had proved himself of late to be a very practical man and thoughtful to a degree. He seemed instinctively to know what would be helpful to me and when to disappear and leave me alone. It wasn't until much later that I realised that, without his help, I would have gone under.

Sam's fair hair had been cut and was now short and jelled into spikes. He had extraordinarily dark eyes, almost black, and dark eyebrows too, which made me wonder whether he was as English as I had always supposed his name to be. He wasn't a tall man, but well proportioned. His hands were particularly beautiful and very small for a pianist. He had once told me that he couldn't stretch far enough to play a lot of Rachmaninov and I'd secretly been pleased as Rachmaninov was not my favourite composer, and reminded me sadly of Daniel's desperate efforts to play the heavily pedalled Romances that had no longer been within his capabilities.

'Almost there,' said Sam and we turned into a drive through a tall stone gateway with a lodge on each side. Surprised to find us going up a long avenue of enormous lime trees, the children looked out of the window and Klara whispered: 'Mummy, look. Is it a palace?'

The house ahead of us was certainly very large and it looked familiar but I couldn't think why. It stood in a park, overlooking a lake with great trees spreading themselves over plushy green grass that made me want to lie on it, it looked so soft and inviting. Not far off a herd of deer looked up as we drove by them and walked off, slowly and gracefully. I wondered if Sam's parents worked here, a thought which was reinforced when we drove round to the back of the house and parked in a walled yard.

Sam turned to me and said, rather shyly, 'My parents live in the stables.'

'Who lives in the big house?'

'No one now ... I was brought up there but it became impossible to run without staff, so my parents converted the stable block to live in. The house and grounds are open to the public. There's a piano museum. But surely you remember coming here? When you left the flat and Daniel gave his keyboard collection to the museum – it must have been about ten years ago?'

That was why the house looked familiar. Daniel had given a harpsichord recital in the music room, which was full of famous old pianos, including Chopin's own instrument.

'Yes, yes. Now I remember. I was expecting Klara. You didn't say it was your home.'

'Well, no. It was Daniel's evening and he just needed me to help and carry things.'

The children got out of the car, unusually quiet. We walked through a high arch in the wall and found ourselves in a cobbled yard with low buildings on either side. On the far side was a blue door with a fan light, and, as we approached, it was thrown open by an elderly woman, who spread her arms wide and gathered Sam into them.

'Samuel, *mein Liebling*! Well done, you're on time.' She had a shrewd, wrinkled face, the same dark eyes as her son and faded hair that must once have been red. Sam introduced me, and she shook my hand and Klara's, but Jo-Jo looked at her suspiciously and stood behind me.

Our hostess led us into a large kitchen with a scrubbed wooden table laid for lunch. The room had been converted from several loose-boxes; the drainage channel still divided the cobbled floor and iron mangers had been left on the back wall.

'How lovely!' I cried. 'Look darlings, horses used to live in here!' The children looked surprised but said nothing.

Our hostess laughed. 'Don't worry. They'll feel better after lunch, I expect. Samuel, Daddy's gone out with the dogs, but he'll be back any minute. Lunch can wait, it's only chicken. I thought the children would like that.' She spoke with a marked foreign accent and something of her speech reminded of me of Daniel's: He would also put a 'k' at the end of words ending in 'ing' when he spoke fast.

We went into a large sitting room where all the sofas and armchairs were covered with the same flowered chintz. There was a worn oriental rug of enormous size on the floor and a great many pictures, mainly portraits of men with shooting dogs, and women with bonneted children, against backgrounds of woods and castles and, in one or two, the great house itself. I sat in one of the flowery chairs and accepted the glass of very dry sherry I was given.

Sam sat down next to his mother, who carried the conversation cheerfully from subject to subject, none of which was embarrassing or controversial. It was my first taste of small talk, the mainstay of English upper class social intercourse. For I had been brought up in a family of intellectuals and Daniel and I had lived amongst people who expressed their opinions forcefully about everything: politics, religion and the arts. There had been no no-go areas. Here, in this charming room with its long windows looking down to the lake and park, nothing controversial was said. I began to feel very peaceful and safe and I wondered at myself.

It fascinated me to watch Sam in this environment. I thought I knew him well, but would never have guessed that this was his background. He listened to his mother, looking a little embarrassed at times, but I could see he was devoted to her. She was, it soon became apparent, completely at home at St Bede's Abbey, but seemed as foreign there as it was possible to be. I wondered where she was from and why she had landed up here. Above the fireplace was a more modern picture than the others, a family group, painted a good many years ago in the garden. Lady Siddal-Gore, much younger then, sat next to a blond man, who I assumed must be her husband, Sir Robert. They were sitting on a garden bench, he tweed-clad and holding a gun, and she, red-haired as I guessed she had been, with a pile of sheet music on her lap. In the picture, three children lay on the grass at their parents' feet: two blonde girls and a dark-eyed toddler, who could only have been Sam.

A tall man came in with two spaniels, whom he commanded to sit. They did so, with much rolling of their brown eyes. Sam leapt to his feet.

'Pa,' said he, shaking hands with his father. 'This is Irena Danuczekova – and Klara and Jo-Jo.' The old man took my hand and then Jo-Jo's, but Klara was busy stroking the dogs. Sir Robert turned to me. 'Lovely to meet you, finally. We remember your husband of course. What a loss, dreadful thing. How are you managing now?'

I had not been expecting this and nor had I been questioned so directly before; his words threw me back into the misery which had, strangely, been dispersed by the interesting circumstances of that day. I heard myself emit a sob and Sir Robert, looking mortified, steered me back to my chair, gently lowering me into it.

'Sorry, my dear. I'm not known for tact. Look, my wife and I will get lunch on the table – you join us when you're up to it. Sam look after Mrs – our guest.'

Sam grinned and whispered, 'Can't manage foreign names – he still avoids saying my mother's,' he whispered as our hosts left the room and the children, their eyes on the dogs, followed them.

Sam sat down next to me, handing me a handkerchief. Accustomed as he now was to my tears, he never failed to look heartbroken himself when I succumbed to them, no matter how often it was.

'Poor Sam – you must be so fed up with this. I didn't mean to embarrass you with your parents. They're so friendly.' I was struggling to stop crying, wiped my eyes thoroughly and blew my nose on his handkerchief – I had given him some of Daniel's the week before when we had run out of tissues.

'What a fantastic place,' I said, getting up and walking to the French windows. 'I had the feeling you didn't want me to come today.'

'Silly of me, I know', he said, 'but none of my friends, none of my working friends anyway, live this way and I suppose I'm, well, not ashamed of it, but embarrassed to have so much more than they have. Can you understand that?'

'Yes, of course I can. But some people would boast about all this.'

'But if you're brought up this way, you haven't done anything to earn it … It's just a trick of fate. I'd rather boast about something I'd actually achieved. If that ever happens.'

Daniel had wondered why Sam, for all his exceptional ability, was completely without ambition or drive. He just loved his music, played sublimely and that was that. Looking around me, I thought that perhaps he had never known the pressure of needing to earn a living.

We went back to the kitchen and sat down. I noticed that, between the mangers, the walls were hung with sporting prints. Lady Siddal-Gore, seeing me looking at them, snorted and told me she would not allow them in the rest of the house. Klara and Jo-Jo were sitting on the floor by the Aga, where one of the spaniels had just climbed into a blanket-lined box and started off a cacophony of squealing from a squirming heap which awaited her. She lay down on her side and rolled over slightly so that her pink teats stood out and six puppies disentangled themselves and scrabbled at their mother, still squealing, until each had a teat, when the noise changed to one of contented sucking. The children crouched by the box and gazed at the dogs.

'Don't fall in love with them;' said Sir Robert. 'You can't have one in London. They're spaniels, country dogs.'

Lunch was great fun. I enjoyed myself and the children did too. Sir Robert was a surprising man, outwardly he fitted all the clichés of the landed gentleman, but I felt there was much more to him than that. He looked at me in a kindly way from time to time as they ate, and his wife reached over several times to press my hand. Sam took the children out to look for bicycles in the cart lodge. As she left the kitchen, Klara looked back anxiously at me and then smiled – I was laughing now and she felt it was all right to leave me for a bit. Jo-Jo hesitated too, then he followed his sister through the French windows.

Seeing the piano museum again finally brought my memory back to life. It was housed in the old library, a beautiful room with a high, vaulted ceiling painted with classical scenes in the Italian manner. The walls were lined from floor to ceiling with bookcases with brass grilles protecting the hundreds of leather-bound volumes and the room was filled with pianos, harpsichords, fortepianos, clavichords, square pianos and virginals – every sort of keyboard instrument. And there was Daniel's painted harpsichord, which he had given to the collection as we had no room for it in our new house. It was painted with rustic scenes full of naked nymphs and satyrs. I used to tell Daniel he should play it with no clothes on to complete the theme. One day he had taken me at my word, pulled off his shirt and sat there, in his wheelchair, naked to the waist. Daniel without his shirt was a beautiful sight, so one thing led to another … I didn't think I'd tell Sam this story, but he was watching me and saw me smile as I traced the design with my hand – the nearest nymph seeming to eye the player as the wind caught her inadequate drapery and exposed her pert white breasts.

'Yes, that's Daniel's harpsichord. They ought to put a sign

on it to say who it belonged to. Look at these Irena – we're so lucky to have all this to enjoy. We need a good curator, really. A lot of these instruments are badly in need of TLC.'

This was a musician's dream. Sam watched my reaction with a pleased smile as I toured the room, excitedly running from instrument to instrument. 'Sam that's Chopin's piano, isn't it?' It was a small Pleyel grand, ornamented with carving, the music stand extravagantly fretted. 'Play something, please play something.'

Sam sat down at the piano, the lid of which was already invitingly raised. He looked at the keyboard for a moment and then closed his eyes and began to play. Chopin, of course, what else. A Berceuse in the minor key. Don't cry, I begged myself, don't cry. This is Sam. It's not Daniel. I did not weep as Sam played, opened his eyes and finished the piece with its great anguished flourish. 'Daniel's hands were too big to play that piano – his fingers kept getting stuck between the black notes. It was rather funny, but he was terribly disappointed. Your hands are tiny for a man.'

'Yes, not the best hands for a pianist. There are things I can't really play.'

'Sam you've got to play more. You know you must share this with people. Daniel desperately wanted the world to hear you.'

'Well, I've left it a bit late now to launch myself, really. I've not been single-minded enough, I know, but I hate those huge concert halls. They make me very nervous.'

'But the more you play, the easier it'll become. You know that's true. It's different if you're a child prodigy like Daniel was, because he didn't really have a childhood with the world he lived in and got used to big audiences at a really early age. That must be why he loved mucking about so much and playing jokes when he grew up. He'd never had that sort of light-hearted time most of us have as children.'

I realised I was talking about Daniel in a normal, calm way, thinking of the fun we had together when I was a young girl and he full of energy and life, and I was not melting into a pool of tears.

Sam opened the long window and we stepped out into the garden. On this side of the house there were throngs of ancient clipped yew and box and wall germander, standing like figures amongst the rose beds. And the long borders filled with bright flowers, their colours flowing one into another, were like great rainbows leading the eye out of the gardens and into the park and the distant fields. I walked outside and wandered almost spellbound among the loveliness of the place, wondering what it would be like to live somewhere like that and be responsible for its upkeep. There was a man on a ladder clipping one of the yews, neatening up the strange heraldic beast it had been cut to represent. Not the gardener's day off, I thought, and then saw that it was Sir Robert. I learnt much later that paying the outdoor staff they needed was becoming less and less possible. Sam's parents cared for most of the flower garden themselves, their old knees complaining and their backs sometimes refusing to co-operate. But they loved it and had been there together for so long that it was natural for them to go out after breakfast, every day of the year, and plan the day's gardening.

Sam told me that his mother was born on the Czech Austrian border and had been shipped over to England with a boatload of Jewish children to escape the Nazis. St Bede's was being used as a hospital at the end of the war and she worked there as a nurse. She had studied the piano in Vienna and one day the young Robert had heard her playing in the music room. He fell violently in love with her and would happily have forfeited his inheritance and the Abbey to marry her. But eventually his parents, who had made the great collection of keyboard instruments, learnt to love Zdenka, who embraced

English country life with such enthusiasm and played the piano so beautifully.

Later, the children paddled in the fountain, whooping with joy. Sam and I sat watching the sun shimmer through the spray as the thrashing arms and legs threw the water into the air where it caught the last rays of the day.

As they drove back down the lime avenue, Irena asked Sam: 'Will you take on all of this one day?'

'Good God, no. Thank heaven I have a very efficient older sister. You know, Helena, who's in the portrait in the hall? What's more, she's married rather a rich man.' And Sam gave an ironic laugh.

Helena, in her portrait, had her mother's strong nose and a very English blondness. She looked up to taking on the estate, Irena mused.

'Luckily my family believed in primogeniture and I'm the youngest. I'd be useless running a huge place like this. There's always something that needs mending and these days we have to satisfy so many regulations – Health and Safety is a nightmare. No, I love St Bede's but the last thing I'd want to do is run it.'

43.   UNCERTAIN JOY

THE DAYS dragged on and turned into weeks. Irena tried to focus on little things, on routine matters which needed only her physical presence, her unthinking acceptance of their existence. Everything now seemed to be bound up in preparations for the memorial concert and she swung between resentfulness and gratitude for the time and effort it was taking. She did not feel well, was unable to keep her food down and was thinner than ever. Something was repeatedly tugging at her mind. At night, she would remember with anguish that last passionate love-making on the floor next to their bed. She remembered Daniel's hands on her, the strength of his arms as he lifted her onto him. And she remembered the way he'd looked at her that evening and his questioning smile as she'd arched her back again and again in the ecstasy of his touch.

Rousing herself one morning, she went downstairs as the children ate their breakfast. When Jo-Jo had left for school in Sam's car and Klara was ensconced in the studio with her music teacher, she went into the bathroom and was sick before returning to the kitchen, shaking all over. She was still sitting at the table, her toast uneaten, staring out of the window, when Magda came in.

'Irena – what is it?' She knew there was more to this silence than usual.

'Oh Mags …' Irena hesitated some minutes before she completed the sentence. 'I think I'm pregnant.'

Magda sat down at the table. 'Have you done a test?'

Irena fished in her pocket and took out a small plastic rod.

'Yes. I've done several. They all come up positive …'

'How far gone are you, do you think?' She herself was trying to do the sums and wondered that Irena showed no signs of thickening about her waist.

'Nearly three months … His back was so sore – we hadn't made love for some time. Then, just before he died …' She gave a sob and paused, not sure she should discuss this with her sister-in-law, but she was the only woman she had any sort of closeness with now.

Magda put her arms around Irena's stiff, resisting shoulders, saying: 'Well, that's lovely, darling. Aren't you a little bit pleased?'

'I don't know what I feel. How can I go through the birth without him? I mean he was always there – with Klara and Jo-Jo …' Strangely, she wanted then to laugh. Daniel had looked so pale she had thought that he would faint, he was far more frightened than she was. 'He couldn't bear blood, could he? He was so brave and stayed all the time – even when they cut me open to get Klara out. I'd never seen him so excited – when he first saw the babies.'

Magda smiled, too. She remembered the telephone calls – his amazement at being a father, his pride in his babies and the time he spent learning to do what he could to help Irena. She had found him once, to her surprise, concentrating hard on changing Klara's nappy, his normally graceful hands rather clumsy, his tongue caught between his teeth as he grappled with the mysterious object.

'You'll keep it, then?'

'What do you mean – keep it? It's Daniel's baby …' Irena burst into tears and fled from the room.

As the day of Daniel's concert approached, Irena found her mood swinging wildly. She watched the changes in her body and the new roundness of her belly and she would talk to the unborn child that was half Daniel, half her, finding, for the first time in many weeks, a little joy, a certain comfort, in the knowledge that she was no longer alone. Sometimes she wondered if Daniel had hoped he might be starting a new life in her that evening when he had pulled her onto him, lying on the floor by the bed. Maybe he knew that this was all he could leave her of himself, the only gift that his death would not take away.

The concert plans were finalized at last. After it was over and Sam had sorted out the last of Daniel's papers, Irena would have Klara's upright brought into the house, lock the door of the studio, and turn her back on a great part of her marriage and happiness. Maybe she would allow the garden to grow up so that it would disappear into a tangled wilderness. She imagined it like the Sleeping Princess's castle, bound around with brambles and creepers and honeysuckle. Once, she had allowed herself to imagine slashing at the vegetation and making herself a space to open the doors again and that she had found Daniel there, at the piano, smiling at her. And, although she knew she was being childish and self-indulgent she had, in her imagination, gone into the studio and closed the door behind her.

The Memorial Concert was only ten days away and Sam was sitting opposite her at the table, proof-reading the draft of the programme. Looking in her bag for a pen, Irena came across a spectacle case she had pushed into its furthest recess and took it out. Sam looked over to her and wondered if Irena needed reading glasses now; she opened the case and, with a shock of recognition, he saw the contents.

'Those are Daniel's, aren't they?' he asked, wondering what Irena was going to do with them. What do you do with things like that when someone dies? No use to anyone else, but too redolent of the man to be thrown away like rubbish.

'Yes. I can't bring myself to throw them away. When I first knew him in Sarajevo he wore big horn-rimmed ones – like Buddy Holly's, you know. The Conservatory staff thought he was far too young for the job – he was head of Keyboard Studies – a really grand position for someone his age …' Sam had heard a lot of anecdotes about the Sarajevo days, the house and Irena's family. It all fascinated him, but this wasn't something he'd heard before. 'Your mother sounds very sweet', he said, not sure if this was something he ought to say. Irena was so easily upset.

'She was English, wasn't she?'

'Well, no, Irish actually.'

'And your father was Bosnian?'

'Yes, and a Muslim, but he wasn't religious. Neither of them was. They were very liberal and had friends from all cultures and beliefs, but then they were musicians, not professional ones, but very good amateurs, and I think musicians seem to be bigger than all that prejudice. Tata always said they were "citizens of the world".'

It was good to be talking with Sam about those happy times, and Irena told him about his mother's birthday party and how Daniel had played 'Great Balls of Fire'. Sam was rather young to know much about Jerry Lee Lewis, but he'd often heard Daniel's musical imitations. He had loved playing the fool at the piano and there was nothing he couldn't do with the keyboard, often playing one composer's work in the style of another: Gershwin in the style of Handel was a favourite of Sam's.

The evening before the concert, Sam brought some Prosecco and two glasses out to the studio. He had a peach in his pocket and squeezed it into the glasses before filling them with the wine.

'Here's to tomorrow,' he said, lifting his glass to Irena. She knew he was terrified of performing in front of such a huge audience, but more than that, playing Daniel's part was still something he was unable to accept without feeling deeply unworthy.

'Sam', Irena was unable to stop herself saying: 'You know it was my fault? I mean what happened to him. He wouldn't have been shot if it hadn't been for me.'

'Have you been believing that all this time?' Sam leant forward in his chair, a look of alarm on his usually calm face.

'Yes. And it's true. He kept going out to Sarajevo when the Siege was making the place very dangerous. A journalist who had taken him under his wing was with him the last time he went – things were a bit less dangerous, but the press were always targets and he was mistaken for one when he was shot. But he wouldn't have gone back if it hadn't been for me.'

'Irena, it was not your fault. Daniel really didn't have to go out on that balcony. He knew that perfectly well. But you see he was already so in love with you and he thought he'd never see you again.'

Sam came and sat next to her.

'Irena, you have no idea, have you? Surely you must know by now that whatever happened to Daniel, whatever sacrifice he had to make or suffering he had to endure, finding you again made everything worth while. Even when if he was tired or in pain, he just marvelled that you two were together at last. You were the centre of his life; not even his music mattered so much.

'Hold that in your poor old heart, Irena, don't beat yourself up any more. You've had something that most people never have in their whole lives – you need to be strong now – for Klara and Jo-Jo.' Irena had not yet told him that she was pregnant. Perhaps that would have been the moment, but instead she smiled gently at him and said: 'Thank you for being such a wonderful friend to him – all those years …'

She saw then that his eyes were full of tears as he stood up, turned from her and said, 'I loved him. I really loved him.'

44.   A FITTING MEMORIAL

THE EVENING of the concert came and Irena went into her room and took her dress from the hanger – her re-modelled wedding dress, with its shorter skirt and low-cut neck-line – and put it on without looking at her reflection. Trying it on the day before, Irena had protested to Magda that it was too revealing, but her sister-in-law remonstrated:

'For goodness sake, Irena, I'm afraid that you are going to be on show tomorrow, whether you like it or not. You'll look wonderful and Danny would have loved that. You want to know he'd have been proud of you, don't you?'

'No', thought Irena, 'I want him back with me again. That's all I want. I don't care about my dress or anything else about this concert. I want Daniel. I don't want him to be dead any more. I'm tired of being so sad and so desperate.' And she pulled the dress on over her head, ran her hands through her hair, which had been recut and shaped by Magda's hair-dresser, and left the room without checking her reflection in the glass.

Magda had predicted correctly that Irena, the least vain woman she knew, would do exactly what she had done. So she sat her down at the kitchen table and went to work, first on her face with her own make-up, then brushing Irena's hair back from her pale face and catching it with two tortoiseshell combs. Then she put her own pearls around her sister-in-law's neck and handed her the box with her engagement ring – the dark opal Daniel had given her for her thirtieth birthday.

'Oh Mummy,' cried Klara, 'you look amazing.' And Irena

looked at herself in the mirror for the first time that evening. Her dress was rather tight and she pulled at it.

Sam who was just leaving, asked, 'Have you put on weight?' He was surprised, for Irena's appetite, always meagre, had been of some concern to him since Daniel's death.

Irena told the children to get their coats from the hall and turned to face Sam.

'I'm pregnant,' she said, simply.

Irena sat between Klara and Jo-Jo in the gallery of the Wigmore Hall, where they had always sat for Daniel's concerts. He had loved the Hall and never tired of talking to the children about the art nouveau decoration, the half dome over the stage with its stylized figures against a turquoise mosaic sky: Dante with his long scroll and Beatrice who seemed to Klara the sort of woman she would like to grow into when she started to play on that stage. As she had no doubt she would one day.

They opened their programmes, where the first few pages were taken up by Leo's eulogy.

Leo Haskell's introduction to Daniel's Memorial Concert programme

I once asked the music critic, Peter Ketner, what it was that made Daniel Danuczek an exceptional pianist?

'Simplicity and clarity', he wrote in his reply. 'But "simplicity" might be misleading; Danuczek is a superb technician, a true virtuoso, so that there seems to be nothing he cannot play with what appears to be great ease. You are never made to feel that a work is anywhere near the limit of his capabilities and, with that huge ability, comes the possibility of clarity and simplicity. He never

fluffs a passage or mishandles a phrase. He is able
to "stretch" the music in some remarkable way to
create what I can only call "space", no matter how
complex and demanding the piece. His ornaments
are not only precise, and that goes without saying
with this exponent, but become essential to the
piece, not an addition but an organic extension of
the structure. His artistry, though, is something far
deeper than mere technique. He said himself that
there is always, in a musician, room for development,
for searching for even greater perfection. With
Danuczek, this is witnessed by the existence of
several recordings of certain works, such as Bach's
Goldberg Variations, which mark the stages in his
career where he has sometimes radically changed his
interpretive opinion …'

I became Daniel Danuczek's agent when he was still
a teenager and already starting to be one of the most
admired pianists on the international concert stage.
Approaching 30 and curious to see more of the world
than the inside of concert halls, he took the position
of Director of Keyboard Studies at the Sarajevo
Conservatory of Music – a pompous title that always
made him laugh – and it was in that city towards the
end of the Siege that he was targeted by a sniper. The
bullets paralyzed his legs and put him in a wheelchair.
No longer able to use the pedals, Daniel was faced
with deciding how to continue in the career he loved.
He was advised that he could either seek a mechanical
solution to this problem or to concentrate on teaching
for the rest of his life. Teaching came naturally to
him and his master classes are legendary, but he was
not prepared to give up performing and I soon found
him concentrating not just on the harpsichord, which
was still within his means, but also beginning a real

love affair with other early keyboard work. Working on the foundations of his wide knowledge of Baroque music, he developed a new concert repertoire on the fortepiano.

As a friend as well as agent, I watched this process with admiration and also cherish the memory of hearing him, when he could not resist playing the old favorites he no longer performed in public, demonstrating a very personal style, which he called 'honkey tonk'.

Daniel met his wife, Irena, in Sarajevo when she was fifteen and already a fine viola player. The horrors of the Bosnian war put an end to the happiness of many families and Irena's life changed radically. After two terrible years, she was able to escape to America and eventually she and Daniel were reunited in London. They did not part again until his death.

Daniel Danuczek was not only an extraordinary musician, but a rounded man, blessed with humility, humour and courage. He will be greatly missed.

Leo Haskell

Irena had told Leo that his piece was far too long, but taken pity on him when he couldn't bear to shorten it, wanting every word to be where it was and Irena had understood why. This was his farewell to a the most rewarding and interesting of his most select clients. A farewell, too, to a dear, dear friend. While Irena re-read Leo's piece, the children went straight to the pictures of their father and the musicians who would be playing that evening. Irena and Leo seldom agreed about which photographs Daniel would have disliked least. At the beginning of his career Leo knew the value of a pretty or handsome face on a CD cover, but they made Daniel uncomfortable. He preferred to be seen at the piano, whether alone or with singers, an orchestra or chamber group. Irena had looked out photographs that went back to when he was a little boy, his face Puck-like and mischievous. Then as a brooding adolescent, with huge blue eyes and the black curls that, once his father had died, were allowed to grow until they could be tucked seductively behind his ears. Then the Daniel of Sarajevo days with his horn-rimmed glasses and enormous smile. More recently he was revealed as a distinguished man with greying hair but the smile was the same. For the front cover of the programme, they had both agreed on a picture of Daniel looking up from the keyboard, his eyes bright and intense with the anticipation and excitement that making music always was for him.

Then she had realised that no picture showed Daniel in his wheelchair, which had become a trade mark for him in the concert world, acquiring a sort of glamour because of its occupant's exuberant arm movements, his swift gliding across the stage and the aura of physical energy he always had about him. A photograph slipped from the pile in her hand and she picked it up. It had been taken on his last birthday, when Daniel and the children had interpreted *Danny Boy* on different instruments: he, in his wheelchair, had appropriated Irena's viola, which he was playing between his knees like a cello and wearing a very 'musical' expression. Next to him, her head thrown back, Irena was laughing as she picked out the tune on the piano. Klara had chosen an antique trombone from Daniel's collection and Jo-Jo had found a pair of bongo drums. This'll do, Irena thought.

Klara gazed intently at the photographs, stroking the images of her father's face with her fingers as she always did when she saw pictures of him, as if she could restore his flesh by her touch.

Zdenka and Robert's seats were at the front of the stalls. Sam's mother nervous but immensely proud; that their son should be playing in this concert and in the role the great Daniel Danuczek had bequeathed to him was an honour they had never dreamed of for their quiet, unambitious boy.

And then the lights began to dim on the audience and, on the empty stage, where seats and music stands, all empty, stood in rows, a spotlight followed Sam as he pushed an empty wheelchair up alongside the piano and waited for the applause to die down. Then he spoke, his voice surprising him by its calm ordinariness.

'Daniel was my teacher, my mentor and, above all, my friend. This concert had been conceived, as you all know, as a tribute to him on what should have been his 50th birthday. None of us, who were close to him, knew how ill he was in the months leading up to his death. He did know and he suspected that he had not much time left. He wrote to me then and I found the letter shortly after he had ... left us ... and in his letter he asked me to play this evening in his place.

'To welcome so many of his friends and fellow musicians this evening is a huge honour for me - an almost unbearable one. When you are listening to this music you will, of course, be remembering Daniel. But please remember him with joy. He was a joyful man ...'

Musicians came and went, filling the hall with the music that had meant most to Daniel. Many of the performers also spoke of their much-missed friend: some paying tribute to his musicianship, and others with personal anecdotes and recollections. There was a good deal of laughter as they recalled the unquenchable light-heartedness of a man who found humour in everything, who always had time for others and their problems and seldom spoke of his own difficulties. They laughed, tears were not far away as the eyes of everyone were drawn often and inexorably to the now flower-filled wheelchair that stood by the piano They tried, between them, to buoy up the spirits of the audience, but there was a great absence, a void in the centre of the evening that could not be filled.

As the first half of the concert came to an end Sam walked over to the chair. Standing beside it, he spoke again.

'Tonight's celebration of the life and music of Daniel Danuczek can't be complete without the people who were more important to him than anything else, his wife Irena and his children Klara and Johannes – Jo-Jo. Irena is a gifted violist and she and Daniel often played together. Just recently I found something that he wrote for Irena early in their marriage. The title of the piece is 'Little Wren' which was one of his private names for her.'

Irena remembered how Daniel had written the piece – for her birthday – and how she had spoilt the first draft by crying all over it and making it illegible. Sam, thinking about Irena's part in the concert and what she might play, came across the manuscript; he knew this was the piece he had been looking for. He took it home and made a few alterations so that Klara's small hands could play the part her father had written for his own much larger ones.

As she had been preparing the piece she was to play with her children, Irena prayed she would not let Daniel down, or poor Sam who had worked so hard in spite of his own anguish and reservations. She looked at her fingers as they rested on the fingerboard of her beautiful little viola. Then the memories of Daniel in the music room of Vila Dolena came flooding back. Almost paralysed then by the overwhelming sense of Daniel's absence, she wondered if her fingers could be relied on to play the right notes even if, as she was afraid it might, her memory failed her. She wanted to run off the stage and go – but where?

Sam adjusted the stool for Klara and pulled up a chair for Jo-Jo on her left. Then Irena managed the few steps that brought her to the waist of the piano and began to tune her viola. As Klara gave her the notes, she was afraid suddenly that her mother would be unable to play and would abandon her at this alarmingly public keyboard. But when she looked up again, Irena had wiped her eyes and was smiling at her daughter as she tightened her bow. Jo-Jo, who was enjoying his new importance, was oblivious to any of this, as he opened the music with a flourish and made much of turning down the top corner of the right hand pages.

Daniel had composed 'Little Wren' for Irena to play with him, the piano part weaving in and out of the viola's, so that neither instrument was dominant, but took the tune in turn, seeming to toy playfully with it before tossing it back to the other player. Klara sat very upright as she played, nodding sternly from time to time at Jo-Jo when he failed to turn a page in time, although she didn't need the music; she had learnt the piece by heart. Page-turning was something Jo-Jo had done, perched on a high stool beside his father, since he'd been able to reach the music rest. Since Daniel's death he had refused to continue his music lessons, but he wanted to take part in the concert and was not reluctant to acknowledge the deafening applause after the piece ended, bowing low and waving at his friends in the audience.

[IRENA]

Finally, Sam and I played Kol Nidri, from the Jewish Prayer of Atonement. My father had transposed it for the viola and Daniel had stood behind me as I mastered the long line of the phrases, the sobbing quality of the bowing. I looked across at Sam as he began to play. Our eyes met and we both smiled, for sad though the music was, for all its power to move us to tears, it was also a triumph of the human spirit expressed in sound.

There was silence as we finished playing and we both stood still, glad that applause was not forcing itself into the thoughts that the piece had left with us. Then the audience stood. A few people at first and then, a row at a time got to their feet and began to applaud. I went over to Sam and took his hand, leading him to the front of the stage and lifted my hand, the way that Daniel used to; the audience ceased their clapping and stamping.

'I first met Daniel, in my home town of Sarajevo, and he came to love Bosnia Herzegovina. Facing the horrors of the Siege, he visited it many times and it was there that his life was changed by a sniper's bullet. When he had recovered, he continued to go back there to perform and to give master classes, always giving the fees to his foundation, the Bosnian Musicians' Appeal. He would, I know, have joined Sam and me in dedicating this evening to all those of our families and friends who have no graves and certainly no concerts to celebrate their lives, but who were people every bit as important, with lives as filled with love and work and purpose.'

'Now, Sam is a modest man, but Daniel knew he was a fine pianist, albeit one who hated playing in public. I want to thank him on your behalf, not only for organizing this wonderful evening, but for braving his worst nightmare – a live audience!'

Sam was standing at my side and I took a few steps back to let him acknowledge the thunderous applause. Flowers were brought to us both, flowers were thrown onto the stage, until we were wading in a sea of foliage and petals as, the clapping and shouting still ringing in our ears, our arms full of bouquets, we went together into the Green Room.

'Dearest Irena. You are the most extraordinary person. I thought you'd funk talking to all those people. And you made that amazing speech. Daniel must be so proud of you.'

'Sam dearest Sam – Daniel has gone now. We must live our lives for ourselves and no longer for him.'

I don't know why I said it; the words seemed to say themselves and I was half ashamed of their harshness. But Sam put his flowers down and embraced me, saying quietly,

'Yes. I know. But tonight I was playing for you.'

He released me and ran up the stairs to his dressing room. I stood for a moment and then, as Magda and the children came in to the Green Room, heading the crowd of friends and fans, I felt the first faint fluttering of Daniel's child within me.

45. SAM'S FUTURE

A FEW DAYS after the concert, Leo Haskell called Sam and asked him to come to his office: 'Twelve noon, Thursday. And I'll book a table for lunch.'

Sam agreed, but resignedly; he suspected there would be decisions that he didn't want to make and praise that he was unwilling to accept if it meant commitments that frightened him out of his mind. Until the memorial concert he'd been able to concentrate on helping Irena back onto a more even keel, he hoped, and giving the children a little security while they learnt to live a fatherless life. Now he was being assailed with TV offers and radio interviews. 'Sit down, sit down,' said Leo expansively, as Sam entered his office, indicating an alarming black leather chair, which reminded Sam of 'Mastermind'. He sat down and leant forward slightly, not intending to make himself too comfortable or to look as if he would be staying.

'So, Sam I have to congratulate you. The concert was superb. I've had a lot of enquiries about you. There's enough interest to get you round the world a couple of times. Were you pleased with the evening?'

Sam had many feelings, but none he intended to share with this man. He looked into Leo's fat, well cared-for face, with its sparse hair made fuller by artful blow drying. But he needed to say something. 'I think it went well. Such things are hard for us all. We want to perform for Daniel and his family, but, at the same time, we would rather do our grieving in private.'

'Yes, I'm sure that is so. But this gives others who are

not part of your close families and friends the opportunity to share something of their own bereavement and sorrow, wouldn't you say?'

'Of course.' Sam waited for Haskell to resume, but the older man said suddenly:

'Daniel rated your playing very highly. Very highly indeed. He would have had you perform much more. Aren't you ambitious, Sam?'

Sam pondered a moment. 'I'm not ambitious for recognition. It's enough for me to know I can interpret music in a way that speaks to my audience, however small. In fact it's the intimacy of, say, the Wigmore that makes performing meaningful for me. To put on a penguin suit and trot out in front of 6,000 people has no meaning at all. And I get appalling stage fright.'

'Well, I can't force you to do anything you don't want to do, but there is a fine career waiting for you if you want to have it.'

'What have you got in mind for me, if I were to go along with you for, say, a year?' He was surprised at his boldness, but sat facing Haskell knowing he must play this man at his own game. Daniel would have wanted him to grasp any opportunity to share his talent with the world and, in any case, what was he now to do? He couldn't hang around Irena and her children any longer. He'd better take off and try to make something of himself while the offers were there.

Leo, gratified and somewhat surprised by Sam's easy capitulation, stood up and reached for his coat. 'Let's eat while I give you a few ideas,' he said, and Sam followed the little man out of the office building.

Irena decided to put her home back as two houses. She and the children would continue to live in The Green House, where she had returned to the bedroom she had shared with Daniel, and she would let the other half. It was a difficult decision, but she had discovered that she was not as well off as she was accustomed to being. The Fazzioli had been sold and some of the money used to pay the builders.

Daniel had not taken much interest in his finances and it was only now that she discovered that he had left a large sum to his charity, and there were other legacies. The various different accounts confused Irena, as she and Daniel had seldom discussed money. Leo came over to help and, as he was making different piles of paper on the table and consigning a good many to the waste paper basket, he picked up a folder and leafed through the contents, sucking in his breath. 'Know anything about prosthetic legs for someone called Kasimir Mehedivić?'

'Yes. He's my cousin. He was blown up and lost both of his legs in Sarajevo – Daniel arranged for him to go over to the States and be fitted with prosthetic ones. Why?'

'Well, here are the bills – have you any idea what these limbs cost? Not to mention long stays with his entire family in hotels, treatment in the Veterans' hospital – no National Health over there …'

Irena took the file from him and looked at the most recent papers inside. 'I see what you mean – the legs were very expensive – and the fittings …'

'Expensive isn't the right word. They've been a constant drain on Daniel's account for some years now and some of these are still outstanding – Mr Mehedivić had running blades last year.' He paused, shaking his head. 'Do you ever hear from this cousin of yours?'

'Yes. He writes quite often and is very grateful for everything. I hadn't seen him since that time in Sarajevo, but he turned up at Daniel's cremation and was walking pretty well. Daniel really wanted him to have those running legs –

Kasimir used to live for his sport and Daniel knew what it was to lose an ability that was very important in his life.'

'Dear Daniel, what a generous man he was, but I suppose he thought he'd go on getting fat concert fees; he knew I'd wangled him some higher ones for his performances next year. But there isn't a huge amount left for you and the children, I'm afraid.'

Irena was neither surprised nor worried by her straitened circumstance; she would make her way as best she could with rent from The Pink House and the music lessons she was now forced to give. The Polish builders came back and, somewhat unwillingly, put her houses back as they had been six years earlier. They were very sad for Irena, having liked Daniel, his eccentricities and good humour. At the end of the original work he had presented the team with tickets to a concert in the park he was giving and provided a picnic supper and wine to take with them. They had been almost unable to believe that the man on the stage was the same person they had shared garlic sausage with in the half-finished kitchen, he speaking Czech and they Polish, and everyone laughing a great deal. Wearing the blue Nehru coat that Irena had chosen for their wedding, he had propelled himself onto the stage, bowed, and pushed himself up to the piano. Gienek leant forward looking alternately at the real Daniel on the stage and the huge screens on which he appeared at either side of the audience. Daniel played the Paganini/Liszt *Campanella*, which he knew was a show-stopper although the piece regularly drove Irena out of the house when he practised it. The audience went mad and the Poles had shaken their heads in disbelief and admiration.

Gienek and his troupe threw themselves into getting the job done as quickly as possible. Coming across Daniel's wheelchair under the stairs where Irena had put it until she could bear to take it to the Red Cross, Gienek wept bitterly and Irena found that she was comforting him, sitting him down in the kitchen and making him a cup of coffee while she tried to reassure him that Daniel had not suffered, that he had been very ill and, had he lived, his life would have been more and more painful and difficult.

When The Pink House was finished, Irena easily found tenants – it was now everything that young people wanting to rent could desire these days, plumbing no longer had a mind and voice of its own, the floors were blond wood, the walls painted in neutral colours. She settled herself and the children into The Green House that was their new home. Klara often looked sadly out at the studio,

'Wouldn't it be lovely if Daddy came back for the summer and I could play out there with him again,' she said one day, her eyes on the window. Irena wondered if she had heard right; Klara had seemed more accepting of her father's death since they had moved.

'What would you play first, do you think?' she asked, wondering where this fantasy might take them.

'The D 940, of course. Daddy loved Schubert – I wonder if he can play it properly again now ...'

Irena remembered then a Saturday in Sarajevo when she'd gone down to the Conservatory with Daniel, who had left a score in the lecture theatre. Pavel, the cantankerous old caretaker, had let them in reluctantly and she had asked Daniel to play for her.

Daniel sat down at the piano and thought for a moment before he stretched his big hands wide over the keys. He began to play a Schubert *Impromptu*, the first one, in the key of C minor. Scarcely pausing as he came to the end of the piece, he continued to play the liquid, shimmering runs of the second *Impromptu*, with its song-like melody and oscillations of key. Lost now in the music and unhindered by the fear of disturbing his neighbours, he played on, through the whole sublime series. Irena had heard the music many times; her father had given her a disc of András Schiff and she had thought them the *apogée* of beauty, but to have Maestro Daniel play just for her and the old man in the back seat was something she would never forget.

Later in her life, Irena read that the music of Schubert 'fits like a glove into the secret codes with which the body transmits its signals to the brain. The brain treats the messages of such music as if they were coming from the heart, not the ear;' And she had begun that morning to know this, to know it without having the words to express that knowledge. The water-like clarity of Daniel's performance seemed other-worldly and Irena wanted him never to stop, to take her into his world of sound with him.

Pavel began to weep, quite silently, as the solitary sadness of the music spoke to his inner being. He wished he could die there, then, reaching upwards from his dreary, lonely, hungry everyday life, to float on that great raft of sound. He was at rest, he was no longer alone, but part of the suffering of the composer, whose own tortured existence had led him to create these exquisite echoes of his inner pain, inviting the listener to be there too, to know his wretchedness but also to hear in the music the intimation – the certainty – of salvation, and of joy to come.

Daniel stopped playing abruptly and looked at his watch. They had been there for over an hour. He stood up, beckoned Irena to follow him and stopped by the caretaker. 'I'm so sorry …' he began, but the man's head was bowed and when he looked up Daniel saw that tears were running down his cheeks.

'Thank you, Maestro,' he said, struggling to his feet, for his aged legs were stiff after sitting for so long. Daniel took his elbow and helped him up. And at that moment there was no gulf between the musician and the man who sat day after day in his stuffy kiosk, or swept the floors with his over-sized broom. Daniel saw in the wrinkled face and the rheumy, red-rimmed eyes that the music had spoken to Pavel and he took the old man's work-worn hand and held it for a moment.

'Any time, any time ... but thanks for being so patient.' He spoke in English, which the caretaker did not understand, but Pavel smiled for the first time that day.

It had started to rain and they had come out without coats. As it was past lunch time and, thinking her parents might be worried, Daniel waited outside a call box while she spoke to them. Then he went in after her and excused himself for keeping her out so long. It was now raining hard; cycling was out of the question that day, so they went, for the first time, to a café together.

Irena's family didn't go to cafés and she was enchanted at the thought of choosing her food from a menu. They sat at a table with a paper cloth and Daniel took off his glasses, which had steamed up in the warm atmosphere indoors, and Irena stole a glance at him as he wiped them with his big handker-chief, wondering how she and her family would fare when he went back to London; she had begun to plan how she might go there too, to study music perhaps. Very hungry by now, they both ate stew and dumplings and sugary pastries. They laughed and the cafe was warm. Irena wanted that Saturday never to end. Then Daniel hailed a taxi and took her home.

The wall between the two gardens had been reinstated, but the studio opened only onto theirs and a fence screened it from the back of the The Pink House. Irena didn't know what she'd do with it. It was still full of Daniel's scores and manuscript paper which were to be collected by a university archivist. Of all places, this was the one that she still could not face. It overwhelmed her with grief and longing, so she almost never went in. She did her best to make a new life in

The Green House, to play her viola, encourage her students and to amuse the children when they were not at school. Often they looked at her strangely as she made jokes and pulled faces at them as Daniel had done. It was not the same, she knew, but she sensed they tried hard to help her by laughing and retaliating with jokes they'd heard at school. Her body was changing all this time, and soon she'd have to face up to the new baby and the new grief he or she would add to her still overwhelming sense of loss.

46.   RETURN TO ST BEDE'S

Sam hadn't been around much since Daniel's memorial evening. He was preparing for his first concert tour and spent long hours at his shiny Yamaha. Sometimes he and Irena said they really must get together for dinner, or go to the theatre together, but they never got around to it, and she tried not to mind. Daniel, with his long years of experience in the concert halls of the world's capitals, would have been excited about the projected tours and been able to help Sam; Irena had nothing of that sort to offer him. The children missed him, but he took them out sometimes, on his own, to eat pizzas and see a film.

When she heard about the overseas tour that Leo had organized, she asked him over. He refused, saying he was very busy, but he told her that his mother had asked for her number and would be ringing her later. He was off the next day to Paris to play at the Grand Palais.

She was disappointed not to see him but only said, 'Bye. Lots of luck – I'll be reading your reviews.'

'Good. You can tell me what they say. My French is dreadful – after all, I only did it for five years at school.'

And that was that. Irena felt bereft – Sam had been such an important part of all their lives and now he was going too.

Then Zdenka rang, her voice warm and strong. 'Irena my dear. Would you like to bring the children down on Sunday? It's ages since we've seen you.'

❈

Arriving at St Bede's in her little car, Irena remembered the day she and the children had spent there the week before the Memorial concert. It had been the beginning of some sort of recovery for her. Not an end, or anywhere near an end, of her grieving – but that day she had been able to put it aside for a few hours and to rest her weary, sad heart for a short while.

Zdenka greeted her as if they had been friends for years, embracing her and the children with a single expansive hug and then linking arms with Irena as they went into the house. While the children were playing outside with the dogs, she told Irena that it was not just for the pleasure of her company that she had wanted to see her, but to put a proposition to her. There were some lodges and small houses on the estate, which had been converted into holiday lets. The season was ending and the little houses were empty. Perhaps Irena would like to have the use of one of them?

Sam had told his parents that Irena's circumstances were not as easy as they had been; that she was letting part of her house and doing some teaching, which she did not much enjoy. Daniel had had such an outgoing personality, such an interest in people, as well as the all-pervading passion to share his knowledge and love of music, that teaching came very naturally to him, but Irena resented the intrusion of pupils into her private domain, where they looked about them inquisitively and needed drinks and conversation.

Zdenka took Irena to see West Gate Lodge. The children had been lent bicycles and followed the battered Volvo to the far side of the estate. Excitedly, they rushed ahead, running upstairs, where they decided between them which room to choose if they went to live there. Finally, they bypassed the cramped kitchen and found the boot room where dog leads still hung on hooks by the back door.

The two women walked out of the sitting room through the French windows to a small stone terrace looking out towards the park. A herd of deer were grazing on the other side of a ha-ha. The Lodge was small but there was a garden with a summerhouse and a bed of newly-dug earth. Irena had always wanted to grow vegetables and thought how lovely it would be to give the children the freedom of this park and live near these kind people.

'It's lovely Zdenka, really lovely. We'd love to take it, but – I'm afraid we couldn't afford a weekend cottage. Perhaps one day ...'

'My dear, there would be nothing to pay – I don't mean you to have the Lodge just for weekends – we'd like you to live there. But I'm afraid there's a proviso attached. You see, we're desperate for someone to run the piano museum – a curator. It's got to be someone who knows music, particularly piano music, though he or she wouldn't need to play, just to know about the instruments and be able to run the place and make sure the pianos are kept tuned and cared for. We've been racking our brains and interviewing a few people. Then Robert thought of you.'

Not Sam's idea, then, thought Irena, not sure if she was relieved. She took Zdenka's hand and said, very quietly, 'I can't imagine anything I'd like more – you know, the job and the Lodge.' She was watching Klara and Jo-Jo chase each other round the garden with an abandonment she hadn't seen since they had last been there. 'The children would love it, but the thing is, well, you see ... ' and she let go of her coat, so that it no longer concealed her expanding form. 'I'm ...'

'But my dear girl ... Sam told us that you were expecting.' Zdenka pulled Irena towards her. 'Surely this would be a lovely thing – to have a pram outside the window here again? And there'd be lots of people to help you. We won't take no for an answer.'

❊

Irena and the children moved into the Lodge at the end of the autumn term and she started at once to learn her new job at the museum. The children were to go to the local secondary school in January and Zdenka had lined up a piano teacher for Klara. He was an academic musician who came over several times a week to do his research, an excellent pianist who sometimes gave recitals there. Christmas loomed, the first of her widowhood and Irena dreaded it.

Zdenka came into the Music Room one morning, when Irena was supervising the piano tuner. Actually, she was gazing out of the window at the winter-bound park and the graceful deer making their way across the frosty grass through the mist that hung over the valley. Turner, she was thinking and trying to remember where that masterpiece of landscape painting had been done and where she had seen it.

'We've just heard' said Zdenka, her voice full of excitement, 'Samuel's coming home for Christmas. He's bringing a special friend – she's called Jean. You'll all join us of course.'

'Oh no. I'm sure you see enough of me,' Irena said hastily. 'But thank you.' She turned back to the piano tuner, who had finished working on Chopin's piano and wanted to show her some damage that would soon need attention. She asked him to look at one of the harpsichords next and turned, presuming that Zdenka would have left them, but the old woman was standing with her hands on her hips, waiting for Irena to finish her discussion.

'I won't take no for an answer. Samuel would be horrified to think of you and the children down in the Lodge having Christmas alone.' She knew that Irena had refused Magda's invitation to spend Christmas in London and had bought a little tree to put in the front window of the Lodge.

It was so long since Irena had heard from Sam and, although she had followed his progress through his letters to Zdenka and Robert, it all seemed very distant from her new life. And this Jean? That was certainly a surprise and Irena was intrigued to see what sort of woman he had thought worthy to bring to St Bede's for Christmas.

Christmas Eve came and Irena managed somehow to get the children to bed. Carol singers had called by, had sung proper carols and come into the Lodge for mince pies and mulled wine It was all very traditional, very reassuring. Klara and Jo-Jo threw themselves into the spirit of things, singing and dancing around the tall tree that had mysteriously appeared on their doorstep, accompanied by a basket of well-worn baubles and a rather wobbly nativity scene, clearly made some time ago by a child.

At last there was quiet and Irena cleared up some of the mess, thinking that no one was there to criticise her house-keeping and she needn't do the rest until morning. She opened the French windows to see if the moon was visible and went out onto the terrace, hugging herself against the cold. It was very quiet and she could see lights in the Stable House. And then she heard a step, a footfall on her gravel path. Sam was standing there, not many feet away from her. She couldn't see his face, but she knew it was him, and he wasn't alone.

'Irena,' he said. 'Is it really you?' and she threw her arms around him.

'Oh Sam – I've missed you so much.'

He laughed a soft mysterious laugh and stepped back to bring his companion forward into the light from the open window.

'This is Gene.' Sam said, and Irena was looking up at a very tall man whose white teeth gleamed in his handsome black face as he smiled and held out his hand.

In the New Year Irena began to enjoy her work and found she was good at it. She made herself overcome her shyness and took groups around the house and museum. Her own excitement over the exhibits and their history made her an enthusiastic and inspiring guide. Zdenka and Robert began to relax; they'd made a good choice with this young woman. They liked her, too, and admired the way she coped with her grief; she talked now about Daniel and their meeting, their life together – once she had even spoken of his death, able at last to do that without being overwhelmed by his absence. He had left a huge hole in her life, in the life of his two children, but they were trying hard to fill it and their existence at St Bede's was full of charm for all three of them. The baby would be with them at Easter and Irena held her hand against her belly as a new, living part of Daniel heaved and danced within her.

Sam kicked off his boots and gave the dogs some water before he padded through to the kitchen in his stockinged feet.

'I see the vultures are gathering,' he said to his mother, pouring himself a cup of coffee.

'Vultures?' Zdenka sat down beside him, 'What do you mean?'

'I've just seen Magda and Jovanka poling up at the Lodge. When's this baby due?'

'Oh Samuel – how horrible you are sometimes!' his mother exclaimed. 'We're all so excited and darling Irena doesn't need a caesarian this time – she's having the baby in her own bed down there. It could be any time now, but she won't rest – she was in the museum this morning before I was up.'

Sam, who had planned his visit to St Bede's some time ago, had forgotten that his presence might coincide with this important arrival. Perhaps he'd go back to London and avoid the shenanigans that were bound to take place, but he still missed Irena and wondered how she would cope with this new birth – Daniel's posthumous child. He decided to go and see her before the action started. He finished his coffee, pulled his boots on again and got onto his bicycle.

Daniel Benjamin arrived in the world with very little fuss in a cheerful bedroom looking out onto the lake, now bordered with yellow and blue iris and huge marsh marigolds. In the months since Irena had known she was to be a mother again – the mother of a fatherless child – she had swung violently between the emotions of panic and excited anticipation. She knew she was constantly being watched and that the kind entourage who bustled about the house cooking, amusing the children and walking her dog, talked amongst themselves. They had her best interest at heart – they all loved her – but Irena felt that there was no one with whom she could share her changeable feelings, even if she'd had the words to express them.

Klara and Jo-Jo climbed onto Irena's bed with her, one on either side, and looked with interest at their new brother.

'What's his name, Mum?' asked Klara.

'Daniel Benjamin – but we'll call him Benjamin, I thought. Benjamin means the youngest one – the last-born.'

'That's a long name for someone so little,' Klara was playing with the baby's tiny fingers. 'We could call him Benjy, couldn't we?'

A knock on the door announced Zdenka, Magda and Miranda, their arms full of flowers. The baby was duly admired and passed around until they saw that the new mother was tired. Then they left her, the new arrival sucking contentedly at her breast.

✻

Magda and Jovanka had gone back to London, and Irena, who had looked forward to having her new baby to herself, could not find the energy to leave the sofa. She sat there all day with Benjy in her arms, needing to summon all her resolve to appear cheerful when the children returned from school. Instead of a joyful time with her new child, she found herself sliding into the darkest grief she had known since the first days after Daniel's death.

Zdenka, who went over daily to the Lodge, found a new Irena who frightened her – pale and haunted, she continually held the baby and tried, often unsuccessfully, to feed him. The Lodge had become increasingly dirty and untidy and, although this in itself was of no importance, the old lady knew it was another sign that all was not well. 'Put him in his cot, darling – go and get some sleep while you can … let me make you some lunch, won't you? You need to eat properly for your milk.' But Irena shook her head. 'I can't leave him … He needs me.'

Leaving the Lodge and wondering how to help Irena, Zdenka remembered a girl called Ludmilla who worked on the farm. Gossip had it that she'd had to leave a young baby with her mother in Bulgaria, where there was no work to be had. Mainly because she was too tired to grieve after a long day bent over the potato fields, she showed no sign of her sadness, until the whole estate were talking about the new baby at the Lodge.

Irena looked out to see who was at the door with Zdenka. She recognised Ludmilla, who sometimes helped her in the garden. The girl had never been inside the Lodge and looked around curiously for a moment. Then she held out her arms for Benjy.

47. REFUSAL

[IRENA]

LEO was a loyal friend and an excellent agent. I had relied on him constantly after Daniel's death, knowing that, for all his hard appearance and sometimes acid tongue, he understood what I was going through. He told me one day, turning away so that I would not see what the revelation was costing him, that there were still times when the sudden realisation that he'd never see Daniel again was almost more than he could bear.

Daniel had many friends, some going back to his school days, but I was a solitary creature and did not mix easily with new people. In a way, my life at St Bede's relieved me of having to try. Ludmilla, who had saved my sanity in the days after Benjy's birth, adored him and looked after him when I was working. She kept house for me at the Lodge, too, and had taken over the cooking of our supper, providing Bulgarian dishes which reminded me of dear Amela's spicy and calorific stews, which Daniel had so enjoyed. The children brought their classmates home from school and I fell into a comfortable relationship with the parents of these friends, an easy tit-for-tat of teas and outings and sleepovers. Otherwise, I was busy, enjoying my work and finding at last the beginning of an equilibrium in my feelings. This was not to say I had got over my grief, but I could now live day by day without the constant tearing of my heart. I did still cry, but quietly, at night and alone.

❊

'Irena,' said Leo after he'd enquired after my health, that of the children and how things were in general. 'I've got a project I need to discuss with you.'

'Oh, I hope it's not a concert. I don't practise enough and anyway, I've got far too much work here. The summer season is starting, we're short of guides and I need to finish the recital programme.'

'Hey, calm down, sweetheart. Not so fast. You haven't let me tell you what this project is.' He laughed his hoarse laugh. 'I need to come down and see you – as soon as possible?'

'I'd love to see you, of course, but can't you tell me on the phone?'

'Ok, but I know what you're going to say. You're going to say no, and you'll be wrong.'

'No to what? You're such a tease – tell me what this is about.'

Leo snorted but went on: 'It's a book. A book about Daniel. I've got a terrific writer and he's as keen as mustard. Let me bring him down to see you if you really can't get to London?'

Oh no, I thought. Not a book. Not having to go through my memories with a stranger and watch him create a person who would not be Daniel, nothing like him.

'You're right, Leo. The answer is 'no.'

But I was faintly curious. Leo had a talent for finding interesting people for his projects and I wanted to know who he had in mind.

'Interesting guy. He's a journalist, foreign correspondent. He's got a couple of books in print and is rated as a writer. I've talked to a lot of people now who know about these things and I think he could do it.'

'Oh Leo ... For one thing it's too soon and for another Daniel as a person had so many facets that I don't think that someone who didn't know him could begin to bring him to life on paper.'

'Well, there you're wrong. They knew each other quite well. They were out in Bosnia together – several times as it happens. Surely you know him – Peter Henderson – he was with Daniel when he was shot.'

'Peter Henderson?'

'Yes, he was out there a lot during the Siege as his first assignment for a newspaper, then kept going back as he was really in love with the place.'

My memory had become very unreliable, particularly when it came to anything that could be painful, but I did remember the name. For some reason, although he and Daniel were frequently in touch, I had never managed to meet him. I'd written to him once to ask him to stay, as Daniel badly wanted to repay at least some of the kindness Peter had shown him, but his work took him abroad most of the time and Daniel was travelling a good deal, too, so they were never able to find a date he could stick to. But I had read some of his articles and there had been an interview when Daniel was playing at the Châtelet in Paris, which he and Peter had obviously enjoyed doing together.

'Oh Leo. You knew very well I would be more interested after you'd said that. I do know who you mean and Daniel always wanted us to meet. All right. Bring him down. I don't know when, though. Weekends are out. I have a free day next Wednesday, but maybe that doesn't suit you?'

'I'll give him a ring. Let you know. Thanks Sweetheart. I think you may find this is something ... Well, this might be less awful than you think. Anyway *ciao* for now.'

He rang off and I got back to what I had been doing. That night I couldn't sleep and thought, 'How could I let Leo even think this could happen.'

This man was just a reporter: there was no way I could talk

through Daniel's life and look out photographs and contact friends in order to produce a piece of sensational journalism. Then I heard nothing and presumed the meeting wasn't going to happen.

On Wednesday morning, the telephone rang as I got back from the school run. A man's voice said: 'Irena Danuczekova? My name's Peter Henderson. You're expecting me this morning but I'm not sure how to find you.'

'But Leo never called me back. I didn't think he was bringing you today after all.'

'Oh, God, I'm sorry. He must have forgotten. He said to go on my own. But if today's no good ...'

I gritted my teeth, but he told me he'd travelled down from Scotland. I didn't have the heart to say I couldn't see him and I had nothing planned that day. Benjy was with Ludmilla and the others had gone on a school trip.

'No. You'd better come, as you're almost here.' And I told him how to find the house, deciding I would take him straight to the Piano Museum which was closed for the day; that way he would see nothing of my home or possessions or any of Daniel's things which lay around the Lodge.

I saw a car draw up and went to the door to greet my visitor. A thin man in a creased Safari suit stood looking up at the statue of St Bede above the portico. He had longish brown hair and a worn leather bag hung over his shoulder. We shook hands on the doorstep and he followed me into the hall under its glass octagon. The tall Roman statues in their niches around the room seemed to interest my companion, as indeed did everything we passed as I led him into the kitchen to fetch the coffee tray I had laid out. He was certainly a reporter, I thought to myself, inquisitive, nosey.

In the Piano Museum, my visitor asked me: 'Do you live here? In this house?'

'No, the children and I live in a Lodge by the main gates.

But my job's looking after this collection,' and I indicated the pianos. He walked over to Chopin's piano and read the notice on the music stand which was a short history of the instrument and a list of musicians who had played it. 'As you see, a lot of pianists come here to play it.' I said. 'Jean-Yves Thibaudet had a film made of him playing Chopin pieces on this piano and talking about it – rather good. He looks like Chopin anyway and wore lace cuffs and things. He told me that it was said Chopin "used the pedals with marvellous discretion."'

Peter Henderson turned back to me: 'Sorry,' he said, 'what did you say?' I repeated it, wondering what he'd been thinking about to miss the little spiel I was used to saying to the groups I took around the museum.

We sat down and I poured him a cup of coffee. Now that I was closer to him, I saw that his cheeks were badly pitted with scars and that he had hazel eyes and a high forehead under the unkempt brown hair. But his face was pleasant enough and the expression wasn't curious, it was friendly. He kept his head turned slightly as we talked and I remembered that he'd lost some hearing when he was blown up. I started to speak a little louder, but he recoiled and sat further back in his chair.

'Mr Henderson,' I began.

'Oh, Peter. Please.' Bother, I thought, now I have to be called by my first name too.

'And I'm Irena.' I said resignedly. He smiled as if he knew what I was thinking and was amused. Then I said: 'Well, I know you're here because you'd like to write a book about my husband.'

'Yes, I would. Leo said you weren't keen – that you'd said no.'

'But you came anyway?'

'Well, you know I'm a reporter. We're not easily put off. And Daniel told me a lot about you – I don't know why we never managed to meet.' He laughed for the first time and looked younger as he did so. I wondered how old he was. A few years older than me, I thought.

'When did you first meet? Was it out in Bosnia?'

'Yes, and the last time we met too, was there. It was after a concert he'd given. I wanted to do an interview, but he was pretty tired – wheelchair access had been problematic and they bounced him around a bit getting him on and off the stage. So in the end we just had a drink. Several drinks, actually – we got a bit drunk. He didn't want to discuss anything except music to start with. But then he started talking about you and how you'd met.' Peter paused for quite a long time and then said, very suddenly and fast. 'But you know, of course, that I was with him when he got shot?'

'I did know. That must have been terrible for you.' I didn't really want to hear any of this, but his face told me that he was not an insensitive man – his own pain was transparent. I asked quickly, 'Are you a musician?'

'No, unfortunately. I never had any musical education, so I felt a bit out of my depth when Daniel started on the technical stuff – particularly on what he couldn't play after he lost the use of his legs. But he didn't seem at all worried about my interviews. He said to let him have a draft of anything I'd written and he'd correct things that weren't right.'

Listening to Peter talking about Daniel I had to admit that he had the knack of bringing someone to life. 'Then I heard he'd died. We'd agreed to meet again and I was to write something for the British press. I ended up doing his obituary for the local Sarajevo paper, *Oslobodjenj*, instead.'

I suddenly remembered when, going through the huge box of letters of condolence, there had been one on paper with the heading of a Bosnian newspaper. It was a very sympathetic letter and insisted I shouldn't even think of answering; the writer just wanted to say that Daniel had been a wonderful friend, he would be terribly missed. I recalled that it was signed *Peter Henderson*.

'I'm sorry I just couldn't manage to answer many of the letters I got. It made me too upset. But yours was special, I remember.'

'Oh goodness,' said Peter, looking taken aback. 'I could imagine – I thought anyway that I could imagine – that you'd feel like that. And now?'

My hackles rose slightly and I instinctively backed away from him. This is how journalists get to you, I thought. All nice and friendly and then, wham, they've got into your mind and your private life. 'I'm sorry,' I said, 'I'm just not ready for a book. I don't know if I ever will be.'

'That's OK, I understand,' Peter said easily and stood up. 'Well, thanks for letting me come, anyway, and the coffee. And it's been – well – very good to meet you finally.'

I had thought he would try to persuade me to change my mind, but he slung his bag back on his shoulder and waited for me to escort him out.

Feeling guilty suddenly and sorry he had made the long journey for nothing, I said: 'Now that you're here, would you like the tour?'

'If you've got time?' Peter followed me through the house, commenting knowledgeably about the pictures and furniture. I noticed again he didn't always answer me when I spoke to him; I realised that it was easier for him to understand what I was saying when he could see my face. We looked out of the tall windows and watched the deer under the trees that Capability Brown had planted two hundred years ago. There was something both intense and at the same time unhurried about the man, and he was easy to be with, to talk to. Now I was on my guard, though, and was careful to talk generally, professionally even. From time to time I caught him looking at me and I wondered what he was thinking.

We had just finished the tour when Zdenka appeared, looking for me. I introduced Peter, not mentioning the reason for his visit but I did say he was a journalist who had come all the way from Edinburgh and had known Daniel.

'Then you must come to lunch over at the Stable House. You can do an article on the Abbey. Would you? We're so desperate to let people know what marvellous things we have here, particularly the pianos, and that there's no government money to stop it all just rotting away.'

Peter was clearly torn. Maybe, I thought, if he stays he'll tell Zdenka and Robert that he wants to write about Daniel and get them to make me change my mind.

'Well, I'd love to, but I've already taken up too much of Mrs ... of Irena's, time. I think I ought to go, but send me some stuff and I'll certainly do my best for a heart-tugging article.'

He had slung his bag over his shoulder and was trying to head for the door, but Zdenka insisted he stay; Robert appeared and said there was no question of Peter's leaving before lunch. Ludmilla brought Benjy over from the Lodge to the Stable House and put his high chair next to Peter, where he ate his lunch appreciatively with his fingers, offering pieces of potato to his neighbour, who accepted them with laudable grace.

'He's got his father's smile, hasn't he?'

'And his appetite! I think he's like him as a person – but my other son, Jo-Jo, really looks like him.'

'Lucky chap. And you've got a daughter too?'

I told him about Klara and her music and he told me he had no children and had never been married, 'Rotten life for a wife – waiting for a war correspondent to come home.' He was a good listener, and smiled and nodded, as Zdenka rattled on in her usual way. He made faces at Benjy who laughed. No-one had told my son about the 'terrible twos' and he was the merriest of little boys. Zdenka lifted him from the high chair when he'd finished his pudding and he trotted out with her into the garden, waving back at us.

'What a star – and you're right – he's got his dad's laugh already.'

Robert wanted to know about the life of a war correspondent.

'You were in Afghanistan?' he asked and Peter's face was suddenly shadowed with sadness, so that I found it hard to look at him.

'Yes, I was, but I was trying to evacuate a house when it was blown up. So I had to come home.'

'Were you badly hurt?' asked his host.

'Well, I was lucky really. Several of my friends were killed that day. I just got these.' He touched the scarring on his cheeks. 'And I lost some hearing in the blast. Just in one ear, luckily.' He indicated his right ear, smiling ruefully. He wasn't feeling sorry for himself, I realized, as he went on to talk about his time in Bosnia. He agonised over the fate of his friends, and had been in despair for the whole country and its disparate, warring people, who had been neighbours and family members until hatred and prejudice and their leaders' thirst for power had driven them from their homes or slaughtered them where they stood.

After lunch Peter sat with Robert in the smoking room at the Stable House, discussing how to put St Bede's Abbey into the public's eye. He struck me as being a patient man, very sympathetic and never rushed, taking his time to evaluate what was being said to him before he answered. I wondered what his books were like. He looked at his watch and said he absolutely must leave. Standing in the hallway, he opened his bag and said: 'I know you probably won't want to read this, but I brought it for you anyway – you can always put it on your second-hand book stall.' He was handing me a paperback, not a new one by the state of its cover. The title was: *Beloved Bosnia: The Years of Pain.* I had tried all day to be restrained and controlled and give nothing away, but he must have seen then the emotion that was flooding over me as tears began to pour down my face. 'I'm so sorry,' said Peter. 'I'm so sorry. I thought you might …,' At last at a loss for words, his face was anguished. 'Don't be upset Irena. I hope I never make you cry again.' An odd thing to say, I thought later.

'No,' I said, taking the book. 'I mean Yes. I would like to read it.'

A few days later, Leo rang me. He scolded me, as I knew he would.

'And what did you think of Henderson?'

'I think he's surprisingly – well, sensitive – as journalists go.'

'And – as journalists go – he went?'

'Yes. He didn't change my mind.'

I made several stabs at reading Peter's book, but the tears came every time until I could no longer read the print. It was full of descriptions that brought back to me the places I had known so well and that he seemed to see with very clear, very empathetic eyes. There was a chapter on a few days he had spent in Sarajevo ten years ago.

> 'This evening I went to a piano recital. The pianist was Daniel Danuczek, who was once on the staff of the Music Conservatory here and shares with me a great love for this city. I had expected it to take place in the Conservatory's newly restored Concert Hall, but, having climbed the seven flights of marble steps that morning to buy a ticket, I understood why it would take place in the Military Hall instead. There, cherubs frolic over the classical doorways and the

audience sits very upright in the original leather and
metal chairs.

Danuczek's playing always astonishes me, but I know
little about music and just sat and allowed the notes
to cascade around me. I wondered how musicians
hear music and wished I could know even just for
a few hours, so that I could understand this most
complex yet most human of all the arts. He is an
extraordinary artist, and a very brave man.

Horrified by reports of the suffering in the then
Yugoslavia and with no thought to his own safety,
the musician visited Sarajevo regularly during the
Siege, where the BBC had enlisted me to protect him
as he accompanied me around the city, desperately
searching for a family he'd been unable to trace.
It was there that, just months before the end of
hostilities, he was shot in the back on the balcony of
his hotel room. Since then he has had to accustom
himself to getting about in a wheelchair, and, just
as terrible for a professional pianist, to finding his
repertoire much limited by his inability to use the
pedals of the piano. Always an inspirational teacher,
he returned to lecturing and giving master classes,
imagining that his concert career was over. He then
gave in to the pressure of his many admirers and
returned to the concert stage – playing the early
music he is still able to perform to his satisfaction
and in which he was already a respected exponent,
bringing into his repertoire many of the lesser
known composers of the Baroque period.

His disability does not deter him from living a life
that would leave most able-bodied people totally
exhausted, and his example has been a great spur
to other disabled musicians, particularly young
people to whom he is something of an icon. At this

point I should mention that Danuczek has a very
light-hearted side and his friends will not forget
his 'honky-tonk' performances, played with mock
seriousness. He has a marvellous sense of humour,
of the ridiculous, and one cannot be with him for
more than a few minutes before one is doubled up
with laughter.

Danuczek is married and has two children. His
wife, Irena, is also a musician. They met when
he was Director of Keyboard Studies at Sarajevo
Conservatory and lodged with her family the year
before the Siege changed this lovely city forever.
They live in London now but he comes back to
Bosnia Herzegovina whenever he can and continues
to give his time unstintingly for musicians wounded
in the war and their families. He recently founded
the charity, Bosnia Musicians' Relief, in aid of which
he frequently gives his concert fees.

I read the chapter several times and formed an impression of the writer that, despite my reservations, I could not
help liking. I thought that Daniel would also have approved,
although he hated being described as 'brave'. He would say
that you're only brave if you have a choice; he had no choice
about being in a wheelchair – he just had to get on with it.

To my surprise, Peter rang me two weeks after his visit to St
Bede's Abbey. I knew he'd written a polite letter thanking
Zdenka for his lunch and sent some notes to Robert following
up their fund-raising conversation; but I had heard nothing
and was annoyed to find myself feeling rather disappointed.

'Irena' he said. 'How's everything? You well?'

'Yes, thank you,' I said formally.

'I've got to be in London for a week or so next month and

I wondered if I could persuade you to come up for dinner, or a theatre or something? I absolutely promise I won't talk about you-know-what,' he said, laughing, but sounding more nervous than I would have expected him to be.

Why not, I thought. He's an interesting person. He and Daniel got on well together. We have things in common. I could leave Klara and Jo-Jo with school friends for the night and Ludmilla would be thrilled to have Benjy to herself. I said 'yes' and then wondered what on earth I was doing.

48. INVITATION TO THE DANCE

W E MET in the foyer of the Sadler's Wells Theatre. I was not expecting Peter to look smart, thinking back to his crumpled khaki suit, but he was wearing a well-cut cream linen one this time and an indigo shirt with the collar open. His hair was smoothly brushed back from his high forehead. I had spent some time wondering what to wear and, in the end, chose a pair of black trousers and a grey silk top. Rather dull, I thought, but that's how I dress. Magda had always said I had dreary taste. Dear Magda – I still saw her when I could, and sometimes stayed in the house she now shared with the painter, Miranda Thesiger. Peter kissed me on both cheeks and led me by the hand to the bar. 'We've got time for a drink. What'd you like?'

I asked for a glass of wine, but he didn't hear my answer and had to ask again. 'Sorry,' he said. 'I can't hear very well in crowds.'

We stood drinking and saying nothing, but I felt quite at ease with him. Our seats were at the front of the dress circle; I hadn't been to the ballet for years and this was one I had been wanting to see – Matthew Bourne's 'Swan Lake'. I was surprised and pleased that Peter had some of my own tastes. 'Hungry?' he asked, as we fought our way out of the theatre. 'Did you eat anything before?'

'No,' I said, and we went to an Italian restaurant, one of a chain and just the sort of place Daniel, who liked his food authentic, would have hated. Peter didn't seem very interested in the menu, but he ordered a good bottle of wine. We sat and ate, saying little, until he looked up at me and said: 'I want to tell you something, and I think you might be horrified or angry or upset, but I've still got to tell you.'

'What is it?' I was afraid the subject of the book was about to come up despite his promise.

'I've fallen in love with you ...'

For a moment I thought I must have misheard. 'Peter ... You don't know me. I don't know you.'

'Did you read my book?' he asked.

'Yes, I did. It was very moving. I liked it a lot ...'

'Then you do know me pretty well. I don't bullshit when I write. What you read is what I am.'

'But you can't be in love with me. I mean, not so soon.'

'Yes I can. And I am. I think I've loved you ever since Daniel talked to me about you. He couldn't stop. He absolutely adored you, didn't he? I don't think for a moment I could take his place – he's a pretty impossible act to follow. But I am in love with you and I want to care for you for the rest of your life if you'll let me.'

'Now I remember!' Irena and Peter were walking under the plane trees that border the Thames Embankment at Fulham, watching the rowers glide by on the black, glassy river. 'Danny rang me and told me about your evening together in Sarajevo after his concert in the Military Hall.'

'He told you how drunk we got?'

'I assumed you had as he told me how many bottles you got through. And he was on strong analgesics, so he wasn't really meant to drink ...' Daniel had never read the small print on the counter-indications section of the packet his pills came in, saying that a certain amount of drink helped to blunt the pain. He wasn't sure of the amount, but was working on it, he'd add.

'And you were in hospital here for a while then? I'm surprised he didn't visit you. He loathed hospital himself, so always went to see his friends when they were admitted and tried to cheer them up.'

'I imagine he succeeded, too – he was very good company. But no, I went back home to Edinburgh and had my treatment there. I only keep a London flat because it's useful when I get in on impossibly late or early flights from God knows where, but I stay as little as possible.'

'You don't like London?'

'I just need somewhere to write and to find people with things to say – journalists and politicians and so on. But I'm not a sophisticated person, I'm afraid – I'm not cultured like you and Daniel. Perhaps you'll find me very dull?'

Even when Irena had moments of doubting what she was doing with Peter, it was not because she found him dull. On the contrary, his knowledge of the world and his keen interest in people and history and buildings – and a lot of other things she had not yet discovered – made him an interesting person to be with. Also, and she could now admit this to herself, she had begun to need him physically.

Since she had been alone, she had tried hard not to think about sex. With Daniel it had been the first time in her life that she was able to give herself wholly to a man and not to be afraid. They had laughed so much, enjoyed themselves so much, that she didn't imagine that she could ever again find anyone who gave her such sheer joy in her body as he had. But when Peter had led her to his bedroom and carefully undressed her after the ballet, she had been overcome with desire for him and he was surprised at her passion and abandonment. It was a delicious thing for him, for Peter had from the beginning desired this little, exquisite woman and thought she would find him ugly, repulsive even. To Irena, he seemed to be another species from Daniel, in almost every way. Scarred and wiry, fast and deliberate in his movements. His blemished face no longer shocked her and she would lie beside him tracing the pattern of the scars with her finger, like a map whose features she must remember, until he no longer flinched and drew away. She had begun to find him irresistibly attractive, so that when they were walking together she would tell him this and laughed to see his surprised flush at the words she was using. He would turn to her and hold her against him so that she knew he too wanted nothing more than to return to bed with her.

They would only have a few days together. It was the first time she had left the children at St Bede's and she wondered, guiltily, how they were getting on. But having no-one to care for was a relief, too, as Peter did not even expect her to cook. He prepared their food quickly and efficiently, but not with Daniel's intense enjoyment. For Peter, food was a necessity but no great pleasure; Irena had always felt the same. They discussed this and agreed that once you have seen – and, in Irena's case, experienced – starvation, there is something obscene about great platefuls of expensive food. Peter was an orderly man; he washed up after meals and put the plates away, always made their bed and bought flowers for the dull sitting room.

'You're so domesticated and tidy. I'm afraid you'll find me a terrible slut.'

'I'm only tidy because my life is such a rush. If a story blows, I have to be at Heathrow for the next plane and I don't like to come back a week later to unwashed plates and general chaos. But you, you have a great musical talent and that's much rarer than being a good housekeeper. We've got to make sure you have time for this in your life. I'm afraid the museum is very time-consuming and you are too tired for practice most days, aren't you?'

'Yes, I am. But I love working there and I've learnt so much

– you know when I began I had no idea about organizing and running somewhere like that. And Zdenka and Robert have been like parents to me – and grandparents to the children. I'm too old to start a real career in music now. I'm just a good amateur.'

'Well, from what Daniel told me, that's rubbish. He said you were one of the best natural musicians he'd ever come across. You mustn't put it behind your other interests. It should come first. Well, after me, of course.' Peter came over to her. 'I hope to God I can be good enough for you.' He stroked her cheek and ran his hands down the silky length of her hair.

She whispered, 'When will I see you again? Please come down soon and meet the children …'

Peter had dreaded this moment. 'I have to go away – on work – for a while. A few weeks.'

Irena sat up, 'But you can't. No. Not now – couldn't you put it off. Please stay, Peter. What shall I do if you go now?'

He took her hands in his and leant forward to kiss her shoulder.

'My sweet – I have to work, I'm afraid. This is an important posting and I want to do it. I want to stay with you, too, of course I do, but this is a story I must follow up. I'm booked to fly out to Kandahar on Friday.'

Irena got up and went over to the window, trying hard not to cry, but her voice was cracked when she asked, 'When will you get back?'

She did not know that this was a question he could not answer, but he had to give her something to hold on to, so he lied, looking away from her and disliking himself for the deception. 'Three weeks or so, I should think. Maybe a month. It's not always cut and dried, but I should be through by then – have seen the people I need to see and got the interviews – and so on …'

Over the weeks that followed, Irena occupied herself as fully as she could. At first there were frequent calls from Afghanistan and the line was so clear that she found it hard to believe Peter was thousands of miles away. They exchanged daily emails: his were love letters and Irena read them over and over, finally printing them out and keeping them in her red bag which was always close at hand. In her replies Irena hid her true feelings: the constant fear she felt for Peter, and her resentment that he should have left her for his work so soon in their relationship.

She took to reading the newspapers – something she had never done regularly before – and scoured the overseas pages for something he had written or any mention of the province to which he had been sent.

She did her best to be active and cheerful with the children but Zdenka watched her anxiously, sensing that something in the young woman's life had changed. Having coffee with her at the Lodge one morning in August, the telephone rang and Irena jumped up, almost fell over the cat, snatched up the handset and took it into the hall. She returned a few minutes later looking crestfallen. The call had not been from Peter and Irena's expression told the old lady all she needed to know.

Three weeks after Peter had taken up his new assignment, a new piano was delivered to the Museum and Irena got up unusually early to supervise its arrival and positioning. It was a lengthy business and mid-morning before she went into the kitchen to make coffee for the removal men. She found Zdenka there, standing with her back to the Aga, a copy of *The Times* in her hand.

'Have you read the paper, darling?'

Irena was reaching up to take down some mugs and had to stand on tiptoe as the shelves had been designed for someone much taller than her. Indeed, Zdenka, who had shrunk somewhat in old age, now had a little block to stand on, which she pushed around the kitchen with her arthritic foot.

'No, I had to leave before it came. Why?'

How tired she looks, thought Zdenka, guessing that Irena wasn't sleeping.

'There's something I want to show you.' and the old lady put the open newspaper on the kitchen table. At the top of the page were photographs of six journalists who were known to be in Afghanistan at the time. Several of them had been captured by the Taliban a few days before; their whereabouts was not known. One of the pictures was of Peter, wearing a khaki hat, his eyes screwed up against the sun.

In the effort to prepare her children for a possible step-father, Irena had shown them a scrapbook that Peter had given her before he left. In it were roughly cut out press cuttings covering his foreign assignments, old teletexts and fading faxes.

'He's really famous, then?' asked Jo-Jo, impressed. The children went on turning the pages until their they came across a picture of Peter looking very young and smooth-skinned standing by a tank and wearing a helmet and flak jacket. The headline read *Journalist Caught in Bomb Blast*.

'Oh – he was quite handsome –' Klara said, surprised.

The children continued to look at the page while Irena read out the report, which ended:

> *Henderson had thrown himself on top of one of*
> *the insurgents whose life he undoubtedly saved, but*
> *in doing so took the full force of the blast in his*
> *face. I went to see him in the field hospital, where*
> *he lay swathed in bandages but making light of*

his appearance – 'I'll be going back to get some
plastic surgery. Might get a new nose and a face lift
while I'm about it,' he joked. Our conversation was
somewhat one-sided as the blast had also blown out
his eardrums and he was having trouble hearing me.
We wish him well and he assures us he'll be back on
duty as soon as he's been patched up.

'How awful. Poor Peter. He must be very brave.'
Irena agreed that he must be.
'When is he coming to see us again?' asked Jo-Jo.
Irena started to tidy up Benjy's toys which were all over the
floor. 'I don't know,' she said, trying not to sound as if she
cared particularly, one way or another.

49. PICKERS' PARTY

S TEFAN and Lidija were to come for two weeks that summer
  as they had done for the past three years when the harvest
was over. Knowing what a difficult and complicated thing
getting these visas was for Lidija, Irena did nothing to change
their plans and was glad of the diversion. Peter had not been
in touch and no-one could tell her anything about him or
where he was. She drifted from day to day glad of any activity
that could occupy her hands and her mind, taking the children out with their friends, supervising their holiday club
activities and cooking copious meals for anyone and everyone.

Irena had grown fond of her secret first child in spite of the
teenager's resemblance to his father, but she hadn't revealed
Stefan's true parentage to her other children. The boy enjoyed
his trips to England and, although he spoke little English, he
and Jo-Jo found ways to communicate and their age difference
seemed to make no difference. Stefan liked nothing better
than to go off with his half-brother to the furthest corners of
the estate where they would build hides and watch the deer.
The only altercations came when the visitor first asked for a
gun – he imagined the deer would make a great barbecue and
found it hard to understand why his request so horrified his
hosts. Of course, they did eat venison and quite often, but
the killing was the result of carefully managed culls and two
boys with guns or crossbows would have been an unwelcome
novelty in the peaceful fields of St Bede's.

❋

'Hurry up. They're lighting the fire – see the smoke?' Jo-Jo and Stefan were already running towards the fruit pickers' encampment where the end of season party was to be held. That night there was a venison carcass to be roasted and a pig as well. The fires crackled as fat from the roasting meat dripped onto them and the smell was delicious. Benjy trotted after the boys and Klara followed with a basket of salad and cakes and sweets, complaining that it was always she who had to carry everything. Laughing, Irena and Lidija picked up their burdens of folding chairs and yet more food.

The pickers' caravans had been parked in the clearing all summer and been home to fifty young people from all over eastern Europe. The children loved their company and Benjy, whose devoted nanny, Ludmilla, lived with a group of other Bulgarian women, regarded the encampment as his second home and the cheerful young inhabitants as his rightful playfellows. The group around the fire had divided themselves into cooks and singers and musicians. Darkness was falling and their faces were illuminated by the flames. They sang songs they had known all their lives in their different homelands. The words didn't seem to matter, as they held hands and began to dance in a wide circle around the fires; but Stefan and his mother stood away a little until Irena led them forward. The music reminded her of her childhood and the gypsies who would come into Sarajevo when they had finished summer work in the surrounding countryside. They too had sung like this, their voices piercing the night, long after she had been sent to bed and, if she craned her head out of the landing window, she could see the fire they had lit in the square and the dancing figures, their faces shining in the firelight, the women's embroidered skirts billowing as they spun round and round, the men naked to the waist and glistening with sweat and oil. Now, in her angry grief to have been betrayed for a second time by fate, she allowed her tears to flow and Lidija watched her sadly, wondering what sort of tears these were. For this graceful woman was the girl she had watched in abuse and starvation for month after month, the courageous child who had been finally subdued and broken as she gave birth, weeping and screaming into the night when she was told that her baby had not survived. Stefan was enjoying himself. He did not mix with the pickers, but stayed close to Jo-Jo, looking at him in admiration as the boy took a guitar from a Lithuanian boy and started to play, his head thrown back and the firelight catching the lenses of his glasses, so that he looked like some bright, unearthly being.

There would be no early bedtime that evening and Irena wished she was not so tired, so exhausted by the weeks of uncertainty and the insistent fear that had begun to creep into her thoughts – the fear that she would never see Peter again. If only she knew. If only there was someone who could confirm either hope or despair.

The telephone rang in the Lodge, but there was no-one to answer it and two hours later a bearded man walked through to the edge of the wood and stood shadowed by the trees, watching the dancers in the clearing by the caravans. He searched for Irena and when he picked her out, standing a little aside, he did not know whether to go to her or not.

'Mummy – look! That man with a beard. He's staring at you,' said Klara.

Irena looked across the clearing beyond the bonfire. She started to walk away from the fire and the singing and dancing towards the woods that surrounded the clearing. She walked very slowly at first but then began to run.

'Zdenka, there's something I need to tell you – to discuss with you. Have you got a moment?'

'Of course I have,'

Irena's voice had sounded urgent, but she seemed unable to open the subject that was on her mind.

Zdenka said, 'How wonderful that Peter is home – and safe. What a time he's had. He's staying with you, isn't he?' Irena nodded.

'Yes, he is. Or was. He's gone back to London for debriefing – and a check-up. He's still not well …'

'What a dreadful experience – and both his companions are safe too?'

Irena nodded and Zdenka waited in silence for her to continue. She could see that Irena was finding whatever she needed to say very difficult. She could help her or she could just wait. She waited. She waited until Irena, her hands the tight little fists they formed when she was especially anxious, finally spoke. 'He's asked me to marry him.' Irena looked down into her coffee cup again.

'My dear girl! Robert and I thought that he'd fallen for you when he had lunch here.'

'But we'd only met that day …'

'But we could see he was already smitten. So … what did you say?'

'I've said "yes".'

'That's wonderful! I think he's quite a special person and he obviously thinks you are. It's quick, but he's fallen hard and maybe you have too. So darling girl, don't look so distraught. Is it Daniel – do you think this would hurt him?'

'I suppose so. I know he'd have wanted me to find someone else – but it's so soon!'

'Not all that soon – you've been a widow for three years now. I know you still miss Daniel, but you really could think about moving on. Maybe this man is the person to help you do it.'

'I don't know if it's fair on Peter. I'm very miserable still a lot of the time and not much fun to be with. And how do I tell the children? They still talk a lot about Daniel, you know. I don't know if they could accept another man in the family.'

'Has Peter been married before?'

When Irena had asked him this, as they lay in his sagging bed and watched the sun set over the Thames outside the window, he'd replied, 'No, not quite. I was in love with a Croatian girl. She worked on the paper I was writing for. She was an editor and we were always arguing about grammar and words.' He paused and then said, looking away from Irena. 'She and her family were taken away one night. I never found out what happened to her – or any of them.'

'Oh poor Peter, how dreadful. Do you still miss her?'

Peter had got up, disentangling himself from Irena's arms, and went over to the window to close the curtains. It was dark outside and she could see his reflection in the black glass before the curtains screened it from her. Then he'd turned back to her and stood there, naked, and railed against the horrors of that war, her war, and the imbecile hatred of one man for another, his muscles tightening and slackening as he re-lived the horror of those days, the pointless violence and the hopeless valour.

'Irena. Irena, my love.' Peter had stumbled towards her, almost falling onto the bed at her side. 'How can we ever forget, how can we go on living with this in our memories?' But he was not demanding an answer, not expecting an explanation. He was simply stating the fact she also knew to be true: that those memories were ingrained in them now, part of the fabric of their personalities and their outlook on all that they saw and experienced.

'No' Irena said to Zdenka. 'He was engaged once. But she died in the Siege – Sarajevo, you know.'

Zdenka sighed: 'Oh Irena. We are all so scarred, aren't we? Me and my family, you and yours. Then Daniel too and now Peter. There is no expiation, you know. Only music for us. We are so lucky to have our music. Does Peter play?'

'No. He never studied music. He likes to listen to it, but no, he's a writer and words are to him what music is to us.' Even in the short time they had spent together, she had been intrigued by the way Peter would keep going to his laptop and she had realised that, where Daniel had gone to his piano many times each day, Peter's keyboard satisfied *his* need to express and communicate his thoughts and feelings – through the written word.

Zdenka came round the kitchen table and put her arms around the young woman. 'And the children – how well do they know him?'

'Not really well. We got them up to London before he left and went to a happening at the Festival Hall. Then they didn't meet him until he turned up at the pickers' party.'

The morning after the party, the children came downstairs to find a clean-shaven Peter having breakfast in the kitchen. They saw that the top half of his face was deeply tanned and the lower part, where his beard had been, very pale. Jo-Jo nudged his sister and they struggled to suppress their giggles. Politely, however, they showed him around the Lodge and Irena remembered how she had not taken him there when he had first come to St Bede's, not wanting him to see that Daniel's presence was everywhere. Peter looked around curiously. There were many photographs of Daniel, some framed but most of them propped up on the top of pieces of furniture or pinned onto the walls. A wheelchair filled with anoraks, gloves and school satchels stood in the hall. Jo-Jo saw Peter looking at it.

'That was our Dad's. He couldn't walk, you know.'

Peter felt uncomfortable. What else would he find here that was Daniel's and how on earth could these things be made to disappear if he was to live with Irena? Looking round the sitting room, he saw the picture hanging over the fireplace. It was a portrait and, he suspected, unfinished. Daniel had been painted sitting at the piano in his wheelchair in the blue studio that Irena had described to Peter. The artist had either chosen to depict her sitter in two positions or had not decided which pose to make permanent, for Daniel appeared to have four hands and two heads – one bent over the keyboard and the other looking out at the observer. The piano he played was a soft, golden colour, and the whole picture seemed full of light.

'That's Daddy' said Klara coming to stand beside Peter. It really looks like him – but he didn't have two heads of course.' and she laughed.

Irena had joined them and looked up at the portrait.

'Miranda – she's the artist – didn't manage to finish it. Daniel should have sat for her again, but – well, he died. It was a commission for the Sarajevo Conservatory, but it wasn't finished enough for them, so she gave it to us. I love it. His expression was just like that lower face when he started to play and was in his own world with the music.'

'And the other one looks as if he's going to make a joke,' said Jo-Jo, pointing to Daniel's second head.

The three of them stood for a while looking at the picture and Peter was relieved that Irena and Klara did not seem sad, but clearly enjoyed talking about their father's portrait.

Miranda had waited over a year before she contacted Irena and turned up at West Gate Lodge with her canvas, which she propped up in the hall. There were boxes everywhere still waiting to be unpacked, and other unhung pictures leaning precariously against walls and furniture.

A grey-haired woman introduced herself as Magda, Dan-

iel's sister. She often stayed at the Lodge, ostensibly to help
Irena. Although she would rise to the occasion when the children were around, she would become increasingly gloomy
amongst the mementos of Daniel, her grief scarcely softened
by the passing of time. Irena had long ago come to realise that
her sister-in-law had been much more than a sister to Daniel.
His death had been a blow from which Magda could not – or
would not – recover, it seemed. So, for the past three years it
had been the widow who had somehow found the strength to
comfort and sustain the grieving sister.

When Miranda arrived, Magda had been about to take
Benjy for a walk in his buggy. She had sometimes wondered
what had happened to the unfinished portrait, and was curious
to see both artist and her painting. Standing with Irena was
a woman of about her own age who wore a long green suede
skirt and a loose embroidered jacket which exactly matched
the pink silk scarf draped around her neck. Her faded blonde
hair was swept up and fastened in a French pleat with a moth-
er-of-pearl comb. She was pointing to the picture and the
hand she extended was long with tapering fingers. 'It isn't
finished, of course. But I wanted you to see it. I felt it … well,
sometimes unfinished work is more interesting.'

Miranda stole a look at Irena who had reached out both
hands and was touching the two painted faces of Daniel,
caressing them, before she turned to Magda.

'It's lovely. Really lovely. What do you think, Mags?' She
saw that her sister-in-law was moved by the painting and
regretted asking her opinion just then, but Magda smiled,
mischievous suddenly, 'Well, his head was pretty big at times,
so painting it twice …' She looked across at the artist, as she
added hastily, 'the hands are miraculous – they seem to be
moving – you can almost hear the music … How clever you
are.'

Benjy, who didn't like to be kept waiting, started to fidget.

Magda turned and pushed the buggy out through the front door.

'Oh Miranda ... I love it,' Irena said, when they were alone, 'but ... this is so embarrassing. I can't afford to buy a picture just now – could we borrow it for a while?' And then the artist told her that it was Irena's, if she wanted it. A present.

That evening the three women had shared one of the remaining bottles of Daniel's champagne. Magda went up to bed early, sensing that perhaps three was not good company that evening, although Miranda intrigued her and she would have liked to have remained to watch the artist and listen to her light, mezzo voice. When she had left them, Miranda told Irena about Daniel's visit to her studio and how she'd learnt about his heart condition.

'I didn't know what to do. I thought I really ought to tell you, but was not sure how, so I waited a while and then rang to arrange the next sitting, but – well – it was too late.'

'How awful for you,' said Irena, 'but I wouldn't have known what to do either. Poor Danny – he was so terrified of being operated on. In the end – well it's taken me a long time to think this out, but I think he died when he had to. He had a great life and gave a lot of happiness to a lot of people. From then on things would just have got more and more difficult for him.'

Irena refilled the glasses and raised hers to Miranda. 'He told me you were one of the most beautiful women he'd ever met.'

'Surely not – he must have thought I was as old as time.'

'Danny wasn't like that. He loved beautiful women – of any age. He said you must have been very lovely when you were young and were still wonderful looking and he laughed because he could see I was feeling a bit jealous. He'd always been a lady-killer – he couldn't help it – and I don't suppose marriage changes people's true nature. He certainly went on noticing pretty women – and,' Irena's eyes danced with laughter, 'he definitely fancied you.' Miranda did not tell the younger woman of her own feelings for Daniel, nor of the grief she'd lived with, knowing that she'd never see him again.

They hung the picture over the fireplace, Irena first clearing away the photographs and pieces of the children's pottery that sat on the mantelpiece. As she did so, she knocked over a small bowl whose contents landed on the hearthrug. Miranda picked it up and examined it.

'It's a piece of bone, isn't it?' she asked, and when Irena didn't answer, she went on, 'It looks like part of a skull ... It's been burnt.' and she'd suddenly looked up at the painting of Daniel in profile.

Irena looked up at it too and smiled.

'You know what it is, don't you? I took his ashes out to Bosnia to scatter. Everything doesn't burn when they cremate someone ... I saw this piece fall out of the urn and couldn't bear to leave it there. I wanted something – physical – of him to keep. Are you shocked?'

Miranda shook her head.

'I'm not shocked. It's rather beautiful – he had such a big strong head I'm not surprised that even fire couldn't destroy it all.'

Miranda had been taken aback by her first sight of the tall, gaunt woman with shoulder-length iron grey hair who had opened the Lodge door to her. She was so very like Daniel. On Sunday, she had offered Magda a lift back to London. Outside her studio, Miranda had asked her passenger in, saying lightly, 'Just scrambled eggs, but please stay ...' Magda had hesitated, but then asked herself why. She had no-one to go home to. Supper was accompanied by too much wine and she had stayed the night.

50. MOVING ON

'DARLINGS, I want to ask you something. It's important– I want you to listen.'

Irena had put Benjy to bed and made a jug of hot chocolate before she sat down with the other children. She was a very informal mother, and Klara looked at her questioningly, sensing that she was about to say something out of the ordinary; Jo-Jo was absorbed in a Rubik cube. She had rehearsed time and again words she would use, but what if they turned against her and hated her for betraying Daniel's memory?

'It's about Peter. Do you like him?'

'He's cool.' said Jo-Jo, not looking up from his puzzle.

Klara said nothing and then, her head turned away from her mother, she blurted out, 'I can't bear looking at him. Luckily he doesn't try to kiss me when he gets here like some grownups do – that would be horrible.'

She looked at Irena then and saw the pain on her face and went on: 'I know that's a horrid thing to say, but ...'

Irena took a deep breath and tried again. 'The thing is – he's asked me to marry him. I know Daddy wouldn't want us to go on being sad for ever. I know he'd like us to be a happy family again – with someone really nice.'

'Fine by me,' said Jo-Jo, but Klara started to cry.

'Alice's mum got married again and they hate their new dad. He says horrible things and won't let them stay up late ... and even if Peter's brave and everything, I just hate looking at him.' Klara stopped, ashamed of herself, and then went on. 'Daddy was really handsome.'

Peter had spent most of his short time at St Bede's with the children. Watching them, Irena remembered that Daniel had felt his disability most keenly when he saw other fathers playing with their sons; it was the only time he felt truly inadequate, but Jo-Jo had never questioned his father's inability to get out of his chair and seemed to have an instinctive understanding of what Daniel could and could not do. Peter, wiry and athletic, ran up the hill and climbed over fences with the kite he had brought back from Kandahar, showing them how to pay out the string and make it dance and pirouette around the sky. They had visited Klara's pony, and Peter, who had never had a high opinion of equines, pretended to be frightened. Klara had shown him how to breathe into its nostrils and scratch its ears. He'd erected an umbrella over the barbecue on an evening when it had rained and the children had laughed, appearing to be happy and relaxed. Altogether, Irena thought things had gone well, but clearly it would take longer than she'd imagined, impatient as she was to start their life with Peter.

Jo-Jo had lost interest in the conversation and was pretending to bowl a cricket ball. Grown-ups were a mystery to him, but no one had ever given him cause to distrust them. Yes, Peter was cool and his mother seemed different now that he was around and laughed much more, he'd noticed.

Lying in bed later, Irena heard a sound as her bedroom door opened and Klara climbed in beside her, something she hadn't done for a long time. Irena put her arms around her and, after a few minutes, Klara said, 'When you and Peter get married, can I be a bridesmaid?'

Irena had decided to sell her Pink and Green houses. They had for some time been let separately and brought in a good income, enabling her to pay for Klara's music lessons and take the children on holiday once a year.

She loved taking them skiing, remembering childhood winter weekends at Pali, the ski resort near Sarajevo, and how she'd revelled in those sparkling days on the snow. She'd been a graceful and fearless skier.

Peter joined Irena and the children in the Alps for a few days. He didn't ski as well as she did, but well enough for them to take some of the easier runs together with Benjy. In the evenings they danced and drank and, when they were sure that the children were asleep, they made love in front of the open window with snowflakes powdering their naked bodies.

'Oh Peter', Irena said, 'I'm sad about my house. We must hurry up and buy another one – together.'

Peter got up, closed the window and pulled the duvet over them. He said: 'All right – there's no hurry, is there? If we can't find anything before the school year begins, Jo-Jo can go back to his old school and Benjy too. Klara will be at the Menuhin all week – and Magda said she would help out. Go and do what clearing up you can when we get back. I need to go up to London on Thursday – I'll join you for the heavy stuff and drive you home.'

They all loved St Bede's, but Peter often needed to be in London. He thought secretly, too, that the Piano Museum took up too much of Irena's time when she could have been playing her viola. Jo-Jo and Benjy were happy enough at the local schools but Klara really needed better music lessons and had passed easily into the Menuhin School in Surrey. London had seemed the solution: there would be enough money from the sale of the Pink and Green houses and Peter's flat to buy something big enough for them all.

Irena's heart was heavy as she cleared out the last of her bits and pieces. The cabinet in Daniel's shower room was locked.

She found the key where she had hidden it and opened the door. Knowing what she would find, she did not look at the contents as she transferred everything into a Provençal bag that Daniel had given her in France: bottles and pills and syringes, which should have been disposed of long ago. The uncertainty that Sam and she had discussed over Daniel's death rose again like a dark spectre. She knew you couldn't just throw away things like that in the dump – maybe they had to go back to the chemist – so she zipped up the bag and carried it with her as she went upstairs to continue her tour. Finding the bedrooms too painful for any careful inspection, she went downstairs again. There, she opened and shut doors and cupboards mechanically, her mind trying to block the memories that each familiar space might hold captive, ready to engulf her.

Finally she reached the kitchen, where she paused in the doorway, expecting to be overcome with the grief that had all but paralysed her when she had fled to the country four years before. She walked briskly towards the back door, opened it and turned back into the room that had been the hub of their lives when Daniel came and went, pulling himself in from the garden and going on his frequent forages in the larder and fridge.

A light wind blew the curtain that still hung in the window but there was nothing there to hurt her now, only everyday memories of family meals and homework and of tidying away the flood of musical scores that followed Daniel everywhere, stuffed down the side of his wheelchair cushion, alongside their bed and in all the kitchen drawers. Now nothing remained of that untidy man except the smile on Irena's face, as she shut the final cupboard door. What she felt then was not grief, or regret, or any sort of pain. Instead she felt a healing flood of gratitude to have known the gentle everyday joy she had lived and that, even as she lived it, she had thanked fate for having put her broken young life in the hands of an eccentric musician who had the skill and humour to piece it back together again.

Everywhere was cleared now, except the studio. She had left that until last, knowing that it would be the hardest place of all.

One side of the garden had been well kept by her last tenants, but the other was overgrown and the studio was draped with leafless creepers which hung dankly almost to the ground across the French windows. Irena took the key from her pocket and turned it in the stiff, resisting lock. No-one had used the studio since she and Sam had boxed up the last of Daniel's files after the Memorial Concert.

Irena had concentrated on locking the doors and then she had pulled the blinds down and gone across the garden without looking behind her. Several families had lived in the houses since she and the children had left but Irena had that end of the garden fenced off and the door was kept locked. Irena had never even shown it to Peter.

It was almost dark inside as a Virginia creeper had grown up over the window, its suckers resisting her efforts to tear it down. There were cobwebs stretched across the corners and between the exposed beams of the ceiling. The floor was thick with dust, but the piano had left its imprint where the feet had dented the wooden floor. The room was not quite empty; Irena had forgotten that Daniel's wheelchair had been pushed in there as she had found herself unable to take it to the Red Cross. There also was the daybed and a pillow still lay at one end on an Indian bedspread in tones of blue and ochre.

'Oh Danny,' whispered Irena, as she sat down on the bed, sending up a cloud of dust which billowed in the air above her, catching the light in thousands of scintillating particles. She watched it swirling around; it seemed in no hurry to settle. She remembered how he'd been playing a Bach *Chaconne* the evening he'd got his new piano, his expensive and beautiful Fazzioli, and how the percussive notes had seemed then to break up in the ruddy light of the sunset and spread it around the azure studio, where, seated at the keyboard, Daniel smiled as he played.

Irena lay down on the bed. She felt Daniel's presence so strongly that she thought that if she put out her hand he might take it. She picked up the bag, which she had put down on the floor beside her, undid the zip and looked at the contents, which brought back the spectre of Daniel's battle with the pain that had blighted the last years of his life. Would she join him now if she filled the syringe and put the liquid into her vein? But Irena had held his ashes in her hands and let them free in a fierce Bosnian wind – all that remained of him was ashes and memories. She lay there, the bag clutched to her chest, and shut her eyes.

For once Peter had managed to park outside The Green House. Klara was in the car with him but had embarked on a conversation on her mobile with a friend.

'You go ahead, Petie,' she said, 'I'll join you when I'm done.'

Peter had only once before been into the two houses, when one of them was being handed over to a new tenant. He had mixed feelings about going in alone.

Daniel had talked so much of his life with Irena that Peter recalled his words almost as scenes he had actually witnessed. He stopped in the kitchen and stood for a moment trying to imagine the couple there together. Daniel had enjoyed cooking, Peter remembered, and could picture him in his wheelchair by the stove with Jo-Jo by his side and Klara fetching things for him while Irena laid the table. He began to like this image and felt he shared for a moment the happiness of the family and their life in that room. There were no vengeful spirits here, only kindly, happy ghosts.

When, in their early days together, Irena had tried to tell Peter about her everyday life with Daniel, she had come to see that Peter had no defence against the great tide of grief that would follow her revelations. She had ceased to torture him with her recollections and he did not know, and feared to find out, how much Daniel still inhabited her mind and heart. He was happy with her. He loved her more than he had thought he was capable of loving any woman. And she – he thought she was possibly as happy as she could be with someone who was not Daniel. Peter feared, too, when he could bear to be honest with himself, that, though she shared her daily life with him, Irena still belonged to someone else. Their lives were busy and creative, she with her music and he his writing. He asked for nothing more now. Sometimes, listening to her play her viola, Peter thought he heard the reality, the soul of Irena, crying out of the beautiful little instrument. He had begun to know something about music, and Irena's playing gradually became a language he could understand. In it he heard her longing and her pain, but also, a revelation to him, the artist's universal joy in the language and beauty of sound.

Peter left the kitchen and crossed the garden to the studio. Through the open window he saw Irena lying on the daybed. He knew that she had designed the studio to remind her of the one where Daniel had lived in the garden of her parents' home: she had painted it the same colour and there Daniel had worked day after day, playing and composing his music. Going in through the French windows, Peter thought at first that it was empty except for the bookcases Sam had built for Daniel and the daybed where he would rest when sitting at the piano became too painful. But there, behind the daybed, stood Daniel's wheelchair.

Irena was lying very still, her face turned away from him.

He had been dreading this encounter on such hallowed ground and, for a moment, an ugly fear leapt into his mind. He sat down beside her, whispering her name.

She opened her eyes then. How serene she looked, he thought with some surprise, as she sat up and put her arms around him. 'Peter, don't you think this is a lovely room?'

'It is.' Peter's arms encircled his wife and he searched her face for a trace of sadness, but she looked truly joyful there, lit by the evening sun and the dancing particles of dust which now swirled anew with Peter's entrance across the neglected floor.

'Mummy!' It was Klara coming across the garden towards them. Irena disentangled herself from Peter and stood up hurriedly, fearing that the girl would hate to see her embracing him in Daniel's sanctum.

Klara came in, her face flushed, 'Mummy, do we really have to sell the house? I really love it here. It's the nicest house I've ever known. Wouldn't you and Peter like to come and live here?'

Surprised, Irena asked: 'Wouldn't it make you sad? I mean because of Daddy?'

'But Daddy wasn't a sad person, was he? I mean he was always laughing and we'd remember that. And anyway, you've got Peter now and he was Daddy's friend so he'd like him to live here with us.' The girl spoke with so much conviction that both Irena and Peter were taken aback by her unsentimental logic.

'What do you think darling?' Irena asked him.

Peter needed to think it over and suggested they lock up and go back to St Bede's. Then they could postpone the sale and look at this new idea from every point of view.

As they were leaving the studio, Klara said: 'Oh, Mummy,' She had seen Daniel's wheelchair and went over and sat down in it. When Daniel had sometimes moved himself onto the sofa or another chair, the children would scoot around the house in his wheelchair; it held no fears for them. It was simply part of their lives. Klara wheeled herself forward a little and Irena wondered whether this was something that would bring back unbearable memories to her daughter.

But Klara just said: 'Let's get rid of this now, Mum. I'm sure someone could use it. It's the really fast one, isn't it?' And without waiting for an answer, she got out of the chair and wheeled it out of the studio, through the house and down the front garden. She folded it expertly and Peter, who had followed her, lifted it into the back of the car.

51. BRAVE NEW LOVE

IRENA went to work the following day in the Museum, but she was distracted and could not settle to anything. Zdenka found her standing by the window, gazing at the parkland.

'You're a long way away, darling' she said, startling Irena out of her daydream.

'Have you got a moment? There's something I need to talk to you about ...' They sat down together and Irena told her that, much as they loved their lives at St Bede's, they would have to leave the Lodge.

'It's strange. I thought it'd be so sad going back to my house. But it wasn't at all. It was lovely – and this was Klara's idea. She adored her father, but she knows he would have hated us all to find the house haunted and miserable. It was such a happy place then and we think it could be again. Klara can have the studio for her music; I'll get her a little piano, but she's so spoilt here for lovely instruments – she'll probably be very fussy!' Irena's smile faded as she reached for Zdenka's hand. 'I feel awful, after all your kindness – can you understand?'

Irena had worked hard to put the Piano Museum back on its feet and to make it an important part of local cultural life, and the work had been her salvation. As for Zdenka, she knew that she and Robert had been extraordinarily lucky to have found this little family to join her team and to have West Gate Lodge so happily occupied, but they had always known that Irena and her family could not stay forever.

'Dear girl – you must do whatever is best for you and Peter

and the children. We've loved having you here, but I think you may be doing the right thing,' and she embraced Irena, partly to reassure her and partly because she felt tears coming and needed to hide them.

Peter, examining his feelings about the ensuing move, was afraid – for Irena and for himself. If she was entertaining an unreal expectation of how it would be to live in her family's home again – with Peter instead of Daniel – it could be disastrous. If indeed she was using the move to try in some way to return to her former happiness he'd see it happening and he would have to leave her to it. But everyone else seemed so confident that they were doing the right thing that he decided not to voice his fears. They would all live in the Green House and the other would continue to be let, unless the day came when they needed to sell it. Meantime, Irena imagined musicians living there, but Peter secretly thought that writers might make quieter neighbours.

The afternoon before they moved, Zdenka asked them all to come and look at something in the great barn. Curious, they followed her as she explained to Peter, 'This is where we keep some of the pianos that people give us – the ones that are no use to the museum. Either not interesting enough or in dreadful condition – or we have that model already.' Irena had often been in there and had been made rather sad by the shrouded shapes of the unwanted instruments, like huge coffins, she had thought. Sometimes they would be lent or used on film sets, but many of them just sat there under their dust sheets. Now, as they went through the great threshing doors into the barn, she saw that the piano tuner was just leaving.

'Finished?' Zdenka asked.

'Yes, all done. Lovely instrument, that one ...' and he

started to replace the cover on the piano he had just been tuning.

'No, leave that,' Zdenka took Klara by the hand and led her over to the piano. 'Klara, my dear, what do you think of this?'

The girl went over and opened the lid of the keyboard. The piano was a Broadwood, an early Victorian drawing room grand with carved legs and a long figured walnut case.

'It's beautiful,' she said, placing her hands on the cream-coloured ivory keys. 'Can I play it?'

'Of course. You'd better get used to it.' Zdenka was smiling, but Klara, who had found a stool by the piano and had sat down, missed the significance of the old lady's words. She began to play, oblivious of what was going on around her, the secretive smiles and the squeezing of hands.

'It's lovely.' She said as she reached a place where the piece might end. 'Really lovely. Is it going to the museum?'

'No,' Zdenka said. 'It's going to London. It's going with you, Klara.'

'With us?' It was a moment Klara would remember all her life. Her mother had said they would get a piano for the Blue Studio but it wouldn't be as wonderful as her father's had been. So Klara was imagining they'd take the upright from the cottage and there'd be room for Peter to have his writing table in the studio, so he could work there too. But now this long, graceful piano with the cream-coloured keys was to be hers.

Peter, touched by the scene in the barn, went outside so that the musicians could coo over the instrument that was causing them such ecstasy. Jo-Jo followed him. The boy was going to be a tall man like his father and was growing to look very like him, too. His constant energetic movements and loping walk were very like Daniel's in the days Peter had first known him. But he seemed a more serious person than his father had been; maybe that was because he watched so carefully over his mother, seeming to feel her every change of mood. He was an unusual boy in this way, perhaps, although Peter remembered himself at that age and how his emotions had been raw and very close to the surface. It was a myth, he was certain, that girls are more aware of feelings and atmosphere than boys, who are simply brought up to conceal them.

'Lucky old Klara,' he said, catching the ball that Jo-Jo had been juggling with since they left the house.

'Yup. But mind you I wouldn't want that life.'

'What life?'

'Being a pianist – or any musician. All that practising. Dad was at that piano all day long. I'd go mad. Mind you, he loved it – that was his thing. But it wouldn't be mine.'

'What do you want to do, Jo-Jo – any idea yet?' asked Peter.

'Yes. A doctor, maybe …'

The family moved into The Green House and Klara and Irena took over the studio, where the brass castors of the ornate Broadwood made new dents in the floor where the Fazzioli had once stood. Peter installed himself in the house, in a small room overlooking the street. He was happy there, only needing a small table and a good many bookcases to make his surroundings exactly as he liked them. Once most of their boxes had been unpacked, Irena and Klara took turns to fill the studio with their music.

The first night he spent with Irena, in the room next to the one where Daniel had slept and died, Peter waited to see whether his ghost would be there with them. Irena came to bed and lay beside him as the light from a full moon lit the room softly so he could see her face. She was smiling at him.

'Welcome home, Peter darling. Be very, very happy here. Please be happy'

'Are we alone?' Asked Peter.

'Yes, quite alone. There's no-one else here. Only the moon.'

Irena woke to the faint sound of a piano coming from the studio and smiled as she listened: Klara was assiduous about practising; her father had instilled in her that she would never make a musician if music didn't start and end each day — even on holiday. How well their daughter played now; it could almost have been Daniel, for the early Bach seemed imbued with the same clarity and tenderness of touch. Irena smiled as she pulled the duvet up to her chin and listened sleepily.

'Peter, can you hear Klara playing over in the studio?' But, unable to hear either the music or her voice, he began to caress her back. He had his arms around Irena when he felt her stiffen. She'd heard Klara's door open and the sound of her feet on the stairs.

Irena shook off Peter's embrace, jumped out of bed and looked out of the window. Klara was walking across the garden to the studio, trailing her hands through the rosemary and lavender that bordered the path. The muffled music continued as she took a key out of her pocket and opened the door; for a moment it became louder and more distinct. Then it stopped as the door was closed again. A shadow glided away from the piano and Klara pulled up her stool, sat down and began to play.

52. SAYING YES

PETER sat at his table looking out at the enormous plane trees which line the river along the Bishop's Park stretch of the Thames. He had always loved this view, with its changing colours as the seasons came and went, but he had just accepted an offer for his Fulham flat and Irena and he were spending a last few days there. Feeling vaguely apprehensive about his life with Irena, now that they had decided to live in her old house, he also felt at a loss as to how to build his future, his working life, from now on. Not to visit places of danger – that was the nub of what she asked of him. To keep away from theatres of war, that was not so difficult, but it was harder to resist setting off for trouble spots where his years of experience so often awakened his instincts for the signs of unrest, quickening his interest and focusing his mind.

He needed to consider his future and his professional life as a writer. The uncertainty of books, their long gestation, made relying on them to support a family too much of a risk. In their early days together, he had secretly begun to draw up the outlines of a book. It was to be Daniel's story. He'd hoped that when they had established a life together, Irena would give him permission to publish it, but she continued to be relentless in her refusal. He could see no alternative to some form of journalism – without danger, without the intrigue he loved and on which he thrived, never knowing what the morrow would bring or indeed if there would be a morrow. He wondered if he could really live another way – the way Irena asked of him.

She had come in quietly and watched Peter for a moment. She'd never seen his hands unoccupied before – never seen him not writing intently, his fingers prodding at the keys of his laptop. But now he was simply sitting, slouched in his chair and staring out of the window. She went up behind him and put a hand on his shoulder. He jumped, for he had not heard her come in.

'Are you all right?'

Peter turned in his chair and took her hand to his lips. He had no intention of letting Irena know what he had been thinking.

'Leo's here. I'm sorry I forgot to tell you he wanted to drop in'

Peter greeted the agent with pleasure, and went to find a bottle of wine.

'Irena, my darling,' said Leo, taking advantage of Peter's absence from the room, his brow creased with anticipation of the reaction his words might bring. 'You're not going to like what I've come to talk to you about.'

Irena's heart sank. Either he had concert work for her, which she couldn't possibly tackle just at the moment, or it was that book again.

'I'll be blunt. It's high time Daniel's biography was written. If Peter doesn't tackle it you may find someone else has done it and written something you would hate much more. Harper & Stanton want it badly. They'll give a good advance – very generous – which is rare these days. I think there's US sponsorship involved. They want it written in a year. I know Peter can do that.'

Peter joined Irena and Leo at the table, putting down three wine glasses. He had not heard what they had been talking about, but Irena had gone pale and was staring at the old man, her eyebrows drawn together, clearly angry.

'Peter, I've brought Irena up to date on the offer for

Daniel's biography. I've told her that if you don't write it, someone else will.' Leo paused and looked across at Irena, who picked up her glass and went to the window. Now we'll have to go over all that again, thought Peter. The book was not a subject he broached very often and when he did it was always the beginning of a row, or an outburst of tears or just a long and painful silence.

He had often tried to explain to Irena that he had loved Daniel, too, and that writing about him would be the most important thing he could ever do. But she had seen only that she would be endlessly quizzed about the parts of Daniel's life about which she had not spoken openly to Peter. She would have to watch while he sifted through his research, help him with questions about music and concert halls. Magda and Sam and all his many friends would be dredged up, too, and the house would be filled with musicians again as it had been when Daniel was still around.

Seeing Peter idle at his writing table in the lodge, as he listened to the news from Afghanistan, Zdenka had shaken her head, 'Poor thing – he's really not satisfied by those articles he's churning out, is he? He wishes he was being shot at, I suppose. Hasn't he got a writing project that would really grab him? Does he write fiction, perhaps?'

Irena had said nothing; she had trained her mind to turn away from this subject.

'For God's sake, please don't let's waste any more time ...' Leo was saying impatiently. Secretly, he was a little afraid of Irena, but the wine was loosening his tongue, so that he spoke to her more frankly that he would normally have done.

She didn't answer, but stood up and left the room, heading

for the bathroom, where she caught sight of herself in the looking glass. What a dreadfully tired and uptight little face she saw. Had grief and frustration turned her into a shrew who had to have her own way if she were not to throw a tantrum? She must surely know by now that Peter's need to write and his thirst for action were like Daniel's need to make music; his commentaries on the world and its history seemed to have a parallel in the interpretation of the music of the past and the painful process of composition itself.

She had seen in *Beloved Bosnia* how he had brought Daniel to life again on the page. She would help him too, perhaps, and relive with him the past she tried daily to forget. And he would blossom again and be the man she had first met in his crumpled suit with a bag over his shoulder full of books and notes and recordings. She shook herself and felt as though a heavy chain was loosening about her shoulders and sliding down the length of her body and legs to the ground. She fancied that all she had to do was to step out of the circle of fallen links round her feet and free herself from the coils that had bound not only her, but Peter too.

She stood for a moment, relishing her strange, new release. The two men watched her enter the room again, wondering what had brought that smile to her face. Then she was walking over to Peter and taking his hands in hers.

'You'd better write that book, darling. What are you waiting for ...?'

EXCITED as he was about his new project, Peter was finding it hard to get started. He flicked through the pages of carefully categorised headings for the research he would need to do. Daniel had sometimes talked about his early memories of Prague, where he was born. Peter intended to visit the city, which he knew fairly well, and try to find anyone who might remember Daniel's family, particularly his parents, Dragan and Anna.

Magda, surprised at first to hear that Irena had finally agreed to a biography of Daniel, invited Peter over.

'Well, you're a brave man. I hope the lions don't tear you to shreds.'

Who these lions might be was not at first apparent to Peter. As a journalist, it should have been nothing new to him to ask the questions others might have avoided, but now he no longer held any conviction that he had the right to invade the still raw grief of this rather alarming woman.

'Could we perhaps begin with your family – in Prague. Just an outline of the lives your parents led there, a bit about your grandparents too ...'

'Well, I'll do my best, but you know Jewish families like ours put down the shutters after the war, the *anschluss* and so on. Whole communities of intellectuals had been completely expunged from Czech life. Most of my relations were either lawyers or musicians – like my parents. Luckily they had connections in Western Europe through their music. Although Jews were forbidden to travel, my parents got away and were hidden with friends in Vienna during the last years of the war. When they returned to Prague there were no family members left, very few friends. I don't, of course, remember the city until the late fifties. It was pretty grim and we were often hungry, but it was all I knew. Daniel was born in 1960 and things weren't that much better, added to which the Soviets were fully in command then and secrecy became a part of everyday life.'

Magda began to relive her childhood, then, in front of Peter. He watched her handsome face as she described the difficulties her gentle, confused parents encountered as they tried to resume their professional lives in Prague – merely wishing to make music for the pleasure of others and to teach it to young people whose lives were not easy as they grew up under the fist of Stalin. She remembered their joy when Daniel was born and smiled wryly as she recalled how jealous she became when his remarkable musical talent began to manifest itself. She had not been party to the decision to defect to London; she never said goodbye to her friends or her school; all was conducted under a veil of secrecy. The family landed at Northolt airport after months waiting for their visas, and were taken in by a singing teacher, a German woman. Like everyone else, she had been enchanted by Daniel and set about finding somewhere for the Danuczeks to live. The large, draughty flat, whose windows faced the Albert Hall on one side and Kensington Gardens at the front, had been empty for over a year and the price was not high. They moved in and, watched by their curious neighbours, set about finding a piano for their son to play.

This was all quite straight-forward. The book would begin with Daniel's background and then his childhood, which was dominated, though gladly, by music, by the piano. He was far from stupid and his English was soon fluent, but he simply did not have time to fit into the school day the many hours of practice which had become his main priority. Also the school wanted him to take part in games, which he hated. It was a while before his inability to catch a ball was explained by his short sight. By then he had begun to play in public. His early career was well documented and Leo provided Peter with all he needed in the way of concert programmes and critiques. The years when he combined his time as a performing pianist with teaching at the Royal College were not demanding to write. Former pupils and retired members of staff remembered Daniel well and there were anecdotes in spades. His character, which had for some years been hidden behind the glamour of fame, began to emerge. There was an eccentricity about him, a quirky humour and a tremendous physical energy. Peter immediately recognised the Daniel he had known, but he had not realised the blow that his parents' death had been to him and how he had, in Magda's view, tried to blunt the pain by playing the fool and by filling his days with long hours of practice at the keyboard. There, in the big, dingy flat that he and his sister had inherited, she witnessed his grief, his remorse, his shame, at not having given more time to the two people who had made such huge sacrifices to bequeath him his life in music.

Seeking to fill in the years between his subject's well documented childhood and his appointment as Head of Keyboard Studies in Sarajevo, Peter had found nothing of interest until he came across a foolscap folder at the back of a file. It was labelled "Sam Siddall-Gore's recollections of DD/Irena's arrival in London. 1997." The sheaf of lined paper was covered in small handwriting that Peter did not recognise, but he remembered meeting Daniel's protégé once at St Bede's when he'd come over from the States to visit his parents.

As a war correspondent, Peter had watched the destruction of Sarajevo at first hand. One hideous desecration following another, as the City Library, the synagogues and churches were reduced to a homogeneous rubble. Amidst the destruction of walls and roofs and the very streets beneath their feet, the population struggled for survival, picked off by sniper fire through their own windows and torn apart in their own homes by mortar blast. These sights and sounds had become the background to his life as he came and went on his missions, month after month unscathed himself, as though protected by some charm, accompanied in the battle-scarred Landrover by his belligerent Scots photographer, Sandy. Barely more than a year into the city's struggle, his boss asked him to take with him a passenger, a classical musician. Peter had scribbled down his recollection of their conversation and of meeting a man who would change his life.

> 'The Conservatory of Music are insisting he come and play there. Could be good publicity for the BBC, but "for God's sake take care of him!" Martin Bell had said, he's a famous pianist who used to work there under Professor Solomon. He's been pestering me for months now to get him out to Sarajevo. Apparently he wants to find some friends who've disappeared – can't get any news of them – so he had the brilliant idea of going to look for them himself. He has two passports, British and Czech, which will help, but I don't suppose he has any idea what's waiting for him.
>
> The following week I picked up my passenger at the airport. We shook hands and loaded Daniel's bags into the Landrover.
>
> 'Here, put this on.' I said, taking off my flak jacket and lobbing it to him. 'They're pretty trigger-happy round here.'

The tall, bespectacled man caught the jacket and looked at it.

'This has got your name on it I'm not leaving you without one – haven't you got a spare?' It was the yellow jacket I regarded as a lucky mascot. There wasn't another one in the Land Rover, but my passenger flatly refused to wear mine. So we both went without; and continued to do so until I could find one big enough for Daniel. The journey from the airport would take a couple of hours the way we went through the mountains. At first he jumped every time there was a flash or gunfire report along the road. I saw he was concentrating very hard not to seem afraid, his face taut, muscles jumping in his cheek and singing sometimes under his breath. I looked at him. He wasn't as old as I had expected – mid-thirties perhaps.

'When are you doing your first concert?' I shouted above the racket of the wheels as they jumped over potholes and spun in mud-filled craters.

'Not sure. I've got to speak to Professor Solomon. But there's something else I need to do here. Someone I need to find,' and he told me that he was desperate to know what had happened to the family with whom he'd stayed the year before the Siege had begun.

Daniel and I became good friends over the course of the next three years. His was certainly a baptism of fire; his first visit ended in horror when we were blown up in the market place. At the end of Danuczek's fourth visit – two years later – forgetting the black-out – he went out onto the hotel balcony which overlooked 'Snipers' Alley', a Turkish cigarette in his hand, and was shot.

Peter had written those paragraphs some time ago. And, re-reading them, he pulled down a shelf-full of files and began to arrange them on the floor around him. As always, he sat crossed-legged on the floor, which would amuse Irena and the children. Asked why he so often did this, he had explained that the tents and sheds and makeshift writing spaces he'd used over his years working abroad seldom had the luxury of furniture. Sometimes there would be a camp bed of some sort and the Land Rover had a stack of blankets in the back, becoming more and more malodorous as the mission went on, so that his companions would swear they recognised their own bedding from its smell. In any case, sitting on the floor had become a habit and he would sometimes think of his school days and posing for the annual school photograph, the older boys standing in rows according to their height, behind the seated staff, and in front the youngest and smallest, all sitting cross-legged.

Immersed in his task, Peter hadn't noticed that Irena was standing in the doorway. 'What a lot of files. Do they go back a long way?'

'Much too far, probably, but I can't somehow throw stuff away – and now I'm glad I haven't. Most of these down here have bits about Daniel, but they're in quite a muddle. Do you want to help me?'

In accepting the fact that Peter had finally started to write his book, Irena had kept her distance, often practising for long hours in the studio and sitting in the kitchen with Benjy as he did his homework. Only when she'd cobbled together their dinner – Irena had never learnt to enjoy cooking, but she now performed the ritual with good grace and Benjy's enthusiastic help – did she call up the stairs to Peter.

Curiosity had begun to overcome her. To start with, Irena had no idea how books were written – it seemed an alarming and almost impossible task to her. Peter's writing was mainly

in the form of articles, swiftly conceived and executed, sometimes in the dining room, so she could see him from the
kitchen. Sometimes she'd ask to read what he had produced,
but war and violence were often his subjects and about these
she had no wish to read or even to think. As the weeks went
by she began to be lonely and wish he would bring his work
downstairs. She was beginning to miss the Piano Museum
and her days seemed long and empty. Maybe her long reluctance to allow Daniel's biography to be written had made
Peter unwilling to give her the pain of being witness to its
evolution.

'Help you? But how?' she looked alarmed and backed away
a little, but Peter reached for her hand and pulled her gently
down until she was sitting beside him on the floor, her legs
tucked under her.

'Well, you're good at paperwork – I've seen you at the
museum. I need to dig out anything that's specifically about
Daniel. Look, I've kept pretty well everything in the way of
our correspondence over the years – notes and letters, mainly.
He was a good letter-writer, wasn't he?' Irena watched Peter
open a fat box file and at once saw Daniel's writing on a letter
which topped the contents. She took it out and read:

> St Thomas's Hospital, London. (Psychiatric Ward)
>
> Mon cher Pierre, (as you're in Paris, lucky you)
>
> Thanks for making time to come and see me again
> in this hell-hole. No, that's not fair – the staff here
> are wonderful. I've just had enough of hospital after,
> what is it? Four months? Anyway, it was great to see
> you and the avocados and anchovies made a fantastic
> addition to the corned beef hash – Tuesday's main
> course and as relentless as turkey at Christmas.
>
> As you know, I was on my way to a session with my
> back specialist, Aziz Hussein. I told you my fears, so

this won't be news to you. Although I've suspected
for a while that my legs were a write-off, Hussein's
prognosis – actually having it spelt out – came as a
bit of a shock in its finality

Magda is in a heap, so I try to look cheerful for her.
Everyone keeps saying how lucky I am that my arms
and hands were not damaged. And I join in saying
'Lucky I'm not a footballer!' which goes down well.
As does, 'I'm used to sitting all day on my bum.'

You'll wonder why I'm not as chipper as I might
be when engaging in this merry banter, so here's a
quote for you from Artur Rubinstein (you've heard
of him, I hope). "The more I play, the more I am
convinced the pedal is the soul of the pianoforte!"
I think HE got it from Chopin, but tant pis … I'll
keep this bit of extra gloom to myself and allow
people the luxury of believing in my future as a
pianist for as long as they can.

Enjoy la belle France and get me something exotic
from chez Fourchon, if you have time. I'm thin as a
pin but as hungry as ever. Which must mean that my
body at least intends to keep going. I both long for
and dread getting home again. But before that, I am
told, I should be rehabilitated at Stoke Mandeville
Hospital. This, I gather, will involve undignified
physical exertions and earnest psychological probing.
I can't say I am looking forward to baring either
my uncooperative body or my very confused soul to
anyone, let alone people I don't know. I may even
have to share a room and play basket ball …

I have to ask, although I probably know the answer.
Any news of Irena? I just wish I knew something.

A bientôt, mon brave.

As ever, more or less, Daniel

'I need to go out for a bit of fresh air, darling. Why don't you read some of this stuff and weed out anything that doesn't seem relevant?' And, without waiting for an answer, Peter was gone, shutting the door behind him.

Irena still held the letter she had been reading and put it against her cheek and then her lips. She felt she could hear Daniel's voice, his laughter and see the mixture of bravado and fear his eyes held when she first saw him again – a few months after Peter had received this letter. She put it down on the floor and began to read through the rest of the file, forcing herself not to be overcome by the proximity in such abundance of bits of paper and card that Daniel had held in his hands. What should she weed out, or indeed, what would add anything that was not far too personal, to a book to be read by people who had never known Daniel? She realized then, what she was asking – no, allowing – her husband to do: to write both intimately and descriptively about a man who also had been hugely important in Peter's life. Could he stand far enough back to see a coherent shape in all these words and their heavy burden of memory?

Peter returned to find Irena immersed in his records and more composed than he had dared to hope, and he bent down and kissed the top of her head. 'Are you all right? This is too hard, perhaps …?

Irena shook her head.

'It's wonderful that you kept everything like this. You must have been very fond of each other.'

'Yes, he was always a breath of fresh air. So elegant and sophisticated in some ways, such a schoolboy in others. I think he liked getting away from the earnest world of classical music from time to time. Like when he played the Lindy Hop and stuff on the piano. And, of course, he found something to laugh at in pretty well everything. Even after …'

'Did it affect your friendship that you'd been with him when that happened?'

Peter looked out of the window for a few moments before he answered. Finally he said, 'Of course I felt terribly responsible – absolutely shattered. But he seemed to want to carry on our friendship exactly as before – remarkable, really. But then he wanted people around him who didn't speak in whispers and avoid the subject of his disability. In his journey to recovery – mental as well as physical – it was important to him to try to understand, to analyse, the changes he would be forced to make alongside his determination to retain as much as possible of the person he'd always been and the life he'd known before. I was a sort of link, I suppose, between the two parts of his life. But it was a while before I realized that his injuries would also force him to re-think his entire musical life.'

Since Peter had become their step-father, Klara and Jo-Jo had continued to talk about Daniel, but casually, and he began to see that this was their father's immortality. He had, in essence, become the sixth person in that house. Uneasy at first, he began to accept that presence in their lives, even to welcome it, for Irena seemed to have found a quietness within her and grief no longer overwhelmed her as it had in their early days together.

Sitting on the floor near his chair reading through the files, moving papers around and making her orderly lists, Irena worked hard, handing Peter the results of her research at the end of each day, without comment, and he was not sure what effect this project was having on her. He did not dare to ask.

As the book began to take shape, Peter was forced to admit to Irena that he had written some of the material some time ago, long before he had been officially given the task of writing Daniel's biography.

'You are a rat,' she had said, coming across a sheaf of type-script headed *'Notes for D D Biog?'* and dated just after their marriage, four years earlier. 'What would you have done with it if I'd never come round to letting you do the book?'

He put his arm around her waist, 'I was going to turn it into fire bricks, so you could warm yourself with it.'

'You do talk rubbish.' She said, laughing. But she found herself increasingly curious to know what he had been writing all that time.

Peter flew to Prague with a list of the few remaining people who might remember Daniel's parents. He had asked Irena to go with him.

'You could help me with the language. Czech is quite like Bosnian, isn't it?'

'I speak Serbo-Croat – not bloody Bosnian. But Klara's got a school recital, you remember?' He had, of course, and felt guilty, but the girl, who was listening to their conversation as she did her homework, laughed and said: 'Mum – I'll be giving hundreds of concerts and, let's face it, he went to sleep in the last one!'

Peter looked shame-faced and gave her pigtail a tug. 'OK, but not while you were playing. You know I'm no good at lis-tening to serious music. Except yours and Mum's, of course.' His step-daughter kissed his cheek.

'We'll look after Mum, and she lets us eat junk food – that's great.'

Before he went, Peter had scribbled a note for Irena about a file he had not yet opened with her, then he wondered if this was not too hard a subject for her to tackle. There were still times when she dreamed of her childhood or of the destruction of her home and would wake shouting and screaming. Jo-Jo and Benjy knew that he had to wait for her to go out if they wanted to watch a movie about war, or anything with gunfire. He had shown Jo-Jo photographs of Sarajevo streets under mortar fire and seen the boy's horror and disbelief when he imagined his mother in such surroundings. Thinking of this, Peter had gone back into his room, screwed up his note, tossed it towards the waste basket and written another, propping the new one up against the screen of his computer.

Darling one, take a rest from all this while I'm away.

I'm going to miss you SO much. Please take care. I love you, Peter.

Two days passed and Peter would be back the following evening. Irena thought she would give him a surprise and do some cleaning in his office. It was then that she found the crumpled sheet of paper which had missed its target and lay under the desk. She guessed why Peter had changed his mind in the instructions he had left. Her hands were shaking as she ran them along the files that were still crammed in the bookcase. *Sarajevo 1, 2, 3* and *4* were there, secured with tapes tied around them. Then she saw a fifth one, *Sarajevo Trials* which had been put on top of the bookcase. Curious, she fetched the library steps and a duster, which she would need if the file had been up there for long. But no dust was disturbed as she brought it down and sat on Peter's chair to open it.

The folder was divided into sections, each one labelled in Peter's small, neat handwriting. Sexual Violence, Victimisation, Refugees, Extermination, Trials. The section on trials was larger than the others and fell open as she rolled off the thick rubber band that held it shut. She found herself looking at a press cutting with a photograph. Why she should be surprised, she didn't know. Daniel had always evaded questions about the perpetrators of his shooting. She did know that their identities had been discovered and, when asked if he wished to see the gunmen tried and punished, he had shrugged his shoulders and changed the subject.

Now, in front of her was a picture of three handcuffed men. Two of them looked defiantly into the camera, the third, much younger, seemed to be studying his feet. The cutting was from a Bosnian paper, and the headline read: KRVIVI TRAGOVI ZLOCINA – *Bloody Footprints of Crime*. She read the article and realized that there had been little doubt about the identity of the men who had shot Daniel – they had been arrested and tried several months later after being tortured and semi-starved in one of the temporary jails outside the city. It seemed that the prosecution had found Daniel, with Peter's help, and demanded that he attend the trial. He had replied to the lawyer and a copy of his letter was in the file clipped to one he had written to Peter on the same day. Irena found herself reading what Daniel had written explaining his reasons for not wishing to go out to Sarajevo for the trial.

Madam

Although I appreciate the time and effort that has gone into finding Lukić, Ateljević and Kovać, I am convinced that there is nothing that would justify my giving evidence against them. I do not seek revenge for the injuries inflicted on me, nor would they in any way be lessened by further punishing the men who shot me.

I have had the good fortune to have lived most of my life in a democratic country and in peacetime. My own opinions, however deeply held, have never forced me to take up arms, let alone against my fellow Londoners. This was not so for these three young men, and they will have found themselves swept along by a great tide of violence and hatred, their minds turned in the single direction of destruction of the 'enemy'. Had I been born in a different place and another time, I would have acted as they did. Whether we call this outflowing of hatred 'ethnic cleansing' or 'civil war' or anything else is immaterial and most of the inhabitants of this once-lovely city had no axe to grind, no dislike of their neighbours, but only a great wish to survive and to live in peace.

It is not for me to lecture you, who lived through the Siege. All I wish to state is that I presume, were I to have been either an invading Serb or a Bosniak resistance fighter, I would have found myself shooting someone at some time. These young men believed that the British Press was their enemy. That evening they saw someone they thought to be a journalist present himself as an easy target on the balcony of a hotel where the press habitually stayed. That it happened to be me, a musician, who was in Sarajevo to give concerts while I looked for a missing family, was just a mistake – an unfortunate one for me.

I am still alive and, although not quite the man I used to be, I have a good life and it would in no way be improved by knowing that I had been instrumental in sending to long imprisonment or, indeed, to their deaths, three men who were simply doing what they believed in.

The letter ended formally and Irena then read Daniel's covering note to Peter, written in haste by the look of his writing.

Dear Peter,

Attached is a copy of my reply to the prosecutor, Danuta Preidzić. I'm afraid that you will not approve of its contents, particularly after the immense amount of trouble you've gone to on my behalf. But this is how I feel, and I will not be changing my mind.

My thanks for everything, of course, and try to understand my reasoning, if you can.

As ever, DD

Peter's visit to Prague filled him with gloom, but it had been a useful trip from the point of view of the first part of his book. Depressed, he decided to take an earlier plane, just giving him time at the airport to buy presents for everyone before he boarded. In London, he took the tube and then, impatient to see Irena, a taxi. Fond though he had become of Klara, Jo-Jo and Benjy, he longed sometimes to have Irena to himself and now there would be an hour or two before the children returned from school. Impatiently he opened the front door. The house seemed very quiet. He knew Irena was in – her bag was in the hall. He kicked off his shoes and ran upstairs.

Irena was sitting on the study floor, surrounded by paper. She turned her head and her eyes opened wide. 'I thought you weren't getting back until tonight … I'm sorry I haven't …' and she put her hand to her hair, which looked as if she hadn't brushed it that day. He saw that she was wearing her pyjamas and bedroom slippers. She did not try to get up, so Peter knelt down and put his arms around her.

'Darling. What have you been up to – I said take a break from this stuff.' Then he looked at the piles of papers and images she had been making around her.

'I got the other Sarajevo file down – I know you put it up there so I wouldn't see it, but …' He would have expected to find her in tears, very much upset, surely, by the endless catalogue of horrors she had been reading, but there was something defiant in her manner.

'Where are the children? They'll be home soon, won't they?'

'No. Magda came with me to Klara's concert and I told her what I'd been doing. She insisted on taking them all back with her for a sleepover. She's obviously more fun than me – they've asked to stay on tonight, so I'm afraid I haven't even had a bath.'

Peter put his nose inside the neck of her sweatshirt and sniffed. 'Lovely. You smell really ripe. Come on – I need a shower too.' and he pulled her to her feet and steered her into the bathroom. 'Little chipmunk ...' He whispered to her.

'Why do you call me that? It's not very romantic.'

'But you have big eyes and a little round face. What could be more romantic – and then you've got wonderful dimples too, of course.'

'Do chipmunks have dimples?'

'Of course. Very fine ones.' He was lifting Irena onto her feet and beginning to undress her. She looked up at him then, as he opened the glass doors to the shower, turned on the water. She watched him remove his socks, first, as he always did and looked down at his bare feet and then the naked legs as he dropped his trousers and pants. Last of all, he unbuttoned his shirt and threw it onto the heap of their clothes and they stood looking at each other before they began to laugh, clinging to each other as they went inside the curtain of water and shut the doors behind them. As they soaped each other, Irena thought of the years she had shared a shower with Daniel, he hanging by his arms as the water sprayed him from all sides and she soaping him and tickling his ribs until he begged her to stop. She closed her eyes for a moment and leant towards Peter, who took her in his arms as the water enfolded them.

In bed, a while later, Peter asked, 'Did you read everything?'

'Yes.' She paused and reached into her bedside table, taking out a some sheets of paper covered in her own writing. 'I found this – it's the letter I wrote to Daniel about my time with Vukašin Milić. Did he give it to you?'

'No. It was down the back of the sofa when we moved. How did it get there?'

'Oh God – it was in one of Daniel's scores. Klara had picked it up and luckily I got the letter out before she saw it. I was going to burn it. Have you read it?'

Peter shook his head. 'I couldn't. It wasn't addressed to me. I know you find it hard to talk about that time and you've told me as much as you can.'

Irena handed the letter to him. 'You might need it. Please destroy it afterwards. I never want the children to read that.'

Peter looked at the letter she had given him and tore it into small pieces. He dropped the scraps of paper into the lavatory and flushed them away.

54.   A SORROW SHARED

S AM walked from Chalk Farm tube station, his eyes narrowed against the setting sun. Magda's directions had
been perfect, and he soon found himself standing in front
of a yellow-painted front door and ringing the bell marked
Bloomfield & Thesiger.

'Sounds like a firm of solicitors, doesn't it?' Magda opened
the door, embraced him warmly, and led him to sit down in
the bay window where the last of the day's light lingered,
flooding the glass-topped table and the family pictures Irena
had given her after Daniel's death, newly framed now and
interspersed with drawings of Klara and Jo-Jo and Benjy and
two other children he did not recognise. Miranda's portrait
drawings, swiftly executed and looking as if artist and subject
were in the midst of an amusing conversation, looked down at
them from the walls.

Sam looked around him as Magda busied herself finding a
bottle of wine in a French armoire which faced the window.
He smiled to himself, seeing her bend down, her round rump
in the air. When the two of them had known each other's
bodies intimately, years ago now, she had been skeletal, and
masculine somehow, gaunt and almost emaciated. It had
been that very thinness, that fine-drawn elegance, pared down
almost to the bone in places, unencumbered by superfluous
flesh, that Sam had come to desire in her. His pleasure in her
body did not delude her. She knew very well that her resemblance to her brother was her trump card as far as Sam was
concerned. She would watch him then as he caressed the long

line of her shoulder and ribs, his eyes tightly closed, imagining that it was Daniel's body and not hers that he felt beneath his questing fingers. Although he had tended his wounded teacher daily in his struggle to regain his strength both of body and mind, Sam had known that their intimacy could never go beyond the touch of a helper, a companion in Daniel's hour of need.

Magda's thick silver hair was cut in a short bob and her smile was welcoming, her voice lighter than it had been when they had last met, but her body had thickened and Sam could not prevent himself from remembering Collette's Chéri when he finally sees the once desirable Léa again after many years and finds a fat old woman with 'arms like thighs'.

Magda was certainly fatter and she exuded an air of cheerfulness. Sam, who remembered her bowed under a pall of constant grief in the months after Daniel's death, was surprised and relieved.

'Oh Sam. It's wonderful to see you. It's been so long. So – tell me everything.'

'Everything? That would take a long, long time. But you look well, darling. You look ...' A truthful person by nature, Sam did not continue, but Magda rescued him, crying out, 'Fat and happy! But I want to hear about you. Are you still with Gene?'

'I am. He's gone to Hay-on-Wye – giving a talk on poets of colour tomorrow. Me – well the music's going well. I don't perform much, but I love the teaching.'

'Ah – like Daniel. But of course he taught you for years, didn't he?'

'And I learnt much more than music from him.' They were both silent for a few minutes while the sun disappeared behind the bare trees on the hill opposite, leaving the sky striped russet and grey over the roof-lines framed by the bay window.

'Do you still think about him?' She asked quietly, seeing that Sam had picked up a photograph of Jo-Jo on Daniel's lap, fast asleep.

'Of course I do. He was irreplaceable, wasn't he? To all of us ... But how's Irena? Do you see much of her?'

'Not as much as before, but Miranda has been drawing all of them. Well, not Peter – he refuses to sit. I like this one – it's absolutely Irena, isn't it?' Magda pointed at the large drawing that hung over the fireplace – a young woman with a long plait falling over one shoulder, holding a viola upright on her knee. Miranda had worked quickly in charcoal as her model was impatient; it certainly was absolutely Irena and Sam's eyes were suddenly filled with tears. He wiped them away briskly.

'She's happy with Peter?'

Magda wanted to answer honestly. If indeed she could. 'I think she's as happy as she can be – now. Peter's a good man, and an unusual man in many ways, but it can't be much fun following someone like Daniel. Sometimes I want to shake Irena – she just doesn't know how lucky she is ... But she can't help it – there's still a sort of emptiness in her, and her eyes look quite blank at times ... The children are fond of Peter and Benjy calls him Dad. They still talk about Daniel, but Irena doesn't say much – although, thank God, she doesn't rush out of the room the way she used to.'

Magda paused, thinking she had said too much and been disloyal to Irena.

'You know Peter's written a book about Daniel, don't you? Oh, of course, you're over here for the launch.'

'Among other things, yes. Is it good – have you read it?'

'No not yet. It's won an award and Peter's rushing all over the place signing copies. I suppose I'll have to read it some time, but I think I know all I need to about Daniel ...'

Magda got up as she heard the back door opening. A tall woman came in, wearing a paint-streaked shirt, a dab of green on her left cheek. 'Ah Miranda – this is Sam.'

Miranda declined the proffered hand, laughing as she wiped her own on the side of her jeans. 'At last. I've heard a lot about you.'

Sam looked rueful. 'Oh, that could be embarrassing'

'No. Only good things. You were a great support to Mags. Particularly after Daniel died.'

'And now she's got you?' It was neither a statement nor a question and, as he said the words, Sam was regretting them.

Miranda got to her feet.

'Don't go away. I must change – herself doesn't like me leaving paint everywhere.' She ran upstairs, her movements those of a much younger woman.

'It's not what you think, you know,' said Magda. 'It's just that women form friendships. We like being with other women. After a certain age and all the mess of middle-aged husbands who push off with something blonde, it's such a relief just to share things with someone I really like – and trust not to bugger me about. And Miranda was lonely, too, and sad. I'm very lucky.'

'Did she know Daniel?'

'She was in the middle of painting his portrait when he died. The picture's rather good – but not finished. She gave it to Irena. But perhaps you saw it at St Bede's? Over the chimneypiece in the Lodge?'

Sam shook his head. The last time he'd seen Irena at his parents' home was on Christmas Eve and Gene was at his side, but he had been far too concerned about introducing his new partner to his family to notice anything in the room. They had driven from the Lodge to the Stable House, Sam silent and apprehensive, Gene his usual unrattled self. Except that he feared he was about to make Christmas memorable for Sam's family in all the wrong ways. Zdenka had sometimes suspected that her son was gay, but she hadn't spoken of it to Robert. Then they'd had the call mentioning 'Jean', or so they thought, and she had been greatly relieved.

Zdenka had imagined an American girl, a musician perhaps, and the sight of the big man towering over Sam at the door, the two of them silhouetted again the snow-covered stable yard so that at first both faces were dark against the brightness behind them, had not been at all what she had expected. Gene, looking around himself with interest, had held out a huge pink palm, and smiled down at her. His teeth were splendid. Zdenka put her hand in his. He looked down at the tiny paw, distorted by arthritis and roughened by years spent working in the enormous walled vegetable garden behind the Abbey, and covered it with his other hand, very gently, as he continued to smile.

Magda recalled him to the present.

'So they had a few sittings and Miranda had a lovely time with Irena and the children – and him, of course. She hadn't expected him to be in a wheelchair when she arrived, but she found him very easy and funny and he put her at ease out in the studio. He seemed very interested in her work, too. Music had always been his entire world and he didn't know much about painting – was pretty short-sighted and he only really noticed things that were very near to him. But her work fascinated him.' As Miranda did, too, Magda suspected.

Irena maintained that Daniel had never strayed during the time they were together. Maybe so. But he had always loved beautiful women and that hadn't changed. Magda's mind went back to the days when her brother was newly out of hospital, angry, hurt and terrified of the future. He had, however, soon discovered with some amazement that he had lost none of his attraction for women: in fact they seemed all the more drawn to him.

'Where's the picture now?' Sam asked.

'In Klara's studio, where Miranda painted it. I imagine Peter was relieved not to have it in the house when they moved in there.'

Sam stayed to supper, which the two women cooked, while he perched on a stool eating scraps of smoked salmon. Their closeness was apparent, but he saw then that this was not a physical relationship; it was a mental closeness, a sharing of opinions and humour and tastes. And he was glad for Magda, to whom he had given as much love as he could to a woman, abandoning her suddenly, in the end, and shamefacedly. She deserved much better.

'Nice piano, Mags,' he said as he opened the lid of the upright in the conservatory at the end of the sitting room.

'Yes. Danny got it for me so Klara could practise when she came to stay. I try to keep it in tune, but it's hardly ever played, sadly. Have a go – if you think it's up to your standard.'

Sam made a face at her and sat down at the keyboard. The two women had returned to the kitchen when he began to play. Miranda grabbed at her side as if she was in pain.

'What is it?' Magda was alarmed and went over to her, but Miranda shook her head. Sam had tucked his right foot in under the piano stool, so that he couldn't use the pedal, and it seemed to the two women that Daniel had joined them in the room.

'Debussy.' Daniel had said, looking across to where Miranda sat just visible behind her easel. 'Honky-tonk fashion. I used to perform this a lot at recitals, but it's out of my range now. I just play it at home for old times' sake.'

Sam untucked his leg and continued to play, his right foot rising and falling on the pedal.

55.   WRITING IT DOWN

PETER stopped writing and looked away from his screen into the eyes of Irena, who was sitting on the floor next to his chair.

'What's up doc?' he asked, reaching out to stroke her cheek.

'You're so lucky, Peter, being able to write. I wish I could.'

'Everyone can write – if they put their mind to it.' He looked at her without speaking for a while. 'You write good letters – or used to – I seem to remember. Not bad emails now.'

'I don't think I could write anything more … I so envy you – you just sit down and out it all comes.'

'That doesn't sound very cerebral. You can type, can't you?'

'Yes. My aunt made me learn. She didn't think a string quartet would keep me fed and clothed.'

'Well, realistic, if prosaic. And now you can vindicate her. You can have my spare laptop. I'll get it ready for you. Just have a go.'

'Oh no, I'd have no idea where to start even … and you know I can't spell in English.'

Peter went over to the bookshelves and came back with the small laptop he used when he travelled. He sat Irena down on his chair and, bending over her, set up the screen.

'I was just saying I so envy you …' Irena went on, 'and there are things I'd like to write about …'

'What things? Anything in particular?'

'I'd like to write about my mother. I miss her so much

sometimes – she had a terrible end and no grave – nothing. I'd like to leave … oh I don't know really … some sort of memorial. I know something about her childhood – she used to talk about that a lot. If I could write it down her life wouldn't just disappear when Hedija and I are gone – no-one else is alive who knew her, you see.'

'So – begin at the beginning … where was she born?'

'Ireland – County Galway.'

'That's a good start. What was her name – oh, Finola, wasn't it?'

'Yes, Finola Deirdre. Lovely names, aren't they?'

Peter fetched another chair and sat down beside Irena. He leant across her and tapped some keys; a glimmering white square filled the screen. Then he typed in capitals, CHAPTER ONE – FINOLA

'OK. So start. I'll make some tea.' Peter left the room.

Irena stared at the screen and then put her hands to the keyboard, spread her fingers and began to type. At first she wrote slowly and carefully, until she got used to the unfamiliar keyboard and she speeded up a little. She wrote:

'My mother was born in Ireland into a large, informal Protestant family who lived in Ballylangrish House, a crumbling Georgian manor in County Galway. In those days you could have bought such a house for a song, before the foreigners and film directors discovered Ireland. To her, it was just home. No one bothered much about cleaning the house or mending the roof. The dampness of the climate – what she called 'soft' weather – caused green slime to ooze from the holes in the slates and down the corners of the rooms, so the furniture was moved around as buckets were strategically placed to catch the rain. The walls were hung with pictures; some were old portraits of her forebears, others were

drawings and watercolours that visiting artists had
given the family in thanks for their often protracted
stays. Lady Gregory, a distant cousin, had written
a poem about Ballylangrish on her way to Coole
with W.B. Yeats, and the piece of yellowing writing
paper was still tucked behind a candlestick above the
fireplace in my Grandmother's bedroom …

Finola and her siblings had a governess who taught
all the children together – a feat I now see to have
been remarkable in an untrained teacher. My mother
played the piano well, taught by a neighbour who
had hear Rachmaninov play in London, and she had
a lovely singing voice.

The freedom of Finola's childhood was brought to
an end when she was sent to Dublin to complete her
education and continue with her musical studies.
There she met a most exotic man, Adam Vidaković,
a visiting viola teacher from Yugoslavia. Her lovely
fairness and sweet voice enchanted the olive-skinned
musician and soon they were secretly engaged. My
grandparents were not ardent church-goers, but
Islam was something very foreign, indeed heathen,
to them. Adam was not, however, to be discouraged.
He had to have the lovely girl; no one else would do.
As soon as she was twenty-one, he took the train to
Ballylangrish and, in front of her horrified parents,
went down on one knee before Finola. Then he
whisked her away to Sarajevo …

When Peter returned with their tea, he saw that Irena was
writing fast. 'You type well.'

Irena paused in her work and looked back at him over her
shoulder. 'You're interrupting me!'

He laughed. 'Well, keep at it and I'll fetch Benjy.'

Irena was still writing when she saw Peter and Benjy turn
the corner into their street, the boy skipping backwards as he

talked to his companion – he instinctively seemed to know that Peter heard better face to face with him. He was sturdier in build than Jo-Jo, with thick chestnut hair and a big mobile mouth. He ran upstairs to his mother who took him in her arms, kissed his two round cheeks and asked about his day.

'Pretty boring – it's just school, you know, Mum. But we're doing a project you'd like – finding as many things in our road as you might find in a country lane. I've started my list – look.' He pulled a crumpled piece of paper from his pocket. 'It starts with dog poo.' Then he looked again at his mother. He didn't remember seeing her typing before.

'What are you doing, Mum? Are you helping Dad with his work?'

'No – he's given me some homework to do.'

'Seriously? Is he going to mark it when you've finished?' He was laughing at the prospect. 'Can I read it?'

'No. Not yet. When it's finished I might let you. I'm writing about your Grandmother Finola. She had a lovely childhood in Ireland. She used to tell me about it.'

'Did my first Dad know her?'

'Yes. When he stayed with us in Sarajevo – you know when he was in the blue studio like the one we have here.'

'Well, don't make any spelling mistakes – Dad's very strict, you know.' And Benjy went off to have his tea.

Irena had started to write and now she couldn't stop. Peter would wake in the small hours of the morning and see the light was on in his office; he would creep in and sit watching her as she wrote, surprised that this small suggestion of his had born such fruit. Half of him was glad and somewhat gratified, but another part of him wished her his again. For she had gone into another world and he could not follow her. Sometimes he would find his wife weeping quietly at the computer, the tears running down her thin cheeks. So he wondered if this exercise were cathartic or merely a painful reliving of terrible things, of unbearable events. 'This can't all be about your mother ... Are you writing about Daniel, too, darling?'

'Yes, he comes into it, of course. But I'm not writing only about him and his life. There's Sarajevo ... but I think it would break my heart if I tried to write about the horrors I witnessed. Anyway there are lots of books about the Siege. You've written some of them! People and places just keep coming up in my memory ...'

'Is it helping you? You seem very sad.'

'I don't know. In a way I wish I hadn't started. And I don't know how to put it together now I've written so many words. And sort of part-chapters and fragments. None of it really adds up to a book. Maybe it never will.' Then she asked him: 'Will you read some of it? Will you tell me where to go now?'

'Are you sure? You don't have to show me, you know. It can be the most private thing there is, this writing business – I just worry that it's making you upset.'

Peter saw Irena return to her work, shuffling through the pages she had printed out for him, holding them at arm's length as he'd noticed she now needed to do. He picked up her bag and looked in it.

'Did you get to the optician last week? I saw you had these in your bag –' He was holding a spectacle case. And handed it to her. Irena took out a pair of gold-rimmed glasses, feeling the familiar shape of the lenses she had so often polished.

'No, they're not mine. They were Daniel's specs. I was turning out his drawers and ...' She held them up so Peter could see how the strong lenses distorted the room framed within them.

'What on earth have you kept them for? I know it's hard getting rid of stuff when someone dies, but a pair of glasses?'

'I just couldn't bring myself to throw them away. He wore

them all the time, so they were almost part of his face. And,' she added, laughing as Daniel would have done, 'they're real gold so they were very expensive.'

Irena took some days to decide what to give Peter to read. She edited a couple of the sections of writing that she had felt flowed most naturally when she had been writing them.

Having chosen her pieces, Irena printed out two copies. Peter was making coffee when she handed one to him. He took it from her.

'What about the red pencil? Won't I need one?'

'Don't be cruel. You can mark grammar mistakes if you like – and spelling. But please don't edit it – not yet.'

'I was joking, actually.'

Irena kissed him and took her coat from the hook in the hall. Peter didn't ask where she was going and she walked swiftly towards the park. The day, which had started cold and misty, was bright now and the autumn trees had only just begun to shed their yellow and russet leaves under her feet. There were no children by the Round Pond as term had begun. An old woman, clutching a bag of bread, was feeding the ducks.

Irena stood for a minute, her lips moving silently, and then she took something out of her pocket and threw it as far as she could. The spectacle case opened and its contents flew out, the lenses flashing for a moment before they disappeared, leaving an ever-widening circle on the dark surface of the water.

Irena still had occasional nightmares, and Peter didn't know if she remembered her dreams when morning came. He would hold her in his arms and wait while her convulsive sobs subsided and sleep came again. This he accepted as a part of the woman he loved and lived with. He had encouraged her to write in the hope that the process would help to exorcise some of her demons, even though he feared that any account of her family and her past must open up the darkest of wounds. Most difficult, more subtly painful for him, was her still sharp grief for Daniel. Surely he must feature large in anything she wrote.

Was it possible to compare the love of two husbands, two men so different? The magic of Daniel, his talent and charisma, his humour and energy – these were qualities that few could match. But Peter knew that just cataloguing his many attractions did not make up the man he had known. Irena had loved him – he had loved her. It was nothing to do with talent or beauty or even compassion. It was simply love, an enduring love.

Knowing that Irena was new to the craft of writing, Peter did not know what to expect as he read the pieces she had printed out for him and it was with surprise and pleasure that he jotted down a note to himself:

> *There's a freshness and honesty in her narrative, interspersed with moments of real insight ...*

56. ASHES TO ASHES

PETER went downstairs to pick up the post. There was an official-looking letter from Bosnia Herzegovina on the doormat. He slit the envelope, hoping it was in English. As he was reading it, Irena looked up from her typing. Peter came and stood by her, his hand on her shoulder.

'Hello,' she said. 'What's wrong?' Seeing the expression on his face, she saved her writing and closed her laptop. Peter led her to the sofa and sat down beside her. He unfolded his letter and said, very slowly: 'You can bury your parents now, darling.'

'Bury them? What do you mean …?'

'They've found them – their remains.'

'But after all this time – how do they know it's them?'

Peter took her hands in his. 'They've been doing DNA testing on the bodies they've dug up …'

'Oh no, oh no, I don't want to hear about it. Please.' And Irena tried to stand up, but Peter held onto her hands and lowered her again to the sofa.

'Darling. Listen to me. This is good news. They've found them and they weren't far from home – in a neighbour's garden. It was peaceful there.'

But Irena could only see the horror of her father's shattered skull and smell his blood on the hot paving stones. She began to scream, her hands covering her ears.

Later that evening, Irena woke to find Peter had put her to bed. Her throat was sore and her eyes swollen.

'I'm sorry darling ...' she began, remembering Peter's news and her hysterical outburst, but he put his fingers on her lips to stop her speaking.

He told her then how he had been following the discovery of hundreds of graves left after the Balkan war had at last petered out. So many people had simply disappeared. Sometimes it was presumed that they had died, but the discovery of mass graves in the woods shocked the world. Then two forensic scientists had begun the DNA tests. At first they met with scepticism. Then, as more and more bodies or body parts could be identified or at least linked with a family group, the bereaved families began to allow themselves to be tested, too.

'I sent them a bit of your hair – from that piece you kept from when you cut it all off.'

'My hair? Why?'

'They tested it against the DNA of the bones they found. And they found a result almost at once. Your cousins were keen to supply their own samples and it was confirmed last week that the remains in the neighbours' garden were your parents and an aunt and uncle and a baby – your cousin's child. Here are their names.'

He handed her the letter and she read it slowly.

It was spring on the mountain side when Peter parked the car by the forest track. Each of the children carried a bunch of flowers and Peter let them go ahead of him.

Klara looked back at her mother. 'Do you think Daddy's ashes are still here, Mummy?'

'They'll have blown about a bit by now – I expect they are all around us.' Klara and Jo-Jo recognised the place. They remembered going there with Sam and how their mother had gone off on her own. At that age they had not understood what they were all doing on that dismal hillside. Now the old

trees were beginning to regenerate and newly planted saplings were coming into leaf.

'So would Granny Baka and Grandpa Dedo like to be with
Daddy, do you think?'

'Oh yes. They'll have great fun together, blowing around
the mountain side.'

Benjy, who had never known his father, had listened all his
life to descriptions of him and jokes he used to tell and how
amazingly fast he could play the piano. He knew that he was
now walking where his father's ashes had been scattered and
his mother was carrying those of his grandparents who had
died long before his birth. His short life had been happy and
secure, but he wished he had known these people himself,
and felt a little sad as he laid his flowers on the ground at
the roots of a newly-planted tree. Klara and Jo-Jo wandered
about until they, too, had found the best places to put their
posies. Peter stood up from where he had left an offering and
Benjy looked curiously to see what flowers he had chosen.
Then he whooped, 'Mum, look what Dad's left!'

Irena turned and saw that Benjy was holding a set of pan
pipes. She looked questioningly at Peter.

'I'm sorry, but I'm not really a flower person – I thought a
bit of music here wouldn't come amiss. I'm afraid they came
from a toy shop – not really up to Daniel's standards.'

'Can I play them?' Benjy had already put the pipes to his
lips and a plaintive air filled the air around them.

Irena went to Peter's side and took his hand. 'That's the
tune Daniel wrote for me – *Little Wren* – listen.' The sound
of the pipes, liquid, defiant and shrill seemed to fill the whole
hillside, wrapping itself around the group of mourners and
lifting up into the ashen, grey sky.

Benjy stopped playing, wiped the mouthpieces carefully
and returned the pipes to the place that Peter had chosen.
Irena, the insistent music still filling her ears, opened the new

red bag that Peter had given her and took out two small boxes. She looked around and, bending, scattered the ashes of her parents on the hillside where Daniel's had been strewn. She turned away and Peter saw her lips moving, but he couldn't make out her words.

They found a café and huddled round a small table studying the menu. The Bosnian descriptions of the dishes had been translated into English – of a sort – and they all began to laugh. Peter watched the family as they chose their food and Irena leant in close to them. She looked serene and untroubled, as she helped the children choose their lunch.

'Mum,' said Klara later, her mouth full of strawberry sorbet, which was dribbling down the side of her cone. 'Haven't you finished your book yet? You've been ages writing it.'

'More or less, but I keep going back to rewrite the first sentence. It's very important to catch the reader's attention – mine just doesn't. It begins, you see, in Sarajevo – on the day that Daddy arrived at our house and we were getting things ready for him.' Klara licked all around her cone with a very pink tongue and considered what her mother was saying. She knew the story well – Irena had often told her how she had dreaded the arrival of the great Dr Danuczek who was sure to be fat and bent and thoroughly unattractive.

'What about the piano – you know – about when they were getting a huge grand piano into the studio for Daddy to play – that was really funny. He told me he had to squeeze around it to get to the staircase – it took up so much room.'

Back in London, Irena was unpacking. The window was open and she could hear Klara practising in the studio. She listened for a few minutes and then dropped the pile of clothes she was carrying and went hurriedly into the study, opened her laptop, ran the cursor to the beginning of Chapter One and deleted the first few sentences.

Peter, who was working on the far side of the room, came over to her.

'Going better now? You probably just needed a break ...'

Irena didn't answer. She was typing swiftly:

SARAJEVO 1991

The piano arrived the day after my fifteenth
birthday. Mama and I watched its precarious
progress through the orchard to the studio, its glossy
black case reflecting ripening plums and apples
under the clear September sky ...

FURTHER READING

Many very moving accounts have been written about the Siege of Sarajevo and, as I was writing *A Place of Springs*, I built up a small library for my research both on the Bosnian War and on music. If you would like to explore either of these subjects in greater depth, some of the books listed below might be of interest.

Barenboim, Daniel. 2008. *Everything is Connected*. Weidenfeld and Nicolson, London.

Bell, Martin. 2012. *In Harm's Way*. Icon Books Ltd. London.

Bell, Martin. 2017. *War and the Death of News*. Oneworld Publishing, London.

Galloway, Steven. *The Cellist of Sarajevo*. Atlantic Books, London.

Gardner, Frank. 2006. *Blood and Sand*. Bantam Press, London.

Glenny, Misha. 1999. *The Balkans: Nationalism, War and the Great Powers, 1804–1999*. Granta Books, London.

Nicolić-Restanović, Vesna. *Women, Violence and War – Wartime Victimization of Refugees in the Balkans*. Central European University Press, Budapest.

Page, Tim. 1992. *Music from the Road*. Oxford University Press, New York.

Rieff, David.1995. *Slaughterhouse – Bosnia and the Failure of the West*. Simon and Schuster, New York.

Reid, Atka, and Schofield, Hana. 2011. *Goodbye Sarajevo*. Bloomsbury Publishing plc, London.

Rosen, Charles. 2002. *Piano Notes*. Penguin Books, London.

Rusbridger, Alan. 2013. *Play it Again*. Jonathan Cape London.

Sontag, Susan. 2004. *Regarding the Pain of Others*. Penguin Books, London.

Straus, Joseph N. 2011. *Extraordinary Measures – Disability in Music*. Oxford University Press.

Tochman, Vojciech. 2008. *Like Eating a Stone – Surviving the past in Bosnia*. Portobello Press, London.

Trebinčević, Kenan and Susan Shapiro. *The Bosnia List*. Penguin Books, London.